Show Me #5

ALSO BY CAROLYN MULFORD

Show Me Mysteries

Show Me the Murder
Show Me the Deadly Deer
Show Me the Gold
Show Me the Ashes

Middle Grade/Young Adult Historical Novels

The Feedsack Dress
Thunder Beneath My Feet

SHOW ME THE SINISTER SNOWMAN

SHOW ME THE SINISTER SNOWMAN

CAROLYN MULFORD

Cave Hollow Press™

A Cave Hollow Press Book

Warrensburg, Missouri 2017

Cave Hollow Press
304 Grover Street
Warrensburg, MO 64093

Copyright 2017 by Carolyn Mulford
Formatting and cover design by Stephanie Flint
Cover Stock Images from Dreamstime

Library of Congress Control Number: 2016960483

ISBN: 0-9713497-9-7
ISBN-13: 978-0-9713497-9-7

ACKNOWLEDGMENTS

Even after decades of writing for publication, I still value feedback. My chapter-by-chapter critique partners, Mary Ann Corrigan and Helen Schwartz, gave me invaluable comments on all aspects of the manuscript over many months and during a quick reading of the whole. With the heavy slogging done, I called on the fresh eyes and keen insights of my beta readers: Joyce Campbell, Judy Hogan, and Fatima Thomas. My sincere thanks for the excellent advice each reader gave.

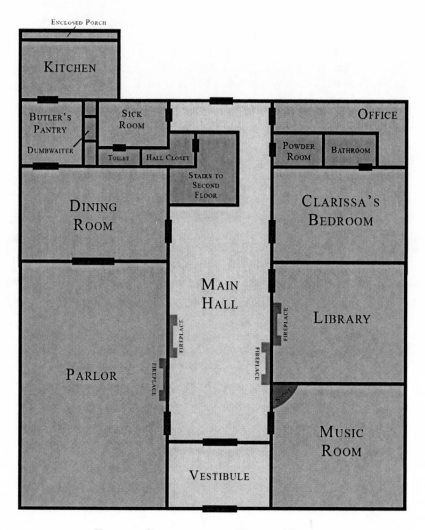

FOUR CHIMNEYS: FIRST FLOOR

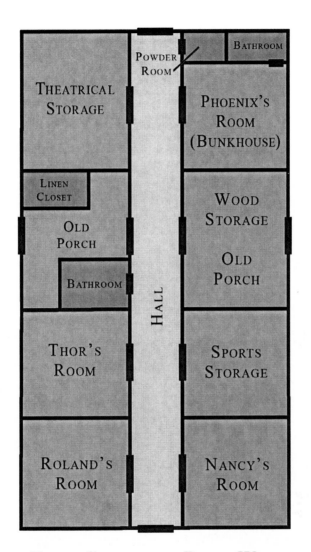

FOUR CHIMNEYS: BACK WING

CHAPTER ONE

The anxious entourage waiting backstage thumbed cell phones while the Laycock Community College president droned on about the honor of welcoming U.S. Congressman Archer Candon and his wife Clarissa, a former music teacher. Relieved of social duties, I pulled up the day's emails to the Coping After Crime Foundation on my phone.

The applications for assistance had snowballed in the two months since I'd turned my late parents' house into the new foundation's temporary headquarters. I skimmed the subject lines: "Despirit for car" (a novel spelling for a common, and usually rejected, request), "Need co-signer on loan" (also typical, always rejected), and "My husband threatens to maim me" (rare and intriguing). I opened the last one.

The congressman's wife, a compact ash blond with subtly applied makeup, touched my arm. "Phoenix, could you please text Annalynn to stall? Neither my husband nor his assistant is answering our calls. They must still be driving in a no-service area."

Numerous pockets of rural northern Missouri fit into that category. "Of course." I exited the email and texted Annalynn, who was onstage acting as emcee.

The advance man peered over my shoulder to see her reply. He wore an Armani suit more appropriate in the Capitol's marble halls than this district's struggling small towns. I guessed that he chose the expensive clothing to compensate for a major professional handicap, a lack of memorable physical characteristics. During my years as a covert operative, such an average body and forgettable face would have been an asset.

I read aloud Annalynn's answer: "Connie sing?"

"Yes, excellent idea." Clarissa Candon nodded to her younger, gray-haired sister, the Reverend Nancy Alderton. Nancy darted down the hall toward the dressing rooms while I texted the reply to Annalynn.

The advance man danced around like a kid desperate to find the restroom. "We can't afford a delay. I've got the AP, the *Post-Dispatch,* the *KC Star,* and a gung-ho documentarian waiting to hear the announcement."

I wondered if all three journalists were actually one man, the local retired newspaper editor. He'd written the paper's front-page story on the music education grant to LCC, but the big-time press wouldn't be here unless it expected something more, most likely Candon's decision not to run next year. Whatever the news, Annalynn would receive good exposure for her unannounced candidacy.

The others had gone back to their phones, so I edged away to reopen my email and its attached application form. Scrolling to the narrative portion, I read, "The first three months I thought I'd married the ideal man. He told me how beautiful I was from the moment I woke up until I fell asleep. I thought he was sweet when he insisted I quit my job and stay home to plant a big garden and fix up the trailer."

Polite applause interrupted my reading. Two students rushed onto the stage to move the grand piano from behind the curtain.

Annalynn said to the audience, "LCC has been selected to develop a new music education program partly because of this theater's fine facilities. Another reason is Connie Diamante, who brought home to Laycock her unique vocal talent and stage experience."

I ignored Annalynn's recounting of our old friend's credits and returned to reading the application. "Over the next few months, Adam found excuses to cut me off from my friends and family. By our first anniversary, he refused to take me anywhere except to the grocery store, where he never left my side. The first time he beat me was when the mail carrier came to the door to deliver a jacket I had ordered."

Connie nudged me and touched her short blonde curls. "Phoenix, come on. We'll start with 'Oh, What a Beautiful Mornin'.' We'll go on from there. Fluff up your hair." She whirled and walked toward the opening to the stage.

"Oh, no," I protested. "You can accompany yourself." I avoided public appearances. After years of operating under the radar in Eastern Europe, I hated that people now knew my face and short black hair from coverage of the homicide cases I'd helped Annalynn solve while she served as Vandiver County's acting sheriff.

The petite minister gripped my elbow and pulled me toward the stage. "Connie couldn't find the sheet music. You helped the students rehearse for *Oklahoma!* and know the songs. You have to play for her."

Connie ran onstage as Annalynn, formerly the second soprano in our high school trio, walked off. She motioned for me to follow Connie and joined the politicians' huddle.

"Go," Nancy ordered. Ten years older and four inches shorter than I, she reinforced her words with a two-handed shove that sent me stumbling onto the stage.

Bloody hell! No escape. Best to play the fool, always a credible disguise. I shielded my eyes to peer at the snickering audience.

Quick to milk a laugh, especially one at my expense, Connie grabbed my hand and pulled me toward the grand piano. "And this is my shy accompanist." She whispered, "For Pete's sake, keep your blazer over your Glock."

I took my place on the bench and stared at the keys, hands in my lap, as Connie introduced the song. When she nodded to me to play, I crooked a finger for her to come over.

She approached cautiously, the hand mike cocked to pick up anything either of us said.

I leaned toward her and said *sotto voce,* "Do you want me to play on the white keys or the black keys?" I had no idea what she'd reply, but Connie loved improv and rarely lacked for words.

She patted me on the shoulder. "Let's be bipartisan tonight. Play on both."

During the tittering, I made a show of flexing my fingers. When

3

she moved back to center stage, I played the introductory chords an octave low.

Connie took two steps toward me. "You're too far to the left. Move to the right, please."

The political junkies in the auditorium chuckled and murmured.

I waited until she returned to center stage and started two octaves high. She rushed to the piano. "Not to the *far* right."

The audience laughed and then applauded.

Out of ideas, I played the song in the proper key. Once we finished, Connie received a big hand.

Annalynn walked onstage and faced the audience. "Would you like an encore?"

Enthusiastic applause.

She turned and whispered to me, "Ten more minutes." Then she walked off.

Connie approached the piano. "What song do we both know?"

None that took ten minutes to sing. I remembered an old gag from our junior high days. I played a dramatic arpeggio and began a simple rendition of "Three Blind Mice."

"Phoenix, that's not appropriate for tonight."

"But it's a political song," I said.

"How is 'Three Blind Mice' a political song?"

I played the music for "See how they run, see how they run."

She smacked her forehead. "The mice are running for their lives, not for public office."

When the laugh died down, she said, "I know. I'll sing the one about what politicians say to lobbyists." She paused. "'I Cain't Say No.'"

Wild applause.

Smart. She'd intended to sing that all along. She had played Ado Annie in summer stock, and I'd helped a student rehearse the song for the LCC production Connie directed. It went so well that she sang an extra chorus. I slipped off the stage while she took bows.

Annalynn, brow furrowed, stood alone in the wings flipping through several sheets of paper.

"Where did the Candon crew go?"

Annalynn looked up. "To the trauma center in Columbia. The congressman's car ran off the road at Star Corner. A medical helicopter evacuated him. Clarissa asked me to announce the grant and tell the audience." My old friend rubbed her right temple. "Our new sheriff will call you when he receives word on Archer's condition. I'll put my phone on the lectern where I can see it so you can text me."

Connie bounced up to us, jubilant at her reception.

Annalynn put on her public face, took a deep breath, and strolled onto the stage.

I answered Connie's unspoken question. "Candon was seriously hurt in a car crash."

"Accident or attempted murder?"

Only the drama queen would think of murder. "Accident, I assume. Anyway, crime is none of our business now that Annalynn's no longer sheriff." Or was it? I opened my email to the application and read, "I'm afraid my husband will hurt or kill me and the good people hiding me. Please help me relocate far away from him."

My phone vibrated. The newly elected sheriff, an old friend, told me the congressman had been declared dead. A tragedy for the Candon family, and a loss that would remind Annalynn of her husband's sudden, violent death six months ago. I hesitated. Could she bear to announce another widow's heartbreak? Annalynn's decision, not mine. I sent a text and watched her open it.

She stood silent a moment. "My friends, I must give you some terrible news. U.S. Representative Archer Candon died a few minutes ago following a car accident." After the audience quieted, she delivered a tribute to the twelve-term congressman so eloquent that even I listened to it.

Connie wiped away a tear. "I don't know much about politics, but I think Annalynn just became a candidate for Candon's House seat."

CHAPTER TWO

During the night, the creak of a floorboard woke me. Annalynn was pacing in her bedroom across the hall. She'd done that almost nightly for the first three months after her husband died but not for weeks. I knew that because right after his funeral, I'd come back to my hometown to visit her and recuperate from a severe wound received during an undercover CIA mission in Istanbul. For both our sakes, I'd become a long-term houseguest. As I debated asking if she wanted to talk, my sensitive Belgian Malinois got up from the green blanket that served as his bed, stretched, and padded over to Annalynn's room to offer comfort.

The next time I woke, Achilles snoozed on his blanket, and Annalynn's door was closed. Apparently she'd decided to sleep in rather than rise early to feed him. Good. She faced a long day of phone calls from curious friends, ambitious politicians, and the prying press. Once again I'd be stuck running the foundation that I'd created to give her a worthwhile paying job. "Stop the pity party," I muttered. "I'll still have a better day than she will."

Achilles jumped up, gave me a puzzled look, and trotted into the wide hall and down the grand staircase for his morning hydration. I dressed in my fall running sweats, went downstairs to the nineteenth-century mansion's modern kitchen to give him a pre-breakfast snack, and strapped on a small daypack to hold water and his leash. If he didn't expend some of his boundless energy each morning, he hounded me all day. The Drug Enforcement Administration had

6

trained him as a working dog, until he flunked out. He was too smart to be nothing but a pet, so I'd scheduled two weeks of full-time training for us in St. Louis in early December. That gave Annalynn three more weeks to transition from Vandiver County's acting sheriff to the Coping After Crime Foundation's executive director before I left. I thought about the application I'd skimmed last night. If the domestic abuse story checked out, I needed to exfiltrate the woman and get her to a safe house right away.

Light frost tipped the grass when Achilles and I left the Carr castle, the town's name for Annalynn Carr Keyser's two-story limestone home. I stretched and flexed as Achilles checked for any varmints trespassing on Annalynn's two-lot property and on the small brick house next door where I'd grown up. He brought me a red Frisbee he'd stashed somewhere and loped down the sidewalk. I stuck the Frisbee in my daypack and followed, sure he was leading me to the park in hopes of competing for catches with a hyperactive terrier that Nancy Alderton was fostering.

To my surprise, when the terrier raced to greet us, he dragged an unknown short, plump, middle-aged woman in a blue parka behind him. She let go of the leash, waved, and collapsed onto a bench.

I took the Frisbee out of the daypack, tossed it high toward the other end of the park, and walked up to her. "Hi, I'm Phoenix Smith. Did Nancy stay with her sister last night?"

"Yes. I'm Nicole Yease. The reverend called me real late to ask me to feed and walk the dog this morning. She said you'd probably be here with your Belgian shepherd to make sure Toby gets a good workout. He's already given me one."

Achilles raced up to me with the Frisbee, and the terrier danced away, apparently hoping for a head start on the next throw.

"I knew the congressman was poorly, but no one expected this," the woman said as I tossed the Frisbee. "Did the sheriff tell you whether it was really an accident?"

Hmm. Obviously the dog walker knew something I didn't. "I haven't heard any details about the crash yet." She wanted to talk, so

I asked a direct question. "What makes you think it may not have been an accident, Nicole?"

"On the radio this morning, they said he didn't brake. He just drove off the road." She ducked her head. "My father shot himself when he found out he had Alzheimer's." She sniffed. "He left a note saying he wouldn't put my mother through that long, living death. I wondered if maybe the congressman felt the same way." She ended with a suppressed sob.

Suicide by car because of advancing Alzheimer's. A plausible scenario. "I have no idea."

The dogs raced up again, and I moved away to let the woman compose herself.

Ten minutes later, when the dogs finally lost interest in the game, I grabbed the terrier's leash and led him to the woman, now stomping her feet to keep warm.

"Thanks," she said, not meeting my eyes. "I'd appreciate it if you don't say nothing about what I said to anybody. The Candons got a right to their privacy same as everyone else."

"Of course. Neither of us wants to add to their grief." From the way her shoulders slumped, she needed more reassurance. "It's good of you to take care of Toby."

She smiled and hurried away with the now docile terrier.

Jogging home, I debated whether to tell Annalynn about my conversation in the park. No, no need for her to know. She'd feel obligated to pass it on to Jim Falstaff, complicating his first days as sheriff and adding to the Candon family's pain.

The sight of a green Buick in Annalynn's driveway reinforced my resolve to keep my mouth shut. It belonged to Annalynn's old friend and political ally, part-time reporter Vernon Kann. The *Daily Advertiser* hadn't been on the porch steps when I left, and I guessed that Vernon and his daughter had torn up the front page and gone to press late to cover Candon's death. Vernon had come either to see if Annalynn knew anything not released to the press or to discuss a strategy for her to win the vacant office.

When I opened the front door, the aroma of coffee pulled me left into the dining room.

"Phoenix, you're looking disgustingly healthy," Vernon said in his slightly loud tenor voice. "I brought bagels and cream cheese with vegetable bits. May I pour you some coffee?"

"Definitely." I took in the dark circles under his eyes, his red bow tie and dazzling white shirt, and the neat part in his silver hair. He was dressed for work. My shower could wait. I took off my daypack and jacket and put them on the chair next to mine.

"Achilles, your breakfast is ready, too." Annalynn came from the kitchen to take her chair at the end of the table. Apparently Vernon had wakened her. Her long brown hair was pulled back in a ponytail rather than her usual French roll, she wore no makeup except lipstick, and she was dressed in teal fleece pants and top. Even so, she looked elegant.

I chose a toasted onion bagel, spread on the cream cheese, added some cream to my coffee, and waited for Vernon to slide into his interrogation.

Instead Annalynn questioned him. "Clarissa said Archer didn't drive at night anymore. Why wasn't Molly, his local chief of staff, behind the wheel?"

"She couldn't drive. She got so sick after they left the last meeting, they went to the closest emergency room. He called the Highway Patrol to escort him to Laycock. Captain Sam Gist, no less, responded. Sam said Archer seemed fine, just a little anxious about running late. Sam led the way down that steep hill at Star Corner at sixty miles an hour, and suddenly the headlights behind him disappeared." Vernon looked at me. "At first he thought Archer swerved to miss a deer."

I smiled. Vernon and I had answered a report of a rabid deer at Star Corner and barely escaped a sniper. "Did you tell Gist no deadly deer hang out at Star Corner?'

Vernon grimaced. "I didn't stay there any longer than I had to, but I saw for myself that the car didn't leave skid marks. Candon never braked." The reporter shifted in his chair. "So far as I could tell with my flashlight, the right wheels went off the blacktop about a third of the way down the hill. Then the car pulled back on, went completely off the road on the left, and flipped over near the creek."

Annalynn put her untouched egg bagel back on her plate. "Heart attack?"

Vernon nibbled on his bagel before saying, "The autopsy will tell us."

The phone rang, and Annalynn went into the kitchen to answer it.

Vernon leaned across the table to whisper, "Something's odd about this accident, Phoenix."

No mention of Alzheimer's. Maybe Nicole had been wrong about that. "The man was almost eighty and planning to retire. He surely had health problems."

Vernon scowled. "He was seventy-seven and did twenty push-ups every morning."

Annalynn rejoined us. "That was Connie. The man making the documentary uploaded footage to some social media site. Phoenix, you and Connie have gone viral with your jokes, and some of the news channels have picked up part of your bit and part of my tribute to Archer."

Scheisse! The omnipresent cameras made it tough for me to keep a low profile.

"I was getting to that tribute," Vernon said. "Annalynn, the way you handled yourself last night gave you the inside track on the nomination to succeed Candon."

Nomination? "Won't the governor appoint someone to serve the rest of the term?"

Annalynn shook her head. "You've lived in Vienna too long, Phoenix. The governor can appoint a senator to serve until the state holds an election. The Constitution specifies that representatives must be elected."

"In Missouri," Vernon said, "that election falls in June, and the nominations may come from the traditional smoke-filled rooms in a couple of months because we don't hold the congressional primaries until August." He squared his thin shoulders. "I know it seems callous, Annalynn, but you have to get on the phone, state your interest in running, and pin down support immediately. Seats open up only about once every twenty years."

She rubbed her temple. "I stayed awake half the night thinking about whether I should announce my candidacy. I won't make a move until I'm sure Clarissa won't run."

How noble. How self-defeating. "Don't be such a Goody Two-Shoes, Annalynn."

"Phoenix is right," Vernon said. "I can name five other people who are already working the phones."

Annalynn crossed her arms over her chest. "I won't join them."

A long silence, until I had an idea. "Nancy will be back from Clarissa's this afternoon. You'll want to extend your sympathy."

Annalynn glared at me. "And ask Nancy whether her widowed sister plans to run for her late husband's office?"

Exactly, but a bit more tactfully. I hedged. "Maybe Nancy will volunteer how much Clarissa loves or hates Washington."

"Not likely," Annalynn said. "Nancy never discusses politics or anyone's personal affairs. My minister keeps secrets almost as well as you do, Phoenix."

The phone rang.

Annalynn sighed. "Would you please check the caller ID, Phoenix? If it's another reporter, don't answer it."

I went to the hall phone. "It's Nancy." I picked up the receiver expecting to be asked to dog sit the terrier for a couple of days. "Nancy, we're so sorry about your brother-in-law's passing. Is there some way we can help you or your sister?"

"Thank you for offering. There is something." She said nothing for a moment. "This is a lot to ask, but Clarissa insists on seeing where Archer—umm—went off the road. She'd rather not ask the police to take her there, but she needs someone to inspect the accident scene with her. And, of course, we want to avoid the press. Could you and Annalynn pick us up at three o'clock at the back door of the church?"

"I'll be glad to. I'll check with Annalynn and let you know if she's not free." I saw Vernon's head turn toward me, his eyes questioning. Let him wonder. "The dogs had a great time in the park this morning."

"Thank you. I knew I could count on you to respect Clarissa's privacy. See you at three."

Hmm. Did Nancy mean respecting her older sister's privacy in seeing Star Corner or in keeping quiet about the congressman's Alzheimer's? Perhaps the indiscreet dog walker wasn't the only one who suspected Candon committed suicide.

CHAPTER THREE

Back at the breakfast table, I forestalled questions about Nancy's call by going into a play-by-play account of the dogs' Frisbee game. Vernon soon turned the conversation to splitting up a long list of political spear-carriers for him and Annalynn to call.

When Achilles came asking to be let out, I escaped with him. I set up six sawhorses for him to hurdle and sneaked back inside to shower and change. The phone rang several times before I pulled on jeans and a turtleneck.

Annalynn tapped on my open door as I ran a brush through my hair. She stepped inside her childhood bedroom, which still held her four-poster canopy bed. "If that rambunctious terrier comes to visit, he's staying in the basement."

I smiled. "Toby's not coming." I relayed Nancy's request without commenting on it.

Annalynn's brow furrowed. "Nancy specifically asked that we both come?"

"Yes." That hadn't struck me as odd. "Do you have something else scheduled?"

"I'll go, of course." She smiled ruefully. "Maybe my six months as sheriff made me suspicious, but I wonder why the sisters need both of us. Do they expect us to see something the troopers didn't?" Her eyes widened. "Are you following your CIA need-to-know rule *again*?"

Perhaps. "Annalynn, you know more about the Candons and the crash than I do."

She groaned. "You sidestepped my question. What aren't you telling me?"

"I don't *know* they need anything but a ride to Star Corner."

She somehow gave the impression of towering over me, even though she was only three inches taller. "But you *guess* that's not all they want."

"Like you, I have my suspicions." I decided against influencing her perceptions by mentioning the possibility of suicide. "For your ears only: I heard a rumor that the congressman had a serious health issue that may have been a factor in the crash."

She took a moment to absorb this. "I haven't heard about anything but his night vision. Neither has Vern. Archer bragged about never missing a day of work. Who told you he had a health problem?"

"An unreliable source." I strapped on my Glock and moved toward the door. "We have foundation business to tend to this morning. Yesterday a woman emailed an application asking us to help her elude an abusive husband."

Annalynn stepped into the hall but didn't go downstairs. "That sounds like a matter for the police to handle, not CAC. Does she live in Vandiver County?"

"I don't think so. The phone number isn't local." I moved on past Annalynn to the stairs. "Aren't you coming to the office?"

"Not until I've changed into business clothes." The phone rang, and she hurried into her bedroom. "And answered calls. You can fill me in later."

Fine. I'd take care of the woman fearing for her life, but I'd be damned if I'd deal with "despirit for car." If I didn't put my foot down, Annalynn would expect me to do far too much of the foundation work. I grumbled to myself all the way through the kitchen, down Annalynn's basement steps, and through the tunnel that connected her house to my much smaller one. Our fathers, war buddies, had constructed the passageway when they converted our storm cellars to bomb shelters at the height of the Cold War.

Before going into my corner office and childhood bedroom, I went out the back door onto the small enclosed porch, opened the storm door, and called to Achilles to tell him where I was.

He barked a reply and raced to show me how fast he could run the hurdles, two of which he'd already knocked over.

I went out to praise him and put the hurdles back up. "Practice, practice. That's how you get to Carnegie Hall."

He ignored my advice and took off after a squirrel sprinting toward a pear tree in Annalynn's orchard.

In my office, I checked my professional and personal email, deleting most of both, before opening the disturbing email I'd skimmed last night on my phone. I saved the frightened woman's attached application and printed out a copy to give Annalynn. This time I started at the beginning, the email address. It came from desdemona@causemail.org. Hmm. Desdemona could be an allusion to the victim of Othello's unfounded jealousy. I'd never heard of Cause Mail. I typed in the URL, and a one-page site opened. The lone paragraph explained that Cause Mail provided email addresses to enable untraceable communication with friends or family in emergencies. It ended with a link that took me to a simple form asking for a name, an email address or phone number, the dates the untraceable email would be needed, and requests for referrals to other assistance. Interesting. A way for people in hiding, probably women or runaways, to contact loved ones without revealing their location.

In her email, the applicant identified herself as Tara Augeri, nineteen, and gave her income as $125 a week plus room and board. She gave no address but listed a phone number in our area code, which covered much of northern Missouri. I reread the opening paragraphs of her account of how her new husband isolated her and progressed from romantic attention to obsessive control.

I paused after the account of the first beating, sure the only unread paragraph would be even more disturbing. It began, "He cried and apologized that night as my right eye blackened and my lips swelled, but by breakfast he was accusing me of enticing men to come to the trailer. He picked up a butcher knife and screamed that he'd kill me if he ever caught me with anyone. I realized then I had to leave him. I had only forty dollars, but I knew my mother would take me in until I got a job if I could get to her apartment. That afternoon I packed some clothes in a garbage bag and started walking in hopes of hitching a ride on a highway a mile away. Adam came back from work early and caught me. He beat me and stomped on my feet and threatened to cut them off with the machete I used in the garden if I tried to leave him again. I was terrified. I could barely walk for days. I'd never have found the courage or the way to leave if some kind women hadn't come by the trailer in mid-September, seen my bruises, and taken me to a sanctuary. They urged me to go to the police, but I saw what happened when the police arrested a neighbor's husband five years ago. He was out on bail the next day. The judge gave her a restraining order. The husband shot her in front of their three kids."

No wonder Tara had opted to relocate. Moving out of state wouldn't solve her problem, though, in this age of computer tracking. She'd need a new identity, a tricky and expensive matter for a young woman with no money and few skills. As an undercover operative, I'd helped exfiltrate several Hungarians and Rumanians, but the CIA had provided the expertise and the cash to establish new identities. The DEA must do similar things for drug informants. Maybe Stuart knew the process and could tell me how difficult doing that for this teenager would be.

The complexity and cost of giving her a new identify struck me. Surely some service organization already dealt with this. CAC's role should be to find that organization and, if need be, finance the relocation. Annalynn might have the right contacts. I felt both relieved at finding a possible alternative and disappointed not to be solving the problem in person.

My mind turned to the puzzle of why the young woman applied to our obscure two-month-old foundation. How did she even know of CAC's existence? If she googled keywords, CAC wouldn't have come up on the first page. Perhaps she sent her message to every possible source of help, not a long list in rural Missouri. Somehow I didn't think so. More likely someone, perhaps the people behind Cause Mail, had referred her to us because they knew Annalynn from her charity work.

I skimmed the application again. No reference to either Annalynn or me or to why Tara had written to CAC. No grammatical or spelling errors either. In fact, the writing stood out for being clear and compelling. Someone better educated than the teenage bride had written it. Could the message be a ruse to test or harass us? Doubtful, but perhaps a little online research could verify the writer's veracity. I googled Tara Augeri. Nothing. She'd called her husband Adam, so I googled his name and followed a link to a social media site I'd never heard of.

At the top of his page were two photos, a baby-faced young man with dark curly hair and a smiling red-haired teenage girl. His last posting had been three weeks ago. It read, "This crappy place got no buses or trains. She left in a car. When I find the dude who took her, I'll turn him into compost."

Three comments contained expletive-filled vents about women's treachery. The site appeared to be devoted to misogynistic rants.

I scrolled down to Augeri's first posting, dated September 17. "Let me know if you see this carrot-haired bitch. She stole my stuff." Eight other messages alternated between pleas for anyone who saw her to contact him and threats to disembowel anyone who touched her.

Convinced the application wasn't a ruse, I did keyword searches for organizations in Missouri working with battered women and domestic violence. I found shelters with assistance programs in the cities and about twenty towns (none of them nearby), numerous court cases, and newspaper stories on three deaths. Most shelters also offered counseling, including on how to deal with the criminal justice system. The state offered a Safe at Home program that provided victims with substitute mailing addresses to use for things like a driver's license. What I didn't find was an organization that established new identities, but perhaps no one would advertise that. To put the issue in context, I went to one of the national advocacy sites and skimmed depressing statistics on "intimate partner violence."

The phone interrupted my research. Annalynn.

She said, "Come have lunch and watch cable news. We may both be on it." She hung up.

I grabbed the folder and hurried back to her house and to the old billiards room. The table had been sent to the basement when Annalynn's son and daughter were small, and a huge television now reigned. Two trays holding chicken vegetable soup and green salads graced the petrified wood table in front of the humongous leather couch.

Achilles was stretched out on the hearth chewing on a fake bone, a sure sign he'd already eaten his lunch.

"The opening tease called Archer a long-serving but little-known congressman," Annalynn said. "The district is so evenly divided between conservatives and moderates that he didn't introduce much ground-breaking legislation."

Knowing nothing about the man's capabilities, I said nothing. Instead I took my seat and dug into the soup. "This is really good, Annalynn."

"Your mother's recipe, of course. I made it between calls this morning."

The report on Candon's death still hadn't run by the time we'd finished eating. I handed Annalynn the folder. "Read the top application and think who could help her."

She'd turned to the second page when a photo of Archer Candon on the House floor flashed on the screen. A voice said, "Congressional leaders expressed shock and sadness at Missouri Representative Archer Candon's death in a one-car accident last night. He was on his way to a meeting in Laycock, Missouri. Local political leader Annalynn Carr Keyser announced his death to the waiting constituents."

Annalynn's aristocratic face filled the screen. Her pleasant voice tight but controlled, she lauded Candon's major contributions to the district for perhaps thirty seconds. The last half showed him shaking hands with a man on a tractor and speaking in front of a campaign poster.

Achilles had dropped his bone and leapt to stand in front of the TV.

I stared at the screen in dismay. The lawmaker was so obscure that news departments didn't have video of him at a crucial vote or hearing on file. What to say? "You did a great job of recognizing Candon's work."

"Thank God I'd prepared to introduce him. I could never have come up with a list of his achievements on the spot."

I reached for the remote.

"And here's our political laugh of the day," the television voice said. "It features Laycock Community College faculty members Connie Diamante and Phoenix Smith filling in as the audience waited for Congressman Candon."

The video opened with me doing my wide-eyed stupid look and asking whether to play on the black or white keys. I was grateful the reporter had misidentified me as a faculty member.

Achilles barked and put his paw on my leg. He knew Annalynn and I communicated on the telephone, but apparently he didn't understand how he could see us in person and on television at the same time.

Annalynn laughed so hard the applications fell on the floor. When she recovered, she said, "That was wonderful. I was talking backstage and didn't hear your routine. You two can be the warm-up act for my campaign speeches."

Connie would love the idea. I had to scotch it now. "Never. Never ever. Don't even mention the possibility."

Chuckling, Annalynn picked up the papers. "Connie is sure to suggest it."

True. Multiple times. "Tell her what a great presence I have on stage, how the camera loves my lustrous black hair and shining brown eyes." Not convincing. "Tell her the audience loves the way I make fun of her."

Annalynn sobered. "Don't be mean, Phoenix." She thought a moment. "I'll tell Connie no one can predict what you'll do, on or off the stage, so I'll leave the warm-up to her, the professional performer."

The phone rang.

Annalynn checked the caller ID. "Oh, Lord. It's the queen of gossip."

"That's for me," I admitted. "Trudy is doing a little job for me." I hurried into the hall to answer the phone there. "Hi, Trudy. How's the project going?"

"Pretty good. I'd never decorated a birthday cake with so many numbers and symbols before. I baked one to practice on. Everything looks pretty good except that symbol that looks kinda like a gate with a curvy top."

"That's pi. Would you like for me to print off a big one so you can see the detail?"

"I'd feel better if you'd mosey over tonight and check the whole cake." She chuckled. "We don't want Beth to give you an F in math."

Trudy was right. I daren't risk a mistake on the cake I'd designed for my former math teacher's seventy-fifth birthday party. "Okay if I swing by between seven thirty and eight?"

"That's good. See you then."

And pump me for any details on Candon's accident and the aftermath. Oh, well. I'd quiz her, too. Connie's nosy older cousin sucked in rumors like a powerful vacuum cleaner.

Annalynn's eyes widened with curiosity when I rejoined her. "You avoid Trudy the way you would ebola. What's going on?"

If I refused to say, Annalynn would think it was a big deal. "Trudy's making the cake for Mrs. Roper's birthday lunch on Saturday." I'd not mentioned my invitation to the family party for Stuart's mother. I didn't want to feed Annalynn's hope that a lasting romance would evolve from the pleasant fling that began when I worked with Stuart, a St. Louis-based DEA employee, on her late husband's homicide.

Annalynn smiled. "An opportunity for you to win over Stuart's kids."

"Right. You can guess how much I'm looking forward to that." Seventeen-year-old Kaysi had written about lonely divorced men falling prey to rapacious cougars on a social media site and had someone send me the link. Fourteen-year-old Zeke had asked Stuart if old people could fall in love. "Tara Augeri is only two years older than Kaysi. Any ideas about how to respond to her application?"

Annalynn put the folder on the table. "The poor girl's in a terrible situation, and she could be right about the futility of a protective order. I don't see what we can do to help her, and I don't know who could. No cases like this came up while I was sheriff."

The statistics I'd read indicated that her lack of cases didn't reflect the number of domestic violence incidents in Vandiver County. I let it go. "I didn't find any organizations on the Web, but surely you know someone who could give us a lead."

The phone rang again. Annalynn glanced at the caller ID. "He can wait." She leaned back on the couch and closed her eyes. After several seconds she opened them. "The only person I can think of is Nancy Alderton. She's lived in Laycock only a few months, but she's been involved in women's issues for years."

I hadn't known that about the First Methodist's new minister, but then I went to church only under duress from Annalynn. I considered a moment. Although I wondered what had caused Congressman Candon's crash, I couldn't do anything about his apparently accidental death. In contrast, the threat to Tara Augeri's life compelled me to take action. "When we go to Star Corner, Annalynn, you take care of the widow. I'll peel off Nancy and talk to her."

Dividing the duties, perhaps Annalynn and I could satisfy our curiosity about the crash and find a way to save the endangered teenager.

CHAPTER FOUR

Leaving Annalynn to continue her calls, I went back to my office to draft a response to Tara Augeri's application. I finally settled for, "We are looking into ways to assist you. I will contact you to outline possible options and arrange a meeting soon. If you must move immediately from your present safe house, please call me at the cell number below. Phoenix Smith, Chief Financial Officer."

Impatient with my ignorance of any options and doubtful that the minister could enlighten me, I went back to my online search for resources. I used every keyword I could think of. A dozen organizations in the twenty counties around us seemed possibilities, until I dug into their websites. They provided temporary shelter and assistance for local and out-of-area women, but none appeared to have the resources to assist with a permanent relocation. Best to prepare to go it alone, I concluded. I emailed a carefully worded request for advice to a retired CIA friend who had established new identities for exfiltrated East German informants in my early years as an operative. I sent a similarly worded message to Stuart, hoping he could tell me how the DEA sets up a witness protection operation.

Relocating and supporting the young woman for several months could strain the foundation's official budget. I checked the offshore accounts that I drew on to finance CAC and pinpointed $50,000 I could access instantly.

At quarter to three I returned to the castle. I heard Annalynn's voice in her home office at the back of the ladies' parlor and went in.

She stood by the window near her roll-top desk. "Vern, I'm not comfortable talking politics in the foundation office." She glanced at me over the carved wood screen that divided office from parlor and waved an acknowledgment. "Okay, I'll think about it. Bye." She rubbed her left ear. "I haven't spent this much time on the phone since college. Do we need coats or jackets?"

"It's in the fifties now, and we should be back before sunset."

I put on a sweatshirt and my hooded rain jacket with pockets big enough to hold binoculars and spare magazines for my Glock. Annalynn donned a short wool navy-blue coat over her light blue sweater. I'd prepared for hiking around in the dead grass and brush; she'd dressed for a social call.

Achilles trotted to the front door with his leash in his mouth.

"He knows I'm upset," Annalynn said, letting him out ahead of us. "It's simpler to take him than argue. You drive my SUV, and he can ride at my feet." She smiled. "Besides, he'll help you find whatever you're looking for."

Huh? "What do you expect me to look for?" I opened the garage door and then the SUV's back door. It was my job to take Achilles' pad off the back seat and brush away any fawn-colored dog hairs.

"You tell me. I've talked to at least twenty people today. No one has said a word about Candon having a health problem." She slid the front passenger seat back to allow more room for Achilles to lie in front of her.

We drove the short distance to the First Methodist Church in silence. I turned into the alley that ran between the church and its overflow parking lot and pulled up with the SUV's right back door next to the basement steps.

Achilles whined and licked Annalynn's hand.

She stroked his head. "He understands how much I dread this. It brings back those first days after Boom's death."

Two women in dark slacks and hooded jackets hurried up the steps. The petite minister opened the SUV's back door and guided her sister inside. Last night I'd thought of expensively dressed and coiffed Clarissa as the sophisticated city mouse and neat, gray-haired

Nancy as the country mouse. Today the country mouse, the younger sister, had taken charge.

Achilles put his front paws on Annalynn's lap and stretched up to inspect the new passengers occupying his regular seat.

"Down," I ordered.

Nancy ducked and pulled Clarissa's head down.

Not sure whether to be alarmed or amused at Nancy assuming the command had been for humans, I drove on down the alley and turned onto the traffic-free street. "We're all clear."

The sisters sat up. Makeup almost obscured the dark shadows under Clarissa's eyes, but the lines in her face had deepened overnight.

Annalynn reached over the back of the seat with her left hand. "Clarissa, I'm so sorry for your terrible loss."

I gave my condolences and then tuned out the heartfelt but trite exchanges. Considering my passengers' concerns, I stayed alert for any vehicles following us. I relaxed only when we reached the two-lane blacktop road leading to the odd six-point confluence of country roads called Star Corner. By now my three human passengers were discussing the memorial service and my bored canine was squirming to get comfortable on top of Annalynn's feet.

"Phoenix," Clarissa said, "thank you for helping me with this fool's errand. I know it sounds silly to search for Archer's missing glove at a time like this, but Pete, my grandson, so admired those Argentine leather gloves. I want him to have the pair as a memento of his grandfather. And Pete has Archer's hands. The gloves fit him."

"I understand," I said, doubting she'd given the major reason for our expedition. "A loved one's small, everyday objects give us a link to them." Hmm. Maybe the glove wasn't just an excuse. People cope with grief by focusing on insignificant things. Perhaps Annalynn and I had both been too cynical about why we were going to the scene of the crash.

Achilles sat up between Annalynn's legs and rested his chin on her arm. He read her moods even better than I did.

We topped the big hill that dropped down to the creek. "That's

Star Corner." Two one-lane roads came in on our side of the creek, and two slightly wider roads angled in near the top of the next hill. Even from here I could see downed saplings and crushed grass where the car had plowed through brush on the far side of the creek.

Clarissa gasped. Halfway down the hill she said, "Archer was coming from the other direction. He went off the road on his left. Would you mind driving to the top of the next hill? I want to see what he saw."

Achilles raised his head to sniff and stare out the window. He whined. Even in a different season, he recognized the place where a sniper almost killed him last June. Or perhaps he smelled trouble.

Annalynn stroked him and murmured assurances.

I parked at the pullout for the school bus stop just as I had then.

Annalynn took a packet of evidence gloves from a container and handed them to me. "If you're rummaging around in the weeds and brush, you'll want to protect your hands."

What had I missed? Why did she expect me to pick up evidence? I took the gloves. "I'll get a bag from the back in case we run across items the troopers couldn't see last night." I opened my door and stepped out.

"Good idea," Nancy said, opening her door. "Archer was driving Molly Dolichek's car. We may come across some of her things."

Clarissa got out. "He had his window partway down." Her stage-quality voice shaky, she paused a moment before adding, "Captain Gist told me the open window indicates Archer was ill or sleepy and trying to stay alert."

Hmm. She'd passed on information to support the accident scenario. I opened the SUV's back door and took out a garbage bag and a bunch of the small paper lunch sacks the sheriff's department used to bag evidence. I'd planned to keep my mouth shut, but I couldn't resist one question: "Did Congressman Candon and his assistant both have the flu or a virus?"

After a long moment, Nancy answered, "They both felt fine when we said goodbye after lunch yesterday. The medical examiner is contacting Molly's doctor about what made her ill."

"Phoenix," Annalynn said, "Achilles refuses to get out of the car. This place frightens him."

I walked to the front passenger door. "You and Clarissa walk down the right side to search for signs of the car veering off the road. Nancy, Achilles, and I will check the left side." I'd assigned myself to the crash side of the road.

Annalynn nodded and walked away.

Achilles sat on the seat with his head turned away from me.

I rubbed behind his ears. "It's okay, *Schatzi*. No bad guys, no danger today." I doubted he understood that. I added, "No bullet-proof vest for you or for me." He knew the word vest and associated wearing it with high risk.

He deigned to turn his head and frown at me.

Okay. Try another argument. He loved showing off his skill at finding drugs and explosives. "Today we're going to *find*."

He tried to lick my face, which he knew I hated.

I moved back out of reach. "Let's go find."

He jumped down, but as soon as I closed the car door, he glued himself to my left leg.

"The car went off the blacktop here," Annalynn called. She pointed to some crushed weeds and walked slowly down the hill about thirty feet. "It came back onto the blacktop here."

I jogged down the left side to join Nancy. We studied the sloping ground by the road until we reached a narrow strip of crushed grass and weeds that progressively widened to the car's width.

Nancy whispered, "What do you think happened?"

I glanced back up the hill where Clarissa stood frozen. "He went off first on the right and managed to pull back on, but he overcorrected." Why didn't he brake? Was he afraid of skidding? Unable to function? I put a positive spin on it. "They were driving sixty miles an hour, so once he went off the blacktop onto the bank over here, he couldn't regain control of the car."

Nancy closed her eyes. "Thank you, Lord." She turned around

and called, "Phoenix says he crashed because he overcorrected."

Clarissa covered her face with her hands, and Nancy hurried up the hill to comfort her.

Hmm. The sisters had brought Annalynn and me along to give an objective interpretation of the cause of the crash, to tell them whether the man had committed suicide by car. I wondered if Annalynn had discerned that. I'd play out the farce. I called, "Achilles and I will look for the glove." I followed the car's path off the road through weeds and brush into an unfenced field.

Annalynn answered, "Clarissa and I will wait in the car."

Achilles barked and loped after them, but he soon rejoined me, as did Nancy.

We said nothing as we approached the spot where the car had rolled and then landed near the creek. Some young evergreens at the side of the road had blocked our view of those final yards when we drove by. I surveyed the damage. Troopers, the medical crew, the tow truck crew, and probably reporters and passersby had trampled the car's path and final resting place. Surely one of them would have found anything that flew out of the car.

Achilles began to search methodically, trotting along the creek from the culvert toward my left with his nose down. He paused, stared at something several seconds, and sat down. He barked and looked back at me without his usual grin of success.

"Good boy!" I put on the evidence gloves, pulled a small paper sack from the garbage bag, and went to retrieve his unexpected find.

A mobile, one of the older iPhones, almost covered by crushed grass. Achilles had seen or smelled it and recognized that it didn't belong here.

Nancy came toward us. "Is it the glove?"

"No, an iPhone." I held it up in my gloved hand. "Do you recognize it?"

"It's not Archer's. He insisted that he and his staff use cells with big screens. Clarissa may know if it's Molly's personal phone. She notices things like that." Nancy turned slowly in a circle. "You're more nimble than I am. Would you mind covering the steeper area?"

"Fine. That sumac will be our dividing line." I had no taste for a pointless search. "Are we really looking for a glove?"

She smiled. "I knew we didn't fool you. Clarissa had to put the possibility of suicide to rest. But, yes, she really is hoping to find his right-hand glove. He was wearing the left one."

The three of us continued to search for several minutes with, to me, uninspiring results. On the other hand, after Achilles completed his circular pattern and discounted finding his usual targets, he enjoyed this new game of searching for anything not in the plant world. He barked for me to come see a hamburger wrapper, a small flashlight, and a paper napkin. Nancy reported finding a notepad and a Missouri map with the route from Archer's last scheduled stop to Laycock traced on it. I picked up two ballpoint pens and a flexible plastic drinking straw. My interest flagged.

"I found the glove," Nancy called, holding it up. "It was under some mashed-down weeds. It's dirty, but it's not torn. Let's call it a day."

Achilles, sniffing around a cluster of gooseberry bushes, barked twice and sat down. He bounced up as I tramped through the bushes eager to see what had sparked this reaction.

He stood sniffing a silver thermos about half the size of the gray one I'd carried to school. He acted as excited as he did when he found drugs or explosives. I picked up the thermos between my thumb and middle finger, unscrewed the top, and flipped up a pouring spout. The odor of strong, bitter coffee drifted out.

Nancy came up behind me. "That's Molly's thermos. She had it with her at the lunch in Macon yesterday. She always brought her own coffee. They tease her about her coffee being so strong she eats it rather than drinks it."

I shook the thermos and heard a small splash.

Achilles barked three times and nudged the hand that held the top.

He disliked some odors, particularly men's cologne, but he'd never objected to coffee before. What had his incredibly sensitive nose detected? Convinced the thermos contained more than coffee, I closed the spout and screwed on the top.

"Molly will be so glad you found it." Nancy reached for the thermos. "I'll give it to her."

I tucked it into the garbage bag. "Sorry." Nancy Alderton was a smart woman. What could I tell her she would believe? "This is the scene of a fatal accident. As a reserve deputy, I'm legally obligated to turn over everything we found here to the sheriff's department to be vetted before it's returned to the owners."

She stared at me, obviously skeptical. "Really?"

I didn't blink. "Yes, but I'm sure Jim—Sheriff Falstaff—will release the items we found in a day or two." Right after we got a chemical analysis of the contents of the thermos to see if Achilles' nose had pointed to murder.

CHAPTER FIVE

Achilles took a final sniff around the gooseberry bushes, barked softly to draw my attention, and trotted onto the road and toward the SUV.

"He's convinced we've found everything from the crash," I told Nancy. I pulled two paper sacks out of the garbage bag. "Put the map and the glove in separate evidence bags."

She frowned. "Those are just paper sacks from the grocery store."

"Yes. These cost the county a lot less than commercial evidence bags."

She didn't move to take the bags. "Phoenix, I asked you to bring Clarissa and me out here as a friend, not as a volunteer deputy."

I doubted that, but I said reassuringly, "Then trust me to do what needs to be done."

She studied my face for several seconds and then took the sacks. "I do trust you. You have no idea how much." She placed the items in the sacks, handed them back to me, and walked toward the road. "I agree with Achilles. Besides, it's getting chilly and late. I'm driving Clarissa home to have dinner with Archer's three sons and their families tonight. She's giving them final say on the memorial service Saturday. I'll stay with her until then."

"Nicole will take care of the terrier?"

"Yes." Nancy looked back over her shoulder at me and smiled. "Unless someone else volunteers."

No way. "Nicole will do a great job." Our short walk up the hill was my last chance to ask the minister about a source of help for the domestic refugee. "I have a question for you. You must deal with a lot of family problems as a minister and know service groups who provide assistance. Where would you send a woman who needs to get far away from a violent husband?"

She pulled up the hood over her short gray hair. "Most shelters accept women from outside their area. Women desperate enough to leave their homes often go to another town to be safe. Shelters try to keep their housing locations for abused women secret, but the word leaks out in small towns, even in cities."

I'd already eliminated shelters as a solution for my young applicant. "A shelter provides temporary refuge. Who around here helps a woman with no resources to relocate and establish a new identity?"

"I don't know. That would require a network of shelters, other nonprofits, and dedicated volunteers."

I needed an entry point into that network. "Who would you call if one of your First Methodist parishioners came in with a black eye and a broken arm?"

"The police, of course."

"And after the police let him out of jail? After he threatens to kill her?"

She pulled the hood more tightly around her face. "Well, Phoenix," she said, her voice muffled, "since I wouldn't know who could help her, I'd call members of my church who might. My first call would be to a compassionate former sheriff with an uncanny knack for unraveling complicated cases."

Strike three. The minister had no more idea of how to assure Tara Augeri's safety than Annalynn and I did.

Achilles barked to announce that we were coming.

Annalynn got out of the back seat and opened the front door. She and Achilles returned to their original places. They were both ready to go home.

"If you don't mind," Nancy said as we reached the SUV, "I'll ask the ex-sheriff if it would be okay for us to take the things we found."

"Of course." Damn! If Connie were here, I could be sure she would catch a subtle clue and back me up, taking pleasure in the improv.

Annalynn lied only in matters of life and death.

Which this could be. How did I let her know? Taking my keys from my pocket, I felt the evidence gloves that I'd peeled off. I slipped the right one on so that Annalynn would see it and know I'd used it. Then I moved quickly to put the garbage bag in the back of the SUV and hop into the driver's seat. I made it there a split second after Nancy took her seat by her sister.

"Clarissa, we found the glove," Nancy said. "And a map, an iPhone, and a thermos." She fastened her seatbelt. "Annalynn, do we need to give the personal items we found to the state troopers?"

I ripped off the glove and tossed it into Annalynn's lap.

Annalynn turned toward the back seat. "I'm not sure, but they'll want to list those items in their report. I'll take them to the sheriff's department this evening. If no one needs to hold them, I'll return them Saturday." She faced me. "Did you photograph the items *in situ*?"

Nice touch. "No, sorry. I didn't even think about it." Home free.

The conversation turned to music for the memorial service.

The minute we dropped the sisters off at Nancy's car, Annalynn took a deep breath and exhaled. "That evidence glove scared me silly, Phoenix. What on earth did you find?"

"Not me, Achilles. He acted like that hospitalized assistant's thermos contains something dangerous." I pulled out of the parking lot.

"Good boy, Achilles." She stroked him. "So, naturally, you opened it."

"Yes. It smells like a strong day-old espresso."

"Archer stopped drinking anything with caffeine years ago. The coffee had to belong to Molly Dolichek." Annalynn sat silent as I drove toward the castle. "You assume someone added a toxic substance to the coffee that made them both ill."

Who wouldn't? "Achilles' nose knows what it knows. The coffee has to be tested."

"Oh, Lord! You've jumped from accident to suicide to homicide.

Clarissa was so relieved when you said he overcorrected." Annalynn poked my arm. "But you anticipated that. You should have warned me they wanted us to look for an indication of suicide!"

"Sorry, but my source didn't seem all that credible." I hesitated to repeat Nicole's words and influence Annalynn's thinking. "Did Clarissa tell you why she considered suicide a possibility?"

"You mean the Alzheimer's that the dog walker told you about and you kept from me? The woman called Nancy to apologize and swear she'd told no one else. Clarissa thought only the doctor and Nancy knew the diagnosis. Archer planned to tell his family next week at their Thanksgiving gathering."

"How did Nicole—the dog walker—find out?" I turned into the driveway and reached for the garage door remote.

"She was dusting and saw notes Nancy had made." Annalynn took the remote but didn't punch the opener. "We're going straight to the sheriff's department. They'll have to give the thermos to Captain Gist. He didn't like us investigating when I was acting sheriff. He'll throw a fit when he hears you want the Highway Patrol lab to test whatever is in the thermos."

All too true. "Can we count on Gist to send it to the lab based on Achilles' reaction? I'd rather ask Stuart to send it to a DEA lab."

"No. Absolutely not. Giving it to the DEA could destroy the chain of evidence. A prosecutor might not be able to use it in court." She groaned. "If it comes to that."

"You're right." I reconsidered. "So am I. Just to be safe, I'll pour a little of the coffee into a sterile container. I'll send it to a lab myself." I turned off the motor to reinforce my words.

She rubbed her temple. "I wish you'd get over being a spy. You expect everyone to conspire, double cross, cheat."

Those expectations had saved my life several times in Eastern Europe and in Vandiver County. How could I convince her we dare not leave the test to the police? "If someone set out to harm the assistant or the congressman, that person poses a danger to others. We can't take a chance that Gist will ignore the coffee or that the overloaded lab will delay the test."

She bit her lower lip. "Most toxicology tests take weeks, especially when you don't know what to test for." She opened her car door. "Okay. Bring the bag. I won't touch it, but I'll sterilize a container. When you've extracted a sample, we'll take everything to the sheriff's department."

Achilles leapt out and raced toward the backyard.

Annalynn unlocked the front door for me, went into the dining room, and draped her coat over a chair. "Give me five minutes or so."

I put the paper sack holding the thermos on the table. I kept the sack holding the iPhone. It would be foolish not to check it, but Annalynn might not appreciate my doing that. "I'm going upstairs. Call me when the container is ready."

I went to my bedroom, closed the door, pulled on a fresh evidence glove, and took the iPhone from the sack. I turned on the phone. Nothing. A dead battery? I could charge it if Annalynn left me alone long enough. I plugged in my laptop, connected the phone to it, and opened an app that allowed me to transfer information from others' phones. While I waited for the phone and laptop to become friends, I brushed my hair and put on fresh lipstick. Annalynn would notice I'd spent time doing that.

"Phoenix," Annalynn called from downstairs. "Ready."

I wasn't. "Be there in a minute." A dozen or so photos of kids playing football and leading cheers popped up on my screen. I closed my photo file and transferred the contact list.

"Phoenix," Annalynn said right outside my door, "at the risk of getting too personal, what on earth are you doing in there?"

"Admiring my classic beauty." I downloaded the text messages and voice mails that Molly hadn't deleted.

Annalynn opened the door, an unusual violation of privacy. "I thought so. You're snooping on that phone. That's not legal even if you were a real deputy."

I unplugged the iPhone from my laptop. "The battery was dead. I charged it enough to make sure it's Molly's phone, not one someone else dropped after the crash." Quite true. I held up the phone so she could see the sliver of green indicating minimal battery life. "It's hers."

"And the information on it is now yours, I suppose." Annalynn shook her head in dismay at my transgression. "That battery better be dead when we turn the phone in. Leave it on while you take a sample of the coffee."

Downstairs, I placed the phone in its paper sack and went to the granite island in the kitchen where Annalynn had put a small glass bottle. To be sure I left enough liquid for the state lab, I poured out a few drops at a time. I stopped when the bottle contained about a tablespoon of coffee. It smelled even stronger in the kitchen than it had in the open air.

Annalynn watched my every move. "From the smell, you'd think it would be as thick as syrup. You're sure you've left enough in the thermos?"

"Yes." I shook it. "Hear that?"

"Good. You put everything back in place while I call Jim to tell him what we're bringing." She went to her home office, out of earshot, to call.

A razor-thin green line still showed on Molly's iPhone, enough power for me to check apps. She used surprisingly few. The screen went black, and I put both sacks in the garbage bag.

Annalynn came into the dining room. "Jim was on his way out, but he's calling Captain Gist to tell him that Achilles found something suspicious. Let's go."

Jim met us in the department's parking lot, his thick whiskers making him look like he'd shaved two days ago instead of this morning. He and Annalynn walked to the back of the SUV to get the garbage bag.

I rolled down my window as he came toward me with the bag. "Hi, Jim. Quintin asked me to pass along his congratulations on your election." Jim and my younger brother had been best buds through junior and senior high school.

"Tell him thanks." Jim grinned. "Gist gave me a two-part

35

message for you. One, thanks. Two, butt out."

I grinned back. "Tell him, 'You're welcome. Don't drop the ball.'"

Annalynn said, "Jim, please omit part two of that message."

"Sam doesn't need to hear it anyway," Jim said. "He's real upset about the accident. I left out the string of profanity he barfed up when I told him my reserve deputies found a suspicious substance." Jim stepped back. "Let me know if you come across anything else. Good night."

And it was night, although not yet six. I pulled out of the lot. "That went well."

"Yes, all things considered." Annalynn checked her phone. "Amazing. I don't know who has given my numbers to all these people. I have twenty messages from party leaders around the state, plus a dozen left on the landline. Excuse me while I start answering them."

When we got home, she hurried into her office, and I went upstairs to study what I'd downloaded from the ailing assistant's phone. I'd email anything of interest to my office desktop, save it to a secure hard drive, and delete it from my computers. I sat in the middle of my bed and opened Molly Dolichek's voicemail. Two short "call me" messages, neither from yesterday. I moved on to the texts. Pretty much the same. With the boss holding a string of meetings, Molly probably spent the day on her business phone.

Next came the contact list. The top entry was Aunt E. What the hell? I knew that number, as I knew every phone number I'd seen in the last year. It belonged to Nancy Alderton. She'd played Aunt Eller in Connie's production of *Oklahoma!* a few weeks ago. No big deal that Molly Dolichek's personal contact list included Candon's sister-in-law's cell number, but why conceal it with an alias?

I scrolled through the next four contacts, all first names only. None had a mailing or an email address. When I saw Hull House, the settlement house founded by reformer Jane Addams, I suspected another alias. I knew I was right when I looked at the phone number. Hull House's number was the one Tara Augeri had listed on her application.

How in heck were these three women connected?

CHAPTER SIX

Hoping to find a clue to the relationship between the teenage abused wife, the congressional staffer, and the Methodist minister, I checked the other phone numbers on Molly's contact list. I didn't recognize any of them. All but two had a Missouri area code, most of them in rural northern Missouri.

Tara's Hull House alias convinced me Molly had played a role in the teenager's flight from her husband. Tara's email name, Desdemona, fit with the pattern of aliases on the contact list. I remembered Nancy, aka Aunt E, saying that she trusted me and that she would go to her parishioners for advice about where an abused wife might seek shelter. She must have prompted the application to CAC and written the narrative. The inevitable conclusion: She and Molly were part of causemail.com or of a network serving abused women. But why didn't Nancy contact CAC herself? Why didn't she tell me this afternoon that she knew Tara?

Before talking to either woman, I wanted more information. I focused on the other names, noting three more from literature and two from history. If the other contacts used their personal phones as Nancy did, tracking down the owners' real names online would be relatively easy. If they used burner phones, the task became formidable.

And what good would identifying the contacts do? These do-gooders surely didn't pose a threat. Helping abused women made them more likely to be past victims than perpetrators.

That thought raised a disturbing possibility: Had Tara Augeri's husband discovered Molly's role in hiding the fugitive and put a toxic substance in her thermos?

I jumped off the bed to go share my speculations with Annalynn. Then I stopped short of the door. I'd witnessed many unlikely events, but that abusive young man poisoning Molly's coffee seemed out of character. Besides, nothing yet proved foul play caused the staffer's illness or her boss's death. From what Annalynn and I had heard from Clarissa and news reports, Molly's doctor attributed her illness to natural causes. Captain Gist had stated that the congressman died from injuries received in an accident. The busy officer wouldn't investigate the death as a possible homicide unless the medical examiner came across something unexpected during the standard autopsy. Or found poison in the thermos.

But toxicology tests often took weeks, and every instinct honed during my years in Eastern Europe warned me not to wait for the test results to investigate the possibility of a malicious act.

The front door slammed, and paws sounded on the stairs. Achilles leapt into the room and did a mid-air turn to avoid slamming into me.

"Hey, boy, what's the rush?" I reached out and touched icy hair. How did his wet hair get past Annalynn? I guided him to the old hooked rug that served as his mattress. "Sit."

"Hi, Phoenix." Connie rushed in and handed me a roll of paper towels. "He was so excited to tell you about the sleet that he evaded Annalynn. What's for supper?"

My turn to cook dinner, and I'd forgotten about it. Annalynn wouldn't care if we repeated lunch. "Chicken vegetable soup." I began to rub Achilles down. I'd need Connie's help to convince Annalynn we should start digging before the test results—mine or the official ones—came in. "I'd like for you to read an urgent application while I fix dinner." I gave Achilles a final rub and brought Tara's application up on my laptop. "Annalynn already knows about this, but I came across some new information that I want to discuss while we eat."

Connie smiled. "You want me to talk Annalynn into paying attention to the foundation instead of her campaign."

"Not instead of, as well as. This can't wait. Just read the application." I hurried downstairs, Achilles at my heels. I fed him before attending to our meal. While heating the soup and tossing a salad, I mulled over ways to make my case for conducting an all-out investigation of these two intertwined cases.

Connie would back me. She reacted instantly, guided by emotion rather than intellect, but she understood people and offered insights that sometimes escaped me. She also thought creatively, coming up with theatrical but effective ways of gathering information. Annalynn, on the other hand, proceeded methodically, insisted on evidence, and considered the implications of our actions. She feared the calculated risks I took to catch criminals. The two balanced my analytical skills and the cynicism that evoked my worst-case scenarios.

Connie came into the kitchen. "No distraught teenager wrote that scary tale and came up with Desdemona for her email handle. Have you verified Tara Augeri's story?"

"Enough to know she's for real, and I'm almost certain Nancy Alderton ghostwrote the application. I'll explain at dinner." I picked up the tray with our salads and silverware. "Pry the phone from Annalynn's ear while I set the table."

Connie returned by the time I put the food in place. "She says not to wait for her."

Go for the dramatic. "Tell her I found a connection between Tara Augeri and Molly Dolichek."

Connie's eyes widened. "The woman who got too sick to drive Candon to LCC?"

"That's the one. Go. I'm saying nothing more until we're all at the table."

"Wow! This is going to be good!" Connie practically skipped toward the ladies' parlor. She came back as I placed a bowl of soup at each place. "Annalynn'll be here in a minute." Connie took her regular place across from me. "Trudy saw you pick up the rev and the widow this afternoon. My nosy cousin thinks you took them to see where Candon died."

Trudy volunteered at the church to increase her access to gossip. By now she'd told half the town where we'd been. If you can't deny a rumor, direct it. "Yes. Clarissa wanted to look for personal items that fell out of the car. Tell Trudy that, but don't let her know that we found Molly's cell phone and thermos."

Annalynn charged to the table. "Spill it, Phoenix. What information did you illegally obtain from that phone?"

"Have you forgotten the concept of deniability, Madam Candidate?" I let that sink in a moment. "Let's agree that this conversation falls under the confidentiality promised to CAC applicants."

"Certainly," Connie said, her eyes shining with excitement. "Come on, Annalynn. You're not sheriff anymore."

Annalynn glared at me without answering.

Connie nudged my leg with her foot. "Annalynn, we'll understand if you want to—uhh—to recuse yourself." Connie patted Annalynn's clenched fist. "Phoenix and I will rescue the poor girl. You go back to answering calls."

I suppressed a smile. Connie's enthusiastic involvement in our official homicide investigations had annoyed me and frightened Annalynn.

She frowned. Then her face lit up, and she reached out to grasp Connie's hand. "All these calls remind me of when I ran for homecoming queen. Party leaders from all over the state are encouraging me to run." She clasped my hand. "I can do it, Phoenix. I can really do it!"

"Of course you can," I said, and Connie chimed in.

After a minute of shared elation, Annalynn sobered. "You two will have to take the lead on this finding a solution for that young woman, but let's discuss the application as the CAC board. You start, Phoenix."

"Tara's phone number is on Molly's contact list under Hull House." I held up my hand to stop their simultaneous questions. "The list includes other historical or literary names. The only other number I recognized belongs to Aunt E."

Annalynn frowned. "Who's that?"

Connie bounced in her chair. "Aunt E for Aunt Eller, Nancy Alderton. She's the one who wrote the application. Who would have guessed she and that congressional staffer are part of a secret rescue squad?"

I reached across the table to give Connie a high five. "You didn't hear that from me, Annalynn."

"No, and I didn't touch that thermos either." She sucked in her breath. "My God! If Achilles was right about the coffee, Tara's husband may have poisoned Molly Dolichek."

Connie's smile faded. "What? You lost me."

I explained how Achilles behaved when he found the thermos, concluding, "So if the coffee contains poison, the person who put it there targeted the staffer. Her boss could have been collateral damage."

Connie pursed her lips. "Hold on, Phoenix. How would a stranger know about her coffee fetish? Or that she carries a special thermos?"

Annalynn had the answer. "Hundreds of people have seen her drink coffee from that thermos. Archer and the staff have teased her about her high-octane habit at events for years. Augeri could have heard about it. He may even have attended one of those coffees."

Then we had to pursue the lead. "Do you know yesterday's schedule, Annalynn?"

"Molly and other staff accompanied Clarissa and Archer to two short coffees with constituents before lunch. Molly introduced him at each place. Archer said hello, shook hands, and posed for photos." Annalynn paused and cleared her throat. "Clarissa said he had the best day Wednesday that he'd had in weeks. She had the staff schedule the events so Archer wouldn't have time to make a speech or answer questions. Because he was doing so well, after lunch Clarissa and Nancy came on to Laycock with Roland Renmar—the advance man so worried about the press last night—to make sure everything was ready at LCC. Archer and Molly attended two more short coffees."

"Let's analyze this." I ticked off the steps Adam Augeri would have followed to poison Molly Dolichek. "First, Othello found out Molly is hiding Desdemona. Feasible. Then he learned where Molly works. Easy. He still had to find out she'd be at those constituent meetings."

"Also easy," Annalynn said. "The schedule was on the news and the congressman's website."

Both of which facts I'd ignored. "Then comes the hard part: Augeri had to know Molly would be carrying her thermos of coffee. Otherwise he wouldn't have come prepared to poison her, let alone managing to do it in a roomful of people."

Connie leaned forward and jabbed the air with her spoon. "What if he'd been stalking the woman, following her in hopes she'd lead him to Tara? Maybe he went to one of the morning coffees, saw the thermos, and dropped in the poison that afternoon."

The obvious hit me. "We need to know where he was yesterday. If he was at work all day, he couldn't have done it."

"Checking alibis is a job for the police," Annalynn said, her tone not inviting disagreement. "If the test shows poison, we have to put aside confidentiality and tell Captain Gist about the application."

I hated the thought of laming CAC by violating confidentiality, but I said only, "I doubt that young man poisoned Molly, but I'm fairly certain someone did. We can't take the chance of waiting for the test results before we check him out. He could try again."

Annalynn rubbed her right temple, a sign of stress. "Okay, but hold off until we hear from Captain Gist about when we can expect the test results. What else can we do *about the application* while we wait for the coffee to be tested, Phoenix?"

"Tomorrow I'll look into ways to establish a new identity for the girl in another state." Right after I checked Augeri's alibi. "Tonight our priority is to learn Molly's specific diagnosis. Maybe we're being too suspicious. Maybe the coffee was just coffee. A former sheriff is the one to ask for that information."

She grimaced. "Gist is almost sure to call to ask what we were doing at Star Corner. I'll see what I can pry out of him. If we're lucky, the medical findings will settle this. What are you going to do?"

I considered a moment. "Look for more information on Adam Augeri online. How big a threat is he? Does he have resources to look for Tara out of state?"

Connie spoke up. "I know Nancy better than either of you. I'll call her to find out where he lives and what else she knows about him."

Annalynn's cell rang. She glanced at it and pushed back her chair. "I have to take this."

When Annalynn disappeared into her office, Connie leaned across the table and whispered, "You and I have to move on this. If we can find out where he works, I'll use a fake identity to check his alibi tomorrow morning. I can make calls between voice lessons."

And give me deniability. "Good. I'll locate a burner phone for you to use. Could you look online for the owners of the numbers on Molly's contact list tonight? I'll open up the file before I go to Trudy's house to look at the cake. If we need to make calls to follow up, we'll split them."

A tingle of anticipation went down my spine. The chase was on.

CHAPTER SEVEN

Connie leaned back in her chair, alerting me to Annalynn's return, and said, "Phoenix, when are you going to Trudy's to see the birthday cake? She's so pleased that you hired her to make it."

An instant later Annalynn's steps sounded behind me. She sat down and picked up her salad fork. "You're going to Trudy's house? You've crossed the street to avoid her ever since you came back to Laycock."

Because I didn't want to risk raising questions about my cover story of gall bladder surgery by swapping medical tales with her. And because she'd snooped in our mothers' closets when she babysat with Annalynn and me as little kids. "Trudy's a wonderful baker."

"Phoenix," Annalynn said in her gotcha voice, "what's so important about Stuart's mother's birthday cake?"

Connie laughed. "Sorry, Annalynn, it's not a tryout as a wedding cake. It's decorated with math problems, all with the same answer: seventy-five. No one but Phoenix would come up with a cake like this."

Unsure whether that was praise or derision, I defended myself. "I want it to be a tiny thank you for all Mrs. Roper did for me as a high school student. I would never have thought to major in math and then economics without her guidance and encouragement."

Annalynn shook her finger at me. "Beth Roper would encourage your relationship with Stuart if she thought you would make a commitment."

"She might, but her grandkids won't. Kaysi and Zeke object to my joining them at the birthday lunch." I couldn't imagine what daddy's girl would post if she knew how determined her father was to overcome my resistance to marriage.

"Beth says Zeke is more open than his big sister," Annalynn said, "and he's always wanted a dog. Achilles will win him over. Kaysi will be off to college next year. She won't be staying at Stuart's condo every weekend the way she does now."

Stuart had mentioned that several times, but never in front of Annalynn. I could guess who had. "I asked you not to talk to Mrs. Roper about Stuart and me."

"For heaven's sake," Annalynn said, averting her eyes, "stop calling her Mrs. Roper. Call her Beth."

"Phoenix, you need to leave in a few minutes," Connie cut in. Having been divorced after thirty years in a less and less happy marriage, she understood my caution about marrying again better than Annalynn did. "I'll clean up in the kitchen."

I still had half my bowl of soup to eat, but I'd lost my appetite. "Thanks. I'll put my soup in the refrigerator and finish eating when I get back." I got up and went to the front window to look out.

Annalynn said, "I'm sorry, Phoenix. I know Kaysi's attitude upsets you. Please sit down and finish your dinner."

"Later." I hurried to the refrigerator. "The street was too warm for the sleet to stick, but I better leave now in case the temperature drops tonight."

My cell rang as I reached the stairs. Stuart. Usually we talked near bedtime. "Hi, you're early tonight. Is something wrong?"

"No, I just wanted to hear your voice. I was watching TV while I ate and spewed water on my shirt laughing at you and Connie hamming it up. You two should form an act."

"Keep that thought to yourself, please." Tossing barbs at each other had given Connie and me an unexpected rapport onstage and in uncomfortable situations.

"I saw Annalynn's tribute to Candon, too. Very impressive for impromptu remarks. Did the family ask her to speak at the memorial Saturday?"

Now I knew why he'd called. He was afraid I'd go to the memorial to support Annalynn and bail on lunch with his kids again. "No, but even if she does, I'll be at your mother's house." I went into my bedroom, Achilles at my heels. "I'm just about to leave to check the cake, but I have a favor to ask. Can you send a sample of coffee to a DEA lab? Or tell me where to send it? Achilles sniffed out a thermos where Candon's car rolled over. He acted as though it contains drugs."

Stuart whistled. "You amaze me with the way you pick up things everybody else misses, but you don't have Annalynn in the sheriff's department to hide your—umm—unorthodox methods now. Please, hon, take the coffee straight to the Highway Patrol."

"Relax, lawman." One of the great things about Stuart was that after he'd figured out I'd been CIA, he didn't ask for details. He also didn't question my ability to deal with trouble, but he gave me his honest reactions. I'd rarely been so comfortable with anyone. I pictured his big, broad-shouldered frame and his pleasant but not handsome face. "We handed it over immediately. Right after I—not Annalynn—extracted a tablespoon of it. I want to make sure we get the results fast. You know how overloaded the state labs are, and Captain Gist may not take Achilles' word that something's wrong."

Silence. "You have a point. I'll see what I can do." He paused. "I expect a reward."

Rewards had proved to be a treat for both of us. "You'll get one." I glanced at the grandfather's clock. "I need to go. Can we talk at the usual time?"

"Call me back when you're wearing something erotic."

I dismissed an erotic thought. "Would you prefer the blue flannel or the green flannel?"

He laughed. "Cancel that motel reservation and come stay with me during all of Achilles' training. I'll turn the thermostat up to eighty so you won't need your flannel pajamas."

"And give your kids one more reason to hate me. Bye." Under

pressure, I'd agreed to consider staying with Stuart a few nights, but he hadn't mentioned my sleeping over while his kids were there. Surely he didn't expect me to cross that bridge. That problem could wait. I woke up the laptop and opened Molly Dolichek's contact list for Connie.

When I took my parka from the closet beneath the stairs, Achilles ran up with his leash. "Stay with Annalynn. I'll be back soon. "

He whined and pressed up against me.

Our trip to Star Corner had upset him, or perhaps he was responding to Annalynn's suppressed tension. "I can't take you to Trudy's."

Connie walked in from the dining room. "Come, Achilles. I'll play fetch with you in the basement. Find us a Frisbee."

He trotted toward the entertainment room, and I hurried out the front door and to my one-car garage next to Annalynn's. My banged-up white Camry liked the cold mist, and the tires clung to the road as I drove to the northwest edge of town where Trudy and her husband lived in an old farmhouse. I turned into the driveway and parked parallel to the back door, the regular entrance. The porch light shone on a long ramp they'd put over the two back steps when a hit-and-run driver broke Trudy's leg last May.

I steeled myself for questions about Stuart. That was part of the cost of hiring Trudy to do my baking.

The back door led to a narrow closed-in porch with a washer and dryer at the far end, snow shovels and salt in the middle, and a bench for taking off muddy boots at the other end.

Trudy opened the kitchen door. "Any trouble on the road?"

"No, it's not slick."

She took my jacket and draped it over a chair at an old rectangular oak table where the birthday cake posed on a cake stand. "The depth of the icing is uneven because I had to keep fooling with all the whatsits. Now that I know how to do it, I'll get it right on the one I bake tomorrow. See what you think."

I liked the round three-layer cake more each step I took toward it. I turned the cake stand to study the details of the chocolate equations on the creamy icing. Everything added up. "I love it. You did a wonderful job on the numbers and the symbols."

She beamed. "I'm still not sure about that pi thing."

Giving pi my full attention, I saw room for improvement. "Do you have a toothpick?"

She brought a container from her work counter.

I took a smooth toothpick and perfected the top curve with it. In doing so, I smeared chocolate into the cream icing. "That would be better, but don't worry if that's too fine a line."

She took another toothpick and cleaned up my mess. "No problem. I want to save this one as the model. I used the spare layer for the taste test. Do you want just a bite, or do you have time to eat a piece and drink a cup of coffee?"

Normally I would have run at the thought of trapping myself at her table, but I was hungry. "A piece with coffee, thanks."

"I gave my Raleigh a slice when he came by. He loved those dark chocolate chips you had me add. He's going to add chips the next time he bakes a chocolate cake at the firehouse."

While she cut the test cake, I poured the coffee, added cream to mine, and sat down.

Salivating when she placed the cake in front of me, I sliced off a bite with lots of cake and a little icing. Pure heaven. "Delicious! You have no idea how I missed American chocolate cake all those years in Vienna. The Sacher torte is highly overrated. Mrs. Roper and I talked about it once. That's how I knew chocolate's her favorite." I dug in.

"Phoenix, I want to ask you something."

Here it came.

"I'm worried about Connie's new job. She was so excited, and you know she needs the money. Now that Archer is dead, will LCC still get that new music program?"

Not what I'd expected. "Don't worry. The paperwork is done and the funds allotted. Besides, Clarissa Candon was the one who originated the idea. She won't drop it."

Trudy nodded. "She taught music for twenty years before she married Archer, and she's a really good singer. None of the Candons ever gave a darn about music."

An unexpected source of information. "You've known them a long time?"

"My husband knew Archer when they were kids. I met Clarissa and Nancy at a church music camp near Marshall when we were teenagers. They were real smart and real nice." She sipped on her coffee. "Archer's death is goin' to be awful hard on Clarissa, but it's probably a blessing in the long run."

"Why do you say that? I understood his family lived long, healthy lives."

"On his mother's side, the Archers. His father lived into his seventies, but in his last years he worried his wife to death and drove the rest of the family to drink."

Careful. "Oh? Why was that?"

She shrugged. "At first people said he was cantankerous. That's what they say about a nasty rich man, I reckon. Then one day a neighbor saw him shoveling snow in his birthday suit. He almost froze off—uhh—his eleventh finger."

I suppressed a smile at the term. "Did he take off his clothes because he had a fever?"

"I don't know, but Archer and his two brothers—they both died years ago—they finally admitted he was senile and put him in a home. I'd never heard of Alzheimer's in those days, but I s'pect that's what it was."

Hmm. So Archer Candon had seen what happened to his father and knew firsthand the stress and anguish dementia placed on a family. No wonder Clarissa suspected her husband committed suicide. I needed to consider this in my analysis of what had happened at Star Corner.

"Speaking of brothers, is Ulysses still teaching astrophysics in California?"

Where did this question about my older brother come from? "Just one post-graduate class. He's working for a company conducting research in space. High, high tech." I pushed back my chair. "This is delicious, Trudy. Would it be okay for me to pick up the cake about ten thirty Saturday morning?"

"Sure." She paused. "How many people will be at Beth's luncheon?"

A sneaky way to ask who would be there. "I'm not sure. It's mostly a family gathering."

Trudy's eyes lit up. "How are you getting on with Stuart's kids?"

Scheisse. Stepped right into that one. "I don't know them. Mrs. Roper was my mentor in high school, and we've always kept in touch." Get out of here. "Thanks so much." I grabbed my coat and fled.

Driving home, I focused on a new possibility. If Archer Candon wanted to kill himself in a car "accident" without hurting anyone else, he had to create an opportunity to drive alone. The only person still with him that night was Molly Dolichek. What if he had placed something in the thermos to make her too ill to drive? And what better way to stage a suicide as an accident than to have a trooper watch it happen through his rearview mirror?

CHAPTER EIGHT

Vernon was walking up Annalynn's porch steps when I pulled into my driveway. He didn't like to drive on dark, wet streets, so something big had brought him over to meet with Annalynn. Had he come as a reporter or a political strategist?

Achilles met me at the door and escorted me to the ladies' parlor. Connie and Annalynn sat on the loveseat, a yellow legal pad face down on the coffee table in front of them. Vernon stood by the overstuffed chair where Connie usually perched.

Greeting them, I went to my chair, slipped off my damp shoes so I could put my feet on the hassock, and waited for action.

Vernon sat down. He ran his left hand back through his silver hair. "Maybe we should talk alone, Annalynn."

I jumped up. "Connie and I will fix some tea."

"And crumpets," Connie added, following me with the legal pad in her hand.

Usually you couldn't pry her out of earshot of a private conversation. She'd found something juicy. I ran water in the teakettle. "Who did you find on that list?"

"An interesting hodgepodge. Molly Dolichek definitely was working on finding a way to get that girl more help. Annalynn thinks some of the numbers, like one at the Missouri Coalition Against Domestic and Sexual Violence, are work contacts, but why would she have them on her private phone with code names?" Connie handed me the pad.

"Phoenix, Connie, forget the tea," Annalynn called.

I put the legal pad on the granite island and turned off the burner before heading back to take my seat in the parlor.

Annalynn gestured to Vernon to begin.

"I got a call from a friend who works for the AP in Washington. A political blog just announced Candon was diagnosed with Alzheimer's two months ago." Vernon waited until it became obvious none of us was going to comment. "I see that surprised me more than it did you." He leaned forward. "According to the blogger, a reliable source speculates that Archer Candon committed suicide." Vernon focused on me. "Could that crash have been a suicide?"

Not the world's business. "How on earth would I know? Ask Captain Gist. He's the one who witnessed it."

Vernon rolled a ballpoint around in his right hand and stared at it. When he looked at me again, he'd morphed from a political strategist into a reporter. "You drove the widow to Star Corner this afternoon. She'd never even met you before last night. Why did she ask you to inspect the crash scene, Phoenix?"

I said nothing, sure he was guessing.

Annalynn blinked in surprise. Then she put on her public face. "I didn't go out there to investigate the crash. Clarissa felt compelled to see where her husband died." She met Vernon's skeptical eyes. "We found where the car went off the road first on one side and then the other. All of us, including Phoenix, assumed he overcorrected."

He nodded. "That's what I concluded when I saw the tire markings last night. Did Clarissa say anything about Archer having Alzheimer's?"

More and more irritated that the press would violate the family's privacy, I jumped in. "Not to me. That Washington blogger's reliable source surely was a member of either Candon's or a doctor's staff. Who else would know about the diagnosis?"

Connie shuddered. "Who would have so little feeling for his family that they would publicize a suicide rumor?"

Vernon turned to Connie. "That's what bothers me. Why would someone come forward with this? It's not as though Candon was a high-profile legislator. My AP friend and I have agreed to share whatever I can find out here with what he can uncover there." The reporter leaned forward. "Connie, your cousin knows more about what happens in people's personal lives than any reporter. Has Trudy said anything to you about Candon having Alzheimer's?"

"No, she barely knows the Candons," Connie said.

I kept my mouth shut.

The phone rang.

Annalynn went to her desk to look at the caller ID. She let it go to voice mail. "Today I've talked to at least twenty people who knew Archer for years. Not one hinted at Alzheimer's. You interviewed the congressman by phone a week ago, Vern. Did you notice any mental impairment?"

"No, I didn't." Vernon sighed. "I probably should have. Thor Stigen, the chief of staff, answered most of the questions, all of those that required details. I didn't think much about it. Archer was exuberant about finally succeeding in inserting a measure for soybean farmers in that must-pass farm bill. He expected to win by a close vote right after the Thanksgiving recess." Vernon stood up. "Even if Archer killed himself, my AP friend doesn't see a political motive for the leak. No candidate to succeed him is going to gain or lose votes over how Candon died."

I spoke my thought: "The usual motive for betraying someone's trust is money."

The newsman frowned. "No tabloid or brainless cable pundit would pay more than a few dollars for the tip, and I doubt the blogger paid anything."

Annalynn said, "I'll get your coat." She left the room.

Vernon lingered by the hall door. "Find anything interesting at the crash scene, Phoenix?"

I stroked Achilles' head. "Candon's missing leather glove and a hamburger wrapper."

The newsman stepped toward me and said softly, "Don't hold out on me. I can't help Annalynn get the nomination if I don't know what's really going on."

I nodded but made no promises.

The minute the door closed behind him, I told Annalynn and Connie what Trudy had said about Candon's father. I ended with, "The congressman must have been in the early stages to function so well, but he certainly knew what to expect later. We can't rule out the possibility he spiked his assistant's coffee so he could use her car to kill himself."

"And risked killing her? I doubt it." Annalynn rubbed her temple. "If he did, Molly Dolichek might not say so. Clarissa said the woman is extremely loyal. Her first job was working for Archer's company. She went from there to working on his campaigns and then constituent services. She's headed his district offices for two or three years."

Connie, always restless, left her chair to pace. "Did you ask Stuart about testing the coffee, Phoenix?"

"He'll let me know how to go about that later tonight." I remembered Connie had left her notes in the kitchen. "You said you'd found some interesting names on Molly Dolichek's contact list. Any of them doctors or reporters?"

"No. I'll get my tablet." She rushed out.

"Annalynn, why didn't you tell Vernon about Candon's Alzheimer's?"

"Clarissa told me in confidence. I could talk about it with you because you already knew." She stood up. "Let's go turn on the TV. If the AP reporter picked up the story from a blog, so will cable news."

The three of us had barely settled onto the huge couch when a young woman in a dress that left no room for breathing read the breaking news: "Congressman Archer Candon's death in a one-car crash on an isolated Missouri road may have been a suicide. A reliable source has revealed that the seventy-seven-year-old legislator had been despondent since being diagnosed with dementia in September. We interviewed Roland Renmar, the late congressman's advance man, via Skype."

Renmar's agitated, raccoon-eyed face came on the screen. He shouted, "Someone has started an unsubstantiated rumor about this courageous, compassionate, Christian man. If you want to know what happened on that dark hill, ask Captain Samuel Gist, the state trooper who saw the accident."

The young woman came back on. "Initial police reports called the crash an accident." She moved on to another story.

The landline rang. Annalynn glanced at the caller ID and headed for the door. "I have to take this."

Connie handed me the printout of the contact list with her handwritten notes on it and the legal pad with Annalynn's handwriting. "Do you think it was suicide?"

"I don't know, and I don't care to know." Unless he was murdered, which meant his killer might go after Molly Dolichek or anyone else who might realize it wasn't an accident. I glanced at the notes. "What's the color coding?"

"Red marks the ones we think are related to Tara Augeri, blue the political ones, yellow the personal ones, and green the two I couldn't find."

I started with red: Big Mama, an organization dealing with domestic abuse; Top Gun, the state attorney general's office; and P. Mason, a law firm in Jeff City. "Molly had covered a lot of bases. I don't understand why she and Nancy came to the foundation."

"Apparently no one came up with a reliable way to protect the girl. Maybe the husband has political connections and nobody wants to touch the case."

Doubtful. Annalynn hadn't recognized his name. "It may be a lack of resources to finance a new identify." I turned to the political list. "I never heard of any of these companies or organizations."

"They're all big in-state political donors. That's why Annalynn thinks they're Molly's office contacts. But look what she called these guys."

"Animal Farm is the Specialty Livestock Association. What in heck is that?"

"The members raise things that aren't traditional farm animals, like puppies, pheasants, and deer."

"Good grief. Deer are running all over the place. Why would

anyone raise them?"

"So hunters can take trophies from a private game area any time of the year."

Not my thing. "Hangover is a member of a wine growers' association. That makes sense. Any idea why she called this renewable energy company Ill Wind?"

"No, but Annalynn says the owners have prime political connections in both parties."

An unpleasant thought hit me. "Are these people Annalynn will have to approach for campaign contributions? Or to run those money-laundering operations they call super PACs?"

"Probably." Connie removed a dream-catcher earring and tossed it on the petrified wood coffee table. "Annalynn will have a lot easier time raising money if Clarissa Candon endorses her for the nomination and gives her the congressman's leftover campaign funds." Connie tapped the paper. "The last one, Gigabite, is Horse Jannison, the founder of a giant tech company. He has deep pockets and was the congressman's pal. We need him."

Annalynn stuck her head in the door. "Phoenix, your cell is about to ring. Please take the call, and be nice." She vanished.

I pulled out my vibrating phone. Captain Sam Gist, the trooper who had ordered Annalynn and me to leave homicide investigations to professionals when she was appointed acting sheriff. I smiled to warm my voice. "What can I do for you, Captain Gist?"

"Dr. Smith, Sheriff Falstaff tells me you're still a reserve deputy for Vandiver County. This is an official request for you to work with my major case squad in investigating Candon's death."

Wow! What a change of heart. "You've tested the coffee?"

"Not yet. The lab may have the test results Saturday, or it may take weeks. I confirmed that the congressman's fingerprints were on the thermos, so it's likely he drank from it. The medical examiner will put a rush on the test. Do you have any idea what your K-9 smelled?"

A reasonable question, one I couldn't answer. "No. The DEA

taught him to recognize several drugs, but he can't specify what he's found." Gist knew that. "I'm sure something besides coffee is in that thermos. Achilles has never reacted to coffee. As far as he was concerned this afternoon, we were playing a game, looking for any object that didn't belong in that field. By the way, I've heard Candon didn't usually drink anything with caffeine in it."

A long pause. "Have you learned anything else that may be relevant, Phoenix?"

So now we were on a first-name basis. I debated a moment. Give and you shall receive. "Possibly. I can't be sure. What caused Molly Dolichek's illness?"

An even longer silence. "The attending physician said stress and exhaustion elevated her blood pressure and her heart rate to a dangerous level. He told me it's a common problem among overweight middle-aged women. She's stable now, but he'll keep her hospitalized for observation at least one more day."

Hmm. It wouldn't be the first time a doctor made the wrong assumptions about a middle-aged woman's health. "I suggest you corroborate that chauvinistic diagnosis."

"You assume she was the target of whatever was in that thermos." His tone was matter of fact. "I've asked a medical examiner to go over the hospital's report." A pause. "I've known Molly and her husband, a great guy, for years. He's disabled, a house husband. She supports him and their two kids. They're both in college now. Molly has plenty of stress at home and in the office. Have you identified anyone with a motive to harm her?"

So not the husband. Gist's sudden respect for my investigative abilities made me uneasy. I weighed my words, wanting to pave the way for siccing him on to Adam Augeri. "No, but her work with abused women could have made a violent man angry."

Silence. "That's the last answer I expected. Do you *know* Molly Dolichek?"

"No, I'd never even heard her name until today. Tell me more about her."

"She's non-confrontational, a conciliator. She never acts without listening to everyone's side—a better trait in a judge than a political operative. When Candon finally gave her the top district job, he warned her not to let the staff run over her. She's more likely to take a couple to counseling than confront some bastard who hit his wife." The captain took an audible breath. "If you didn't have such an uncanny knack for solving cases, I'd ignore what you just told me. Do you have a name?"

"One, but he's a very long shot. His name came to me as confidential information in a matter unrelated to the crash. I'll check his alibi tomorrow morning. If he wasn't on the job yesterday, I'll give you his name. She may have seen someone that day at one of Candon's coffees who would be a much likelier suspect."

Connie and Annalynn both leaned over me to try to hear Gist's side of the conversation.

Gist issued an order: "Give me the name and what you know about him, Deputy Smith. I'll check his record myself tonight. If I don't find anything, it'll go no farther. If he's got a record, *I'll* decide who's gonna check his alibi."

As good an offer as I was going to get, and he had access to information that might take me hours of trickery to find. "His name is Adam Augeri. If you don't find an adult criminal record, look for a juvenile file."

"Address?"

"The name and his propensity for brutality are all I have. I don't know even know the county he lives in."

"I'll email you Augeri's record tomorrow morning. As soon as I receive a full report on your search of the crash site. Report to me if you learn anything. *Anything.*"

I put away my phone and pondered Gist's uncharacteristic request for my help and his skepticism that Augeri or another abuser had poisoned the coffee. The officer had expected me to suggest another line of investigation. Of course. "Captain Gist wants me to take the flak for investigating whether Archer Candon committed suicide."

CHAPTER NINE

Connie shook her head and frowned. "If the captain wants you to investigate whether the car crash was a suicide, why would he insist you give him Augeri's name?"

"To avoid being obvious," I said. "If it really was an accident, Gist would much rather I receive the blame for bringing more anguish to the family by suggesting otherwise."

Annalynn sighed. "He asked me about the Alzheimer's rumor and the suicide speculation. I told him that unless it was a homicide, the cause of death is the family's business. I'm sorry for suggesting he call you, Phoenix, but obviously I can't be involved in this investigation."

Irritated that she'd passed the hot potato to me without asking, I shot back, "Don't be naïve. You already are. Clarissa Candon made sure of that. After all, until the election a few days ago, you were the best-known sheriff in northern Missouri."

"In the whole state," Connie said. "If it turns out that the crash wasn't an accident, people will expect you, Annalynn, to lead the investigation."

Annalynn pressed the fingers of each hand to her temples. "I can't do it. I can barely handle all the political maneuvering that's going on. Please, Phoenix, you have to find out what happened, even if it means buddying up with Gist." She turned on her heel and hurried out of the room. Her steps sounded on the stairs. Her bedroom door closed.

"Wow!" Connie plopped down on the couch beside me. "I didn't realize how much Candon's death has upset her. It brought back her anguish when the deputies said Boom committed suicide."

"Yes, but it's more than that. Annalynn's dreamed of being in Congress since high school. After she married Boom, she settled for political grunt work, the school board, charity events. Now that she has the chance to run for office, she's afraid she'll blow it."

Connie fiddled with her earring. "Something else is going on with Annalynn, too."

"Oh?"

Connie leaned close to whisper, "She's interested in a man."

What on earth was Connie talking about? "Who would that be?"

"Damn! I thought maybe you knew." She tiptoed to the door and checked the hall and stairs. "When I went into the ladies' parlor after I cleaned up in the kitchen, I heard her talking on the phone to someone."

"Annalynn has been on the phone all day. What did she say that was so special?"

"Something about having soup for supper, and how he'd probably want a rare steak and a piece of rhubarb pie after that. You have to know someone well to know they like rhubarb pie. But it wasn't what she said as much as the way she said it. Her voice was—intimate."

I loved rhubarb pie, but I couldn't think of anyone else who did. "She must have been talking to Walt."

Connie shook her head. "Believe me, Phoenix, this was not the tone you use when you talk to your son. I was so surprised I dropped my ballpoint. She told him she had to go and hung up. I asked her who was on the phone, and she said 'an old friend.' And she smiled. All over."

My first reaction was that Connie's imagination was working overtime, but she'd spent years interpreting Annalynn's moods. "I can't even make a wild guess. Let's get to work." I picked up Connie and Annalynn's notes on Molly Dolichek's contact list. They didn't yield anything else. "Did you talk to Nancy?"

"My call went to voice mail. Annalynn says the farm doesn't get cell phone service. Tomorrow morning I'll call the landline." Connie picked up her earring, a sign she was ready to leave. "I know you don't want to let on that you recovered the contact list from the iPhone, but we could save a lot of time by asking Nancy who's working on Tara Augeri's safety."

"Do it. Nancy's sharp. She won't be surprised." I thought a moment. "Any idea why she didn't approach one of us directly?"

"Maybe she didn't want to ask as a personal favor. What will you be doing tomorrow?"

"I'm going to find out everything I can about Adam Augeri." I handed her the pad. "Let me know when you reach Nancy. I'll decide which of these people need follow-ups then."

She glared at me.

I amended my statement. "*We* will discuss our next move."

"That's better. You're going to need my help, Phoenix. Just the way you have on our other cases." She stuck her finger in my face. "Admit it."

Surrender now and fight when it counted. "I'm going to need your help." I couldn't resist adding, "Just as you needed mine for your performance last night."

She brightened. "We were a major hit. I've been thinking—"

"Don't." Now I glared.

She smiled. "We'll see. Goodnight."

As soon as she left, I wrote my report and emailed it to Gist. Then I checked the security system, turned off the lights, and followed Achilles upstairs. He paused at Annalynn's closed door, and I motioned for him to come into my bedroom. She'd talk to me when she'd sorted out her thoughts and emotions. Or she'd open her door and let him in to offer nonjudgmental love.

Looking forward to repartee with Stuart, I put on my green-flannel pajamas and snuggled under the covers with my phone to call him. I opened with, "What are you wearing?"

"My coat, damn it. I'm leaving for the hospital to talk to an injured undercover agent." A door closed. "I've thought about the congressman's accident, or whatever it was. The Highway Patrol will go at it full throttle, especially now that Gist realizes his crew missed something. If you're not satisfied with the way he's handling it, bring your sample Saturday, and I'll get it analyzed. Talk to you tomorrow."

My disappointment reminded me that Stuart had become an important part of my life. Staying with him during Achilles'—really my—training would be a good test of how hard it would be to meld our independent lives. Forget it. His teenagers made even brief cohabitation impossible.

I fell asleep while pondering Annalynn speaking to a man in an "intimate" tone. In the thirty-five years she'd been married to her beloved Boom, she'd never mentioned being attracted to another man, and she certainly hadn't said anything about it since his death six months ago.

When I awoke to a dark, damp morning, Annalynn's door stood open and Achilles had gone. I dressed in sweats and opened my laptop to check my email.

Gist had written, "Adam Augeri has no criminal record, not even a speeding ticket. He's been employed full time since he graduated from high school by Lassell Furniture Renewal, an upholstery business south of Browning. He's not a person of interest at this time."

In other words, ignore Augeri and focus on whether Candon found a way to make suicide appear to be an accident. But I couldn't forget that the young man had a clean record because his terrified wife hadn't gone to the police. Where in heck was Browning? Missouri had scores of tiny towns you never heard of unless a tornado, flood, or other disaster hit them. I looked up the employer's website. A photo showed a red barn.

I went downstairs, and Achilles herded me to the back of the ladies' parlor.

Annalynn hung up the phone. "Vern's AP friend hasn't been able to identify the leaker yet. The suicide rumor is turning Archer's death from a five-inch newspaper story into hours of cable news chatter."

She stared down at the phone. "Vern agrees that it's better for me to keep out of the investigation and leave it to you."

The fact she'd asked the newspaperman told me she had doubts about not working with me. I decided to push her a little. "Stuart thinks we should trust Gist to handle it."

She jerked her head around to stare at me. "Surely you don't agree with that."

I hesitated. "I didn't when I came in here, but if the media swarm— well, neither one of us wants that kind of attention."

She sighed. "Sam Gist knows his job. I have no qualms about leaving it to him to prove that Archer did or didn't stage an accident. His family might be better off not knowing. But what if it was murder? What if someone killed Archer and Molly was collateral damage? Worst of all, what if someone set out to kill her and caused Archer's death?"

"Gist says she's a conciliator, not the kind of person to incite a relative or coworker or acquaintance to kill her." A rather naïve position for a cop. I accepted the leash Achilles put in my hand. "An angry, violent man like Adam Augeri might go after anyone. I'll check him out for CAC today. If Gist doesn't come through, we'll take another look at Candon's death. Agreed?"

"Agreed." She rubbed her eyes. "I'll be on the phone all day with people who knew Archer and his staff. I'll see if I can pick up anything about Molly or the people at the coffees."

"Good. How far is Browning?"

"Let's see. It's between 36 and Milan on Route 5. At least an hour's drive. Why?"

"Augeri works at an upholstery place near there. I intend to find out whether he was on the job Wednesday."

She said nothing for a moment. "I know better than to ask you not to go. You're bored with doing paperwork." She glanced out the window. "The weather's too nasty for your morning run. Let's have breakfast. I want to fill you in on the political situation."

I ate my oatmeal with blueberries and forced myself to pay

63

attention as she ran through the major players: five likely rivals, twenty potential supporters, a dozen influential newspaper editors and television reporters. Halfway through, I opened the basement door for Achilles so he could entertain himself by moving his toys to new hiding places. I wondered if that was his way of keeping himself in training to find things.

Finally I said, "Annalynn, I have a photographic memory for numbers, not names. Please make me a cheat sheet—your list of names I should know with enough information to tell me what topics to bring up or avoid."

"Of course. Vernon has been working on a campaign playbook for weeks."

"Good. I'm going to the office to check calls and email, and what that upholsterer has to offer. I want to have a plausible story when I walk in."

"I have a dining room chair with a tear in the cushion stored downstairs. You can take that." She put her hand on my wrist. "You take too many chances. That young man could be very dangerous. Don't you dare leave the house without your bullet-proof vest."

About eleven thirty, I pulled into a parking lot in front of a red barn with tall rolling doors in the center. On each side of the upholstery shop's big doors were regular-sized glass doors and plate-glass windows. A light was on in the window to my left.

The rain had stopped, but the clouds hovered low as I went to the Camry's battered trunk to take out the damaged seat I'd detached from Annalynn's chair. With it as my cover story, I'd skipped a disguise. No one here was likely to connect me to the Vandiver County sheriff's department, especially without a Belgian Malinois at my side.

A middle-aged brunette in a red sweatshirt with a quilted cutout of an overstuffed chair was talking on the phone at a broad counter. She shifted her gaze from a muted wall-mounted television tuned to a news channel and nodded to me.

I put the chair seat on the end of the counter and strolled down the first row of hanging eight-inch square cloth swatches. The pseudo early-American prints struck me as suitable for chairs in a modest family room. If these unimpressive samples represented the store's most desirable products, I'd have trouble playing the role of a serious customer and drawing the woman into conversation. I started down the next row, plain colors and a better quality cloth.

The woman hung up the phone. "Hi, there." She picked up the seat. "What a shame this was damaged. I haven't seen this fine tapestry cloth in years. You'll never find an exact match."

"Oh? Has it gone out of style, or has the manufacturer gone out of business?"

"Both, I'm sorry to say." She picked up the seat, bustled from behind the counter, and motioned for me to follow her toward the back. "I carry a cloth with a similar texture in solid colors. One may match the muted scarlet in the pattern. That could work if you need to recover, say, half your chairs."

An interesting approach. I followed her to the back and fingered the cloth swatch she'd mentioned. Not top quality, but not bad. Offer her the opportunity for a big sale. "I have twelve chairs. All of them show some wear. If I can find a sturdy cloth with a really pretty pattern, I'd consider having the whole set redone."

She beamed. "Do you want a similar pattern or a completely new one?"

"The chairs are antiques. I prefer a traditional rather than an ultramodern pattern."

We spent almost twenty minutes studying swatches. I occasionally heard pounding, whirs, and voices coming from the room behind us. No one came into the showroom, and I could find no natural opening for asking about the employees. Unlike most local sales people, she stuck strictly to the business at hand and asked for and gave no personal information.

"Sorry," I said as we reached the end of the options. "I don't like any of these patterns well enough to sit on them for thirty years."

"Then let's take a gander at wholesalers' online catalogs. I can order anything you like."

"Yes, let's do that."

A big man in a red hooded sweatshirt opened a side door. "Honey, is that nephew of yours coming in today or not? We need some help back here."

"Adam slept late because of his cold, but he swore he'll be in by noon. He offered to work tomorrow to make up for being out the last two days."

Bingo! Adam Augeri hadn't been here the day someone tampered with Molly Dolichek's thermos. What's more, his aunt's defensive tone indicated he'd missed work before.

"He damned well better show up," the man groused. "We're backed up."

The woman gave the man a shushing look. "See the fine old chair covering the lady brought in? How long would it take you to recover a dozen of these seats?"

He stepped forward and reached for the seat. As he studied it, the sound of a cable news channel came through the open door. "Nobody's made this for years. Must be antique chairs. Do you worry they're going to give way every time you sit down?"

The man knew his stuff. "They're solid. The previous owner loved woodworking. He took excellent care of them."

"Won't take long then, once the cloth comes in. If I got any help." He spun on his heel and left, closing the workshop door.

The woman went behind the counter and brought up a laptop. "Give me a couple of minutes to see what I can find."

"Of course." I waited until she'd typed in a Web address. "I gather that was your husband. Is this a family operation?"

She didn't look up from the screen. "Yup. My husband's brother and his boy work in the back part time, and his wife and I split our time between back there and out here." She shook her head and typed in another Web address.

"Plus your nephew who overslept?"

"Yup. He's a good worker. When he's here." She typed in a password and stared at the screen.

I glanced at my watch. Adam Augeri was already two minutes late.

"Several possibilities here," she said, turning the screen so I could see it. "Do you like any of these patterns?"

I enlarged three of the more promising ones. "Not enough." I'd keep looking until Augeri showed up. I moved on to the next nine patterns.

Ten minutes later, an old green Ford pickup parked next to my car. A short, curly-haired young man in a red sweatshirt jumped out and hurried in. "Sorry I'm late, Aunt Honey," he muttered, head down, and went through the side door.

Hmm. Face haggard but no redness around his nose, no sound of stuffiness in his voice. He'd gotten over his "cold" in a hurry.

She glanced at her watch and knotted her brows a moment before turning her attention back to me.

I enlarged three of the patterns. "I like these two, but I can't really tell without seeing and feeling the cloth." I went on to the next page and spotted one I really liked. "This one looks quite promising. Could you give me a price on recovering all twelve seats with this?"

Ten minutes later I gave her one of my untraceable email addresses so she could notify me when the samples came in and walked out with full-color printouts of my selections. I walked around to the passenger side to stash the chair seat and to see if Augeri had a gun rack. He did, but the rack didn't hold a rifle. I shivered at the sight of a gleaming, well-sharpened machete.

CHAPTER TEN

The machete in Augeri's pickup didn't prove he intended to cut off his wife's feet, but the bright blade certainly supported her claim that he'd threatened her. Forcing my eyes to turn from the weapon, I got in my car and back on the road. How did you defend yourself against a machete?

While I was still pondering this, my phone rang in my purse. Few people had the number, so I turned left onto a narrow gravel road to take the call. Captain Gist.

He said, "Mrs. Keyser told me where you went. Can you talk?"

"Yes. I just left the upholstery shop. Augeri missed work the last two days on a flimsy excuse. He works for his aunt. From what I saw, she'd give him an alibi if he needs it."

"Forget about him. I drove Molly home from the hospital and asked her about her work on ITV—that's intimate partner violence. She said she works with women's groups on legislative strategy, not with abused women."

She'd stonewalled him. "I have proof that she was involved in Tara's rescue."

"Uh, yes, but not on purpose."

The bastard had held out on me. "What in hell does that mean? What happened?"

"Molly told me in confidence, but she also said Mrs. Keyser's foundation is helping the girl, so I'll tell you. Back in September, Molly and a trainee were going door-to-door stumping for some local candidate and ran across this terrified young woman. She'd obviously been beaten. No one saw them take her away. Augeri has no idea how his wife got out of there."

That two months gave Augeri plenty of time to hear two campaigners had been stopping at houses that day and to discover their identities. "Did they take her to a shelter?"

"No. Molly didn't know of a suitable one, but she knew a farmer in another county who needed a temporary worker. The girl is safe there for now."

So Molly didn't trust the trooper enough to tell him where she'd hidden Tara. Using my poor-ignorant-woman tone, I said, "We'd appreciate any advice you have on relocating her."

He didn't answer for a moment. "I'd advise you to report the case to the sheriff's department in her county and let him contact the proper social service agencies."

Useless advice, which could be why Molly didn't tell him more. I moved on. "Did you ask Molly who could have tampered with the coffee?"

"No, and don't you either. She accepted her doctor's diagnosis that her blood pressure shot up because she's been working so hard. In fact, don't talk to her at all. If the test turns up a toxin, which is highly unlikely, I'll question her myself."

Idiot. She needed to be on guard right now. I said sweetly, "It's very thoughtful of you not to add to her stress, but if someone tried to poison her, she could still be in danger."

"She'll stay at home and rest several days. We'll know for sure about the coffee before she's out and about." He cleared his throat. "It's quite likely your dog raised a false alarm, Dr. Smith. I asked Molly if she thought Candon might have drunk some of her coffee. She laughed at the idea. I also talked to Roland Renmar, the advance man. He stayed with the team until after lunch and then drove Mrs. Candon to Laycock. He doesn't remember seeing the thermos or any mysterious strangers. He was impressed that Molly knew the name of every single person who showed up. She would've noticed if Augeri was skulking around."

But Achilles had smelled something disturbing in that coffee. Working with Gist was proving even more frustrating than working around him. I tried another tack. "By now, the medical examiner must know whether the congressman's stomach contained any coffee."

"From eyeballing the contents, he doesn't think so. He'll have an analysis later today. I'll let you know what he finds. Meanwhile, see if you can pick up on anything that might indicate suicide." He disconnected.

Bloody hell! He wanted me to quiz Candon's family and staff unofficially, sparing him the job of asking uncomfortable questions. No thanks. I'd wait for the autopsy results. Meanwhile I'd go home and focus on relocating Tara.

Not wanting to back across the highway to reach the right lane, I looked ahead for a place to turn around. Pastures with close-cropped brown grass bordered the road on both sides. The road ran down a long hill and up another one. At the top of the ascending hill, a driveway led back to a house trailer almost surrounded by trees. Plenty of trailers around here, but this one could be the Augeris' home.

When I reached the top of the hill, I saw the remains of a large garden. The one Tara had mentioned? I pulled into the driveway. The place looked forlorn on this cold, misty day. I drove closer to the trailer and saw a large padlock on the door. Was this to keep her in when he found her? I doubted it. From my online research, I'd gathered that fear rather than physical barriers held abused women prisoner. Should I pick the lock and take a look around? No. I could learn nothing there that would help the girl at this point. Besides, if passersby saw my car and told Augeri, he might connect the woman in the upholstery shop to his wife's disappearance and complicate my relocating her.

I backed out and drove toward the highway. A white cargo van zoomed over the hill behind me and stayed on my tail until I turned left onto the highway. When it turned right, my mirror showed me Lassell Furniture Renewal on the back. Damn! The driver almost certainly would mention seeing my banged-up Camry near his coworker's home. I'd been foolish to go against my training and skip elementary precautions—a disguise, a false identity, a rental car with fake plates. I watched for Augeri's green pickup until I turned off Highway 36 onto a narrow blacktop road that led to Laycock via Star Corner.

Approaching the crash site, I accelerated from fifty to sixty, the speed Candon had been traveling. When I crested the hill, a red SUV blocked my lane twenty yards ahead. A man stood in the other lane. I braked as hard as I dared on the damp road and hit the horn. He dove down the roadside bank on my left.

My tires started to lose traction. I released the brake and swerved around the van going faster than I liked. I turned back into my lane and stopped parallel to where Candon's car had landed.

A youngish blond man in a red puffy vest staggered to his feet.

Heart pounding at the close call, I stepped out of the car. "Are you hurt?"

He rubbed his left knee. "I've got a booboo."

Anger followed relief. "Didn't your mommy tell you never to block the road?"

He crossed to the vehicle, took an industrial-size video camera from the back seat, and lifted it to his shoulder. "And the driver is Phoenix Smith. Did you come to examine the scene of Congressman Candon's death, professor?"

Bloody hell! He was the press. "You fuckin' fool. You almost made this a death scene for both of us." Hoping the expletive would keep him from using the video, I stepped back in my car. I'd never seen him before, but he'd recognized me and called me professor. He must be the aspiring documentarian who had sold the footage to cable news and misidentified me as LCC faculty. The last thing I wanted now was to have my face on cable news again.

I pulled out. Bad luck that he was there, but I'd learned one thing: Gist had been driving too fast in these hills considering the dark, shoulderless road and the vision-impaired driver following him. Perhaps the good captain hoped to clear his own conscience by having

71

me prove Candon had driven off the road on purpose.

Another complication in an already complex situation. Time to fall back on my experience as a covert operative. I certainly wouldn't go on another fact-finding outing without a simple disguise, a fake ID, and a car rented from Clunkers on Call. I thought about the machete. And taking Achilles with me as a backup. How in the world could I disguise him?

My stomach began to growl. Breakfast had been almost six hours ago. By the time I walked into Annalynn's front door, I was in a foul mood.

Achilles waited for me with his leash in his mouth, eager to go out.

I knelt to give him some loving. "Sorry, boy. We'll go for a run later."

"Hi, Phoenix." Connie stuck her head out of Annalynn's bedroom door at the top of the stairs. "Does Augeri have an alibi for Wednesday?"

"No, and he carries a machete in his gun rack." I stood up, took off my coat, and walked down the hall toward the coat closet. "Did you ask Nancy what Molly's done to place Tara?"

Connie came part way down the stairs. "Nancy didn't have time to talk about it on the phone. She'll give us the full story in person tomorrow after the memorial service."

Scheisse! At the same time as the birthday lunch. For a moment I considered using Tara's plight as an excuse for skipping lunch with Stuart's kids. No, I had to talk to them sometime, and not going would hurt Stuart and alienate his mother. "I'm not going to the service." I hung up my coat and stomped toward the kitchen.

"Oh, yes, Beth Roper's birthday lunch with the young savages is tomorrow." Connie followed me through the dining room. "By the way, I didn't call Nancy. She called me."

Connie waited for me to ask her why. Out of pure contrariness, I didn't.

She told me anyway. "Clarissa asked me to sing three solos with the church choir at the memorial service. We'll drive over early enough to rehearse at eleven. The church is providing a light lunch for the family and the politicos coming from out of town."

Lunch with antagonistic teenagers or egomaniacal politicians? A tough choice. I forced myself to respond properly to Connie's news. "Congratulations. Singing there will give you good exposure." I opened the refrigerator door and took out eggs and the accessories for an omelet. "Have you had lunch yet?"

"Annalynn and I finished the soup. We've been going through her suits and dresses for something appropriately funereal yet striking to wear tomorrow. With all this hoopla about whether Candon committed suicide, you can bet the TV cameras will be there." She put on water for tea and went on and on about the merits and demerits of Annalynn's top five options for her on-camera appearance.

I dutifully noted that wearing red as women on the Hill tended to do at any televised joint session might make Annalynn appear overly confident that she would be the candidate. Then I tuned out. Frustrated that I'd reached a temporary impasse with both the CAC and Candon investigations, I wondered what I could hope to accomplish this waning Friday afternoon. Whatever I learned in the next few days, one task took priority: making sure Tara was in a safe place. My online research had netted me little on finding someone else to handle relocation. I ran through a mental list of my CIA contacts for one who could fill me in on the legal complications and the best places to hide a lone teenager with few job or life skills.

Connie clinked a spoon on her teacup. "You're ignoring me, as usual."

I didn't bother to deny it. Out of habit, I didn't tell her my real concern. Instead I gave an excuse she would accept. "I was thinking about what to wear to the birthday lunch." I picked up my plate and nudged Achilles off my feet. "I'll finish lunch in the office. You and Annalynn don't need my advice on clothes."

Connie sighed. "I don't think she needs my advice on anything. It's like she's entered a new dimension populated by people I don't know. Between calls from politicians and reporters, she's never off the phone long enough to hold a conversation." Connie followed me into the kitchen and rinsed out her teacup. "No sweatshirts tomorrow. Wear one of those beautiful wool sweaters you had shipped over from Vienna. Teenage girls respect clothes."

"Okay." Obviously Connie thought I needed her advice. I hurried through the basement tunnel to the foundation office. Achilles, his leash in his mouth, stuck right by me. I spent an hour researching witness protection programs and women's networks likely to be helping abused women start new lives. I learned little. People had become cautious about what they put online.

I'd just turned off the computer when Annalynn came in and sat down in the chair in front of my desk. "Any word on the coffee?"

"Not yet. Gist doubts Achilles' nose." I sensed she'd come to tell—or ask—me something.

She twiddled her thumbs. "Nancy just called. Clarissa has invited me to come to Four Chimneys, the Candons' antebellum home, after the service. She's going on with the press conference Archer had scheduled at three o'clock. Nancy wouldn't even hint at what it's about."

"Can you guess?"

"Yes, but as you would say, I don't *know*." Annalynn shifted in her chair. She didn't usually needle me that way. "Nancy was upset that you won't be there, too."

Hmm. "Because of Tara's need to relocate or because of the question of how Archer Candon died?"

Annalynn picked up a pencil and rotated it in her fingers. "I'm not sure. Maybe both. Someone came into the room—Nancy was on a landline—and she was very guarded in what she said." She put down the pencil and met my eyes. "Phoenix, I have such a bad feeling about that poor girl and about Candon's death. Is my experience as sheriff making me super suspicious?"

"No. I hear alarm bells, too." I tried to explain why to her and to me. "Tara's email and Adam's rants online, plus that machete in his pickup, convince me he will hurt or even kill Tara if he finds her. According to Nancy and Molly, the girl is safe for the time being. I doubt that. As to Candon's death—I'm not certain about anything right now. It could have been an accident, suicide, collateral damage, or murder. If the coffee contained a poison, the only one of those we can eliminate is an accident."

She smiled wryly. "So you figure the odds are three out of four that it wasn't an accident."

"I didn't say that."

"Yes you did." She rubbed her right temple. "Clarissa also invited me to come to the farm Sunday for a late lunch and a meeting of major campaign donors and other 'interested persons.' That's code for possible candidates."

"Great! Why aren't you elated?"

"Because Clarissa's grief stirs up my own. Besides, if someone caused Archer's death by poisoning that coffee, she'll expect me to solve that case as we've done others. Phoenix, I'd like for you to come with me Sunday as my economic adviser. No one will question that. We'll take Achilles, too."

My cell phone rang. Gist. I put it on speaker as I answered and said, "You have the test results?"

"The lab detected a small amount of coffee in the stomach. It raises questions, but the examiner needs an additional test. We should have conclusive results on that and the coffee in the thermos within twenty-four hours. Needless to say, this is completely confidential."

Achilles had been right. "Of course. Please call me as soon as you get the results."

"You'll be among the first to know." He disconnected.

Annalynn groaned. "Not an accident. One possibility down, three to go."

CHAPTER ELEVEN

Annalynn and Connie left for the memorial service soon after Achilles and I returned from a somewhat late morning run on a cold but sunny day. Concerned that Augeri or his online pack might be savvy enough to track me down using my car license, I'd carried a spare magazine for my Glock and kept watch for a green pickup.

I cleaned up and dressed in my dark green slacks and variegated green wool sweater, a compromise between my usual jeans and sweatshirt and my expensive business clothes. With a few minutes to spare, I went over to the foundation office to check for any calls or email.

Achilles followed and sat watching me rather than roaming around as he usually did. He sensed my anxiety.

I reached out to stroke his head. "You're my secret weapon with Zeke. Bring your Frisbees, please."

He darted from the room and across the hall into Annalynn's office. A moment later he brought me a red Frisbee.

"Good boy. Bring me another Frisbee."

We went through this two more times, each Frisbee taking him more time to retrieve.

I dialed Mrs. Roper's number. "Hi, it's Phoenix. Is there anything you'd like me to pick up on my way over?"

"No, but do come as soon as you can. I'd like to hear all about your new foundation before the kids get here. Oh, will Achilles be comfortable on my back porch? It's enclosed."

"He'll be fine there." As long as I came out to reassure him every few minutes. "I'll see you in about half an hour."

I put the Frisbees, a chew toy, a water bowl, and some treats in my daypack.

Achilles brought a newish tennis ball to add to the mix.

Wearing my Glock might alarm my former teacher, so I carried it in my leather purse with a gun pocket. The coffee sample for Stuart went in the purse, too. I didn't trust Gist to share the test results.

On the way to Trudy's to pick up the cake, I gave myself a pep talk. Stuart and Mrs. Roper would demand the kids behave courteously. I just had to keep my temper and be pleasant. Show an interest in them without being intrusive. Be modest but confident. I'd done this with hundreds of hostile or insultingly dismissive people both as an operative and an economist.

Leaving Achilles in the car, I hurried to Trudy's back porch. I wanted to get in and out without satisfying her appetite for gossip.

"Come in, come in," she said opening the kitchen door. Beaming, she gestured toward the cake on the table. "I wanted you to check it before I put it in your pretty cake carrier."

I studied every detail. "I thought the first one looked great until I saw this. It's perfect."

"I boxed up the practice cake for you to take home. Annalynn and Connie will want to see it." Trudy eased the glass carrier into a dark plastic bag, tied the top, and lowered the bag into a rectangular cardboard box. "The two cakes fit in the box pretty well, but I wouldn't make any sudden stops." She blocked my path to the cakes. "Did Clarissa ask you to find out whether Archer committed suicide?"

"No." Good. She'd asked a question I could answer honestly.

"Why do all those guys on TV talk like keeping his disease a secret was something sinful? It's none of their business."

"They say Candon's constituents had the right to know. From what I've heard, no one here or on the Hill thought he wasn't doing his job."

"Yeah, I guess a bad memory is a good thing for a politician. I heard Ronald Reagan had Alzheimer's coming on before he left the White House."

I stepped around her to pick up the box. "I have to go. Achilles will start barking if I leave him alone in the car much longer."

With the box on the floor wedged between the front and back seats, I drove to Mrs. Roper's house, the same one where I'd babysat for Stuart and his little sister and presided over the Math Club's meetings. Mr. Roper, a jovial bank mortgage officer who wore khakis rather than jeans at home, always brought us a plate of his homemade peanut butter cookies. He'd died at least five years ago. The couple had given their children a happy home and Stuart good training for marriage. Yet, his marriage had fallen apart.

Parking in front of Mrs. Roper's detached garage, I took the daypack out of the back seat and put the short carrying strap between Achilles' teeth. Then I lifted the bag holding the cake out of the box, placed one hand under the cake carrier, and followed the paved walk to the back door.

Mrs. Roper, dressed in black slacks and a pumpkin-colored sweatshirt with a turkey on it, opened the porch door before I could knock. "How sweet of you to bring the cake, Phoenix." She stepped back. "Come in, both of you. The sun has been shining on the porch all morning, so it's nice and warm."

Achilles followed me in, dropped the daypack, and sat to offer her his paw.

She smiled and bent slightly, sending her glasses sliding far down on her long nose. "Stuart said Achilles is smart. I didn't know he's also a charmer."

Only if he liked a person, and he liked only the people I liked. Geez. What would he do when he met Kaysi? "Happy birthday, Mrs. Roper."

She frowned. "For heaven's sakes, Phoenix, call me Beth. Let me take the cake into the kitchen while you get Achilles settled."

I handed it to her. "No peeking." I unzipped the daypack and dumped out Achilles' items in the sunniest spot on the porch. We both sniffed appreciatively at the aroma of pot roast.

He whined when I told him to stay and went inside.

The house looked much as I remembered it. My tension faded away as I told her about the foundation's aims and the kind of requests we received. Then she gave me the latest news of several classmates who'd left Laycock as I had. When I offered to set the table in the small dining room, the silverware and plates were in the old buffet right where they used to be, although the plates had a different pattern.

A car door slammed out front.

"There they are," Mrs. Roper said. She reached out and pushed a strand of hair off my forehead. "Just be yourself."

My tension mounted.

Zeke, dressed in blue sweatpants and a matching Royals sweatshirt, burst through the front door and into the living room with a big grin on his face. "Hey, Gram, happy birthday. I smell roast. Let's eat." He thrust a small package into her hands. "This is from me. You can't open it until we're ready to cut the cake." He spotted me and the grin faded but didn't disappear. "Hi."

His sister strolled through the door, pausing a moment in a model's pose. She needed Connie's advice on entrances. The seventeen-year-old wore form-fitting black slacks with a striking pseudo-silk yellow and black leopard top, almost assuredly a designer brand. Her long blond hair was in a complex upsweep more suitable for a prom. She handed her grandmother a small box with an elaborate bow. "Happy birthday, Gram. It's your favorite candy. Don't open it until we leave or Zeke will eat it all."

"Thank you both," Mrs. Roper said. "This is Phoenix Smith, an old friend of mine and of your father's."

Without looking at me, Kaysi said, "How do you do?"

Before I could respond to this formal inquiry, she hurried into the hall powder room.

Stuart, dressed in jeans and a Cardinals sweatshirt, stepped inside with a large white box that held a warm rose-colored robe. "Wow, that roast smells wonderful." He handed the gift to his mother and kissed her on the cheek. He stepped over to me and kissed me on the lips, not lingering but making a statement. "Did you bring your wonder dog?"

"He's on the porch. And he's probably thirsty. I didn't fill his water bowl."

Zeke sprinted toward the porch. "I'll do it."

Not sure how Achilles would respond to all that energy, I hurried after the boy. "Let me introduce you first. He's nervous around strange men, especially in unfamiliar places." I went through the door to see boy and dog standing frozen, each studying the other warily. "Friend, Achilles, friend." I put my hand on Zeke's shoulder. "This is Zeke. He'll play Frisbee with you."

Achilles darted to a wicker chair, took a yellow Frisbee from the seat, brought it to me, and went to the outside door.

Mrs. Roper said, "Go ahead, Phoenix. I'll call you when we're ready to put the food on the table."

I opened the door. Achilles shot out and loped around the backyard to give it his usual sniff test. Smelling nothing alarming, he stopped at the back of the yard and waited for me to throw the Frisbee.

I tossed a high one. "Let's play keep-away, Zeke. You go to the back of the yard. We'll throw it back and forth, and he'll jump to intercept it."

Zeke grinned and ran toward Achilles. "Keep-away, Achilles, keep-away."

Achilles let Zeke take the Frisbee and trotted toward me while watching the boy.

In a few minutes boy and dog were joyously competing to receive my throws. When they wrestled on the ground for possession of a dropped one, Achilles let go and licked Zeke's face.

With all the noise of laughter and barking, I didn't realize Stuart had come outside until he touched my shoulder.

"One down, one to go," he said softly. "Hey, Zeke! Time for lunch."

"Come, Achilles," I called. "You and Zeke can play later."

Zeke handed Achilles the Frisbee. "Does he really understand what you say to him?"

Should I brag? No. "He understands 'play' and 'later.' I used your name a lot while we played to start teaching him 'Zeke.'"

Stuart greeted Achilles by offering him the expected biscuit. "Phoenix signed them up for a private two-week course at K-9 Grad School in early December."

I cut in before he could say anything about inviting me to stay with him. "The training is mostly for me. I want to find out what Achilles already knows and learn the right way to teach him more." I went into the porch, Achilles at my heels, and picked up his water bowl. "I'm sure he's ready for a drink now, Zeke."

"Sure." He went into the kitchen.

I lingered. Achilles wouldn't drink the water Zeke brought unless I signaled it was okay.

Sure enough, Achilles sniffed the water and looked up at me for approval.

I nodded and handed Zeke a plastic bag of treats. "Please give him up to three, one at a time, while I wash up." I went inside and to the half bath off the kitchen. The reflection in the mirror there pleased me. I didn't look young, but my short black hair was attractively windblown, my brown eyes clear, and my cheeks lightly flushed from the exertion. A stranger would never guess Stuart was six years younger than I was.

While Mrs. Roper and Stuart carried the food into the dining room, I took the glasses from the buffet and filled them with ice water.

Kaysi sat at the table making a show of smoothing out the white cloth napkin I had folded into a tricornered hat. She inspected her fork as Stuart pulled out my chair, which was on Mrs. Roper's right directly across from Zeke.

Suspicious, I sat down with care and sprang up as I heard a distinct creak.

Mrs. Roper gasped. "Oh, Phoenix, I'm so sorry. I'm afraid the chairs got mixed up. That's the one I have to take for repair."

Stuart grabbed the chair and, face grim, switched it with the one at the end of the table. "It would be a terrible thing if we should have any accidents on Mom's birthday."

Everyone but Zeke watched the red creep into Kaysi's face.

I relaxed. She'd taken considerable effort to appear a woman, but she'd struck out at me like a little kid. Better to kill her with kindness than to strike back.

Zeke's curiosity about Achilles provided a conversational safety zone for several minutes. Stuart followed up with questions about Mrs. Roper's bridge club. Then she asked Kaysi about a new group she'd organized called Cyber Defenders.

Kaysi's face went from sullen to animated. "Any student who's being bullied online can come to us confidentially. We'll track down the bullies. If they won't stop when we ask them to, then we find ways to block or counteract them."

Mrs. Roper frowned. "Why isn't the school taking care of this?"

Kaysi shrugged. "I don't know. I guess it's because it doesn't happen at school. Besides, a lot of the girls would rather we handle it."

A noble idea, but fraught with unforeseen consequences. Not my place to say that. I glanced at Stuart. He didn't appear concerned. I was. "How many students have come to your group for help so far, Kaysi?"

She took the last bite on her plate.

Mrs. Roper said, "I was wondering about that, too."

Kaysi directed her words to her grandmother. "I started it because some guy was posting really nasty things online—anonymously— about one of my friends. Four of us worked together to figure out who he was and bombed him until he shut up. Word got around, and three other girls and one gay guy came to us. We've stopped the bullying every time."

"Good for you," I said without thinking. Careful. "I suppose if someone poses a physical threat, you can gather evidence to take to the police. St. Louis must have an active cyber force."

"Yes," Stuart said, finally breaking his silence. "If you like, Kaysi, I can help you develop a reporting form so that each of the Defenders

82

records her findings the same way."

Kaysi patted her lips with the napkin. "I'll place that idea before the group."

Zeke leaned back in his chair. "I'm ready for the birthday cake."

Stuart stood up. "Stay right there, Mom. Kaysi and Zeke will clear the table while I bring in the cake and coffee."

Kaysi moved quickly to pick up her own and her father's plates. "Did you make carrot cake, Gram? That's my favorite."

"Wait and see," Mrs. Roper said. She reached for my plate and put it atop hers.

Hmm. A preventive measure in case Kaysi planned to accidentally drop my plate in my lap? Mrs. Roper always stayed a step ahead of her students. I picked up the butter and plate of dinner rolls to take to the kitchen.

Mrs. Roper placed a restraining hand on my arm. "You stay and talk to me. I turned on the radio to check on whether that big storm front coming from the northwest will dip down to us. It won't, thank goodness. We rarely get snow before Thanksgiving. But I digress. The point is, I also heard that the Candon family is holding a press conference after the memorial service. That seems very odd to me. Do you know why?"

"No, but Annalynn and Connie will be there. I'll get a report at dinner."

Kaysi came back from the kitchen and put small plates and forks from the buffet at each place.

Mrs. Roper said, "Thank you, dear." She turned back to me. "We won't have to wait for their report. Evidently it's a slow news weekend. The cable channels are carrying the press conference live." She paused. "Is it too much to hope Clarissa Candon will announce she's going to support Annalynn for the nomination? I've heard that Candon had considerable money left in his campaign chest. That would give Annalynn a tremendous advantage."

Her assumption that Annalynn was running surprised me. "Does everyone expect Annalynn to run?"

Mrs. Roper smiled. "Everyone with any sense."

That eliminated many people, but they didn't vote anyway.

Zeke brought in a tray with four cups of coffee and a glass of milk and put them in place.

Carrying the cake with the glass cover still on, Stuart began to sing "Happy Birthday." When we'd finished the song, he put the cake in front of his mother. "Hold on a moment. I want to take a photo when you take off the cover." He took his phone off his belt carrier.

She smoothed down her hair and removed the top. "Oh! Oh! Look at this!"

Kaysi jumped up from her chair and went to her grandmother's side. Grinning, she studied the cake. "Wow! The answer to every equation is seventy-five." She pulled her cell from her pocket and took a series of pictures. "That's so clever, Gram. I'm posting this on Instagram. I'll say your birthday cake has pi on it." She returned to her chair with her thumbs flying.

Mrs. Roper beamed. "Print out copies for me. It's so lovely that I hate to cut it."

Zeke laughed. "That's the nerdiest cake I ever saw. I hope it's chocolate."

Hmm. Should I admit I was the nerd who designed it?

Stuart held up his coffee cup. "You'll be able to taste the nerdiness, too. The cake has seventy-five pieces of dark chocolate in it. Cheers for our three math nerds."

Mrs. Roper picked up the knife. "It's my birthday, so I get a piece of pi. Thank you so much for the best birthday cake I ever had, Phoenix."

"Shit!" Kaysi's whispered exclamation carried to my end of the table.

Zeke reddened. "I like nerds, two out of three anyway."

Mrs. Roper said calmly, "Kaysi, you're excused to load the dishwasher."

Beet red, the girl bolted to the kitchen, and Stuart, fists clenched, rose to follow her.

I flashed back to how crushed I was when my hot temper and sharp tongue disappointed my adored father. I grabbed Stuart's arm and said softly. "It's okay. Sit down and have some cake. She's caught in that awful middle ground between being daddy's little girl and a woman who defends those under attack."

"Wise words," Mrs. Roper said. She leaned close to whisper. "I'm afraid you're going to have to remind yourself of that for a while." She raised her voice. "Tell us about the music program Connie is going to direct at the college next summer. Zeke may want to apply."

After fifteen minutes of normal conversation, Zeke went outside to play catch with Achilles, Mrs. Roper set about directing Kaysi in making a carrot cake, and Stuart and I collapsed side by side on the living room sofa.

He drew me to him.

After one very nice kiss, I pushed him away. "Business before pleasure. Gist is holding out on me. I need to know exactly what was in that coffee as soon as possible."

Stuart pulled back a few inches. "I'll do what I can. Do you suspect suicide? Or murder?"

I'd debated that question well into the night. "If Candon committed suicide, he risked killing Molly Dolichek in order to stage a car accident. Which could have injured rather than killed him. It's unlikely, but, considering his Alzheimer's, I can't discount the possibility."

"And if he didn't?"

"Then someone tried to murder her and make it look like death from natural causes. That's why testing the coffee is crucial."

He frowned. "That sounds more like someone who knows her well rather than the machete-wielding young husband."

"Yes, but Gist insists that he do any questioning—if he decides it's necessary. We're losing valuable time. I'll interrogate her colleagues informally at that meeting tomorrow."

He sighed. "I won't insult you by saying be careful. If a killer figures out you're after him, ... well, don't drink any coffee."

CHAPTER TWELVE

Mrs. Roper cleared her throat and bustled into the living room, trailed by Kaysi.

I wondered how much they'd overheard.

Mrs. Roper sat down in a small recliner that had a reading lamp on one side and a small pile of books with a television remote on top on the other. "It's time for the press conference."

Kaysi planted herself between me and the TV. "Would you like another cup of coffee?"

Was this enforced politeness, or had she heard us mention poisoned coffee? "No, thanks."

She took a chair slightly behind us, just out of our line of vision.

The commercials ended. The host, once a real reporter, gave some headlines and said, "We are joining a press conference called by Clarissa Candon, widow of Missouri Congressman Archer Candon, at Four Chimneys, the family's plantation house."

On the screen, Annalynn stood in profile before three mikes on a lectern. "Good afternoon. I'm Annalynn Carr Keyser. Congressman Candon called this press conference last Tuesday before coming home from Washington, D.C. He planned to share news with his family this weekend and with the public today. Clarissa Candon has found the courage to read the announcement that they wrote together."

As Annalynn stepped away and Clarissa came forward, the camera pulled back. It showed a long table lined with pots of red, white, and blue flowering plants. Two tall middle-aged men, younger versions of Archer Candon, stood in front of white window drapes to the left of the lectern. A matching third brother stood on the right. Annalynn moved past him and stopped.

Clarissa placed a single sheet of paper on the lectern. "Archer's sons, the great pride of his life, have agreed that he would want his constituents to hear his final announcement." She had begun with the clear voice of a polished speaker. She paused and pressed her lips together. Then she read, "Serving my friends in District 6 has been a high honor, a great pleasure, and a grave responsibility. Over the last few months, I have become less and less capable of meeting that responsibility." She took a deep breath. "I've continued to serve my district because of the extraordinary competence and dedication of my staff." Her voice wavered. "In July, I entered an experimental program for those ..." After a moment, she turned away and held out the paper to the two men to her left.

Both, faces contorted, shook their heads.

She handed it to the third man. He handed it to Annalynn and embraced Clarissa.

The camera turned to the audience, seven reporters, including Vernon Kann, and thirty or so people, including Connie and Nancy, standing behind them. The camera moved back to the table. In the background a tall young man standing in front of a large mirror opened a swinging door and said something. Could he be Pete, the grandson with the hands like his grandfather's?

Public face in place, Annalynn studied the paper. A line on the screen identified her as Vandiver County Sheriff Annalynn Keyser. "In July, I entered an experimental program for those suffering from dementia. The disease's progress has slowed but not stopped. I can no longer do the work I was elected to do. Therefore I will resign on December 31 so that the voters can choose my successor."

Annalynn glanced at Clarissa, who had covered her face with her hands, and the camera again pulled back for a long shot. Annalynn continued, "I leave this office with much regret, but I look forward to spending my last days in the place I love most with the people I love most."

The swinging door opened about halfway, and the young man reached through it. In the instant before the door closed, the mirror showed a small redheaded woman handing him a glass of water.

Thanks to Adam Augeri's posting online, I recognized his wife. "Bloody hell!" I clapped my hand over my mouth and swore under my breath as I envisioned the upholstery shop's TV tuned to the same news channel.

Annalynn said, "The Candons will not take questions today."

A commercial came onto the screen.

I bent down and reached inside my purse for my cell phone.

Stuart leaned close and said *sotto voce*, "What in hell did you see?"

"Not what, who." I punched in Connie's cell number. She and Nancy had to get the girl out of there before Augeri could reach the farm. The phone went to voice mail. "Connie, Desdemona was caught on camera. Four Chimneys isn't safe. Bring her back with you." But Connie and Annalynn could be halfway home before they had cell service. I disconnected. "I need the Candons' unlisted landline number."

Stuart turned to his mother. "Could we borrow your laptop?"

Kaysi ran from the room. "I'll get it." She was back in an instant, but she didn't hand the laptop to me. Instead she put it on the coffee table in front of us and knelt with the screen facing her. "The Capitol Hill office will have it." Her fingers flew over the keys. She dictated the number.

I dialed it on my cell. Voice mail. The office was closed until Monday.

I dialed Captain Gist. Voice mail. *"Scheisse!"* Had he gone to the farm, too? At the beep, I said, "News channels showed the abused wife, a redheaded teenager, during the press conference. Can you have someone watch her husband until I can get her out of there?"

Molly Dolichek would know the number. I dialed her cell. Voice mail. I couldn't leave a sick woman this disturbing message. I disconnected.

Kaysi said, "No record of the home number online. Is the redheaded girl Desdemona?"

I nodded. No point in hiding it.

Stuart rubbed the back of my neck. "Relax, Phoenix. She couldn't have been on more than an instant. I didn't even notice her. Surely her husband isn't the type to be watching that press conference."

"True," I conceded, "but the TV at his workplace is set on that channel, and he or someone there may have seen Tara. She was on camera during an emotional moment. Besides," I censored my words, "her husband has posted her picture on at least one site frequented by equally twisted men. Every time this channel or another one replays the press conference, they'll include the part where she's on camera. Sooner or later, machete man is bound to hear about it."

"Phoenix," Mrs. Roper said, "who is this woman and why is she your responsibility?"

I didn't mind telling Mrs. Roper, but Kaysi's generation had no sense of privacy. I kept my reply general: "Desdemona applied to the foundation for help in hiding from a violent husband."

Kaysi turned the laptop screen so I could see it. "Is this Desdemona?"

How had Kaysi found the photo so fast? She had to have known exactly where to look. "Yes." Geez. "And that's not the site I dug up."

Kaysi turned the laptop back around. "This one is mostly wackos from Missouri, Kansas, and Iowa. I know a bunch of others where Adam Augeri might have posted. The Cyber Defenders can watch those the rest of the weekend to see if anyone reports she's at Congressman Candon's farm."

An unexpected source of expertise. Too bad I couldn't trust her.

Stuart beamed with pride. "Great idea, sweetheart."

Careful. I said, "Yes, and a generous offer, but I can't ask teenage girls to spend hours monitoring these awful places."

Kaysi flushed. "You think we're just a bunch of daddy's girls who can't handle adult problems."

So she'd overheard what I said. I struggled to find a reply.

Mrs. Roper rescued me: "Phoenix is afraid the parents won't approve."

I relaxed at the out she'd given me.

Stuart said, "We've all signed off on Cyber Defenders. One of the mothers is a tech whiz who has made sure the girls have set up barriers so they won't be identified."

Back in deep doo-doo. "I have one other concern, Kaysi. Adam Augeri threatened to cut off his wife's feet if she ran away. He's had two months to boil. As you can tell by reading his posts, he's a lethal threat to her and those who help her. Anyone who gets involved must maintain absolute secrecy. No bragging to friends at the mall. No posting hints online. No writing essays about your adventure for English class."

Stuart nodded. "Phoenix is right. The police should be monitoring these sites, not—uh—citizens. We better leave it to Captain Gist."

I sighed. "You know I can't count on him." I debated a moment. Connie and I couldn't monitor all those sites, especially while we were at the farm. Besides, I felt sure Kaysi would proceed no matter what I said. Safer to know what they were doing than leave them on their own. "Kaysi, please contact your group and sketch out the situation without giving them any details. Explain what's at stake and the necessity for secrecy. If the parents approve and the Cyber Defenders will monitor sites as professionals would, then I'd greatly appreciate your help."

She ducked her head and began to type.

I excused myself and dialed the sheriff's department to explain the situation to Jim and ask him to contact Gist. Jim listened and promised action.

When I came back, Kaysi sat next to Stuart on the sofa looking at the laptop screen. She smiled for the first time since I met her. "We're in, Phoenix."

I extended my hand. "Good. I'll give you the basic facts the Cyber Defenders need to know."

Stuart stood up. "Mom, let's have a little more cake while these two work on their case."

As soon as the two were out of earshot, Kaysi said, "I'm doing this for Tara Augeri, not you."

My hope for *rapprochement* plummeted. But our personal issues weren't the priority. Was she woman enough to recognize that? I spoke slowly and precisely: "Fine, but you must take Tara's situation seriously. Please understand that if your group slips up and reveals her location, her husband might maim or even kill her."

CHAPTER THIRTEEN

The warm, sunny day had turned cloudy and cold by the time Stuart and the kids left for St. Louis (taking all the leftover roast and half the cake), and Achilles and I returned to the castle.

I was freshening Achilles' water when, to my surprise, Nancy Alderton replied to my call to Connie about Tara being caught on camera. Nancy was riding back to Laycock with Annalynn and Connie. As I'd feared, they had driven miles from the Candon farm before receiving service.

"We appreciate your concern," Nancy said, "but both Four Chimneys and Archer's son's home—that's where Tara is staying— have fancy electronic surveillance systems. I'll call Junior and warn him not to let Tara go outside alone."

Not enough. Persuade, not dictate. "Worrying about Tara places an additional emotional burden on a grieving family. It's not fair to them to leave her there."

"The three of us talked it over," Nancy said. "We agree it's best to leave Tara there tonight. Annalynn has offered to bring her back Monday and let her stay in the castle until you can relocate her."

The right idea, but the delay alarmed me. "Monday? Why not tomorrow?"

"Clarissa has asked Annalynn to come tomorrow afternoon and stay overnight to meet with Archer's staff and some other political people."

Damn! "Nancy, that gives machete man forty-eight hours to find out where she is." I considered a moment. Annalynn had turned in her service weapon and not rearmed herself. "You three come on home. I'll go get Tara right now."

"Wait!" Annalynn had taken the phone. "I knew you'd say that. Phoenix, both houses are well back from the road, the gate to the road is locked, and they have outdoor lights. Besides, anyone can see from the cars that several people are there. Only a crazy man or a fool would approach her in front of all those people."

That didn't reassure me. "Are any of those people armed or capable of facing down this dangerous kid?"

Nancy answered, "The Candons hunt and shoot varmints. The family she's staying with knows the situation and, if necessary, would pick up a rifle to protect Tara. Besides, it's too risky to leave Tara alone in the castle tomorrow night and most of Monday."

I agreed reluctantly and disconnected. I went upstairs to check my laptop for a reply to the relocation questions I'd emailed to my former CIA colleague.

My cell rang. Captain Gist.

He said, "I got your and Jim's messages. I was at the farm, and I never saw any red-haired girl. Are you sure it's her?"

"I just confirmed it. Can you assign someone to watch Adam Augeri?"

"No, but Jim is filling in the sheriff in that county. He'll handle it."

If that county was as short of deputies as Vandiver County, the sheriff couldn't stake out Augeri more than a few hours. That might suffice. Or it might not. "How secure are the houses on the Candon farm?"

"I can't say about Junior's house, but Four Chimneys—the main house—has excellent security. I know because I advised Archer on the system when they renovated the place five years ago." Gist said something indistinguishable to someone else. "The medical examiner just emailed me the test results on the coffee in the thermos. Hold on."

Maybe Stuart wouldn't need to take my sample to the lab after all. I paced and paced, waiting for Gist to come back on.

"Not sure what to make of it," he said. "The coffee contained a normal amount of sucrose and an excessive amount of trimethylxanthine."

"Sucrose is sugar. What's the other one?"

"Trimethylxanthine is a white alkaloid. The examiner is going to test the congressman's blood to see if he ingested enough to affect him. I'll get back to you tomorrow."

"Hold on." I still didn't know what was in the coffee, but it sounded ominous. "Now that we know Molly stashed Tara at the Candon farm, we have to take seriously the possibility that Adam Augeri found out how his wife escaped and where she is. Surely he's become a viable suspect for tampering with the coffee."

"I'm not the amateur, Dr. Smith. I've got men collecting photos and any surveillance tapes of Candon's meetings Wednesday." He disconnected.

His attitude reconfirmed my suspicion that all he wanted me to do was ascertain the probability of a suicide. I went to my laptop and, after a struggle with the spelling, I entered trimethylxanthine in the search engine and found the more common term, caffeine. Why in hell hadn't Gist said that? Molly was known to drink strong coffee. What did excessive caffeine mean? One thing for sure, Gist had held back information.

I called Stuart's cell. Kaysi answered.

I couldn't ask to speak to Stuart while he was driving. "Please tell your father that Gist reports the coffee contains excessive caffeine."

"That's why people drink coffee," she said. "Oh, I get it. Somebody dumped in an overdose of powdered caffeine."

"That's not established yet." Her guess made sense. I knew nothing about powdered caffeine, but obviously an overdose could give even a devoted coffee drinker nausea and an accelerated heart rate. A couple of sips, on the other hand, might be enough to disorient a caffeine-sensitive older man.

The phone went silent for a long time before Kaysi said, "Dad says lots of brick and online stores sell caffeine powder as a stimulant. Overdosing is a problem, particularly with students. We'll drop off your sample at the lab on the way home. Measuring the powder shouldn't take long, but tracing the source could take weeks."

"Thanks. One other thing, I'm not happy about this, but we're going to leave Tara where she is tonight. Annalynn and I will go there tomorrow for political meetings and move the girl to a new location Monday." Kaysi needn't know Tara would be in the castle. "The most crucial time for monitoring Adam Augeri's postings will be the next twenty-four hours." I couldn't risk being incommunicado at the farm. I'd take my special cell phone. I hated to give the curious, online-savvy teenager my unusual number. "I'll email your father the Candon's landline number and an emergency cell phone number before I leave Laycock."

"Okay. Bye."

Annalynn's house phone rang. Connie. I answered it.

"It's your turn to fix supper, Phoenix. We'll be there in forty minutes. Bye."

Saturday wasn't my turn to cook dinner. It was Connie's. Let them eat cake. No, they'd had a tough, tiring day. Besides, casual questioning at the table could tell me whether to overrule Annalynn and pick up Tara tonight. I decided to prepare one of my mother's busy-day twenty-minute meals, fried sliced potatoes with eggs and bits of ham or bacon stirred in and a tossed salad.

That left me time to check my email. To my relief, my former CIA colleague had replied to my query on relocation. His reply took me ten minutes to decipher. The gist of it was that setting up a lasting false identity took time and expensive expertise. My contact recommended working with organizations assisting abused and sex-trafficked women to place Tara in a safe house until we could establish the new identity in a suitable environment. He added an alternative solution: Encourage the husband to have a fatal accident. Appealing but unfeasible.

Achilles barked to remind me he was ready for dinner. I hurried to the kitchen, fed him, and washed three smallish potatoes. As I peeled them, I thought about a suitable environment for a teenager who had few job skills and needed a support system. College, of course. Out of state. Blend in with the crowd. Hold it. I didn't know whether the girl could do college work, but I could fake a transcript to get her in somewhere not too fussy. She could last a semester, giving me or more knowledgeable people time to find a long-term solution.

Achilles ran to the dining room window and barked a greeting.

I put a skillet on a burner and brought olive oil from the pantry.

The front door opened, and I heard Nancy's voice.

"I don't smell food." Connie had projected her voice as if she were on stage. "Phoenix?"

"Dinner will be ready in fifteen to twenty minutes," I called, digging into the bag for a fourth potato. "Set the table, please, Connie."

She tossed her coat over a dining room chair and hurried through the kitchen to the powder room in the back.

I heard the door of the hall closet open and close and then Annalynn and Nancy going up the stairs.

Connie came back through the kitchen and peeked into the dining room before saying softly, "You have to let Annalynn off the hook for doing foundation work. She's competing with at least five other people for the nomination. She has to concentrate on that."

Damn! Right when I thought I'd be rid of "despirit for car" and her ilk. And it would only get worse if, no, *when* Clarissa backed Annalynn. "The whole point of setting up CAC was to give her a decent income and a prestigious job. Nonprofits are not my thing." I wasn't all that fond of peeling potatoes either.

"Most theaters are nonprofits, but not on purpose." Connie took the plates from the cupboard. "You can easily afford to hire someone. The applications come in online or in the mail. You can hire someone who wants to work from home and doesn't need an office here."

Not a bad idea. "Give me a name."

She took the plates and silverware into the dining room. "You can't expect me to do everything."

Or to cook dinner. I turned on the burner, poured a little olive oil into the skillet, and starting slicing the potatoes. "Did you talk to

Tara today?"

Connie came back and filled the water glasses. "Barely. When Nancy told me Tara was working in the kitchen, I sneaked in long enough to introduce myself and tell her we—CAC—will be there tomorrow. She's barely five feet tall and could pass for fifteen." Connie peered into the skillet and stepped back when I brought a box of eggs from the fridge. "Gee whiz, Phoenix. That's not much of a meal for company."

Annoyed, I snapped, "It's your turn to cook tonight." Forget it. "How long has Tara been at the farm?"

"Since she escaped. Molly explained the situation to Heather Candon, the daughter-in-law, and took Tara straight to Heather's house. It's on the same farm but somewhere behind Four Chimneys, the old house where Clarissa held the press conference. Heather was looking for someone to help pick and put up vegetables and fruit. Lately Tara's been helping feed and water the herd and clean Four Chimneys. It worked out well for both sides."

Hmm. Then why had Nancy asked CAC to relocate the girl? Maybe the senior Candons didn't want a stranger to witness his decline. "Did Clarissa ask Nancy to contact CAC?"

"No, Molly did. Clarissa didn't know anything about it. She still doesn't."

"No wonder Nancy doesn't want me to remove Tara tonight."

Annalynn walked into the kitchen. "Umm, potatoes and eggs. I loved it when your mother fixed those. I'll toss a salad."

Five minutes later, Nancy, her face taut, joined us and took a chair across the table from me. She said a short, generic grace, not at all like her prayers from the pulpit. After the amen, she made no move to eat. "I called Archer's son to warn him to watch for Tara's husband. Captain Gist had already called. They're old friends. Junior will check the security systems for both houses and alert his brothers to take any alarm seriously. They're staying at Four Chimneys tonight."

"Good," Annalynn said. "Superior numbers always help."

Nancy drew a deep breath. "There's more. Captain Gist told Junior that Molly may have become ill because someone added powdered caffeine to her coffee. The examiner is checking to see if Archer drank some of it. Junior and I decided not to tell Clarissa until the police know whether the coffee could have affected Archer's driving." She shifted her gaze to me. "You knew something was wrong when you found that thermos. Why didn't you tell me?"

Tell the truth but not the story to this human lie detector. "I knew only that Achilles smelled something."

Nancy raised a skeptical eyebrow and focused on Annalynn. "Captain Gist said Phoenix is working on the investigation. Annalynn, did you accept Clarissa's invitation because you're investigating Archer's death?"

"No," Annalynn said. "I'm going there to seek support to run for Archer's seat."

I didn't want to tell Nancy that Gist brought me on to find out whether the crash was a suicide. "Relocating Tara is my priority. We'll have to do it in steps. Nancy and Annalynn, you know the state's leaders on women's issues. Surely one of them can direct us to people running safe houses in other states. I'll take Tara to one until I can establish a new identity for her."

Connie pouted. "And what do I do?"

The answer sprang from my subconscious: "You become a redhead and take your daughter to enroll in a college in January. I'm sure Nancy can persuade"—or I could pressure—"LCC to produce a transcript to send to admissions offices."

Connie beamed. "I'll be the third act."

"That's an absolutely brilliant plan, Phoenix," Nancy said. "Thank you."

Right. A brilliant plan. With one big catch. I had to sneak Tara Augeri off that farm before her husband could swing his machete.

CHAPTER FOURTEEN

My table companions relaxed and enjoyed the simple meal. Only Annalynn followed my parents' custom of sprinkling vinegar on the potatoes and eggs. All three chuckled when I brought in Trudy's practice cake. Connie, like Zeke, immediately labeled it a nerd cake. I was grateful for Nancy's presence. It forced Annalynn and Connie to delay their questions about my encounter with Stuart's kids.

I drove Connie and then Nancy home and returned anticipating a grilling from Annalynn, but she was on the phone in the ladies' parlor. I hurried upstairs to my laptop to learn more about caffeine overdoses.

A British site said a strong cup of coffee contains between fifty and a hundred milligrams of caffeine, and many regular coffee drinkers safely consume six to eight hundred milligrams a day. A cup of Molly's famously strong coffee must contain at least a hundred milligrams. So the equivalent of eight cups a day wouldn't bother her. But how much more than that—ingested in a couple of hours—could she tolerate? Damn Gist for not defining excessive.

I read news articles about students who had died from accidentally overdosing on powdered caffeine and went to the Food and Drug Administration site for reliable information. The feds emphasized the danger of an accidental overdose. No wonder. A teaspoon of the stimulant approximated the amount in twenty-eight cups of coffee— three times most devoted coffee drinkers' daily tolerance. How would I administer an overdose? Pretty simple. Empty out a paper packet of sugar, spoon in the white powder, seal the packet with a small piece of tape, and slip it in your pocket. With a few seconds of private access to the thermos, you could empty the packet, drop it into the trash, and walk away undetected.

So what happens when you drink the coffee? Lots of sites listed the symptoms of caffeine toxicity, including rapid heartbeat, vomiting, and disorientation. Those fit what I knew about Molly's illness.

Because Archer Candon didn't drink coffee, almost any excess caffeine would have affected him. So focus on Molly. How much caffeine powder would she need to consume to send her to the emergency room? What would a lethal dose be? Not knowing such variables as her age, weight, and health, I could find no definitive answer online.

That left me with no choice but to use vague numbers—hated those—and guesstimate. First known: The thermos held two cups, and less than half a cup remained in it. Candon didn't normally drink coffee and probably did no more than sip. Estimate: Molly drank at least a cup.

Hmm. A coffee addict would drink way more than two cups a day. The thermos contained only her afternoon supply. How fast would her body absorb caffeine? I scrolled through sites and learned the stomach absorbs caffeine in forty to sixty minutes. The drinker feels the effects only after it reaches the bloodstream. Those effects last four to eight hours. Conclusion: She had drunk the tainted coffee from one to four hours before becoming ill. That verified an after-lunch poisoning. She would remember when and where she filled the thermos.

But Gist had forbidden me to talk to her. Annalynn wouldn't do it. If Gist stayed mum, I'd enlist the help of the Reverend Nancy Alderton.

The stimulant constituted a clever murder weapon. The doctor hadn't recognized the cause of Molly's symptoms and tested for a caffeine overdose. By the time anyone had an inkling her illness didn't come from natural causes, her body had destroyed the evidence. Did hospitals keep patients' blood after dismissal? Doubtful, but the doctor might be able to estimate the time of ingestion and narrow the pool of suspects. The advance man—Roland somebody—had remarked that Molly knew everyone's name. She'd be able to list most of the people at those two afternoon sessions.

Or she already had. I went to Candon's website and then to his calendar page. Sure enough, his schedule for Wednesday came up, and with it a dozen photos of him posing with constituents. Photos Gist had elected not to mention. I enlarged each photo and searched for Adam Augeri's baby face. I zoomed in on two dark-haired young men but couldn't tell whether either was Adam. The big monitor in the basement office would yield a better view.

Closing the laptop, I ran down the stairs.

"Phoenix," Annalynn called from the parlor, "I'm ready."

Ready? For what? "Give me five minutes. I'm going downstairs to look at photos from Candon's meetings Wednesday afternoon. Augeri may be in one of them."

"I'll come with you. It would be wonderful to identify him and bring him in as a person of interest tonight."

We hurried downstairs to the bomb shelter, constructed in our childhood, that the Keysers had converted into her late husband's home office a decade or so ago. I sat in Boom's giant ergonomic chair to bring up the photos. The faces were much clearer than on my laptop. I found the two young men. "Augeri's not there."

Annalynn peered over my shoulder. "That doesn't mean he wasn't at the coffees. What about surveillance footage?"

"Gist is handling that, and he won't share." So be resourceful. "Some of Candon's supporters would have taken photos and posted them online."

"I know some of these people. Which are the afternoon photos?"

I scrolled through the schedule. Coffees at nine in Milan and eleven fifteen in Kirksville. Lunch at twelve forty-five in Macon. Coffees in Marceline at two thirty and Brookfield at four. "Scratch the morning places." I explained the absorption rate and added, "We need to know when and where Molly last filled the thermos and whether she sipped on her coffee for hours or drank it in a few minutes."

"Sam Gist must have asked Molly those questions by now. Please leave investigating the caffeine to him."

"I can't. He's clammed up, and I need to know asap whether Augeri poisoned the coffee. If he did, he's smarter and more dangerous than I expected." I stood and moved over so Annalynn could sit in the desk chair and have a better view. "Can you tell which photos show the Marceline crowd?"

She took the chair. "These two. I recognize a half dozen people, including Bernadine Platt, one of my rivals for the nomination. She drove a long way to be at that little coffee." Annalynn reached for a pad and pencil. "I doubt that you'll find anything but selfies of them with Archer, but I'll write down their names."

I studied the group photos and noticed the same two middle-aged and one young woman in all of them. Had to be part of Candon's entourage. "Which one is Molly Dolichek?"

Annalynn pointed to a well-rounded woman with shoulder-length rather frizzy brown hair and a big smile. "She's always smiling. At first I thought it was fake, but Vernon says Molly always expects the best in spite of the evidence. I can't imagine anyone who knows her wanting to kill her. It must have been that Augeri boy." She pulled up two other photos. "I know only three people at Brookfield. The short man with the moustache is Jerrald Nussbaum, another rival." She wrote down those names. "People had to sign up for the lunch in advance and pay fifty dollars. Augeri could have used a false name and mailed in cash, but I assume Molly would have recognized him."

"He would have stood out like a worm among snakes, from the looks of these photos. We can be fairly sure he wasn't at the lunch."

Annalynn handed me the list and turned off the computer. "I have the prep materials for tomorrow laid out upstairs. Come quiz me before you look for other photos."

For a moment I didn't know what she was talking about. Then I got it. "You're cramming the way you would for a test. Will all the potential candidates give a speech, too?"

She grimaced. "I wish. Writing a speech would be much easier than preparing to answer questions on education, agriculture, highways, health insurance, gun control, homeland security, immigration, deficits." She threw up her hands and walked out the door. "And then come the international issues. I really need your help with those. The meeting will be one giant final exam."

Good grief. "I'm going to need another sliver of chocolate cake."

She suppressed a smile. "How was the birthday party?"

"Mrs. Roper and Kaysi both loved the cake." Enough about Kaysi. "Zeke played with Achilles every moment he wasn't at the table. Stuart thought it went well."

To my surprise, Annalynn asked no more. The campaign was already taking over her life.

We studied until eleven o'clock. My only breaks came while Annalynn took phone calls and I talked to Stuart—a whole five minutes with Annalynn shuffling papers on my end and Kaysi muttering in the background on his. Finally Annalynn went up to bed with her notes in her hand. I went downstairs to check for photos posted by the people on Annalynn's list. I turned up nothing but stiff poses with Candon and awkward selfies.

When I woke in a dim light Sunday morning, Achilles stood by my bed with his leash in his mouth. I got up and looked out the window. In the backyard, grass protruded through a light layer of snow. My iPhone's weather app predicted an inch of snow for Laycock today and two inches tomorrow. Same for Kansas City. Maryville, in the northwest corner near the Iowa border, expected six inches today and twelve tomorrow. I didn't know how far from there Four Chimneys was, but I feared it might get the same snowfall as Maryville. Annalynn's SUV had four-wheel drive, but I'd pack a winter driving kit.

"Sorry, Achilles. No run today." I put on my robe and slippers, went downstairs, and let him out the back door.

As usual, he ran to the hummingbird feeders first in hope that the birds had come back. Then on to the orchard, his favorite toilet. He romped around in the snow so I went back upstairs to dress and call

Stuart before he had an audience.

"Zeke really liked you," he said when he answered the phone.

"No, he really liked Achilles. I'm the tolerable appendage." I'd be happy if Kaysi saw me that way. "Stuart, I applaud the girls for wanting to defend kids being bullied online, but that's a risky business. I'm worried about their monitoring those vicious sites."

"So am I, but after they started the Cyber Defenders—without telling us, by the way—I talked to the other parents. We decided the girls were safer if they would come to us at the first hint of trouble. The techie mother set up special email accounts to protect them— and to keep tabs on what they do. So far, so good."

"This isn't high school. Adam Augeri has said he wants to carve up Tara. He also may have tried to kill Molly Dolichek. I need to know now whether the powdered caffeine constituted a lethal overdose."

"We'll know late today. What's your emergency cell number?"

I gave it and the Candon's landline number to him.

"I see why you didn't want to give your cell number to Kaysi. She'd search for hours to find out where it comes from. Oh, she gave me an update after you and I talked last night. The Defenders found machete man's postings on ten sites. He's looking for his wife all over the country. Kaysi says the tone has changed over the last two months. At first he claimed they loved each other and he wanted her back. Now he's threatening her and anyone who helps her."

"He's sounding more and more like he could have gone after Dolichek."

"You have reservations?"

"It's hard to buy the idea that he learned she carried around a thermos of her own brew, and even harder to see him, a stranger, dropping in the powder without anyone noticing."

"Well," Stuart said, drawing out the word, "answer me this: Could you have done it?"

Of course. "I didn't even know about powdered caffeine. From what I've learned online, students seem to be the major users."

"Augeri's not a student. How do you suppose he learned about it?"

A good point. "Ask Kaysi's crew to watch for any reference to caffeine in his postings."

"She just came in. Hold on." A long silence. "They already did that. No hint of it."

Scheisse! A teenager had been a step ahead of me—again. "Give her my thanks. Talk to you later."

Annalynn, still in her robe, tapped on my open door. "Good morning. Anything new?"

"No sign of Augeri in the photos. No mention of caffeine in his posts. His recent ones indicate that he's spiraling out of control. Still, I don't see a man who beat his wife and carries a machete trying to kill someone with powdered caffeine." I dropped him from *the* suspect to *a* suspect.

Annalynn pondered a moment. "Does Gist think Augeri poisoned Molly?"

"The good captain didn't initially. I don't know what he thinks now." I went to the closet and took out my spy suitcase. Even if Augeri hadn't targeted Molly, he definitely posed a major threat to Tara. "I want to get to the Candon farm as soon as possible. When can we leave?"

"Not until noon. Nancy and Connie are riding with us. They're cutting short both the sermon and the choir and taking their bags to the church." She pointed to my suitcase. "Why are you taking that instead of an overnight bag?"

"I'm packing a few extras." Every makeshift tool I had on hand. "Annalynn, I'd feel more comfortable if you asked Jim to give you your service weapon back."

Her mouth dropped open. "No, Phoenix, no. I'm not the sheriff anymore. I can't wear a holster to this meeting, and I don't want to carry a gun ever again. Surely you and Achilles and the armed Candons can defend Tara from one addled young man."

I tossed Achilles' and my bulletproof vests into the suitcase to demonstrate my concern. "Annalynn, Augeri may not be the only one who goes to Four Chimneys with murder on his mind."

CHAPTER FIFTEEN

Annalynn crossed her arms and hugged herself as though chilled. "You suspect an insider, not Augeri, doped Molly's coffee."

"We can't afford to discount that possibility." I opened my dresser and took out two pairs of my warm ski socks. If Augeri showed up, I preferred to confront him outside rather than in the house with vulnerable—and talkative—bystanders. "I know you want to dress up for this meeting of politicos, but take warm slacks and sweaters, not a Chanel suit. It's going to be really cold, and old houses are usually drafty. I'm taking sweats to wear as pajamas." I could jump out of bed and throw on my parka if the alarm went off at night.

"My house isn't drafty, and Four Chimneys was quite comfortable yesterday," Annalynn said defensively. "I suggest *you* take something light in case the place is overheated."

A bad start to the day. I went to the closet and took out a pair of ski pants to wear while patrolling the perimeter. "I'm less concerned about what you wear than what weapon you carry. After all the publicity you received when we solved those homicides, everyone in the state knows you were the sheriff. Any criminal and most civilians will assume you're armed."

"No gun. After all, Molly was the target, and she won't be there to protect." Then the retired sheriff sighed. "Fine. I'll carry one of your little secret weapons. A pen that shoots tiny bullets? A tube of lipstick that sprays tear gas? A siren to wear on a bracelet?"

"Those are so twentieth century," I said dismissively. "Give me your iPhone. I'll turn it into a stunner."

Her eyes widened. "My iPhone! Really?"

"Well, with a special case and an app. Unfortunately it works only once and at close range."

The doorbell rang.

Annalynn rushed into her bedroom. "Vernon. He's early. Could you get the door, please?" She stopped with her bedroom door half closed. "Or did you teach Achilles to ring the bell when he's ready to come back in?"

Why bother? He could bark. I checked the camera view of the front porch on my iPhone. "It's Vernon with his laptop and a folder." I hurried downstairs and opened the door.

Achilles, hair flecked with snow, rushed in ahead of Vernon.

"Stop, Achilles. Wet. Come on in, Vernon, while I clean his paws and rub him down." I took Achilles' towel from a hat rack by the door. "Annalynn will be down in five or ten minutes."

"Good." He took off his John Deere cap. "I want to talk to you first."

"About what?" I cleaned the paw Achilles lifted for me.

"Who tried to kill Molly Dolichek."

That got my attention. Was he playing me, or had he heard about the powdered caffeine? "Why do you say that? Her doctor said her illness came from natural causes."

"He's not saying that now." Vernon hung his cap and jacket on the rack. "Come on, Phoenix. Annalynn could be going into a snake pit today. We have to work together."

Was he trying to get details from me by implying that someone on staff had drugged Molly? I studied his face. White and drawn. He knew as much as I did. Maybe more. I led the way into the dining room. "Someone overdosed Molly's coffee with powdered caffeine Wednesday afternoon, but I don't know where, when, who, or how much. Do you?"

He sank into Connie's chair on the far side of the table. "I know how much: 2000 milligrams. And no, I won't tell you my source. How close to lethal is that?"

"Too close." I sat down across from him. "Did your source name any suspects?"

"No, and I spent half the night trying to come up with a motive. She's uncommonly well liked for a political operative. As far as I can tell, no one had anything to gain." Vernon ran his fingers through his neat silver hair, giving it a bed-head look. "I don't know much about Molly's personal life. She could be having a torrid affair."

Annalynn spoke behind me: "She doesn't have time for that. Phoenix located a young man who has a grudge against Molly for something unrelated to her work."

He cocked an eyebrow at me.

"He's a possibility," I said dismissively. "I told Gist about him."

Vernon said, "If I were an objective crime reporter who didn't know any of these people, I'd investigate the poisoning as an inside job."

Annalynn went into the kitchen. "If I were still sheriff, I'd question Molly on her personal life."

Wishful thinking. Hmm. I connected some threads. An insider had revealed Candon's personal life, his dementia, to a political DC blogger. The revelation had no political relevance. Instead it fed rumors that the death wasn't an accident. "Vernon, did your AP friend run down the blogger's source for the suicide story?"

"No. After the announcement at the press conference yesterday, nobody cared."

Which played into the leaker's hands. "Tell your friend he should care. That story diverted attention from the reason for Molly being ill and directed it to why Candon died."

"Of course!" Vernon opened his laptop and signed on to our wifi. "If the police thought Archer committed suicide, they wouldn't suspect Molly was the real target. I'll email the AP Washington bureau to go after that anonymous source."

I rubbed Achilles behind his ears. "If you hadn't found that thermos, boy, no one would have known it was attempted murder."

Annalynn ran water into the teakettle. "I've lost my appetite and my taste for coffee this morning. Will you both settle for tea?"

Vernon and I assented. Uninvited, I walked around and read over his shoulder as he wrote and rewrote a message to the DC reporter. I admired his skill at conveying the urgency without giving away the nut of the story.

"By the way, Phoenix," he said as he finished, "I've seen the bit that you and Connie did at least ten times on news programs. My grandson tells me you're big on YouTube, too."

Scheisse! I wouldn't be able to go anywhere without someone with too little to do recognizing me.

Annalynn brought in cups of tea on a tray and picked up the folder Vernon had brought. "Thanks for the notes. I'll study them on the drive to the farm. Phoenix, did you see the birth announcement from the Volckers on the coffee table in the ladies' parlor?"

In short, get lost. "No, I missed it." I went into the parlor pleased that the couple, exceptional deputies from the neighboring county, had included us on their mailing list. They'd enclosed a photo of themselves with William Frederick Volcker, six pounds and seven ounces. He'd inherited Wolf's blue eyes and Willetta's tightly curled black hair. A handwritten note said she would be on maternity leave until February. Nice to receive good news.

Achilles brought me his leash again.

I looked out the window at large feathery flakes. Those rarely lasted, and the really cold weather hadn't come in yet. "Okay, we'll take a short run." If we didn't, he'd not be able to sit still on the drive to the farm or, even worse, when we went into the antebellum house. "You can wear your new coat and boots." Leaving him at the front door, I went upstairs to get winter gear for both of us and to belt on my Glock.

Strapping the new black waterproof dog blanket on Achilles turned out to be easier than I expected. He didn't associate it with danger as he did his Kevlar vest. On the other hand, putting the black booties on his paws proved to be a two-woman job, and Annalynn had to help. I'd ordered them custom-made to fit his paws and to close snugly over his lower legs with Velcro. He hated the sound of the Velcro being pulled apart, and he recognized none of the words I used trying to explain their purpose to him. I put on my après-ski snow boots—better to wear sipping *gluhwein* than running—to show him we needed special footwear today.

Annalynn, who had pooh-poohed the idea he needed winter gear, laughed so hard at the bootie battle that she could barely hold onto the final unshod paw.

Fed up with both of them, I said firmly, "Annalynn, control yourself. Achilles, hold still or we won't go."

He obeyed. She didn't.

We went out the front door with Annalynn and Vernon joking about my buying Achilles baby clothes. Looking over my shoulder as Achilles walked gingerly beside me toward the sidewalk, I saw they were watching from the window.

He soon picked up his pace, running well ahead of me and darting into a yard to lick snow from a gnome's face. Then he trotted past me with his alert look.

Wearing a hood that obstructed my peripheral vision, I turned around to jog backwards and saw an old green pickup turn into a driveway. Bloody hell! Augeri had been waiting for us to come out. I pulled my baseball cap with concealed rearview mirrors out of my jacket pocket, turned back around, and put the cap on in place of the hood. "Come, boy. I see him."

Head raised, Achilles stayed by my side.

At the corner I turned right toward the park. The pickup remained in the driveway with the motor running. After half a block, with the pickup not in sight, I called Achilles and darted into a driveway lined with bushes. I crouched behind a car and held Achilles close to me so his tail wouldn't stick out. We remained there about two minutes, both of us listening intently. I started to stand when I heard a vehicle turn onto the street. I ducked down below the level of the car's roof but stood high enough I could see through the windshield and back glass.

The green pickup crept down the street past our hiding place.

I couldn't see the driver's face, but I recognized Augeri's license plate. He hadn't even looked at my face when he came into the upholstery shop. How had me identified me? He couldn't have, but his aunt could have seen me on television and aroused his suspicion about the purpose of my visit. On the other hand, he must not know Tara was at the farm yet. Otherwise he'd be there. If he'd connected me to her, he might well stick around and follow me to the farm. Better to accost him here and either provoke him to attack me or convince him I knew nothing about her.

First I had to draw his attention. "Come, Achilles." I sprinted through the backyard and ran full tilt down an alley parallel to the street. I slowed to a jog as I reached the end of the alley and turned right onto the street. The pickup had turned left and continued to creep along. I couldn't very well run after it. I stopped and brushed the snow, now falling in small flakes, from Achilles' head and tail.

The pickup's brake lights went on. Then the driver sped up and turned right.

By the time we reached the park, he was trailing us again.

The terrier tore toward us, and the dog walker waved from a child's swing.

"Go play, Achilles. Stay close." Turning my back to block both the woman's and the driver's view, I took off my right glove and slipped my Glock out of the holster and into my deep pocket. After a moment I took off my left glove and stuck my gloves in the left pocket. If I had to rack the Glock, I didn't want a glove to interfere. I strolled over and leaned against one of the swings' support poles so that I faced the woman and my magic cap afforded me a view of the street behind me. "Good morning, Nicole. I see you still have dog duty this morning."

She beamed and pushed her hood back an inch when I called her by name. "Yeah, the reverend was still writin' her sermon." Nicole reached into her coat pocket and brought out a tennis ball. "I'm no good at throwin'."

My magic cap showed Augeri strolling down the sidewalk, his

hands in the pockets of his jacket and a black ball cap pulled down over his eyes.

No machete. But he might have a switchblade in one of those pockets. I wanted to see his hands life size, not just in my viewer. My right hand on my Glock, I took the ball with my left hand and turned to toss it in his general direction. He kept walking as the dogs raced toward the ball. Achilles reached it first and dashed to me while the terrier hung back for the next throw. This time I tossed the ball farther, and the terrier grabbed it as it rolled onto the sidewalk.

Augeri jumped and stepped back, pulling empty hands from his pocket. He watched as the terrier sped toward me and stopped just out of reach, inviting me to take the ball from him.

Normally I would have, but I preferred to keep my eyes on Augeri's hands.

Achilles knocked the ball from the terrier's loose grip and brought it to me.

Augeri hadn't moved. Time to engage, maybe find out why he'd followed me. I threw the ball hard enough it would bounce into the street. "Hey, a little help, please," I called.

"Sure." He grabbed the ball with his left hand and held it a moment as the dogs waited for his throw. He drew back his arm, lunged forward, and hurled the ball toward the far side of the park.

The dogs raced after it, Achilles well in the lead.

"Thanks," I called. Flattery might help me get a read on him. "You must play baseball."

"Center field." He walked toward me, his gloveless hands at his side, pride on his face. "We met Friday, sort of, at the upholstery shop. My aunt saw you playing the piano on television Friday after you came in."

I smiled as though pleased to be recognized. "My fifteen minutes of fame." Damn! My pulling into the trailer's driveway had made him suspicious enough to look me up on YouTube and find out online or by asking someone local where I lived. No way he could have discovered my connection to Tara, and his presence here indicated he still didn't know where she was.

He stopped about some thirty feet away and blew on his hands. "Are those your dogs?"

"Only the big one." As Augeri knew from following me. "He likes meeting his buddy here." Dispel the boy's vague suspicions with friendliness. "Care to toss them a few?"

"Sure."

Nicole had pulled her hood forward and readjusted her neck scarf to cover her nose as well as her chin. Was she warding off the cold or hiding her face?

Achilles ran to me with the ball and then went to Nicole, a woman he barely knew.

Certain he sensed tension, I watched her through the screen on my cap bill. She stroked Achilles' head but watched Augeri. I flipped the ball to the short but sturdy young man when he came within twenty feet, a safe distance. If he pulled a knife and ran at me, I could down him and move out of the way.

He threw the ball high, and the terrier ran after it. Achilles didn't move.

The kid wouldn't make a move with Achilles standing by. What could I learn from him? "I remember now. You're the nephew who came to work late. Do you have family in Laycock?"

He faced me, the sliver of a smile on his full lips. "No, my wife does. She went for a walk in the snow early this morning. I thought she might be here in the park. Have you seen her?"

A skilled liar. I pointed to the far side of the park. "A woman with a beagle walked out of the park right before you came."

"We don't have a beagle. Just a black cat."

The kid was quick. I turned to Nicole. "You were here before I was. Did you see anyone else?"

She shook her head no.

He thrust his hands in his pockets. "Guess I better move on then. So long."

"Bye." Ignoring him as he walked away, I brushed the snow off the swing by Nicole and perched on it. Talk about something everyday. "You were telling me how you roast vegetables. I like sweet potatoes and cauliflower, but I draw the line at celery."

She blinked a couple of times at my strange words and glanced toward Augeri, moseying toward the sidewalk and still in earshot. She said softly, "I like turnips."

"Yesterday I went to a birthday lunch. We had a delicious roast beef cooked with half a dozen vegetables. Cooking them together cuts down on the pans to wash."

Nicole watched Augeri cross the street, now walking rapidly, and pulled her scarf down a bit. "That was one of the best pieces of chocolate cake I ever had. How did you get along with Stuart's kids?"

Now I was the one dumbfounded. My opinion of Nancy plummeted. "What did Rev. Alderton tell you about the birthday party?"

Nicole shrank into her coat. "Just that I could have the piece of arithmetic cake you sent home with her. I heard about the party at the church."

Bloody hell! The whole town was following my relationship with Stuart as though it were a soap opera. Few would be so loose-tongued about it in front of me as this naïve woman. I felt guilty for intimidating her. "It's okay. I hadn't realized how interested people are in my"—I bit back *affairs*—"in my activities."

I checked to make sure Augeri didn't lurk somewhere behind us. "Why are you afraid of Adam Augeri?"

She ducked her head. "I'm not supposed to talk about it."

Great. Now she became discreet. I could respect that, but I couldn't allow it. I stood over her. "He's a dangerous man. Why is he in Laycock?"

She kept her head down. "I don't know."

Pull back. I'd frightened her. I guessed people had been bullying her most of her life. I patted her on the shoulder. "He's looking for his wife, and he wants to hurt her. I'll tell Nancy how well you kept our secret."

She exhaled in a big whoosh and looked up at me. "You got to help her. He'll kill her if he finds her." She blinked away tears.

Surprised by her emotion and her conviction, I patted her on the shoulder. "I'll see that he doesn't." She must have some personal connection to Augeri or his wife. "How do you know he wants to kill her?"

"I know. I seen this before." She wiped away the tears with a gloved hand. "He came to the shelter in Marshall looking for her about six weeks ago. I was coming out the door, and he grabbed my arms and wouldn't let go. He didn't believe me when I said she wasn't there. The other women drove him away, but he watched the shelter all night from down the street."

"Parked in a green pickup?"

"That's right. How did you know?"

"That's what he's driving today. You did a good job of covering your face so he wouldn't recognize you." I took my mobile from an inside pocket and called Jim to alert his deputies and the LPD to watch for Augeri. A traffic violation could keep him occupied for hours. "Let's go. I want you to walk home with me just in case. He already knows where I live. If he's not around, I'll drive you home."

Her eyes widened, but she came with me. "I have to get the dog home soon. I mustn't be late for church."

"We'll walk fast, and I'll cut you a big piece of cake to take with you."

"Thank you." She smiled. "You'll make a great stepmother."

A chill went down my spine. Facing Augeri's machete today frightened me less than living with Kaysi's hostility for years. After all, I could shoot him.

CHAPTER SIXTEEN

Walking back to the castle, I coaxed a bit of Nicole's life story out of her. After ending a bad marriage distinguished by heavy drinking, she'd stayed sober for five years. She'd lost her minimum-wage job in July because of illness and been evicted in September. Nancy had hired her recently as a live-in housekeeper and general helper.

During the rehearsals of Connie's production of *Oklahoma!,* I'd seen the minister's compassion and skill in counseling a troubled teenager. I hoped she'd used good judgment in giving the hapless Nicole a home.

Augeri's green pickup didn't follow us, so I cut Nicole a chunk of cake, drove her home to leave the terrier, and then dropped her off at the church.

Back at the castle, Achilles watched me take off my boots and coat and remained relatively still while I removed his.

Annalynn came from the parlor dressed in dark-blue wool-blend slacks and a light-blue cashmere sweater. She also wore a pendant, the outline of a gold heart holding a cloisonné American flag. Seeing me staring at it, she touched it. "For luck. Father gave it to me on my tenth birthday." She petted Achilles' head. "How did he like his new shoes?"

"Better than I expected." I checked the booties. They were dry inside. I dropped them into the little plastic bucket in which we stored his slobber-encrusted tennis balls. "Augeri followed me to the park this morning. Judging from what he said and did, he had only a vague suspicion that I could lead him to Tara."

"He wouldn't have come here if he already knew she's at the Candon farm."

"Right. To be on the safe side, watch for his green pickup. I don't think he'll approach a former sheriff, but if he does, you need a weapon."

"I'm not carrying a service weapon." She sighed and handed over her iPhone. "How long will it take you to turn this into a stunner? I should leave in about ten minutes."

"That's enough time, but it doesn't replace a Glock." I went upstairs, downloaded the app to her phone, and snapped on the special cover. The stunner provided limited protection in up-close encounters, the kind to avoid, but it was better than nothing.

Annalynn came to my bedroom door. "That storm may move south far enough to make driving difficult on the way back. Could you please gather extra snacks, drinks, and blankets to carry in the SUV while I'm at church?"

"Sure." More and more I was getting stuck with the paperwork at the office and the odd jobs in the house. I handed her the phone/stunner. "Slide up the little button on the cover. You have to have it right against the person, and the blast will disable someone only about twenty seconds. Just time enough to whack him over the head and run like hell."

She felt for the button with her thumb. "I left my notes on the people who will be at the farm on the dining room table." She turned to leave and stopped. "Thanks, Phoenix. I couldn't have succeeded as sheriff or found the courage to enter the race without you." She reached out to squeeze my hand. "In those first few weeks after Boom's death, I wouldn't have been able to get through the day without your support."

Ignoring our families' custom of not demonstrating affection for anyone but a child, I hugged her. "Your father would be so proud of you."

"Of us," she said, returning the embrace and stepping away. At the door, she stopped again. "I dreamt about him last night. He told me not to give up, to remember that no one could represent District 6 better than I can."

I smiled. "As usual, the judge is right. I'll see you at noon."

My stomach reminded me that I'd had nothing but a cup of tea this morning. I went to the kitchen, fixed a bowl of oatmeal, and ate it while looking through printouts and photocopies giving salient information on Candon's staff, five potential rivals for his seat, and his top ten in-state political donors. Too many people to remember. I focused on the money people that Molly's contact list called Ill Wind, Hangover, and Gigabite. Her choice of nicknames indicated her cheerful smiles concealed considerable cynicism. Or simply realism.

My cell rang. Sheriff Jim Falstaff.

He said, "A deputy noticed the green pickup at that shooting range outside of town, so I came out to check on it. The driver had already left, but he fit Augeri's description."

Bad news. "What kind of gun did he carry?"

"None when he came in, but I'm pretty sure he had a handgun when he left. He shot targets with a guy known to sell cheap revolvers in the parking lot during gun shows. He denied he sold anything to his pal John Adams."

Maybe buying the gun rather than checking on me had been his main reason for coming to Laycock. "Can you hold the salesman?"

"No, I had to let him go. I'll radio the Highway Patrol that Augeri is probably armed and traveling west on 36. If we're lucky, he'll go over the speed limit and they can pull him over. For God's sake, Phoenix, be careful."

I agreed with his concern. Purchasing a gun indicated Augeri had moved to another level, a lethal one. "I may need backup. Could I pick up Annalynn's service weapon?" I'd put it in my suitcase rather than argue with her about carrying it.

"I'll do the paperwork and drop it off on my way home." Jim disconnected.

The mini biographies in front of me now held little interest. I scanned the money people's bios, downloaded them onto my iPhone, and closed the manila folder. Rinsing my dishes in the kitchen afterward, I realized I'd been too quick to ignore the suspects besides Augeri. If he didn't poison Molly, then the most logical suspects were the other three staff members and the two would-be candidates who'd attended the coffees. Our visit to the farm would be no picnic.

I tucked my special satellite phone into one of the inside pockets of my custom-made loden blazer. I had to rely on Stuart, Vernon, and, regrettably, Gist to provide information that would warn me which of those five suspects to watch.

The farther northwest we drove, the faster the snow came down. It covered the painted lane markers, forcing me to guess where the shoulder was.

"We turn off on a blacktop road to the right in about half a mile," Nancy said from the back seat, where she and Annalynn had been talking softly. "Soon after that we lose cell service."

I glanced at Achilles. "I'll pull over after the turn so we can make our last phone calls and let Achilles out." He'd grown restless and unsettled riding at Connie's feet over the last hour. He didn't like being confined so long, particularly with the window closed. It didn't help that Connie ignored him to text cancellations to her voice lessons and talk to her little grandchildren in Oregon.

A stop sign showed me where the road was. I turned off and stopped, putting on my emergency blinkers. I left the motor running as I undid my seat belt and squirmed into my parka.

Annalynn's phone rang. She looked at it and said, "I'll stretch my legs, too." She was into her coat and out of the SUV before I opened my door.

Achilles trotted after her as she hurried up the road, the phone at her ear.

I stayed near the SUV to make my own calls. First, Sam Gist.

His cell rang eight times before he answered. "I'm dealing with a storm emergency. I'll call if I have something to tell you." He disconnected.

Jerk. Next, Stuart.

He answered after one ring. "Hi, Phoenix. The good news: No sign of Augeri online since last Wednesday. The bad news: The clip showing his wife in the mirror played on at least two of the Sunday political talk shows. Anything new on your end?"

"No." Why worry him? "We're about to go into the no-service zone."

"You have your—uhh—your company phone charged?"

"Yes, and I brought extra charges with me just in case."

"Good. You may need them. The latest weather report says the front has shifted. The cold from the north and the moisture from the south will clash right over you about six o'clock this evening. They're forecasting eighteen to twenty-two inches across northern Missouri by morning. You may not be able to drive out of there tomorrow."

"If we're not able to get out, Augeri won't be able to get in. Bye." I walked toward Annalynn to talk over our options of an early or late departure.

She stood with her back to me. She laughed softly. An intimate laugh, an affectionate laugh, a flirtatious laugh. She said, "I can't wait. *Au revoir.*"

Good grief! Annalynn hadn't said that since we took French in high school. Connie had been right about Annalynn being interested in someone. I couldn't ask straight out who it was. "Can't wait for what?"

She jumped. When she turned around, the cold didn't account for the red in her cheeks. "Can't wait for this snow to stop falling."

I let the obvious lie go. "It's going to get much worse. We have to leave by four thirty or risk being stuck at the farm two nights."

She brushed the snow from her phone and put it in her coat pocket. "I don't dare leave the field to the others. We'll have to risk getting snowed in."

"Okay by me. Would you mind rubbing the snow off Achilles while I make one more quick call?"

"Of course. Come, Achilles."

I called Vernon. "Any word from the AP reporter on the leaker?"

"No, but he's on it."

"Did you identify a likely suspect? I counted five people with easy access to that thermos Wednesday afternoon." I corrected myself: "Six if you count Molly and nine if you count Nancy and the Candons."

"I'm making calls, but I haven't found the ghost of a motive yet."

He had a better chance of narrowing the field than I did. "I still have a company phone that has a strong satellite connection. I'll call you tonight around nine." Whenever I could use it without being heard or seen. I didn't want anyone, including Connie, begging to use my phone.

"I expect to have something by then. I don't know what, but something. And Phoenix, don't try to drive out before the plows clear the roads. For one thing, you'd get stuck. For another, staying there will give Annalynn a chance to impress people who underestimate her. You get to know people pretty well when you're trapped together."

Not a consoling thought. "Understood." I disconnected and went back to the SUV. The wind had come up, blending fresh and fallen flakes into a white mist.

Ten minutes later I turned left at a big No Hunting sign. If the narrow, bumpy road hadn't been bounded by dead weeds, I wouldn't have been able to see it. For the next twenty-five minutes I strained my eyes and gripped the wheel.

"Turn right at those three big evergreen trees," Nancy finally said. "Four Chimneys' front gate is less than a mile from here."

A hard place to find if you didn't know the area.

After the turn, fresh tire tracks showed me the way. My tense shoulder muscles relaxed as brick columns and an open wrought-iron double gate came into view. I stopped worrying about Augeri. Unless he learned of Tara's hideout within minutes, he wouldn't be able to drive here in this storm. Meanwhile Molly was resting at home, Gist's responsibility rather than mine.

A big red Ram pickup with a cab-high canvas cover over the bed blocked the lane inside the gates. A tall young man—Clarissa's grandson Pete?—in a camel-colored Carhartt coat jumped out of the cab and waved us into the last vacant spot in a three-sided shed. A rented blue Cruze, a black Lexus, and a red Dodge minivan occupied the other spaces.

The kid helped Nancy, who barely came to his shoulder, out of the SUV. "Sorry, Aunt Nancy. I only got room for three more in the cab. I'll come back for the fourth person and the luggage."

I released the door to the back and got out. "No need for that. Achilles and I will ride in the back of the pickup with the luggage."

Achilles came across the driver's seat and jumped down beside me.

The boy glanced at Nancy. "Does Grandma know about the dog?"

Uh-oh. Farm dogs usually lived in the barn and stayed out of the house. A lie sprang to my lips. "He's a medical service dog. He goes with me everywhere."

Nancy smiled. "Don't worry, Pete. I'll explain to Clarissa."

Connie chimed in, "Dr. Smith doesn't like to talk about it, but she's allergic to lead and other metals. Achilles alerts her when they're present."

Yes, bullets and machetes.

The boy went to the back, gathered up all the bags except mine and chucked them into the pickup bed.

I pulled out my suitcase.

He took it from me as if it weighed five rather than thirty pounds, slid it well back into the pickup bed, and cupped his hands to create a step for me. As soon as I was in, Achilles leapt up after me. We huddled together amid the bags as the pickup moved slowly up the long drive.

My phone vibrated in my concealed pocket. I managed to get to it. Stuart. His call signaled trouble. I answered.

He went straight to the point. "Ten minutes ago, one of the online bastards told Augeri to watch the Candon press conference online."

Bloody hell! "Thanks. Fortunately we're in a blizzard here. Augeri shouldn't be a problem until the snowplows come through. Gotta go before someone sees me on the phone." I disconnected, tucked my phone away, and buttoned my parka.

The pickup stopped, and the cab doors opened. I pushed the luggage from the back to the edge of the bed and jumped out as the first-class passengers climbed out.

A stout woman in a red parka with a fur-fringed hood came around the corner of the pickup. The paleness of her face emphasized the bright red lips stretched into a big smile. "So sorry we took up all the room in the cab." She thrust out a gloved hand. "I'm delighted to finally meet you, Phoenix. I'm Molly Dolichek."

Scheisse! Now I had two people to protect. Why on earth hadn't she stayed home? I smiled and took her hand. "My pleasure."

CHAPTER SEVENTEEN

The other passengers came to the back of the pickup to gather their bags. I took the opportunity to step back and look over the place. We'd driven up a slight incline. With the blowing snow, I now could barely see the shed where we'd parked, even though it stood only about three hundred yards away. Twenty or so small trees— ornamental cherry trees like those on D.C.'s Tidal Basin?—lined the lane as it approached the house's circular drive. Five vehicles, one the pesky documentarian's red SUV, had parked around the circle's edges. Two massive snow-enhanced evergreens, the old-fashioned cedars common here, stood on each side of the circle, their dense low-lying branches providing protection from the north and south winds. And a great hiding place for an enraged young man. I would have to check the perimeter before dark to figure out where Augeri could hide if he managed to find the place.

Achilles barked from the pickup bed. He stood over his blue backpack.

Had he sensed my tension, or did this strange place make him uneasy? "Come, boy. I'll bring your bag." I reached for it as he jumped down.

Pete Candon grinned. "And I'll bring yours."

"Thanks. Usually we both carry our own, but I packed extra food for him and ski clothes for me so I can take him out to run." The perfect excuse for reconnoitering.

The boy's face sobered. "Let me know when you're ready. I'll show you around." He leaned down. "Are you armed?"

So he knew Tara's cover had been blown. "Yes, and so is Adam Augeri. Tell your parents." Pete looked so scared that I hastened to reassure him. "Even if Augeri could drive here in this storm, he wouldn't approach Tara with all these people around. By the time we leave Monday, Captain Gist may have picked him up." Or not. And Augeri was obsessed. "We'll talk about precautions later."

Achilles glued himself to my left leg as we walked up a recently shoveled walkway toward Four Chimneys, a two-story brick house with four large casement windows on each side of the wide front door. Tall brick pillars framed the door and supported a balcony little wider than the French doors leading to it. I guessed that the balcony's New Orleans-style wrought-iron railing had been added well after the house's construction in 1848. Smoke fought the snow to rise from two of four chimneys, two on each side of the gently sloping slate roof.

Pete opened the front door and ushered me into a vestibule ending in a set of double wooden doors leading, I assumed, into the main hall. He put my bag among the others and went outside.

The pickup's five other passengers were hanging their coats on hooks in the vestibule across from an old church pew. Several pairs of boots sat on a runner under the hooks, and a box of knitted slippers sat at one end of the bench. So did two rolls of paper towels. Clarissa cared about her floors.

Molly introduced me to Doreen, her driver today and her co-worker. She'd been in most of the Wednesday group photos.

One of the double doors opened enough for Archer Candon's advance man to step through. Roland had replaced his Armani suit with a green and brown British-tweed jacket. Rhinestone stars twinkled in the flag pin in his lapel. At LCC Wednesday night, I'd guessed Mr. Nondescript to be in his late thirties. Now, black bags under his brown eyes—today behind rimless glasses—made him appear older. He did a double take. "Molly! Great to see you. Clarissa said you wouldn't be able to come."

"I couldn't miss this, Roland." Her smile remained in place, but the hand that stuffed her gloves in the pocket of her coat trembled. She hung up her coat and sank down on the bench.

He patted her on the shoulder with an awkwardness I hadn't expected in someone who constantly dealt with the public. "I'm really glad to see you, but don't overdo it." He turned his attention to Annalynn, switching on a smile fitting for his PR persona. "Welcome. You certainly came out of the storm camera ready."

Annalynn touched her flag pendant. "The press is here?"

"Yes and no. A documentary filmmaker is taping the meeting. Clarissa agreed to let him come only if he videos each attendee. She wants a copy as a remembrance of Archer's staff and supporters." He glanced at me, probably wondering why I was here, before focusing again on Annalynn. "Walk in, stand by the fireplace, and introduce yourself. Your name, current position, a bit of your history in politics perhaps. If he asks you anything, include the question in your answer." He opened the door.

Annalynn held back. "Molly, it's a bit chilly out here. Would you like to go first? "

"Yes, thank you," Molly said, struggling to her feet.

"Of course," Roland said, holding the door open for her. "Back in a moment, ladies."

Doreen pulled on knit slippers. "I tried to talk Molly out of coming. Aside from everything else, she's in caffeine withdrawal, and the doctor absolutely forbids coffee."

Annalynn tore off a paper towel. "Let's leave Achilles' booties on and spare Clarissa's beautiful hardwood floors." She wiped the snow off his booties and her boots.

Roland opened the door. "Any time you're ready, Annalynn."

"Knock 'em dead," Connie said. She ran her hands through her short blond curls as the door closed behind Annalynn. "Should I talk about my work on the Candons' music education program?"

"Sure," I said, "if they give you the chance. Annalynn's really the only one the documentarian is interested in."

Roland slipped through the door and said softly, "Doreen, we're meeting in the library. Could you please go on in and bring Molly a plate of food from the dining room before you do your bit?"

"Sure thing," she said, and they left.

Molly presented an unanticipated problem. I motioned to Nancy and Connie to join me near the outer door so I could speak without being heard if the advance man lingered within earshot. "I'm not going on camera. We don't want Augeri or his twisted online buddies to see on the news that I'm here." I hesitated, but my allies had to know the threat. "Augeri will soon find out that Tara was at Four Chimneys yesterday. He bought a pistol this morning." The alarm on their faces prompted me to add, "If he has any sense, he won't show up here."

Connie grimaced. "He's too obsessed to be sensible. What's the plan?"

I didn't have a clear one, but basics are basics. "Someone should stay with Tara at all times. With Molly, too."

Nancy nodded agreement. "We can take turns staying with Tara while she's here. Heather, Archer's daughter-in-law, will make sure she's not alone in their house or outside. I'll suggest that Clarissa assign staff members to stay with Molly."

I couldn't risk Molly being guarded by the person who tried to kill her. I'd have to say more. "That's not a good idea. We don't know for sure Augeri went after Molly. If he didn't, one of the staff or visitors here may have poisoned her coffee sometime Wednesday afternoon."

Roland opened the door. "Connie, Clarissa would like for you to talk about the music program she's sponsoring in Laycock. Can you describe it in about two minutes?"

"Of course," Connie said. "Phoenix is always demanding that I summarize complex information."

When the door closed, I said to Nancy, "I know of five people who attended the afternoon meetings and came here: Molly, Doreen, Roland, Bernadine Platt, and Jerrald Nussbaum. Anyone else?"

"Horse Jannison came to the luncheon. He's an old friend of Archer's and runs one of those super PACs. He gives other money, too." She shook her head. "Phoenix, you're wrong to suspect any of these people." She closed her eyes and inhaled deeply. "Have you considered that Archer may have put that powder in Molly's coffee to make her too ill to drive?"

Even the dead man was a suspect. "It occurred to me that he could have created an opportunity to drive himself to Laycock." Perhaps I'd dismissed the idea too quickly. "Is that what Clarissa thinks?"

"No, she says Archer wanted very much to cast his last vote for an agriculture bill next week. That was to be his—his last hurrah." Tears filled her eyes. She turned her face away.

Achilles licked her hand.

She stroked his head. "He looks ferocious with that damaged right ear, but he's so sweet."

"He's nervous in this unfamiliar place." As was I. Opening the backpack, I offered him a choice of treats. "Nancy, I need to check out the house, learn my way around without being obvious about it. Could you give Connie and me a tour?"

Before she could answer, Roland opened the door, this time without the PR smile. "Who's next?" He stared at Achilles.

Achilles stared back.

"He doesn't talk to the press," I said. "Neither do I. We'll pass."

"Don't worry, you'll look good on camera." When I didn't move, he frowned. "Don't be shy. All you need to do is give your name and say that you work with Annalynn at the foundation."

Nancy moved forward. "Dr. Smith doesn't wish to take part in the documentary. I'll tell the young man." She brushed past Roland.

He tugged down his dark-brown shirtsleeves, exposing gold Capitol-dome cufflinks. "Dr. Smith, I have to advise you to never pass up a chance to publicize Annalynn's work at the foundation. It compensates for her lack of experience as an elected official."

A good point, one I had to counter. Stick close to the truth. "Part of my work is investigating applications for the foundation. I avoid going on camera."

He stared at me, mouth open. "And you're part of her campaign staff?" He stared at me a moment and pointed toward my holster. "Are you carrying a gun?"

Maybe it didn't hurt for Candon's staff to know I was armed. "Yes. I'm on call as a reserve deputy during this storm emergency."

"Okay. You're not part of the Candon staff anyway." He peeked through the door. "All clear."

I checked to make sure my boots were clean and gave Achilles his backpack. As we went through the door, the blond documentarian swung the video camera to his shoulder and aimed it at us.

Achilles dropped the bag and leapt over it with a deep growl in his throat.

"Down!" I rushed forward to kneel beside him and grab his collar. "Put the camera on the floor so he can smell it. He thinks it's a weapon." I wrapped my arms around his shoulders and neck. "Good boy. Brave boy. It's okay. No gun. No gun."

He whined and tried to lick my face.

The cameraman lowered the camera to the floor slowly.

The noise had attracted a dozen people, most of them holding wine glasses. I retrieved the backpack and walked to the camera with Achilles pressed against my left leg. "Smell, Achilles," I said, kneeling between the camera and its owner. We were so close to a fireplace that I felt the heat of burning logs.

Ignoring the camera, Achilles studied the crowd with eyes and nose.

Annalynn stepped forward to stroke him. "Achilles is very gentle unless someone threatens Phoenix. Shall we adjourn to the library?"

No one moved until she walked down the wide hall past another brick fireplace, this one dark, and through a wide doorway. A couple of people lingered.

The cameraman said, "Is it okay if I pick up my camera now?"

"Only if you don't point it at me or my dog."

"Most people love to talk to me." His eyes got that same hunter's look that Vernon's did when he worked on a story. "What do you teach, Dr. Smith?"

Carolyn Mulford

Better to answer him and dull his curiosity. "Nothing. I'm on leave from my job as an economist in Vienna—that's Vienna, Austria, not Vienna, Missouri. My specialty is matching venture capitalists with Eastern European start-ups."

A short, wiry man with well-styled salt-and-pepper hair raised his wine glass to me and said to the cameraman, "Come on, Fellini. The storm has us running late, and a lot of folks want to get out of here before the blizzard moves in."

The documentarian hurried into the library.

Nancy, holding a plate in one hand and a coffee mug in the other, came through a door between me and a broad stairway. "You must be starving, Phoenix. Please help yourself to the buffet and bring your food into the library."

The man with the wine glass hesitated at the library door. "Heather bakes a wonderful sourdough bread, and you'll never find buffalo barbecue like this anywhere else." He held out his hand. "Horse Jannison. Gotta get in there now, but I'd sure like to talk business with you tonight."

"I look forward to it." Horse was Molly's Gigabite, and he'd been at the lunch Wednesday. He went into the library, and Achilles and I went left into the dining room. The drapes that had been closed during the press conference yesterday now stood open, giving a full view of a thick curtain of snowflakes, a white expanse, and then rows of fruit trees.

A tall, broad-shouldered woman with a brown braid falling to her shoulder blades and a short, freckle-faced, redheaded teenager—Tara—were clearing the long table. I hadn't expected her to look so young and so vulnerable.

The girl froze a second when she noticed me. Then relief replaced fear on her face. "I saw you on television. You're Phoenix! I'm Tara." She put down two dishes and held out a tentative hand toward Achilles.

He offered his bootied paw, and she smiled as she shook it.

"Heather Candon," the woman said, wiping her hands on a faded

130

floral-patterned apron. "We farm the place and live in the house behind here. Thank you for coming."

Achilles offered her his paw.

Heather smiled. "I've had six dogs, and I could never teach one to do that. Plenty of food left. Tara, would you bring our guest a mug of cocoa?"

Tara gazed at me with wide, guileless eyes. "Would you like marshmallows? They're big homemade ones."

"One, please." The girl reminded me of a puppy.

As soon as she went into the kitchen, Heather whispered, "Nancy said Augeri has a gun."

"Yes, and a machete. Can he find directions to the farm online?"

"No, but a photo of Four Chimneys is on the official website."

I looked over my shoulder to confirm no one could hear us. "Augeri may not be the only threat. One of the guests may have poisoned Molly Dolichek. "

"That's what Sam Gist said." Heather shook her head. "I can't believe that. Molly takes ages to make decisions, and even longer to change her mind, but she's fair and good-humored. She annoys people sometimes, but no one hates her."

A familiar refrain. "Perhaps the poisoner didn't act out of hate. Greed and fear rank pretty high as motives for murder."

Tara backed through the swing door from the kitchen, a tray in her hands.

Heather said, "Be sure to try the buffalo barbecue, Phoenix. I like to dump it on a baked potato myself."

Tara put the tray with a place setting and a cup of cocoa on the table. "We'll have cake and pie and homemade cookies after the auditions."

Auditions? So that's what Clarissa called the candidates' session in the library. I began to fill my plate from assorted dishes. "Where do you find buffalo meat?"

Tara glanced at Heather, who nodded, and said, "In the pasture."

Obviously a family joke. I didn't get it.

Heather enlightened me: "I've been building a herd for ten years.

Bison meat has less fat than beef. We sell mostly to restaurants in Kansas City and St. Jo right now. Pete can show you the herd, if you like."

"I'd like that." A good excuse to inspect the surroundings.

Connie stuck her head in the door. "Annalynn wants to know if you brought a copy of her report on the economic feasibility of building a new jail in Vandiver County."

"No, but I can quote the key figures." I'd written the whole thing for Annalynn's signature. I picked up my tray. "I'll be back for dessert." I walked into the hall. Ten feet wide and running from the front door to a door leading to the back wing, it formed an elongated room.

Achilles trotted over to pick up his backpack.

My phone vibrated. Had to be important. I put the tray on a small table, stepped to the back of the hall to pull out the phone, and read a text from Kaysi: "aa knows 2:43." My translation: Adam Augeri posted on finding Tara three minutes ago. I hit "tx" and put the phone away. In normal weather, Augeri would be roughly an hour's drive away on back roads. In this weather, even with a four-wheel drive he'd be on the road at least two hours. After he figured out where the farm was. He couldn't get here before five o'clock. Almost dark.

I returned to the dining room. "Heather, please tell Pete I'd like to go see the herd at four thirty, if that's convenient."

She nodded.

Headed into the library with my food, I formed a tentative plan. By five o'clock I'd have the lay of the land, including sheltered viewpoints for me and hiding places for anyone who got past the fence. I shivered at the thought of what the next twenty-four hours might bring.

CHAPTER EIGHTEEN

Two dozen people had crowded into the library, a room about eighteen feet deep and twenty feet long. Sitting on loveseats, stuffed and wingback chairs, and padded folding chairs, they faced a large stone fireplace quite unlike the two brick ones in the hall. Embers yielded only tendrils of smoke. Annalynn and a tall, slender blond man approaching fifty—definitely a runner and probably a skier—perched on a semicircular foot-high stone wall. He wore jeans and a blue wool sweater that matched his eyes, but he had an air of quiet command.

From the photos on the Candon website, I recognized two potential nominees sitting to his right. As I looked for a chair, I took their measure. The one with the bushy moustache was Jerrald Nussbaum. Annalynn's notes had told me he hadn't hit sixty, but he appeared older. He folded arthritic hands over a potbelly and stretched out his denim-clad legs in a show of confident masculinity that the orange glint in his brown hair belied. Or perhaps he simply wanted to show off his cowboy boots with the U.S. flag. Bernadine Platt, a trim, middle-aged, long-haired blonde with impossibly long eyelashes and sculpted eyebrows, tugged the bottom of a charcoal-gray wool dress down over her knees. She wore a flag pin (a politician's badge), a long single strand of pearls, and three-inch black heels. Her concession to the storm had been black tights. Her hands were clasped in her lap. To hide trembling?

Surely Annalynn would face stronger opponents than this.

Connie waved at me from the back corner and pointed to a folding chair by a small round table. I edged my way there along a wall lined with half a dozen bad nineteenth-century family portraits and a dozen large photos of Archer Candon with people acting joyful or important. With my tray secure on the table, I noted the shoulder-high, built-in shelves lining the back wall under a row of small casement windows. Hard for someone to climb in one of those.

I paid little attention as Clarissa got up from a floral-patterned wingback chair near the fireplace to thank everyone for coming to discuss issues that the next nominee would have to address. I savored the barbecued buffalo and sourdough bread as she mentioned candidates and party officials who hadn't come because of the weather or prior commitments. She obviously had been quite capable of speaking for her husband when he had a bad day.

Connie leaned over to whisper, "Annalynn wasn't on the original invitation list."

So the political establishment hadn't even considered her in the running. Her speech at the college must have impressed Clarissa. Others would need much more. I studied Annalynn's face. She listened intently, her profile giving the appearance of being younger than she was and much more poised and attractive than the younger woman. Vernon's notes had said Bernadine had worked as a public school history teacher/basketball coach for ten years and resigned after her second child was born to found an online tutoring company. Her husband was a coach at a rural consolidated high school.

Clarissa patted the blond man's shoulder, a gesture of genuine affection. "As always, Thor has stepped forward to move the discussion along." She sat down.

So the Nordic runner was Candon's chief of staff, an agricultural chemist who had switched careers to work on a House agricultural committee. He'd landed his current position three years ago after his wife, a lawyer, became a senator's top aide.

Thor unfolded his tall frame from his low seat on the wall. "Archer and I planned this unofficial gathering. Clarissa asked me to carry on despite the—unique circumstances." He glanced at the three people sitting on the wall to his right. "Each of our—uhh—guests will have two minutes to introduce themselves. Then I'll ask them questions concerning three areas of special interest in this district: education, agriculture, and infrastructure. In our last few minutes, we'll throw it open to questions." He gestured toward the sprawling man, now hidden by the people sitting in front of me. "You first, Jerrald."

Jerrald's head became visible. "You all know me. I was all-state on my high school baseball team in Brookfield. I went to college a couple of years and didn't much like it, so I joined the pit crew of my uncle's NASCAR team for five years. Then I got my chance as a driver. Everybody in the state knows my record. People still come into my auto parts stores—I got six of 'em—and ask me about my races. I ran unopposed for county commissioner twice. I'm a down-home guy who cares about his neighbors."

I remembered Vernon's notes. This caring guy didn't pay his staff members living wages unless they belonged to his family. His major asset was name recognition among older NASCAR fans, including donors. He'd probably been handsome once, but illness or a fondness for beer had left his face flabby. He'd be effective in a room of good ol' boys, but Annalynn would outshine him in a town hall or a TV debate.

Bernadine went next. She, too, made the rookie mistake of staying seated. I could see nothing but the top of her head. After her first few hesitant words, her well-modulated voice sounded confident and animated. She talked for three minutes, most of that time about her business success.

When Thor signaled for her to wind it up, she concluded, "I know firsthand the failures of our public schools. I understand what this country needs to do to prepare our young people to contribute to America's greatness."

Hmm. I smelled the stench of economic self-interest. She was advocating diverting taxes from struggling public schools to private tutoring firms like hers. Her limited pitch would appeal mostly to the bigots who preferred schools segregated by race, religion, or income.

Annalynn rose to speak. "I'm Annalynn Carr Keyser. The Carrs came to Vandiver County about the same time Archer Candon's ancestors came here."

I reached out to restrain Achilles, who had jumped to his feet at the sound of her words. He relaxed and sat, which meant he heard no angst in her voice.

"Public service has been a tradition in both families," she said. "I served on the school board while my son and daughter attended public schools. Over the ten years I was president, we raised standards and test scores at all levels. We also raised high school graduation and college admission rates. Even so, our tax rate remains relatively low. With dedicated leadership, we can improve education for people at all economic levels."

Connie marked a score in the air with her finger.

"Six months ago my husband gave his life to protect our community from the meth epidemic." Annalynn paused a moment as two women gasped. "To discover the truth about his death, I asked to be appointed acting sheriff of Vandiver County. With the help of friends in and out of law enforcement, I served six months. I learned unexpected lessons about how crime devastates society, and especially our citizens with limited resources. Phoenix Smith, Connie Diamante, and I have founded Coping After Crime Foundation to address problems the government and other nonprofits do not."

She reached down to stroke Achilles. Unnoticed by me, he had gone to her. "I've also discovered what wonderful friends dogs can be." She straightened. "These last terribly difficult months have driven home a lesson first learned from my father. Each one of us has a responsibility to do what we can to improve the lives of our loved ones and of our community."

Connie started the applause. Molly Dolichek picked it up on the other side of the room, and it spread throughout.

Startled, Achilles whirled to face the audience.

"Achilles, go to Phoenix," Annalynn said.

I realized that he hadn't had any water since we left home. I grabbed his backpack and my tray and hurried toward the kitchen.

He inspected the audience a moment before following me.

Tara and Heather had completed the clean-up and were slicing cakes and pies on a high worktable in the large, modern kitchen. They greeted me and continued working.

I rinsed off my dishes at the sink and filled Achilles' water bowl. "Sorry to be late with my dirty dishes. I enjoyed the meal."

Heather pushed away a cherry pie cut in eight identical slices and reached for a lattice-topped peach pie. "Pete put your and Connie's coats and bags in the bunkhouse."

Huh?

Tara tilted her head in a birdlike movement that reminded me of someone. "That's what we call the bedroom with bunk beds. It's the last one on the right in the back wing. It has its own bathroom."

"Thanks." She acted at home here, more like part of the family than an employee.

Connie rushed into the kitchen. "Thor jumped to audience Q&A, and those big-money people are going for the throat. Annalynn may need your help with numbers."

I walked with Connie back into the dining room. "A genuine interrogation?"

"The donors had to have planned it together. The guy Molly called Ill Wind on her contact list helped Jerrald expose himself as an ignoramus about Missouri's alternative energy programs. Annalynn and Bernadine did fine."

"It was an obvious question, at least to Annalynn and Vernon."

Connie stopped at the door leading into the great hall. "The wine woman just asked Bernadine her view on some proposed legislation to encourage wine exports."

I didn't see the problem. "Annalynn's ready on that. Is she nervous?"

"No, but I am," Connie said. "Get in there."

I strolled down the hall and into the library and took my seat in the back.

Annalynn stood at ease in front of the fireplace. "Thanks to an ideal climate and soil for the Norton grape and the expertise of German immigrants, Missouri led the nation in wine production in the late nineteenth century. Our wines won prizes in Paris and Vienna. The destruction of vines during prohibition disabled our industry for years, but now our wines can compete with both domestic and international products. We need to make that obvious." She smiled. "One of the bonuses of finishing my term as sheriff is that I'm no longer constantly on call and can allow myself a glass of Missouri wine with dinner again."

Why had Connie been alarmed? Annalynn was in her element.

Horse Jannison, aka Gigabite, said, "As sheriff, you studied the economic feasibility of building a new jail big enough to house a hundred to two hundred prisoners from other counties. What conclusion did you reach?"

"That the county's limited resources and the trend toward decreasing prison populations made the construction of a large, expensive building a risky investment. I recommended remodeling a city-owned building as an emergency annex instead."

A good summary. She didn't need the statistics.

Horse said, "A lot of people in Vandiver County disagreed with your recommendation. I'd like to hear the numbers that support your decision."

"I can't give you exact numbers off the top of my head, but the expert who conducted the study—*pro bono*—can. Phoenix, do you mind?"

I stood up and, out of the corner of my eye, saw the camera swing toward me. I lifted my hand in a casual gesture that obscured my face. "How much time do I have?"

Horse tapped on his Rolex watch. "Two minutes."

I decided to go into my professorial mode and snow him with figures. By the end of the first minute the camera had refocused on Annalynn, and only she, Horse, and Ill Wind were listening. I finished. "Any questions?"

"I got one," a Candon man in a sheepskin coat said from the library door. "Who wants to get out of here tonight?"

Most hands shot up. Not Annalynn's. Not the other two candidates'. Not Horse's.

Candon motioned toward the dining room. "Then grab a dessert and some coffee or cocoa and be ready to ride in twenty minutes. I've put a snowplow on my pickup to break a path out of here. The snow has stopped, but the front will hit us in an hour or so."

If we could drive out, Augeri could drive in. And the fresh tracks would lead him to us. Now that Annalynn had outshone her rivals, did she really need to stay? This was our last chance to take Tara to safety. And Molly Dolichek. If she had any sense, she'd leave with her driver. I searched for them among the people hurrying from the room.

Molly and her smile hadn't moved. I wove between the chairs toward her.

"No, Doreen," she said to her co-worker, "you go ahead home. I have to stay to convince them our workload will stay too heavy to lay off office staff. I'll hitch a ride home tomorrow."

A noble but foolish decision for a woman that frail. Should I tell her to leave? I had no authority to do so, and Heather had remarked on Molly's stubborn streak. She'd left us no choice. We were stuck here to protect her.

CHAPTER NINETEEN

Nancy waited for me in the great hall. She whispered, "I'll stick close to Molly until dinner. Connie and I will herd her and as many others as we can into the music room after that."

"Good. I'm taking Achilles out for a few minutes." I had to broach a delicate subject. "For safety's sake, Clarissa and Molly need to know about the powdered caffeine and the likelihood Augeri will coming looking for Tara and possibly for Molly."

Nancy closed her eyes and tilted her head back. "You're quite right. I'll tell Clarissa as soon as I can talk to her alone. It will be better for her to tell Molly."

Molly came out of the library, and Nancy took her arm to walk into the dining room.

I took the daypack from Achilles, and we walked to the end of the great hall, through a wide wood door, and into a fifty-foot-long, dimly lit corridor. The only natural light came through transom windows over doors spaced nine or ten feet apart. I wondered if the wing had been servant quarters, or even slave quarters. Shivering in the chilly air, I quickened my steps.

The last door on the right opened not into a bedroom but into a small powder room. "Not last room. Last bedroom," I told Achilles, going to open the neighboring door, which had no lock. Good thing my suitcase had a lock worthy of a store's safe.

The bunkhouse had two sets of bunk beds, one against the east wall and one against the west. Between them was a space about six feet square. The lower bunks had been made up. Sheets, blankets, and towels were on the upper bunks. Our bags sat in front of an antique oak wardrobe in the right corner. A matching three-drawer dresser with an attached cloudy mirror stood against the hall wall. Thanks to a radiator between two casement windows on the north wall, the room was warm, at least compared to the hall.

Connie came out of a narrow accordion door in the back left corner. "That's one compact bathroom, and our room looks like a homeless shelter. Easy to see where we rank."

"Never mind. The less seriously the other guests take us, the more likely they are to let information slip." I opened the combination locks on my suitcase. "I'm going out to reconnoiter with Pete. Nancy is watching Molly. Your assignment, should you choose to accept it, is to charm Candon's two male staffers, Roland and Thor."

Connie perked up. "Okay. What am I trying to find out?"

I pulled Achilles' bulletproof vest and his coat out of my bag. "Any reason someone at the afternoon coffees would fear Molly Dolichek. Or profit from removing her either temporarily or permanently."

She held up her hands, palms out. "Don't say it!"

"Say what?"

"What you usually do. That I have to be subtle, to hide what I'm after." She stared into the cloudy mirror. "Who should I be? Dumb *a la* Marilyn Monroe? Country girl awed by big-city sophisticates? Cougar prowling for fresh male meat?"

I swallowed my impatience with her melodrama. She'd elicited a lot of information using improv techniques. "Suit yourself. Just remember that you'll have to play the same role until we leave here." I took off my jacket and holster. Careful. Connie had no idea I'd been shot during a CIA mission in Istanbul. I had to hide the scars while shedding my light sweater. I turned my back to take it off and put on a thermal shirt, my bullet-proof vest, and a warm wool sweater.

"Loyal sidekick with great flare," Connie said. "I'll play myself. Are you going to stick with eccentric financial genius?" She picked up Achilles' vest. "You're really worried about this Augeri guy."

"Never underestimate a malcontent with a gun and a machete." I put on my warm socks and ski pants. Blocking Connie's view, I moved my special phone from my loden jacket into my zippered pants pocket.

Someone tapped on our door. I opened it. "Hi, Pete. Achilles and I will be ready in two minutes. Come on in. Connie is part of the foundation so you can speak freely."

He'd been a confident young adult with me. Facing Connie, he turned into a bashful teenager, ducking his head and murmuring, "Thanks for singing yesterday, Ms. Diamante." He dropped to one knee to stroke Achilles. "I sure hope he gets along with our border collies. I brought them with me so they'd get to know each other. They're waiting outside."

Achilles whined as I strapped on the vest. He knew it meant trouble. He didn't object to the black coat.

I slid my Glock into my parka pocket's makeshift holster, put on snug thermal gloves, and pulled on the parka. "Let's go."

At the sturdy back door, Pete stooped and took a key from under the mat. "This one's for you. It works on all the wing's outside doors."

I pointed to the security box. "I'll need the code to go in or out without setting off the alarm."

He punched in the numbers.

"Got it," I said, opening the door to blowing white snow and lowering charcoal skies. The front would hit us soon.

Achilles bolted out ahead of me, paused at the sight of two black-and-white collies rolling in the snow, barked once, and loped toward them.

They sprang to their feet and barked in tenor and bass.

Pete yelled, "Steel! Iron! Quiet."

They shut up and watched Achilles, their poses curious and cautious but not hostile.

He slowed to a walk, and the dogs advanced on each other. They began their rituals.

Pete pointed to an old but well-maintained red barn about fifty yards straight ahead. "I keep my snowmobile in there. We'll take it."

I thought of the noise. "I don't want to advertise what we're doing."

He grinned. "My snowmobile is quiet. I built a battery-powered electric motor for it as part of a school project last year." He started toward the barn. "I bought the body in a junkyard, and Dad's been helping me fix it. The ride will be kinda rough. Granddad said he won't ride with me until I get the springs fixed." His voice caught. "Sometimes I forget he's gone. I think Grandma does, too. Just for a moment. She loved him a lot."

His last words carried both conviction and defiance. Had some of the Candons never accepted the second wife? Would Kaysi ever accept me? "I admire the way your grandmother has carried out your grandfather's plans in spite of her grief." The boy had little experience with grief. "Don't expect her to be able to maintain the self-discipline. She'll need your support."

"She's got it." He strode toward the barn, his long legs carrying him ahead of me.

He slid back a twelve-foot-wide track door in the center of the barn and switched on a light. Unused stalls lined the sides of the barn, leaving a wide, open area in the center.

I followed him in and stepped onto a partial basketball court with a standard basket and backboard and a free-throw line. A net bag just inside the door held several basketballs. "You must be a serious basketball player."

"I'm on the high school team, but I'm not into it like my two older brothers." He pointed to some old farm machinery behind the backboard. "When I was a kid, we cleared everything out and gave shows in here at family get-togethers."

A built-in ladder led to a six-by-six hole over the machinery. "What's in the loft?"

"Antique tools. Some stage flats. Miscellaneous junk." He took a blue tarp off a dented motorcycle on skis. "I painted it white so it wouldn't stand out in the snow." He turned on a switch, eliciting a soft purr, and guided his creation through the door.

I pulled the barn door closed and then perched on the seat behind him and gripped his waist. I couldn't see anything but his back.

He drove us south. "The only way somebody can get anywhere close is by coming in through a back pasture. The gates and fences by the roads are electrified."

"Roads? Are there two entrances?"

"Yeah. Our driveway comes out on that road you were on before you turned north toward the front gate. The road curves, so it's less than half a mile from our house. Our mailbox stands by the gate, but you can't see our house or Four Chimneys from there."

Achilles barked and raced along beside me.

"It's okay, boy," I assured him. "Pete, take it slow, please. He'll be upset if he can't keep up and I'm out of his sight."

"Sure."

He stopped a few seconds later in front of a sprawling brick ranch-style house. Three large cedar trees on the side and a row behind it sheltered the house not only from the wind but also from prying eyes at Four Chimneys.

I reached out to stroke Achilles, and the two collies came to get their share of attention.

Pete said, "Steel and Iron sleep in that enclosed breezeway between the house and the garage. They have a doggie door, so they can get out to go after any surprise visitors." He pointed to a large shed some fifty feet to our right. "That's the machine shed with our big equipment. We keep it locked."

The snow hadn't quite covered the pickup's tracks coming from the shed and turning onto the lane ahead of us. "Are there any other outbuildings?"

"Nope. We tore them down when we built the machine shed." The snowmobile moved forward. "Our orchards are on your left behind our house. You can see them from the Four Chimneys dining room. The fruit trees' trunks aren't big enough to hide a person. The main buffalo herd is in the pasture to your right."

I stared down a long hill but saw no animals. "Would a buffalo attack a person?"

"You don't want to test them. We don't go into the field on foot."

Note to self: Avoid the buffaloes.

Achilles ran to the fence with his nose on the alert and stared toward a long three-sided shed near a creek at the bottom of the hill.

Pete stopped. "The weather doesn't bother them, but we have a couple of sheds where the calves can take shelter."

I spotted dark shadows across the creek in the dimming light. "Let's go on to the gate."

After going over a small rise, we reached the gate. I got off to inspect the wire fence and the pipe gate that blocked access from the road. Signs warned that the fence was electrified. "Do you turn off the power to open the gate?"

"Nope. We use a remote control like the one you have on a garage door."

Achilles moved closer to the gate.

"No, Achilles, no! Hurt! Come. Pete, how strong is that current?"

"It wouldn't kill a man or a big dog, but he'd get a nasty shock."

I turned around to face the way we'd come. The rise, the distance, and the coming darkness blocked the view of both houses, but I suspected the top floor of Four Chimneys could be seen from the top of the rise on a clear day. A gust of cold wind blew snow into my face. "What's on the far side of Four Chimneys?"

"The yard, the garden, electric fence, the pasture for the young bulls we'll sell for meat or breeding. The fence and the bulls oughta keep Augeri from reaching Four Chimneys from that direction."

Fresh flakes blew in on a steady, ice-cold wind. Until morning at least, Tara was protected from her vicious husband by a blizzard, buffaloes, and electric fences. I wished I had such strong allies in the main house protecting Molly Dolichek tonight.

CHAPTER TWENTY

With the snow falling heavily, Achilles didn't object to going back inside. He fussed only a little when I put a dry set of booties on his paws to protect Clarissa's waxed wood floors and the lovely old Persian carpet in the library. The booties also had the advantage of letting him move around almost soundlessly. I changed back into my light sweater and loden jacket, leaving the bullet-proof vest on.

Walking down the wing hall, I heard no one. When I opened the door to the great hall, I heard a murmur of voices from the library. The walls of the old house had to be thick to obscure the sounds of a dozen people so well. I went past the staircase and into the dining room to get a piece of pie.

Tara and Heather were setting the table for dinner, functioning as a practiced team. I guessed that the escapee's desire for protection rather than the farmwife's need for productivity had led to the teamwork. Obviously both had become comfortable with it over the last two months.

Tara said, "The pies are in the safe in the butler's pantry."

I knew the safe was an antique kitchen cabinet but humored her. "Your pies must be very precious."

She smiled shyly. "It's a pie safe, a cabinet with little air holes in the doors. The air can get in but the flies can't. I left a plate and a fork for you on the second shelf."

"Thanks." I hated to see the two women stuck with feeding a group of strangers. "Would you like another pair of hands in the kitchen?"

"No, thanks," Heather said. "After three days of cooking for twenty-three Candons, supper for a dozen is a snap." She whispered, "Nancy is waiting for you in the library."

I chose a piece of peach pie, stepped through the archway into the kitchen to pour myself a cup of coffee, and proceeded to the library.

Annalynn's two rivals, Jerrald and Bernadine, talked with Thor, the chief of staff, in the far corner. Their heads close together, they spoke in low voices. Molly and Nancy sat in wingback chairs near the fireplace.

I perched on the low stone wall in front of the fireplace and put my coffee mug beside me. "I've never seen a wall like this. What's its purpose?"

Nancy shrugged. "Ask Pete. He's giving a tour at six." She headed for the door. "Excuse me, ladies."

Achilles stretched out by me and lifted his head to stare at the flames.

"Phoenix, you pique my curiosity," Molly said. "How does an economist specializing in Eastern Europe end up in Laycock?"

A question I'd asked myself many times in the last few months. I told my usual cover story. "I grew up there and came back to sell my parents' house. I've stayed to help Annalynn establish the Coping After Crime Foundation." And run for office.

Molly sipped on a glass of water. "And to work on Annalynn's campaign?"

"If she becomes the candidate." I hadn't expected such directness.

Annalynn's rivals broke off their conversation with Thor and nodded to Molly and me as they walked out of the library. They had left their plates and cups on a bookshelf rather than taking them to the dining room. Did they think they were in a hotel?

Thor, his coffee mug in his hand, nodded to me and took the chair Nancy had vacated. "Phoenix, isn't it? Annalynn tells me you're her economy and international affairs adviser. I hope you won't be too bored with our discussions." He turned to Molly. "You must be exhausted. Would you like to postpone our meeting?"

"If you don't mind, I'd rather wait until tomorrow morning." The smile didn't hide her exhaustion. "I brought my laptop so that I can pull together figures on our projected workload before the June election. You won't see anything surprising. Could we talk about eight thirty?"

"That's fine." He turned his attention to me. "The mill doesn't stop grinding because we no longer have a miller."

Molly nodded. "Archer's death barely affects our workload in the D.C. or the district offices. We still have the same requests for help with grants and veterans' benefits and internships and a letter from the President wishing a happy hundredth birthday. The same number of questions about crop insurance, flood insurance, health insurance. The same sales pitches for special interests and favorite causes."

"The only thing we don't have," Thor added, "is a vote in Congressman Candon's committees or on the floor. All the work and no influence."

Nancy stuck her head in the door. "Molly, Clarissa would like a word with you."

Molly handed her glass to me so that she could use both hands to push herself up. Nancy hurried over to take Molly's arm and lead her from the room.

Thor watched them leave. "She looks terrible," he said softly. He ran his left hand down over his face, his own fatigue evident. "I hope to God she doesn't have another cardiac episode while we're stranded here. Only Molly would insist on coming to this meeting half dead."

"I never met her before today. What's she usually like?"

"Ebullient, always cheerful. That's probably why some people underestimate her political street smarts."

"In my experience, many men underestimate almost any woman."

"That's what my wife says." He rubbed his eyes with his knuckles. "Molly's deliberate in reaching conclusions, but she identified Archer's Alzheimer's before the D.C. staff did."

Maybe because she knew his family history. "When did your staff realize how serious his problem was?"

"A couple of us became concerned last spring. Thinking back, I should have realized it during the campaign last year when he started reading any remarks that went beyond a greeting." Thor smiled ruefully. "We groused that Clarissa controlled his schedule and stayed at his side at every appearance. We blamed her when we should have given her credit. In July, he told me he wouldn't run again, and I realized he wasn't just slowing down. He was never—uh—a visionary." Thor shifted uncomfortably in his chair.

His openness surprised me, but stress and exhaustion hamper judgment. Maybe he would divulge who leaked to the blogger. "Did all the staff know about the experimental treatment?"

"No, just me, his press secretary, and his scheduler. Or that's what we thought until some bastard leaked it and implied Archer committed suicide." His fair skin flushed with anger, he stood up. "Sorry, but I'm beat. If you'll excuse me, I'm going to rest my eyes before dinner." He strode from the room on his long runner's legs.

Hmm. Thor hadn't thought highly of his boss but had been a loyal staff member. He'd obviously been answering—or evading—questions from Bernadine and Jerrald earlier. Maybe Annalynn could coax him into divulging more about office politics. At least he'd taken his cup with him. I cruised the library collecting napkins, dishes, and silverware while Achilles cleaned up piecrust crumbs from the floor. Then we went to the kitchen.

Heather was browning meat, and Tara was chopping up vegetables at the tall worktable. Achilles sniffed appreciatively but didn't approach the gas stove.

"The pie was delicious," I said as I put the paper and crumbs in a giant trashcan by the back door and the dishes in the sink. I stared out the side window toward the orchard. A light outside showed a deluge of middle-sized flakes, the kind that can fall for hours. Right now I valued the security that the storm provided—maybe. "Tara, does Adam's pickup have four-wheel drive?"

"Yes." She glanced out the window and fumbled as she picked up a stalk of celery. "He's coming here to get me, isn't he?" Her voice shook, but she continued to work.

"We have to assume that, but I'm here to make sure he doesn't come near you." I pulled the tail of my jacket away to show her my holstered Glock. "I hope the storm will hold him up until we can drive you out of here."

Heather reached over and rubbed the girl's back as though comforting a child. "And we have a foolproof security system, don't we?"

Tara nodded, but her face had gone pale. "He'll hurt anybody who gets in his way." She chopped the celery into small pieces. She paused and looked at me. "He doesn't own a gun. He doesn't like guns."

Which made his purchase this morning all the more dangerous. Apparently Heather had withheld the information to keep from frightening the girl even more, but she needed to know. "He bought a handgun this morning."

She dropped the knife, leaned on the table with her elbows, and covered her face with her hands. "My mother was right. She said once they start, they just get meaner and meaner."

Heather enveloped her in a hug. "It's going to be okay, sweetheart. If Adam shows up here with a weapon, Phoenix and Sheriff Keyser will take it away and see that he goes to jail for a long time."

No way I could guarantee that. I said nothing as Heather went back to stirring the hamburger and Tara to chopping celery. May as well get the worst out there now. "Tara, did Adam carry a machete on his pickup's gun rack?"

Her eyes widened. "No."

"Did he ever carry a rifle there?"

She shook her head vigorously. "He wouldn't shoot a rifle. He doesn't see good far off. He's a terrible shot."

Good news. He'd have to come close to pose a danger.

Nancy came into the kitchen. "Phoenix, could I speak to you, please?"

I followed her into the dining room.

Footsteps sounded on the stairs, and Nancy whispered, "Clarissa told Molly about the powdered caffeine. Molly wants to talk to you in her room, the one behind the stairs. It's one of the few with a lock on the door."

When we went into the great hall, a knock sounded on our left. Glancing that way, I saw Horse, the major contributor Molly called Gigabite, waiting at her door. I turned right and walked across the hall into the library. Nancy turned left to go past Horse into the back wing. Apparently she ranked low on the political totem pole, too.

"Molly," Horse called, knocking again. "I need to talk to you."

She opened the door. "Not now, Horse. I have to rest."

"Yeah, sure, of course. After dinner?"

I heard the door to the back wing open.

"I have some work to do tonight," Molly said. "Tomorrow morning at eight in the library?"

"Good. Get some rest." Horse came back down the hall and turned into the dining room.

Whoever had come in from the back wing didn't follow.

"You look like you should be in bed, Molly," a man said. "Are you going to be okay?"

"I don't know, Roland. I'm going to Columbia to see a cardiologist Wednesday. I have to rest now, but we *must* talk before the meeting tomorrow morning. I want to discuss some figures you reported and some rumors I've heard."

"Okay. See you in the library at seven thirty?"

"Fine."

Her door closed, and the door to the back wing opened and closed again. So staff members also ended up in the back wing.

I stepped out of the library.

Horse came from the dining room holding a scotch on the rocks. "Join me for a drink?"

"Thanks, but I'm on the wagon right now because of a medication."

He took a sip. "Archer's death and this whole situation drive me to drink. Holding the seat will be tough no matter who our candidate is. To make matters worse, Molly's going to have even more say in running the office. She's good with people, but she's sloppy as hell with the business end of it. Now that her ticker isn't ticking right, the office will be an even bigger mess."

I wondered whether he based his opinion on gender expectations. "I'm afraid she overestimated both her strength and her obligation to be here."

"Right." He studied me. "You're wearing an Austrian loden jacket. Annalynn tells me you've specialized in Hungarian start-ups. I'd like to run some ideas past you."

He wanted free advice. A pay-off for supporting Annalynn? I'd had to make such trade-offs for years. I'd had enough. I managed a warm smile. "Perhaps we can chat after dinner."

Jerrald came down the steps smoothing down his moustache. He pointed to the drink. "Is there any more of that?"

"Sure," Horse said. "Clarissa never serves hard liquor, but Archer kept a few bottles in the butler's pantry. I knew someone would want to drink with me. See you later, Phoenix."

The two men went into the dining room, and I hurried to Molly's door in hopes of getting inside before anyone else came along. I knocked softly and said, "It's Phoenix." I waited half a minute and tried the door. Locked. Good. I knocked again.

A few seconds later, she opened the door. This time she wasn't smiling. "Come in."

Achilles and I slipped in, and I turned the deadbolt behind me. The long, narrow room was quite warm, but Molly shivered in an Irish fisherman's sweater.

She sat down on the single bed placed along the wing wall and enveloped herself in a faded patchwork quilt. "Please sit down."

A glider sat near a small square table in the back corner under the only window. Like the windows in the library, the bottom of the window was at least four feet from the floor. "I know you're exhausted and alarmed. Feel free to lie down."

She did so, and I pulled the quilt over her stockinged feet. To give her time to collect her thoughts, I looked around. "An unusual room." I gestured toward a *garderobe* almost seven feet tall and five feet wide that stood against the back wall. "How on earth did they get that huge wardrobe in this small room?"

"It's built in," she said. She took a deep breath. "Did that awful Augeri boy really try to kill me and end up causing Archer's death?"

Maybe to both questions. To calm her, I kept my tone businesslike. "We don't know yet. Someone, possibly Adam Augeri, dumped caffeine powder in your thermos. Archer drank some of the coffee, and that may have contributed to his driving off the road." Move on to the vital questions. "Did you refill your thermos Wednesday afternoon?"

"Yes. I carry one of those two-cup coffeemakers when I travel. I remember brewing a fresh pot in Macon after lunch." She closed her eyes. "Did I make one later in Brookfield? I can't remember."

"Did you make the coffee and pour it into the thermos yourself?"

"Certainly. I measure very precisely." She licked her lips. "That coffee has become sort of my trademark, an icebreaker." She drew the quilt to her chin with trembling hands. "I didn't see Augeri. I saw his photo at the trailer. I wouldn't forget that face."

I dreaded the thought of dismissing him as a suspect. "Did any of the meeting places Wednesday afternoon have back or side rooms?"

"They all did."

"Was your thermos ever out of your sight in another room?"

She moaned. "Yes, in every single place. I left it in my tote bag with my coat in Macon. I left it on the kitchenette counter in Marceline. I have no idea where it was in Brookfield."

By the time she reached Brookfield, the last stop, the powder had started taking effect. So the poisoner struck at Macon or Marceline. Annalynn had commented that Bernadine Platt had driven a long way for the Marceline meeting. Definitely a suspect. The NASCAR guy had only been in Brookfield. Eliminate him as a suspect. "Molly, who would gain from"—I couldn't say killing—"from making you ill?"

"No one!"

"Think about it. Does anyone besides Augeri hate or fear you?"

"No!"

Somebody tried to kill her. Surely she couldn't be so unaware that she didn't suspect someone. "Perhaps you know a secret that could cost a friend their marriage, or a colleague a job, or a candidate an election." I thought of Horse. "Or a donor a bribery or fraud charge."

She pushed herself upright. "You're saying someone in this house wants me dead."

So Molly had connected the people at the Wednesday meetings to the houseguests. "I'm saying we must consider all the possibilities, and you have to be very careful." From what others had told me about her, I judged that she needed time to consider what I'd said. "To be on the safe side, I don't want you to be alone except behind a locked door." I pointed to a narrow accordion door in the back left corner by the front of the wardrobe. "Where does that lead?"

"To the world's smallest toilet. The door you came in is the only way in and out of this room."

"Good." I checked the tall casement window. Definitely put in long before standardization. With the bottom a good seven feet off the ground, no one was likely to come in that way. "Connie or I will come by for you on our way to dinner. Whenever you're out of this room, she, Nancy, or I will stay near you." I got up, and Achilles, napping by the *garderobe,* sprang to his feet.

"It has to be that Augeri boy," she said, but her voice lacked conviction.

"Anything you say to me will be confidential. If I'm to protect you, you must tell me who may have a motive."

She opened her mouth to speak and then put a trembling hand over it. She finally dropped her hand to grip the quilt. "I can't—I won't accuse anyone without a good reason."

I anticipated a long, tense night.

CHAPTER TWENTY-ONE

Connie, curling her eyelashes in front of the foggy mirror, jumped when I opened the bunkhouse door. "Being trapped here in the snow gives me the willies," she said. "Anything new?"

I closed the door behind Achilles and me. "I talked to Molly. She obviously suspects at least one person, but she wouldn't name anyone. I'm ninety-nine percent sure the caffeine went into her thermos right after lunch or at the first coffee after that. That eliminates the NASCAR guy as a suspect."

"Does it eliminate Augeri?"

I considered. "No, but I don't see how he would have found out about Molly's coffee habits. Even if he did, I doubt he could have gone into those coffees without Molly noticing him. From what I've learned, only three people knew about the thermos, were with her at the right time, and could have dropped in the powder without being noticed." I ticked them off: "Bernadine the potential candidate, Horse the money man, and Roland the advance man."

Connie turned away from the mirror to face me. "And who has the strongest motive?"

"I've no idea. Each one scheduled a meeting with her tomorrow about some issue. Horse is upset about the way she handles the office's financial records, but I don't know what the others' problems are."

"I do," Connie said smugly. "Roland wants Molly's job. He told Thor that Bernadine called him Tuesday afternoon to complain about Molly again. She didn't invite Bernadine to the lunch at Macon and

155

to some earlier Fourth of July celebration. Clarissa dislikes conflict. She told Roland to placate the woman by inviting her here." Connie leaned close to the mirror to check her work. "My money is on Bernadine. Poison is a woman's weapon. It's non-confrontational."

"Missing a lunch and fireworks is hardly a motive for murder." Connie got huffy if I didn't value her gleanings. "Unless Molly's snub means she has some dirt on Bernadine." I freshened my lipstick.

Connie ran a brush through her hair. "How much influence could Molly have on choosing the next candidate?"

"I have no idea." I thought about it. "She knows a lot of people, including the district's major political players. But from a remark Thor made about her being underestimated, I doubt the party officials listen to her. We should ask Annalynn about how Molly could help or hurt a potential nominee."

"Speaking of Annalynn, she rushed out of the SUV to return someone's call in private. Do you have any idea who it was?"

"No, but I overheard enough to agree with you that she's interested in someone. He can't be a new acquaintance. He has to be someone she's known a while."

Connie fingered a flame-shaped earring that matched the flame-colored blouse she wore over a light-yellow turtleneck. "Maybe a high school or college boyfriend?"

Memory couldn't bring up anyone. "I doubt it. She met Boom her first week on campus and didn't date anyone else. She never had any serious interest in anyone in high school."

Connie grinned. "Oh, yes she did. She had a major crush on an older guy. She talked to me about him for months. She didn't think you or her mother would approve."

Amazing on two counts: Annalynn had told me everything, or so I thought, and I'd rarely agreed with Annalynn's snobbish mother on anything. "I give up. Who was it?"

"Annalynn will tell you if she wants you to know." Connie made a zip motion across her lips and stepped to the door. "Time for the tour. What are we looking for?"

"Ways to break in, places to hide if you're already inside." I took a tennis ball out of Achilles' mouth and tossed it on an upper bunk before going into the hall. His tail drooped, and I stroked his head. "Stay close. We may need to find." He perked up.

Roland came out of the first room down from the main building on the dining room side. He waited for us. "Joining the history tour, I assume. Are you Civil War buffs, too?"

A chance to obscure my reasons for checking out the layout. "I'm intrigued by some of the unusual antebellum architectural features, like that ledge in front of the fireplace."

He opened the door into the great hall. "I've been here four or five times but never heard an explanation for that."

In the great hall, Pete fit a fresh log into the fireplace while Bernadine watched. He closed a metal screen and stood up with his back to the front door. "Grandma asked me to tell you some of the things I learned writing papers on family history." He cleared his throat self-consciously. "The hall fireplaces and the double chimneys on each side of the roof are unusual, but the builders used a common design in the 1840s." He gestured to his left. "On this side, the parlor, the dining room, and the butler's pantry. Plus the sick room that's tucked in under the stair landing. It's behind the butler's pantry."

Interesting. Molly's bedroom was the sick room.

Pete gestured to his right. "Over here are the music room, the library, the master bedroom, and a small office. Let's start with the parlor, which is twice as big as any other room in the house." He opened the large door next to the vestibule. "They had weddings and funerals here, and balls and parties spilled over into the great hall. We don't use the parlor much in the winter. It's hard to heat, mainly because the original windows let in the cold air."

As we filed in, I glanced around the formal room and took care to keep my face neutral. By Austrian standards, nothing here reached historical status. By almost any standards, nothing approached museum quality. What had I expected? The place had served as the home of prosperous but not famous people. The outstanding thing about this long, cold, overstuffed room was that eight or nine generations of one family had gathered here.

The awe on Bernadine's face suggested she didn't realize that the Early American chairs, loveseats, and tables were reproductions. She oohed over the white wallpaper dotted with green willows, an adaptation of an old pattern. Two clusters of wingback chairs in a matching willow pattern sat in front of a stone fireplace with an incongruous marble mantle. The rather crude painting over the mantle portrayed a flatboat on a river at sunset.

Bernadine asked Pete if the artist was George Caleb Bingham, one of Missouri's, and the country's, most renowned painters in the nineteenth century. I wondered whether she was trying to flatter or didn't know how ignorant the query sounded. She didn't seem embarrassed when Pete explained that an ancestor had copied a Bingham painting.

I edged past an authentic horsehair sofa—undoubtedly preserved because no one wanted to sit on furniture so uncomfortable—to reach the front windows. I pulled back the green drapes that matched the wallpaper's willows and peered out a tall window. Its size and weight would make it hard to open from the outside, and the rows of wood panes made breaking the glass useless. A pole light in the circular drive revealed thick snow drifting up to the bumpers of the cars. The howling wind threw white missiles at the windows. Adam Augeri surely couldn't drive here through this tonight.

Pete's words caught my attention. "The windows all have a simple defense against burglary. You stick pegs into holes so the window won't open wide enough for someone to crawl in. The whole house is built so air will circulate and cool it off in the summer."

I checked the window. Metal pegs about six inches above the lower casement guaranteed no one was coming in that way.

Pete opened pocket doors at the far end of the room, and we moved on into the much smaller and warmer dining room. He talked for a minute about four nineteenth-century soup tureens on display in an attractive walnut china cabinet from the same period. No one asked any questions, so he led the way into the butler's pantry.

Bernadine rushed to admire the pie safe on our left. Connie studied the china in the shallow, ceiling-high, glass-faced cabinets along both walls to the right of the swinging door. Roland stifled a yawn.

Pete pointed to the drawers in the lower part of the cabinet against the dining room wall. "The only original keys we have left are the ones to lock up the silverware." He grinned and opened a cabinet door. "We lost the keys to the liquor cabinet, so help yourself." He turned from the cabinet to the pantry's back wall. "This is my favorite thing in the whole house." He pushed back a panel in what looked like solid wood to reveal a space about a yard high, a yard long, and a yard deep. "It's a dumbwaiter. In the early days, they used it to send the food up from the kitchen and cellar. Until after the Civil War, they did the cooking and baking in the basement or in a detached kitchen right behind the house. When cooking stoves became common, they built a kitchen and a little porch onto the back of the house."

Roland peered into the space, stretching his neck to look up. "How's it powered?"

"With an electric motor," Pete said. "We go down to the cellar from the porch, so the dumbwaiter is still handy. We use it to bring up food from the freezer and move the laundry up and down. When I was a kid, I rode it between floors." He closed the panel. "I know Ms. Diamante is anxious to see the music room. Let's go there next."

I stepped back to let the others go ahead. With the alarm box inside the kitchen rather than on the porch, someone could break into the basement and ride the dumbwaiter up. I made a mental note to check the locks on the porch and basement doors later and followed the others back through the dining room into the great hall.

Pete turned right toward the front door. "The music room was also the ladies' parlor, a place where the wife would receive guests. It's the only room on this floor with its own stove."

Annalynn stepped out of the library. "Phoenix, a word, please."

"Of course." As the group went into the music room, I walked with her to the hall fireplace. "What is it?"

She glanced over her shoulder. "Do you know anything about Horse's reputation in the business world?"

I'd never heard of the man until a couple of days ago. "Just what Vernon said. He made his first millions with a tech company designing and maintaining proprietary business-management software. He diversified, creating software for government agencies and then buying up innovative tech companies whose founders were bad managers. He's amassed a fortune."

"Yes, but is he an ethical person?"

"Vernon didn't say." I glanced around to make sure no one was within earshot. "He's on my possible suspect list with Bernadine, Roland, and Augeri. What's bothering you?"

"He's asking a lot of questions about your work in Vienna." She licked her lips and frowned. "He hinted that some good leads on Eastern European investments would encourage him to be generous with campaign contributions."

I smiled at her naïveté. "That surprises you?"

She grimaced. "I hadn't expected him to start talking money so soon or be so open about his price. Phoenix, I want to be clear. Don't feel obligated to advise him in order to help me."

Easier said than executed. "Don't worry. I've handled his type before, many times." Another concern crossed my mind. "Be careful to keep your distance. He's still young enough to want some— cuddling and old enough to expect to get it if he does you a favor."

Her mouth dropped open. "I haven't had to worry about that for years."

Because she'd been married to a former pro athlete willing and able to pulverize anyone who made a pass at his wife. Widowhood gave her a new vulnerability. Best to prepare her. "If he starts touching you even casually, tell him that he's pale or flushed—anything to make him worry about his health. And just like in high school, don't let him back you into a corner."

The opening bars of "I'm Just a Gal Who Cain't Say No" sounded on a piano in the music room.

Bad choice of songs, Connie. "If he gets frisky, as Mom used to say, you better prop a chair against your bedroom door tonight."

Annalynn's eyes widened. "Are you serious?"

"Is a corporate king used to getting what he wants?" Was I being too cynical? No. "You're new to this game, and you're a recent widow. Men are going to test you in a lot of ways. The more confidence you show, the more you'll be respected." And resented.

Annalynn stared at me a long moment. "I can handle Horse." She smiled. "My mother didn't teach me how to cook, but she educated me in the genteel dismissal of unwelcome attention." She stroked Achilles. "If all else fails, Achilles will provide backup." She walked toward the library, and her backup went with her.

The tour group emerged from the music room.

Connie motioned to me from the door. "Phoenix, take a quick look before we go upstairs."

I joined her and peeked in. A grand piano commanded my attention.

Connie pointed to a floor-to-ceiling stove coated with green ceramic in the corner. "Don't you have one like that in your apartment in Vienna?" She whispered, "What did Annalynn want?"

"To ask me about Horse," I whispered back. I raised my voice. "Yes, but mine is covered with white tiles with blue *fleur de lis* patterns."

We went back into the hall to join the group, now standing by the staircase.

Pete said, "The interesting thing about the back wing is that the doors are an equal distance apart, but the rooms are different sizes." He grinned. "And not all the doors lead to rooms."

Everyone but Roland immediately questioned his meaning.

Pete said, "The third door on your right leads to a porch. People worked and slept out there during the summer. We store firewood there. We converted part of the porch on the other side into a bathroom and part of it into a linen and storage closet."

And I'd thought I had only one outside entrance to worry about in the back wing. "Do the former porches have locked outside doors?"

"Yup," Pete said, "and they're hooked up to the alarm system."

He bounded up the steps three at a time.

Heather came out of the dining room. "We eat in ten minutes, son."

"Okay, Mom. I'll just show them the game room and the library." He reached a wide landing and turned left into a room.

We followed, Bernadine leading the way and Roland bringing up the rear.

I lingered a moment in the upstairs hall to gaze out two tall adjoining windows toward the barn, invisible in the snow and darkness, and over the roof of the one-story back wing.

Pete pointed to an old pine floor-to-ceiling wardrobe near the middle of the game room. It stood about five feet wide and three feet deep. "Guess what's in that."

I calculated that it stood directly above the north end of the butler's pantry. "The dumbwaiter."

"Right. This room was a playroom and dining room for the little kids. The cook could send their food up from the kitchen. The dumbwaiter is a shelf with no sides, so you can reach it from either side of the cabinet." Pete slid a door in the upper half of the cabinet to one side. The shelf held a plastic laundry basket filled with sheets. "My uncle's family stayed here last night, so we had to change the sheets this morning." He pushed something inside the door, and the laundry basket moved down out of sight.

Bernadine picked up a faded rag doll from a scarred, built-in pine shelf that held two other dolls, a top, a metal train car, and a piggybank. "Are all of the toys and games antiques?"

"Naw, just old," Pete said. "You're welcome to play the board games or put together the puzzles that are on the shelves in the back." He went into the hall. "These windows open like French doors. That lets the air circulate. At the other end, real French doors lead to the balcony." He looked at me. "From there you can see the front gate."

Good thing I'd brought my night-vision binoculars. After dinner I'd check for signs of car tracks on the road, if the heavy snow didn't block my view.

Bernadine brushed past me. "My bedroom is the corner room next to the balcony, and I have a lovely stove like the one downstairs. Do any of the rooms on this floor have fireplaces?"

"No," Pete said, "heat from the fireplaces on the first floor came up the chimneys and warmed the rooms—a little. Now we have central heating."

Bernadine beamed when she heard no one had a fireplace. I guessed that she considered her corner room the primo guest room.

Pete hurried on downstairs. "We'll finish in the library."

I followed. "Do you know why the fireplace has a stone wall in front of it?"

Eyes shining and face earnest, he stopped by the library door and said, "Yes, I looked and looked and finally found it in an 1877 diary. A baby crawled too close to the fire and got burned. That's when they built the wall." He led the way into the library and to the back corner, walking behind the guests sitting by the fireplace. "The ledgers and bound files on the three bottom shelves give the history of the house and the family." He faced us and raised his voice slightly. "One of the most important things I found was that the first mistress of this house, a Quaker, insisted that the Archers own no slaves. They freed their slaves, hired most of them, and helped them buy their relatives." He paused. "Four Chimneys was part of the underground railroad."

Roland plucked a white handkerchief from his British tweed jacket and cleaned his glasses. "I've never read about an underground railroad in northern Missouri."

Pete pulled out a frayed ledger about fifteen inches high. "The family never talked about it, probably because their neighbors would have been mad even years later. One of the Quaker's daughters wrote about it in 1879. Fugitive slaves—and Missouri had a lot of them— came through here on their way to Kansas and Iowa, both free states. Every county in Missouri had patrols looking for runaways. This farm was one of the few places around here that gave them food and shelter."

The advance man still looked skeptical. "Archer never mentioned that to me. It's not in his official bio."

I jumped in. "That's a proud heritage you've uncovered, Pete.

Your ancestors showed great courage in acting on their convictions."

He took down a foot-long wood box sitting on a shelf two feet above the family papers. "During the Civil War, and after, bushwhackers came here several times. The family and their workers used those upstairs windows to fight off a dozen men once. Not the James brothers." He opened the box to display an antique revolver. "Things got so bad that my Quaker ancestor, Lucretia Dunkin Archer, sometimes carried this five-round 1849 Pocket Revolver."

Roland snorted. "I understood Quakers didn't believe in violence."

Pete grinned. "The rest of the family was Presbyterian, and she never carried the revolver loaded." He reached into the box and held up a marble-sized lead ball. "We have two dozen balls and enough black powder and caps to fire them. Grandpa cleaned and oiled the gun and fired it every New Year's and Fourth of July." His lower lip quivered.

Clarissa spoke from the library door. "That's your job now, Pete. Everyone, we're going to have a simple farm supper: chili, vegetable soup, a green salad, and cornbread. Please come help yourselves and choose a seat at the table."

Horse, Thor, and Jerrald had gathered around to see the revolver. Connie and I stepped back, but Bernadine and Roland didn't budge.

Jerrald pulled back the revolver's hammer. "How about showing us how to load this?"

Bad idea to load a weapon kept in an unlocked box. I said, "Maybe it would be better to explain it than do it."

Bernadine smiled at the boy. "I'd love to see how you handle the black powder."

"I'll load one cylinder," he said, reaching up to the highest shelf and retrieving a powder horn, one that a cow had once worn.

Achilles pressed against me and whined. Alarmed at the smell of the black powder?

I shared his unease. If one of the three suspects in the house had poisoned Molly Dolichek, access to the antique revolver could encourage the would-be murderer to try another weapon.

CHAPTER TWENTY-TWO

As Pete poured black powder from the horn into a tiny measuring cup, I resolved to come back at my first opportunity, pocket the weapon, and empty the cylinder. Meanwhile I'd show my disinterest. "Excuse me. I have to go feed Achilles."

Connie joined me in the great hall and walked with me into the back wing. She gestured toward the first door on the right. "This is Nancy's room. Roland is across from her. Thor's next to him." She opened the door next to Nancy's room and flipped on the light. "Sports and camping equipment. Maybe I'll borrow a baseball bat at bedtime." She turned the light off, went to the next door, and opened it. Beyond the stacked firewood stood a sturdy metal door. "I don't see a security system box."

"The one at the back must be wired for all three wing entrances." I opened the door across the hall and turned on the light as a blast of frigid air hit me. A narrow hall led to a metal door with a major lock. An unlocked sliding door on the right opened into a linen closet. One on the left opened into a small bathroom.

Connie opened the door across from the bunkhouse. "Look at this! Clarissa kept the artifacts from her days as a music and drama teacher. Makeup boxes, wigs, sheet music, a mannequin dressed in a uniform from—umm—maybe *The Pirates of Penzance*. Even a sword."

Connie continued to explore the storage room while I served Achilles his supper and murmured assurances. The strange place and people had upset him. Or perhaps he sensed the tension and stress among the houseguests, including his own humans.

Connie joined us. "Do you remember those old Mickey Rooney and Judy Garland movies at the Laycock Cinema on Saturday mornings? The ones where they put on a show in a barn?"

"How could I forget? They were so true to life. Why?"

"You saw the inside of the barn here. Could it be used as a theater?"

"A small one. It doesn't resemble those spacious interiors in the movies. Why?"

"Clarissa wants to start a summer theater program for college students here as a follow-up to the program for high school students at LCC." Connie dashed into the bathroom. "It's getting late. I'll wash my hands and escort Molly to supper."

Ten minutes after she left, I walked to the dining room with Achilles carrying his dessert, a bone chew, in his mouth. The Candons had moved the long table into the center of the room. On a small table by the windows, a half dozen ceramic soup bowls sat between two big crock pots. Everything else was on the large table, and the only unoccupied chair stood at the end by the parlor door. Archer's seat? I didn't want to sit in that. His son and daughter-in-law sat near the middle of the table. Pete and Tara weren't in sight. I apologized to Clarissa for being late, filled a bowl with chili, and reluctantly took the empty chair.

Horse, sitting to my right, broke off a conversation with Bernadine to hand me the cornbread. "What would you be doing on a Sunday night in Vienna?"

An easy question and a happy thought. "Attending a concert."

He leaned toward me, shutting Bernadine out. "And tomorrow morning?"

Not a happy thought. "Attending meetings. One after the other all day. My only breaks would be to answer urgent messages."

He passed the large glass salad bowl to me. "I take it you're not going back to that job."

I'd been debating this for months while circumstances prevented my return. Now I spoke with conviction. "No. I'm ready to move on. After the Berlin Wall fell, Eastern European business growth fascinated me. Challenging and unpredictable, and critical to political as well as economic development." Sure he wouldn't believe me, I told the truth. "The last five years have been rather dull."

"But profitable?" He leaned back and took a bite of a cornbread dripping butter.

Insight: He saw Annalynn as an investment. The less she needed his capital, the more he would want to invest. I leaned toward him and lowered my voice to say, "Wildly profitable, but after you earn the first twenty or thirty million, the thrill is gone."

He roared with laughter, attracting the attention of the whole table. He choked on his food, and Bernadine pounded on his back.

Pete rushed through the swinging door and cupped his hand to say something to Clarissa. She jumped up and motioned to me to follow her.

When I caught up with her in the kitchen, she held a portable phone to her ear. "What is it, Sam?" She frowned and shook her head. "I don't understand what that means. You better talk to Phoenix." She handed the phone to me. "It's Captain Gist."

I took the phone and moved toward the back door out of earshot of the dining room. "Phoenix Smith here." Clarissa had followed me, so I held the phone so she could hear, too.

Gist said, "The blood test showed traces of caffeine."

I waited, but he said no more. I wasn't about to let him get off the phone without knowing how the medical examiner interpreted those results. Force Gist to confirm or deny. I lowered my voice and cupped my hand around my mouth so the kids couldn't hear. "Then the test indicates a criminal action led to the congressman's death."

Clarissa gasped.

Gist growled, "I didn't say that."

"But that's what you meant."

"For God's sake, woman, somebody in that house could be the person who tampered with the coffee. Don't advertise that we know what happened."

"Right." I met Clarissa's eyes. "We won't tell anyone."

I needed information on another danger. I turned around so the kids could hear. "Captain, did an officer pick up Adam Augeri for possession of an illegal weapon?"

Tara shivered and jumped back from standing near the window.

"No," Gist barked. "A hunch doesn't establish probable cause. The deputy reported Augeri returned to his residence at two o'clock. He answered the phone there at four o'clock."

Right before the snow stopped. "When was the last time he answered his phone?"

"That's the last report I received," Gist said impatiently. "Don't you know we got a blizzard raging for the next twenty-four hours? Nobody's going anywhere."

We'd be snowed in tomorrow and quite possibly until sometime Tuesday. I had to focus on the suspects here. "Do surveillance tapes or Web postings show him or anyone else acting suspiciously at the Macon and Marceline meetings?"

"We've got nothing. You better—"

The phone went dead.

I hit the off button, waited a few seconds, and hit the on button. No dial tone. "He was cut off. Clarissa, is this your only land line?"

"No, we have one in the office." She looked at her grandson. "Run check it, Pete."

"Walk," I corrected. "Don't arouse curiosity."

Clarissa, Tara, and I stood in tense silence until the boy came back.

"No dial tone," he reported. "Trees probably took the lines down."

Pete's father charged through the swinging door. "What's going on?"

Clarissa held out her arms to him. "The medical examiner confirmed that your father didn't commit suicide. We didn't find out anything else before the phone went dead."

Caffeine in the blood didn't preclude suicide, but I couldn't say that to the man's family.

Junior hugged her. "I didn't think Dad would go to meet his Maker without a fight." He kissed her forehead, whirled, and charged into the dining room.

Clarissa hurried through the door after him. "Junior, no! Wait!"

"Everyone," he shouted, "the medical examiner says that Dad didn't commit suicide."

Scheisse! I hoped Augeri rather than one of our dinner companions had poisoned Molly.

Clarissa, her face white, opened the door. "Phoenix, please come explain about the coffee and warn them about the possible intruder."

Smart. Talking about Augeri would divert them from the coffee. Mind racing, I took my time walking back to my chair. "Most of you know that Archer didn't drink anything with caffeine. Well, driving to Laycock, he sipped on Molly's strong brew. That may have disoriented him enough that he went onto the shoulder, overcorrected, and crashed."

No faces betrayed guilt. Waiting for the buzz to die down, I wondered how to convince the poisoner that we hadn't detected the caffeine powder. Hard to do. So imply that we suspected no one but Augeri. "As Clarissa said, I have to warn you about a possible intruder, a violent young man armed with a machete and a pistol." That got everyone's attention. "You've all seen Tara, the redheaded young woman helping with the meals. Molly found her bruised and terrified during a door-to-door campaign, rescued her, and brought her here to hide from her husband. Tara applied to Coping After Crime for assistance in relocating. Before we could arrange a safe place, her abusive husband saw her on television during yesterday's press conference."

A tear glistened on Molly's right cheek. "I'm so sorry to have put anyone in danger."

Heather put her arms around Molly's shoulders. "You—we—did what any caring person would do. We won't let Adam Augeri get near you or Tara."

Good. Heather had mentioned the connection between Augeri and Molly.

Thor stood up and called for quiet with the authority of the chief of staff. "How can we help, Phoenix?"

His positive response to the situation relieved me. "By keeping your eyes open. The security systems for the grounds and the houses will alert us if he tries to get in. If the alarm goes off, stay wherever you are with the door closed. Achilles and I will assume our roles as reserve deputies and intercept him. Believe me, I'm a far better shot than Augeri is."

Roland waved his hand. "That's all well and good, but what happens if the security system doesn't work? What's he look like?"

"He's short, five foot six or seven, baby-faced with brown curly hair." No one but Tara reacted to the description. "Did any of you notice someone who looked like that at any of the meetings on Wednesday?"

Molly and Bernadine shook their heads no. Roland frowned and shrugged.

Horse said, "Hell, I couldn't tell you who was in the library this afternoon."

Their reactions argued against Augeri being the poisoner, but at least I'd established him as a suspect. "No heroics. If you see him, take cover and raise the alarm." To ease the tension, I added, "The way this heavy snow is drifting, no one will be traveling tonight. He's unlikely to reach here for another twenty-four hours."

Their faces relaxed. Then the lights went out.

CHAPTER TWENTY-THREE

Someone shrieked as complete darkness enveloped the dining room. Silence fell at the table, and I jumped as the wind howled and slammed something against the windows.

Achilles put his nose on my left knee. I stroked him and hoped he didn't detect the chill running down my back. I should have anticipated a power outage when the phone went dead.

"Relax," a man said. A match scratched, and a hand moved a tiny flame to light a candle. The hand lifted the candle, revealing Junior's face. "Enjoy dinner by candlelight." He reached over and lit another candle.

A flashlight went on, and Pete said, "I'll get a lantern, Dad."

Bernadine leaned forward, her profile silhouetted by the second candle's light. "Did—do you suppose the man with the machete cut a wire?"

"No, no," Clarissa said. "The electricity goes off during storms occasionally. We're prepared for it. If the lights don't come back on by the time we finish supper, we'll turn on the generator and—uh—other equipment."

Bloody hell! No home generator could power this big house overnight. If the power didn't come back on, the downed lines doomed us to a dark, cold night. Repair crews would come late to this low-population, low-priority rural area. The security system would be down, and so would the electric fences. I needed a Plan B.

Pete returned and stretched to his full height to hang a battery-powered lantern from the contemporary chandelier above the table. All the food and faces became visible again.

I wondered if the others were worried that Augeri could break into the house undetected.

Connie said cheerfully, "I love dining by candlelight. It makes even Phoenix look ten years younger." Her face sober, she leaned forward to address the advance man, who sat across the table from her. "Tell me truthfully, Roland, do I could look a day over thirty?"

Head down, he didn't respond.

"No more than twenty-nine," Thor said. "If I didn't know better, I'd think that distinguished man at the end of the table is Warren Buffett, the Sage of Omaha."

Horse grinned, obviously pleased. He nudged Bernadine, Annalynn's only female rival, with his shoulder. "And I'd mistake this pretty lady for Julia Roberts." He shifted to face me. "I've been trying to remember who you remind me of, and now I've got it. She's a political consultant I met in DC last summer. Her husband grew up in Missouri."

Scheisse! He was talking about my ex-husband's forty-year-old wife.

Connie smothered a laugh. "Does she act like Phoenix?"

"No one acts like Phoenix," Annalynn said, "especially when she and Connie go on stage together. Connie, tell them about the time the three of us sang at the Rotary Club lunch."

A perfect distraction. Connie told a great story, usually with all the laughs coming at my expense. Besides, Annalynn loved hearing about the few times she did anything unorthodox. I played along. "No one wants to hear Connie's creative version of that performance."

"Creative? You mean factual." Connie dabbed her lips with her napkin and took a sip of water. "Here's what happened. The head Rotarian invited our high school trio to provide the after-lunch entertainment. Phoenix envied my voice and resented that I always sang the lead, especially when we sang 'Swing Low, Sweet Chariot,' that beautiful old hymn."

I rolled my eyes and took a bite of salad. While Connie talked, I studied the other diners, hoping someone's expression would reveal worry that the medical examiner had discovered the cause of Archer's accident and, in consequence, Molly's illness. The only ones leaning forward and giving Connie their full attention were Thor, long-shot candidate Jerrald, and Nancy.

A gold cufflink flashing in the candlelight, the advance man slumped in his chair, not bothering to pretend to listen. But then he'd acted depressed during the candidates' talks in the library. Not surprising. He'd just lost his boss and, most likely, would soon lose his job.

Molly, her food barely touched, played with her fork and cast furtive glances around the table. She, too, faced unemployment, but I wagered she worried less about her job than her life.

Horse, in contrast, appeared at ease. Why not? He had come to appraise the possible nominees and offer the one he anointed a pittance from his millions. He leaned forward to stare past Bernadine at Annalynn, her face regal and seemingly serene in the dim light.

Bernadine sat straight, her hands in her laps and her eyes on the windows. She laughed a moment behind Thor and Jerrald. Did the storm and the violent young man out there somewhere frighten her? Or had she sensed that she had little chance of leaving the farm with endorsements from Horse and Clarissa, the only two who mattered to the party's decision makers.

Clarissa, immobile, gazed at Connie with that dutiful expression of interest political spouses wore at events.

Seventeen-year-old Pete Candon and Tara Augeri, only two years older, had left the room. Now they came in from the hall, each carrying a sizable cardboard box that they placed on the serving table.

Connie reached her punch line, "So while I was soulfully singing the hymn, Phoenix and Annalynn were doo-dooing the backup—to the tune of 'Born to be Wild.'" She held up her hand to hold her chuckling listeners' attention. "But that's not all. Flash forward to a church choir rehearsal two months ago. I asked Phoenix, the woman whose memory puts an elephant to shame, to sing the first verse of 'Swing Low, Sweet Chariot.' She claimed she didn't remember the words because she always sang backup."

My turn. "And right there by the altar, Connie called me a pain in the apse."

Horse led the laughter, sounding like an ass. "I make a motion that the trio performs for us tonight."

Nancy called out, "All in favor, say aye."

Only Annalynn and I voted nay.

Clarissa pushed back her chair. "Pete has started a fire in the stove in the music room. We'll have our coffee and dessert there." She walked over to the small table. "When you choose your pie or cookies, take a flashlight from the box. Later you may want to take a lantern to your bedroom." She lifted a lantern out of a box and turned it on. "If need be, we'll provide portable heaters for the unheated bedrooms."

Damn! Northern exposure would make the bunkhouse cool down fast.

Bernadine raised her hand. "Does my stove work?"

"Yes," Clarissa said, "and Molly's room won't require a heater either. The rooms in the back wing will be the coldest."

Horse grinned. "When I was a kid, we kept warm by sleeping three in a bed. I'm willing to try that method tonight." He leered at Bernadine, who smiled nervously and leaned away from him.

Junior got up, went to the serving table, and took a heater about eighteen inches high out of the box. "I need to go take care of my own house, so I'll show you how the propane heaters work. I'll put them and the fuel canisters out in the hall for you to pick up. One canister may last the night if you run the heater on low, but I'll show you how to change them just in case."

I gathered around with most of the others to watch Junior go through the steps. He emphasized that we should keep the space around the heaters clear and turn them off when we left the room.

Annalynn, sandwiched between Jerrald and Horse, said, "I've heard that unvented heaters consume oxygen and create carbon monoxide."

Junior tapped the side of the heater. "The oxygen depletion sensor shuts the heater off, but it wouldn't hurt to leave your door to the hall open a couple of inches."

Heather dropped a pile of dark sweat pants and tops by the heater. "If you're cold, you can wear these. And we have half a dozen sleeping bags."

I envisioned a shadowy figure, anonymous in sweats, creeping around the dark house to sabotage a heater and cause an "accident." Good thing the lock on Molly's door didn't depend on electricity.

Nancy poured a cup of coffee and thrust it toward Horse, forcing him to step away from Annalynn. "We'll worry about the heaters later. Let's relax with our dessert in the music room."

Horse reached around the heater to retrieve the last piece of blackberry pie, my favorite. "I do a little singing myself, mostly barbershop quartet."

Others quietly selected a piece of pie or a homemade cookie and followed Clarissa, lantern in hand, out of the dining room. I picked up an oatmeal cookie and a flashlight and stared out the window into total darkness before going after the pack.

Thor, his height and blond hair making him more visible than the others, waylaid Roland by the great hall fireplace. "You and I should carry in enough wood to last the night."

Jerrald turned around. "I'll lend a hand as soon as I eat my pie."

I envisioned a stick of firewood striking Molly's head as she came from her room. Stupid. Not stupid. Dismiss no possibility. Trust experience and guard against even the most unlikely scenarios. I reached down to stroke Achilles, who had pressed his shoulder against my leg. He was reflecting my unfocused fear.

Nancy met me at the music room door and herded me to the piano bench. "Time to play for your supper, Phoenix."

For a minister, she was darn pushy. Did she resent it that I rarely came to church? What the heck. I'd diddled at the piano at many international parties during my years as a covert operative. Strangers assumed my brains were in my fingers and talked freely in front of me. Besides, playing for others to sing built goodwill and gave me the right to ask for favors. Maybe fooling around now would help the diners forget my Glock and make my suspects underrate me. I played an arpeggio. Nice sound and touch.

"Let's hear that Rotarian trio," Horse said.

"I'd prefer a duet," said Annalynn from an overstuffed chair by the front windows. "Our trio disbanded when we graduated from high school."

"Come on, Annalynn." Connie grabbed her hand and tugged. "We harmonize whenever we go anywhere in the car."

And we'd sung the odd combination on a shopping trip to Columbia in September. We could make it work. I hit a chord. "Don't be shy, Annalynn. Connie will drown us out here just the way she does in the car."

Achilles had planted himself to my left where he could watch my hands on the keys. He wouldn't interrupt my playing, but whenever Connie sang, he sang along. To prevent his adding his tenor, I took his head in my hands. "No singing, Achilles. No singing."

With Connie standing in the curve of the grand piano and Annalynn behind me, we gave a half-professional, half-amateur performance that elicited enthusiastic applause.

Annalynn hurried back to her chair. "This part of the trio has retired."

Thor stood up. "Excuse us. We'll bring in some firewood and rejoin you."

Roland and Jerrald jumped up. Horse, the oldest of the men but certainly fitter than Jerrald and possibly Roland, followed suit a moment later. Only the women remained. Bernadine wasn't among them. Damn it! I'd lost track of one person.

Nancy turned on another lantern. "How about a duet?"

With all my suspects running around in the dark, I needed to get to the library and pick up that pistol. If I started playing for Connie, I'd be here for an hour. I thought of an alternative. "My tenor and I have been rehearsing one number." I stroked Achilles' head. "Sing with me."

Nancy laughed as I played the introductory bars to an old pop song, "How Much Is That Doggie in the Window." I sang the words, and Achilles barked on cue. The laughter that followed his barking surprised him, but he never missed a beat.

I stood up. "I've warmed the bench for the next act. Now it's time for me to take my tenor outside." I strode to the door before anyone could object.

Achilles came with me, but he paused at the door and whined in hopes of enticing Annalynn to go with us. He didn't like his people separated in a strange place.

A lantern at the end of the great hall showed the door to the wing had been propped open by a piece of firewood. Male voices sounded in the wing hall.

I ducked into the library and used the fire's flickering light to find my way to the shelf that held the little wood box with the loaded weapon. I could see nothing in the dark corner. I ran my hand along the high shelf until I felt the box. I lifted the lid and reached in.

Someone had beat me to it. The antique revolver was gone.

CHAPTER TWENTY-FOUR

Reasons for the revolver's disappearance flitted through my head. One of the Candons hid it to prevent anyone from handling the valuable antique. Tara took it to protect herself from Augeri. Molly borrowed it to frighten off the wannabe killer. All possible, but I feared the worst: The poisoner stole it to make another attempt on Molly's life. If so, Adam Augeri hadn't dumped caffeine powder in the coffee. A houseguest wanted the woman dead. Molly had opened her door to everyone who knocked. If she hadn't pocketed that revolver, I had to guard her tonight.

Hearing steps coming down the hall from the music room, I hurried from the shelf to the door in time to see Connie's blond hair go by in the dim light. "In here," I called softly.

She reversed. "What is it?"

"The revolver is missing," I whispered. "Molly can't stay alone tonight, not even in that locked room." It had no place for a guard to sleep. We'd have to move her. "We'll smuggle her into the bunkhouse."

"The bad guy will be watching you. You and Annalynn hold everyone in the music room, and I'll take Molly back to our room."

Connie's plan made sense, but it put her and Molly both in danger. "Too risky."

Male voices were coming toward us.

"Not if Achilles comes with me." Connie hopped into the hall and projected her voice. "I'm going to get some sheet music from Clarissa's storage room so we can sing some Gilbert and Sullivan."

And I'd thought only my British friends would consider that

entertainment. "I'm not sure whether Achilles will be able to refrain from joining in." A good reason for Connie to leave with him.

The four men came in the back door single file, the first three with an armload of firewood. Roland used a dolly for his load, keeping his expensive jacket pristine. Connie and I stepped out of the way. When they passed us, she went into the back wing.

Horse put his load in the box by the hall fireplace and removed the piece of wood holding the door open. "Leave the key to the porch on the library mantle. We may need to bring in more wood during the night. The forecast was for a low in the teens, but the wind chill will make it feel like zero."

I groaned. "The sooner I take Achilles outside and get back in the better."

Roland stopped the dolly at the library door. "Why not leave the key in the lock?"

"I'd prefer the mantle," I said. "If Augeri should get in the house, I don't want him to find a key in a door."

Jerrald and then Thor dropped their loads into the box. Thor said, "Phoenix, the four of us can take turns standing guard tonight."

"Thank you for the offer." To create an opportunity to gather them in one room and allow Connie to hustle Molly into the bunkhouse, I said, "In half an hour, let's interrupt the songfest long enough to draw up a schedule."

"I'll suggest that to Clarissa," Thor said. "We need to discuss distribution of the heaters, too." He went on into the library.

Roland brushed a little piece of bark off the left sleeve of his expensive tweed. "Phoenix, I don't think you—anyone—should go outside alone. Would you like for me to go with you?"

I suspected the advance man was more concerned with getting out of unloading the firewood than my safety, but it would give me a chance to talk to him alone. "Thanks. Achilles and I will put on our coats and meet you at the back door in a couple of minutes."

Picking up one of the battery-powered lanterns, I went into the back wing. The air there had cooled, and the bunkhouse was cold enough that I welcomed my parka. Achilles didn't object when I put his blanket on him. I guessed that he wouldn't want to stay outside in the freezing night for long. I took the lantern into the hall.

Roland stood by the back door wrapping a wool scarf around his head babushka fashion and tucking the ends down the front of a black dress overcoat. "I left my parka in my apartment in Virginia. Thank God my dad had the foresight to bring me a pair of his boots yesterday." He took a key from his pocket and inserted the latter in the lock. "The same key works for all three of the doors back here." He fumbled with it, twisting it this way and that several times before the lock clicked.

I turned off the lantern and set it down by the powder room door. Its light, visible through the transom window above the door, had announced our presence to anyone watching. "A light makes a good target, so turn off your flashlight before you open the door."

He dropped the flashlight and bent to pick it up. "I don't know how you can be so calm about the possibility that psycho is out there." He switched off the light.

"I doubt that he is, but taking chances is foolish." In the darkness, I opened the door and ran my hand along the edge of the storm door until I found the knob to open it.

Achilles darted out.

I followed, raising my hand to shelter my face from a gust of wind driving icy snowflakes. I heard but couldn't see Achilles moving to my left and sidled along the edge of the building. A faint light, surely Connie's flashlight, shone from the window of the storage room. Then it disappeared. I also detected a faint light through the trees that sheltered the farmhouse.

The storm door banged, and Roland swore under his breath. "Where are you?"

"Next to the building. If we move more than a few feet away, we'll get lost."

"Would you really shoot the guy?" He edged toward me.

"If necessary." An alarm went off. Augeri posed little danger in this blinding snow, but that same snow gave my companion an opportunity to attack me with no one the wiser. Keep him talking. "Where does your family live?" I took ten steps forward, ten steps to my right, and ten steps right again. Even as my eyes adjusted, I could barely make out the building now directly ahead of me.

"Jeff City." His voice came from near where I'd been standing. "Dad has worked for two governors and I don't know how many departments. My son and daughter go to high school there. Cathy didn't want them to change schools. She refuses to live in DC."

Maintaining two homes had to be expensive, but from the looks of his clothes, money wasn't a problem. "What does an advance man do?"

"During Archer's last campaign, I handled local press and logistics at his stops." He stomped his feet and clapped his hands. "After the election, he shifted me to D.C. to liaison with Missouri-based special-interest groups. I come back home regularly to help Molly with special events and with contributors she doesn't know how to handle." He paused as the wind blasted us. "That's most of them. Horse Jannison told Archer to fire her months ago."

If Horse hadn't criticized Molly earlier, I would have dismissed Roland's complaint as self-serving, an opening bid for Molly's job if Annalynn succeeded Archer. A light moved in the bunkhouse bathroom window near where I stood. A fuzzy silhouette of Annalynn's head and shoulders showed through the shade. What was she doing there? Better hang a towel over the window to conceal us from a shooter.

"What are your plans, Phoenix? Will you run Annalynn's offices here or go to D.C.?"

So he was interested in working for her. "I'm not political."

Achilles barked somewhere to my left. Could he be lost? "Come, boy," I called. "Roland, go on in and get warm. I'll be right behind you."

"Thanks. I'm going straight to the fire." The storm door and then the hall door opened.

A moment later, Achilles nudged my hand. He held a foot-long stick in his mouth.

"No fetch," I said firmly, feeling my way to the door.

He brought the stick inside anyway.

I closed the door, turned on the lantern, and brushed the snow off our respective coats. Roland had disappeared with the key, so I locked the door with the one under the rug and then pocketed it. I used toilet paper from the powder room to wipe up the snow and water droplets and went into the bunkhouse.

Annalynn crouched over a heater. She glanced up. "I'm moving in with you tonight. I left a spare canister on the dresser and put one in place. I learned how the only time I went on one of Boom's hunting trips in Wyoming. This heater looks safe."

"It's a potential weapon. Check it every time we come back into the room." I filled her in on the plan to spirit Molly back to the bunkhouse. After I took off my and Achilles' coats, the three of us walked down the shadowy hall toward the main building. The singing of "A Policeman's Lot Is Not a Happy One" from the *Pirates of Penzance* greeted us as we entered the main building.

Roland, now wearing black sweat pants and a hooded sweatshirt, was warming his hands at the hall fireplace. He'd taken off his glasses.

Achilles dropped his stick into the wood box and walked with us into the music room just as the song ended.

Clarissa rose from the piano bench. "Now that we're all here, let's organize for a night with no lights, no hot water, and no heat."

Horse cleared his throat. "What about the generator?"

She sighed. "It powers only the kitchen, a heater in my bedroom, the freezers in the basement, and the heating elements for our water pipes. At least I can offer you a hot breakfast with coffee tomorrow morning. Heather brought some frozen cinnamon rolls up from the basement freezer for me to put in the oven. Unfortunately we don't have enough heaters for every bedroom. Nancy will stay with me."

"And I'll bunk with Connie and Phoenix," Annalynn said.

Horse waggled his eyebrows. "My room is warmer."

Annalynn ignored him. "Perhaps two of the men don't mind sharing?"

Thor said, "We have to keep the fires going tonight. I'll stretch out in a sleeping bag in the library."

"Me, too," Roland said. "I don't trust those heaters."

I gave Achilles a signal, and he went to the piano and put a paw on middle C and D.

"Oh, good grief," I said. "He wants to sing. Connie, would you please take him back to our room while we assign shifts? And maybe you can drop off Molly as you go."

Molly stood up with difficulty and accepted the arm Connie offered.

I took Achilles' collar and led him after them. In the hall, spooky with the flames throwing shadows, I knelt by him and whispered, "Guard Connie, guard."

When I came back in, Thor was speaking softly in Clarissa's ear. She nodded and looked at me. "You represent the law, Phoenix. What do you want us to do?"

Normally I would have laid out a schedule in half a minute, but Connie needed time to talk Molly into moving into our cold corner and to get her there. So I summarized Tara's case again, stressing the danger Adam Augeri posed to Tara, Molly, and anyone who accosted him. Then I asked who knew how to keep a fire going.

Thor, Horse, and Annalynn held up their hands.

We settled on Roland taking the eleven to one o'clock shift by the fire in the main hall, waking Thor early for the one to three shift if the fires threatened to go out. Thor would stoke the fires until Jerrald took his turn from three to five, and Horse would replace him in time to build up the fires for the morning. Annalynn and I would be responsible for the back wing all night, an easy assignment as Achilles would warn us if anyone came near the outside doors. Bernadine, Nancy, and Clarissa would have coffee and a hot breakfast ready by seven.

Clarissa, in the show-must-go-on spirit of a good hostess, went back to the piano to sing Broadway hits with Nancy and Horse, a good amateur baritone. Roland slipped away after the first song and the rest of us after the second. I saw lantern light in the library and peeked in. Roland sat reading an oversized book by the fire with a blanket around his shoulders. I hoped the book would keep him awake until one.

Annalynn and I went upstairs to bring down her overnight bag and the blankets on her bed. Passing Molly's door, I checked to make sure it was locked.

Connie, looking quite self-satisfied, sat on the bunkhouse floor near the heater massaging cream into her face. She put a warning finger to her lips and pointed to the lower bunk to our left.

I motioned her to come into the hall and moved a few steps from the door to whisper,

"Is Molly okay?"

"Just exhausted, and scared. She was afraid to fall asleep alone in that room tonight because she's a really deep sleeper. She once slept through a tornado."

Annalynn joined us in the hall. "I'm worried about her. Her color is awful."

Connie poked me. "You're in the other lower bunk. You check on her every couple of hours. She said to shake her awake tomorrow morning in time to dress for a meeting at seven fifteen, but I think we should let her sleep. An odd thing: She brought a thick manila folder and put it under her pillow."

Annalynn hissed, "And you both will leave it right there."

Achilles whined from inside the bedroom, and I opened the door to quiet him.

Annalynn brushed past me. "I'm going to bed before this icebox gets any colder."

I needed to call Stuart and Vernon for any updates. "Achilles and I will make the rounds to check the outside doors and windows before we settle in."

I started in the storage room and moved up the hall, knocking before going into the bedrooms. Achilles sniffed around and found nothing of interest. All being secure, I went into the great hall. I checked the window in the small office and tapped on Clarissa's bedroom door.

Nancy opened it, and the warm air told me Clarissa's heater did a much better job than ours. Nancy promised to check the windows there.

Thor was going over a spreadsheet in front of the library fireplace as I checked those windows. Roland, wrapped in a blanket, sat in a recliner in the music room with a lantern on a side table to light his reading. He'd put his glasses back on.

No one occupied the other rooms, and I went through them quickly. In the kitchen, my last stop, I pulled out my phone to call Stuart. No service. I was on my own.

Going back to the bunkhouse, I heard nothing but the wind.

Annalynn, reading with a flashlight, occupied the bunk above me. She whispered, "How are you going to keep Achilles away from that heater all night?"

I took his green blanket from atop my suitcase, folded it in half and in half again, and put it on the foot of the bunk. "Tonight, and tonight only, he'll sleep on my bed."

He hopped on the bunk, hunkered down to keep from hitting his head, and stretched out on his blanket.

Confident we'd have a quiet night, I took my sweats into the bathroom, placed a towel over the shade to block a view of my silhouette, and undressed at record speed.

Annalynn and Connie turned off their flashlights as I came back into the bedroom. I hadn't gone to bed at ten for months, but I didn't hesitate to crawl in, wish them goodnight, and turn off the lantern.

Achilles wriggled until his body was against my legs and his head toward the door.

He woke me with a low growl a little after midnight.

I reached for my Glock and my flashlight and struggled out of my cocoon. I heard nothing except the howling wind. I tiptoed to the door, and Achilles blocked my way.

Definitely something wrong. "Back. Heel," I whispered. With infinite care, I turned the knob and eased the door open two inches. Not a sound to hint at human movement. Not a whiff of air to indicate an open door. The only tiny bit of light came from the transom over the back door a few feet down the hall. I stood there and counted out two minutes. The wind had died down, but still I heard nothing in the house.

I tiptoed to the bunkhouse window and looked out on a black-and-white winter scene worthy of an Ansel Adams photograph. I couldn't see the moon, but the snow reflected an eerie light. Stepping into the bathroom, I lifted a corner of the towel I'd put atop the window shade and then the shade. The blowing snow had almost filled my footsteps from three hours ago. In the cinematic darkness, the barn loomed large and foreboding, appearing closer than it had in the daylight. Could Adam Augeri have arrived during the respite in the storm and sheltered there? I strained my eyes but could see no sign of disturbed snow.

Achilles yawned and returned to his blanket on the bunk. He hopped off the bed when I tiptoed back to the door. I listened for a minute and then slipped into the hall. Moving slowly in the dark, I checked the wing's outside doors. All secure. Maybe Achilles' keen ears had heard Roland or Thor adding wood to the fire.

I went back to bed but lay alert for an hour.

Nothing else disturbed my sleep that night. I woke at six forty-five in near darkness. The cold air—around fifty degrees?—discouraged me from getting up. I dozed for a few minutes, forcing myself up only when Achilles licked my face. He knew how much I hated that.

I gathered my warmest clothes and went into the bathroom to dress even faster than I'd undressed. When I came out, Annalynn went in.

Achilles waited for me by the door. I pulled on my parka and slid my Glock and my special phone into the pockets. As I stepped into the dim hall, the door to the main house opened.

"Phoenix," Bernadine called, "something's wrong." She held up a lantern. "Molly is late for our meeting, and she doesn't answer her door."

I hesitated a split second. We might well be here another night.

No one should know Molly was sleeping in the bunkhouse. "She's probably in the bathroom. Give her a few minutes."

"But she looked so ill last night. What if she had a heart attack? Don't you have some kind of police master key so you can open the door?"

Molly had left the key on the dresser. I could get in. "I have a key I can try. I'll be there in a moment." I stepped back into the bunkhouse.

Connie peeked out from under a blanket. "Now what?"

I picked up the key and glanced over at Molly, still sound asleep. "I'm going into Molly's bedroom and come out to report she doesn't feel well enough to get up yet. You keep her in here until I give you an all clear." I closed the door and walked toward the main house, Achilles at my side. When we entered the great hall, he growled low in his throat.

Bernadine stepped back from Molly's door as he moved toward it and barked. What in hell was wrong?

Bernadine's eyes widened. "Is he smelling illness?"

Why would she ask that? Oh, yes. I'd claimed he was a medical service dog. "Could be. You better go into the library and wait." She half ran into the library. I stepped back into the wing and called, "Connie, tell Annalynn I may need help, please." For what, I didn't know.

I located the keyhole by feel, unlocked the door, and edged into the room with Achilles right behind me. I could see almost nothing, but I smelled black powder. I locked the door, fished a flashlight out of my pocket, and shone it on the bed. A figure lay under the old quilt, which didn't quite cover the top of a head with frizzy brown hair like Molly's. Who was asleep in the bunkhouse? No one else here had hair like that.

I leaned over and spotted a nickel-sized hole in the quilt at about where the ear must be. Then I saw the antique revolver on the bed about three inches from an open hand and red-sleeved wrist.

CHAPTER TWENTY-FIVE

I stared at the 1849 Pocket Revolver and the hand.

What's wrong with this picture?

I aimed the flashlight at the hand. No adult's flesh was ever that pink. Or that plastic. Was someone playing a joke? Better not treat it that way. I pulled out my phone and took a series of close-up photos, a staple in homicide investigations. Then I drew my Glock and inserted the barrel under the edge of the quilt to pull it back from the head. A wig on a mannequin dressed in a red uniform. The red brought to mind not blood but *The Pirates of Penzance.*

Only Connie would substitute a prop from a Gilbert and Sullivan operetta for Molly.

But Connie hadn't put that bullet hole above the ear.

A tap on the door. "Phoenix?"

I dropped the quilt back in place and let in Annalynn, locking the door behind her. The room had lightened enough to show a long form under the quilt. "Take a look." I focused the flashlight's beam on the revolver and then on the hole in the quilt. "Think like a sheriff."

She gasped. "My God! Who is it?"

So Connie hadn't shared her staging trick with Annalynn either. "A mannequin supplied, I assume, by Connie, but the bullet hole is real."

Annalynn bent over the bed and focused her flashlight on the tableau for a minute or so. "Someone staged a suicide. Did you find a note?"

"I haven't looked yet."

She swung her flashlight's beam to the glider chair, the tiny table, and the closed wardrobe. No piece of paper.

An oversight? Perhaps not. "With the power out, no one could print out a suicide note, and a bad forgery of Molly's handwriting would arouse suspicion. Besides, the only door to the room was locked with—supposedly—the only key. Most people would assume she used the gun beside her to shoot herself."

Annalynn said nothing for a moment. "But not a police officer who knew someone had tried to poison her five days ago. The person who shot—uh—it, had to be desperate to sneak in here and fire a gun, especially with guards down the hall and us in the back wing."

"Maybe we're not as famous as you think." How big a chance had the shooter taken? "At dinner I said Archer drank the coffee and became disoriented. I didn't say someone had tampered with it." I flashed back to getting out of bed during the night. "Achilles must have heard the shot. He woke me a little after midnight. The wind was howling. That could have masked the sound of the gun firing. Besides, the walls are thick, and no one was sleeping next to or above this room."

Annalynn bent over to sniff the revolver. "It's definitely been fired. Don't black-powder guns send up a lot of smoke?"

"Yes. It would leave residue on the shooter's hands and clothes."

She grimaced. "Too bad we don't have a test kit here. By the time Gist brings one, the shooter will have washed or burned the clothes." She bit her lower lip. "Who was on guard at midnight?"

"Roland. He was stationed by the hall fireplace so he could watch and listen for anyone trying to break in the front door or a window. Or he may have been in the music room." I envisioned the hall. "The fireplace is at least twenty-five feet away, and the fire was probably crackling and popping. Thor would have been asleep in the library, also by a noisy fire."

"If Achilles heard a shot all the way from the bunkhouse, surely one of the men heard it, even if they didn't realize what it was at the time. We have no authority, but shouldn't we separate and interrogate them?"

I considered a moment. "No, at least not officially. For one thing, we should keep this from the group, let the shooter think we're hiding Molly's death. She'll be safer if the guilty person doesn't realize she's alive." I ran my beam along the floor of the small room hoping the shooter had left a clue behind in the dark. Nothing. "During breakfast, we should chat with all four guards and the sisters—they were the closest to this room. Meanwhile, we need to figure out how the shooter got in here."

The first place to check was the window. Locked. Standing on tiptoe, I peered down at the ground. A moderate snow was falling, but surely not enough had come down in the last few hours to obscure all signs of footsteps or a ladder. "The shooter didn't come from the outside."

Annalynn turned the flashlight on the toilet's narrow door, open about an inch. "The storage closet under the stairs shares a wall with this bedroom. Maybe that accordion door leads to the closet."

"I doubt it. It's a small toilet." I crossed to the door in six steps, used a tissue to open it wide without leaving fingerprints, and inspected the entire space—perhaps five feet long and little more than a yard wide—with my flashlight. Definitely not up to code.

Annalynn watched over my shoulder. Molly's toothbrush and toothpaste sat on a foot-long, four-inch-wide shelf over a doll-size sink to our right. Opposite the sink, on the wall against the wardrobe, a bath towel and washcloth hung on a long towel bar. I leaned over the toilet, which was to my immediate left, to run my light up and down the wall that abutted the hall closet. No crack, no hinges, no sliding door. "I can't see a door, but I'll sneak into the closet and check from that side during the morning meeting."

To be thorough, I used the tissue to open the wardrobe. Molly had hung a navy-blue pants suit in the narrow section for hanging clothes. A pair of red pumps sat beneath the suit. An orange-red sweater, doubtless matching her lipstick, lay on the highest and shallowest of four large shelves. Her coat wasn't here or hanging in the bunkhouse, so it must still be at the entrance.

Annalynn stepped back and flashed her light on the bedroom door. "The person had to come through this door. Either someone had another key or knew how to pick the lock. You're an expert on locks. How tough would it be?"

"Fairly tough. Very tough, under the circumstances. I could do it in a minute or so if I had a light to see and no one down the hall watching and listening for a break-in."

Achilles trotted to the door and barked. He needed to go outside, and he saw no reason to stay in this room.

I did, but staying here now would arouse suspicion. "I'll come back later and do a thorough search. Right now we need to go out and tell everyone the same story."

"Which is?"

Lies come back to trip you up. "The truth, or at least part of it. Everyone but the shooter will believe us."

Annalynn smiled. "Molly is too weak to talk to anyone. You'll bring her some breakfast later. If she feels up to it, she'll come to the meeting after that." She sobered. "Will she?"

"No. Much too risky." I thought a moment. "When everyone is occupied, I'll take Molly to the farmhouse. Heather's family can guard her and Tara as long as necessary."

"I don't think Molly has the strength to walk in this deep snow."

She'd been foolish to come yesterday, but Captain Gist had hidden from her how much danger she would be in. "I'll arrange a ride on the snowmobile when I take Achilles out."

He barked his readiness to go.

"Good. I'll tell her what we found here. Let's go."

I unlocked the door and blocked the view of the fake body as Achilles darted out and Annalynn followed. By the time I'd locked the door, half the household had clustered around us.

Clarissa grasped Annalynn's hand. "How is she?"

"She's quite cold," I said, hoping the shooter would interpret that to mean dead. "She's going to stay in bed for a while. I have to take Achilles outside." I opened the door to the wing and hurried toward the back door behind Achilles.

"Molly's terribly weak. She has to rest," Annalynn said as the door closed behind me.

As I neared the back door, Connie stuck her head out of the bunkhouse, her eyes wide with curiosity.

"Very funny, that mannequin," I said, "and very effective. Keep Molly hidden. Annalynn will explain." I unlocked the back door and opened it enough to scan the surroundings for footprints and any sign of a hidden shooter before I allowed Achilles to slip through.

Connie whispered, "Molly's in the bathroom getting dressed to go meet Bernadine. What do I tell her?"

The door from the main house opened, and Roland, wrapped in a blanket, walked toward us. "Hide her," I hissed to Connie. I waved at Roland. "No need to come out with me this time."

He nodded and went into his bedroom.

When his door closed, I stepped into the bunkhouse long enough to open my suitcase and take out Annalynn's gun and holster. I handed it to Connie, rendering her momentarily speechless. "Tell Annalynn to carry."

I hurried outside where Achilles was jumping to make his way through a drift more than three-feet high instead of taking an easier path through snow half that deep. With all the energy he was expending, he wouldn't need his long run this morning. He was headed for the evergreen trees, apparently his designated toilet.

I took a meandering route toward the barn between the worst of the drifts and then angled left toward the farmhouse. By the time I reached the evergreen trees, my nose tingled with the cold and my body was overheated from the effort of walking in the deep, clingy white carpeting.

Iron and Steel barked and came to greet me, their tension turning to tail wags as I called their names and Achilles plowed through the snow to intercept them. The three frolicked around me as I kicked my way through a three-foot drift to the house's door.

Heather opened it before I could knock and pulled me into a tiled foyer at least twenty degrees warmer than the bunkhouse. "Is something wrong?"

She drew me into a large, modern kitchen and thrust a cup of hot coffee in my hands. I told her what I'd found, and she swore Archer had lost the other key to Molly's bedroom last summer. I explained my idea of hiding Molly in the farmhouse until Annalynn and I could identify the would-be murderer.

Heather answered immediately, "Sure. We can guard Molly and Tara together. You could tell from your reception that our dogs won't let anyone come close without raising a fuss. I should have brought Molly home with me last night when the power went out. We heat mostly with wood, and we have three generators."

A sensible, decisive woman. The kind of supporter Annalynn needed. "I'm going back to eat breakfast. When the rest go to the meeting, I'll say that I'm going on patrol on Pete's snowmobile and transport Molly over here on that. Or at least I will if Pete agrees."

Her body tensed and her eyes grew dark. "Tara would go into hysterics at the idea of Pete leaving the house. So would I, for that matter. You'll have to drive Molly yourself. I'm not letting Tara or Pete out of the house until Augeri is behind bars or on a slab."

Junior spoke from behind me. "None of us is leaving the house until then. According to the radio, the snow will blow out of here before noon. It's already stopped a few miles south of us. I figure that if Sam doesn't catch that lunatic on the road, he'll show up here this afternoon." He glanced up at a shotgun on a rack over the kitchen door and then at me. "That snowmobile is Pete's prize possession. You sure you know how to operate it?"

"Yes, I've driven them before." In Europe. "Pete showed me how his works yesterday."

The Candons exchanged barely perceptible nods. "I'll get the key." Junior walked away, his slippered feet making no sound.

If Junior Candon spotted Augeri on the farm, Tara would be a widow. My CIA friend had recommended that solution, but I didn't think it was one this family should have to live with. I said nothing but thanks as Junior gave me the key.

Outside, the three dogs romped around me as I walked to the barn to make sure the snowmobile hadn't been spirited away. It remained in place. I walked back to the big house, stepping in my own steps where I could.

Achilles didn't want to come in, so I left him outside with his new friends.

I slammed the back door and stomped my feet to announce my arrival.

Annalynn opened the bunkhouse door and said loudly, "Any sign of an intruder?"

I didn't answer until I was in the room. "No way anyone got in the house from the back last night."

Molly sat up in her bunk and swung out her legs, clad in sweat pants. She reached for a pair of leather boots.

Annalynn lifted the bottom of a blue-and-white Norwegian ski sweater to show me the tip of her holster. "No one came in the front, according to the men. They all swore they stayed awake and heard nothing but the wind. They also said they patrolled through the unoccupied rooms in the main house to keep warm and alert during their shifts."

Hmm. "So a guard wasn't in the great hall at all times."

"No, but it wouldn't take more than a minute to walk through the parlor, dining room, and kitchen. If you were right about that lock, no one without a key had enough time to sneak into Molly's room."

Surely someone had found the other key. But that didn't solve the problem. "Even if you had a key, you'd have to sneak back out without being heard."

Molly moaned. "You're saying someone I work with meant to shoot me. I can't believe that. Are the phones working? I have to talk to Sam Gist."

Annalynn walked over to pat Molly's shoulder. "Believe me, we'll turn this over to the good captain as soon as possible. Meanwhile, we'll keep you safe." Annalynn looked at me. "I sent Connie to breakfast ten minutes ago. She'll ask the sisters and Bernadine how they slept. One of us should join the group now."

"You go. I'll stay here to wait for Achilles to come in."

Molly pulled a folder from under her pillow and riffled through some yellow sheets of paper. She removed a couple of sheets and glanced at them. "Last night before supper I printed copies of my workload projections. Could you pass these out at the meeting, Annalynn?"

She hesitated.

Achilles barked at the back door.

"Go ahead," I said to Annalynn, stepping into the hall. "Tell them Molly gave you the projections to study last night." I unlocked the door and let Achilles in.

Annalynn met me in the hall, her hands empty. "I'll come back for the folder when everyone gathers in the library." She left.

Molly rushed into the bathroom.

Sick with fear? Still in denial? Intimidated by me? I curbed my impatience. I picked up the folder on Annalynn's bunk and glanced at the yellow sheets. Standard office workload analysis. I put the folder back on the bunk.

Sounds of retching or dry heaves came from the bathroom. I preferred not to interrupt that. I could wait a few more minutes to interrogate Molly, but not much more than that. However ill or resistant she might be, she was going to tell me who wanted to kill her and why.

CHAPTER TWENTY-SIX

Molly still hadn't come out of the bathroom when Connie returned fifteen minutes later with a glass of milk and a banana. She reported that Bernadine had complained the wind kept her awake half the night but seemed no worse for it. Clarissa, on the other hand, looked exhausted and admitted to being awake from two thirty to five thirty, about the time Nancy woke up.

Not much help.

The meeting would start in a few minutes. I decided to go eat a quick breakfast and observe the suspects for myself before transporting Molly. I replaced my parka with my ski jacket and hustled through the cold halls to the kitchen.

Jerrald and Horse, both bleary eyed, nodded to me from the small table by the window in lieu of speaking. They wore hooded navy-blue sweatshirts and slumped over their coffee. Salt-and-pepper whiskers showed Horse hadn't shaved. Jerrald had, and a fleck of icing from a roll had stuck in his moustache.

"Good morning, Phoenix." Nancy, also in blue sweats, hopped down from a kitchen stool at the worktable and removed a tray of cinnamon rolls from the oven of the gas stove. She peered at me with obvious concern. "How are you feeling? Annalynn told me you chill easily."

That aftermath of the shooting last April had almost passed. "I'm fine. I brought warm clothing, including these ski clothes." In comparison to the bunkhouse, the kitchen was warm—at least sixty degrees. I poured coffee from an aged percolator into a paper cup, added milk from a pitcher on the worktable, and accepted a warm roll on a paper plate. Inhaling the heavenly aroma of cinnamon, I wondered what I could learn as I ate.

The petite minister appeared rested and at ease, so I judged her to be unaware of last night's attempt on Molly's life.

The two glum men's presence gave me a chance to explain my absence from the upcoming meeting. I said, "It's not so cold outside this morning. After breakfast, I'm going out to patrol the fences on the snowmobile to see if Augeri could be on the property."

Horse put another chair at the two-person table. "You shouldn't go out alone. One of us"—he looked pointedly at Jerrald—"will go with you."

I had to scotch that idea fast. "No need. Achilles and the Candons' collies will alert me of any strangers." I sipped my coffee. "We had a quiet night in the back wing. Any action in the main house?"

Jerrald shook his head. "Not on my shift. Roland admitted he almost—uh—he got scared once near the end of his shift. He heard something hit a window in the parlor, but it was just a small branch." The former NASCAR driver drained his coffee cup and chuckled. "My big moment came when a piece of wood popped in the fireplace. For a second, I thought I'd heard a gun. To make it worse, I heard you coming downstairs, Horse."

That would have been around five, well over four hours after Achilles woke me up.

Horse rubbed his eyes with his fingertips. "If I stayed right by the fire or the stove, I got sleepy. If I walked around, I got chilly. I stepped into the parlor about six o'clock to look out. The place was freezing. Last night reminded me of what I hated about the good ol' days on the farm."

So the guards had all moved around the first floor. The shooter could have come downstairs to Molly's room without being seen, which did no good without a key.

Thor came into the kitchen. His crow's feet had deepened, but he'd shaved and appeared alert. "Please bring your coffee into the library and we'll start the meeting. I put a heater in there an hour ago, so it's the warmest room in the house." He turned to me. "Did Molly say anything to you this morning about her workload projections?"

I took care to tell the exact truth. "She made copies last night before the power went out and gave them to Annalynn."

Jerrald scowled.

I interpreted that to mean he felt out of the loop. If I'd read the tea leaves right, he'd soon be so far out he couldn't see the loop.

"Good," Thor said. "With Archer gone, we—his staff in the district and DC—come under the supervision of the Clerk of the House until the election. I'll need to report Molly's stats along with those from the Hill office."

Horse snorted. "Better check her figures. She's not good with numbers."

He'd said something similar yesterday. I needed to follow up with him and Molly on that. Carrying my roll and coffee, I followed the men out to the great hall and turned left to go to the bunkhouse as they turned right to go to the library.

Connie and Molly sat side by side on a bunk with their heads together.

It struck me that I hadn't seen Molly smile since I'd talked to her about the powdered caffeine in her coffee last night before dinner.

Connie stood up. "A complication: Molly's coat is still in the front entrance."

"No problem." I emptied the pockets of my ski jacket and handed it to Molly. "This and a blanket will keep you warm and conceal your identity if anyone looks out a kitchen or upstairs window." I transferred my Glock and phone to my parka pockets and put it on. "I'll drive the snowmobile right up to the door in about three minutes. Molly, be ready to move when Connie signals the all clear."

Connie followed me to the back door and said softly, "I've been thinking. We might get caught if we keep pretending to take things to Molly in that bedroom. How about I go to the library in a few minutes and say you've taken Molly over to the other house?"

I hadn't thought of that, but it made sense. "Good idea. The only person who won't believe you will be the one who fired the shot. If anyone asks why I moved her, say it's warmer there and Heather will keep an eye on Molly." I opened the door a crack and checked for any observers. Nobody visible. "I don't want the houseguests to see us on the snowmobile."

Achilles whined, anxious to go out again.

I opened the door wide, and we hurried out into big, lazy flakes. Nearing the barn, I glanced back at the big window on the second floor hall. No one in sight. At the barn door, I listened for any movement inside. Achilles wagged his tail and barked a question. I opened the door, pulled out the snowmobile, and closed the door. No one stood at the second-floor windows.

I had no trouble starting Pete's creation and driving it to the back door. We were out of view of any of Four Chimney's windows, so Connie helped Molly onto the seat behind me, secured her tote bag between us, and tucked the blanket around her. The gauge warned me the battery was running low, and I breathed a sigh of relief as I pulled up to the farmhouse.

Iron and Steel came out of the breezeway to bark a greeting, and Heather opened the door.

Her son pushed past her and helped Molly dismount. "Everything okay?"

Sure Pete meant the snowmobile, I said, "It runs great, but I wouldn't ride it far until it's recharged." I got off, and he got on.

He stared at the gauge. "Shucks. It had a full charge yesterday afternoon. The cold must have affected the battery. I'll put it in the garage. It's warmer than the barn."

I went inside.

Molly sat at the kitchen table by the window, tears on her cheeks. A capped bottle of pills sat in front of her. "I don't understand why this is happening."

Heather put a cup of coffee in front of Molly, who grasped it with both hands.

"No coffee," I ordered. Time to establish my alpha status. "She'll have hot lemonade with honey. In a room where no one can see her through a window."

Heather smacked her forehead. "Of course. Sorry." She took the cup. "Molly, you can rest on the couch in the den until Tara makes up the bed in my oldest son's bedroom. With the vertical blinds closed, no one can see a thing."

I took Molly's hand to help her up. "Which way?"

Tara, looking even smaller and paler than last night, appeared in a door leading into a dining room. "I'll show you." She came over to take Molly's arm. "I'm so glad Adam isn't the one who tried to kill you. I felt awful."

Molly drew in a sharp breath but said nothing.

The young woman lacked a filter, or a brain. I glanced at Heather.

She smiled. "Would you like hot lemonade, too, Phoenix? And some fresh bread with homemade blackberry jam?"

Breaking bread together broke down social barriers. "That sounds lovely." I watched Tara and Molly walk through the dining room and down a dark hall to a room on the left. "Is Tara a bit—uhh—disabled?"

Heather ran water in a teakettle. "More disadvantaged, I'd say. She acts as naïve as a ten-year-old, but she's really not. She understands what she reads and calculates things like the supplies needed for canning with no trouble." The woman put the kettle on the burner of a gas stove. "Tara's good about following instructions, too. She's been a great help, as least after the first week. Until then she was afraid to be more than a few feet from one of us. She's still scared to go outside alone, and she's refused to leave the farm." Heather opened the oven, took out a loaf of bread wrapped in foil, and cut a slice. "Right before supper, Sam called Junior and told him not to shoot Augeri unless he's carrying a weapon."

Which we knew he was. The captain had given Junior permission to fire on the abusive husband. I said nothing. I'd been taught a basic rule: If you have to shoot, shoot to kill. The baby-faced young man posed a threat to Tara and others. I had to stop him, but I preferred to send him to jail rather than to hell. "Killing someone takes a toll on you—then and later." How would an economist know that? "Just ask the wounded warriors from our armed forces."

Heather stared at me. "I know the cost, or at least I can imagine it. That's one reason none of my family is going outside." She cut another slice of bread. "Molly called Sam after she talked to you last night. He told her not to tell you anything else. He said you're a great shot but not a trained officer and have no official legal standing here."

Thanks a lot, Captain Gist. "If I'm going to stop whoever wants Molly dead, she has to tell me which person to guard against. We can't wait for the captain to gallop through the drifts with a posse of forensic experts to find black powder residue on the shooter's clothes. Please help me make her understand that."

"I'll try, but she's a Missouri mule." Heather placed the bread on two plates and put those on a tray. "Remind her that she brought Tara here instead of to the police for a good reason." She added butter, jam, silverware, and two cups of hot lemonade to the tray. "Good luck."

"Thanks. If anyone comes by and asks about Molly, say she's here but can't see anyone. We want everyone but the killer to think she's alive."

I carried the tray down the hall to the dusk-dark room. Molly was stretched out on a couch with a blanket over her and her eyes closed. I put the tray on the small tile-topped coffee table in front of the couch and turned on a battery lamp. She didn't open her eyes.

Playing possum wouldn't work with me. I slammed the door. "Time to talk. Who poisoned your coffee and shot a lead ball into your surrogate?"

She opened her eyes. "I honestly don't know. Until last night, I had no idea anyone tried to hurt me." She sniffed and pushed herself up on her elbow to reach for a box of tissues on the coffee table. "When you said someone shot that dummy, I thought it was a joke. How could anyone think that giant doll was a real person?"

Time to ease up a bit. I handed her a cup of lemonade and pulled a hassock up to the coffee table so that I faced her. "The room was dark. The shooter would have taken great care not to wake you with a noise or a light. I didn't realize the figure was a mannequin this morning until I shone my flashlight on the hand."

She nodded. "That's what Connie said. She acted the whole thing out for me."

Give Connie a point. "How could someone get into that room?"

"I've no idea. I locked the door, and Connie checked it."

So had I. "Obviously someone found a way, someone who fears you enough to want to shut you up forever. You must know who that is."

She blew her nose into a tissue and crumpled it. "I don't know. I swear to you in God's name I don't *know* who hates me so much."

Perhaps a matter of semantics here. "You don't know, but you suspect."

She lifted the cup to her lips but didn't drink. "Sam said I shouldn't talk to you about it."

"Captain Gist isn't here." I remembered Heather's tip. "You didn't trust him to save Tara from Adam. Instead you went to Heather. Then you, along with Reverend Alderton, came to the foundation, to Annalynn and me. If you trust us with Tara's life, why not trust us with yours?"

Hands trembling, she put the lemonade on the table. "It's not that I don't trust you. I have an obligation to keep certain work matters confidential."

"No obligation is more important than saving your own life. Think of your family." I buttered a slice of bread that I didn't want and added a teaspoon of jam.

Molly pushed herself upright and drew the blanket around her shoulders. "Does the foundation's rule of confidentiality apply here?"

The attempted murder had nothing to do with the foundation. "Of course." For good measure, I added, "As Captain Gist doubtless mentioned to you, I'm a reserve deputy, a volunteer, not an officer of the law."

She nodded once, and then again. "I'm starving. I was too upset to eat last night at dinner."

So she'd decided to talk. I handed her my slice of bread.

She grabbed it, took a big bite, and chewed. "This would be perfect if I had a cup of coffee." She held up a hand. "I know. No coffee." She took another big bite.

I prepared another slice. I'd pried a lot of information from people, mostly men, by plying them with liquor. This was the first time I'd used blackberry jam.

She accepted the bribe. "You can't tell Annalynn."

Holy hell! Had I stumbled on something big? "I'll respect your confidence." If I can.

She put the bread down and leaned toward me. "You see," she said barely above a whisper, "I have to do a lot of things in my job that—well, I don't approve of. A big one is keeping a special record of constituents' contributions to—to finding solutions to their problems."

Not what I'd expected. How naïve of me. "You mean that you keep a secret set of books for campaign contributions and lobbyists' gifts."

She drew in her breath sharply. "That's not what I said. The Hill office tracks the big money. Last election, Archer's campaign cost almost a million dollars, and nearly a fourth of that came from PACs—political action committees—and Horse set up a super PAC, one of those that pretends to be a nonprofit and keeps donors' names secret. We're not allowed to coordinate with them. I had nothing to do with those."

Was she going off track deliberately? "So you don't keep records of campaign contributions, just the lobbying money between campaigns."

Her hand steadier, she picked up the lemonade again. "Phoenix, we're never between campaigns. One starts when the other ends.

And the big lobbyists are the major campaign contributors. I just don't deal with the registered ones, the ones that spend at least $12,500 a quarter and have to file a report."

I had lots to learn, but not now. "So what records do you keep?"

She nibbled on the second slice. "Small amounts from Missouri business and advocacy groups. Mostly they request certain wording in regulations or want statements inserted into the *Congressional Record*. Sometimes groups contribute a service, like publishing Archer's speeches in their newsletters. They're used to almost no laws on giving to state legislators, and they don't want to get involved in filing with the federal government."

So the congressman and his staff had rationalized breaking federal laws as following local customs.

Her expression went from defensive to defiant. "I don't like it, but after all, a lot of these people are Archer's old friends. Besides, most of my day goes to finding assistance for deserving constituents, like veterans needing health care."

I nodded sympathetically. "We all have to compromise our values sometimes." Especially in the CIA. "The world contains much more gray than black or white."

She thought that over a moment. "That's true, my job has thirty shades of gray. That's one reason I'm extra careful not to accuse anyone without being certain they're guilty."

Experience had taught me to appear to accept whatever rationalization people chose to justify their bad behavior. "That's admirable." And could be fatally foolish. Confident she wanted me to force her to talk to me, I said, "Unfortunately, we don't dare wait for Captain Gist or a hundred percent certainty. I'm going to list my three top suspects. Please confirm whether they—uhh—wish you ill."

She closed her eyes and took a deep breath. "Yes, time is running out. Who are they?"

Finally. "Bernadine."

She exhaled and gave a slight nod.

"Roland."

A more emphatic nod.

"And Horse."

"Yes. All three."

That didn't really help me. "Let's start with Bernadine. She drove a long way to attend a coffee Wednesday. She also went over your head to get an invitation to the meeting here."

"She hates me, but I don't think she'd shoot me."

"Why does she hate you?"

Molly pulled the blanket around her. "For telling her the truth. A couple of years ago, she asked me for advice on running for the state Senate. Her only campaign experience was helping a friend run for mayor. I suggested she work for other candidates for a cycle or two to gain experience and exposure and then go after the nomination for a state House seat. She got huffy. She said I wanted her to do all that work for other people instead of running herself."

Hardly a motive for murder. "Bernadine seems to have a more recent grudge against you."

Molly sighed. "She accused me of not inviting her to events where she could meet party bigwigs and political donors. I found out that she hired Roland to arrange invitations to events in Jeff City where she could meet the right people. His moonlighting was one of the things I wanted to talk to Archer about Wednesday, and to Bernadine and Roland about this morning."

An unexpected connection. "Did Roland advise Bernadine to go after Archer's seat?"

Molly hesitated. "I doubt it. She approached me last August after the rumor went around that Archer wouldn't run again. She said that I should support a woman—her. When I didn't jump at the opportunity, she walked out." Molly paused. "She'd seen me use my thermos before Wednesday."

Discouraging a candidacy seemed thin motivation for murder even for an ambitious politician. "What about Roland? What does he have against you?"

She grimaced. "Lots of things. He expected to get my job. Roland's

205

father, Horse, and Archer played poker together. During the last campaign, Archer hired Roland to arrange venues, identify toilet stops, set up short interviews with the local press. Then he offended several longtime backers by demanding that they triple their contributions. After the election, Roland's father asked Archer to name Roland a 'special constituent liaison.'" Her hand trembling, she spread more jam on the bread.

Standard office politics. To keep her going, I said, "Did he encroach on your territory?"

"No. He moved to D.C. He expected to spend all his time going to fancy restaurants and cocktail parties with lobbyists."

That explained the expensive clothing, not a big asset in rural Missouri.

Molly sneered. "Roland didn't realize a lot of lobbyists, especially the ones masquerading as advisers, are experts. They expect to deal with a staff member who knows what they're talking about. Plus he made promises Archer couldn't deliver on. Roland's wife hated the place—living miles out in Virginia, the terrifying traffic, her kids in school with all 'those people.' She moved back to Jeff City and filed for divorce."

Roland hadn't mentioned that. Too private. Or perhaps he was in denial.

Molly pushed her plate away. "He told Archer he had to work with special constituents here to save his marriage. We didn't need him, but Archer assigned Roland to spend half his time in Missouri. He hates reporting to me, and his reports are incomplete and inaccurate—unacceptable. I tried to tell Archer that Wednesday in the car, but he didn't understand. I intended to give Roland a chance to explain his numbers this morning before I decided whether to recommend that Thor keep him on or fire him."

The family and job situations explained Roland's depression. So far as I could see, murdering Molly wouldn't solve either problem.

My concern for Molly's health grew as her face became drawn. I had to move on. "What's your relationship with Horse?"

"Not good. He considers politics and poker men's games. He came here ready to back the NASCAR hero."

Horse's attitude toward women came as no surprise, but I gathered Jerrald had lost ground. "Horse indicated that he has a specific beef with you. What is it?"

She stretched out on the couch again, her face whiter than it had been only a minute ago. "Strictly confidential?"

"Boy Scout oath." A safe one since I wasn't a Boy Scout.

"He's accused me of mishandling some money he contributed under the table. Archer was to use it to encourage other representatives to—you don't need to know that." She reached for a tissue and wiped sweat from her forehead. "I think I may pass out."

I ran to the kitchen to fill a glass with water and dampen a tea towel.

Heather followed me back to the room with the bottle of pills in her hand. She reached for Molly's wrist as I lay the towel on her forehead and helped her sip the water.

Molly closed her eyes. "I'm sorry. I feel—seasick. I have to rest." She opened her eyes. "Phoenix, you'll find everything I know in my notes."

"What notes?"

"For my meetings with our three suspects this morning. On my computer in a folder labeled Munchausen."

I hadn't seen a computer in her room or in the bunkhouse. "Where's your computer?"

"Under my sweater on the middle shelf in the wardrobe."

"The computer's not there." And the sweater had been on the top shelf.

"It doesn't matter. I printed them out with the workload projections. They're all in the folder I gave Annalynn."

And she took to the meeting. I jumped up.

Heather took the glass of water from my hand. "You take care of the papers, Phoenix. I'll take care of Molly."

Hurrying out the door, I feared Heather had the more difficult job.

CHAPTER TWENTY-SEVEN

The wind had picked up again, throwing pellets rather than flakes into my face as I followed the snowmobile's tracks back toward the barn. Ahead of me, charcoal clouds raced northeast toward Chicago. Behind me to the west, the sky lightened to the color of concrete. Could a faint blue be far behind? I checked my phone. Still no service.

Achilles and his collie friends hip-hopped around me in the snow until I reached the door of the back wing. Iron and Steel turned back, and Achilles followed them. I decided to let him play this morning. We'd be watching for Adam Augeri this afternoon and quite possibly tonight.

Inside, I brushed the snow off, replaced my parka with my warm loden jacket, and hurried down the gloomy corridor. When I opened the door into the great hall, the group was emerging from the library. Half of the guests wore sweats top and bottom. Bernadine wore dark-blue sweat pants with a red-and-blue plaid blazer over a white turtleneck with the mandatory flag pin on the collar.

Clarissa, clad in a stylish green fleece outfit (without a flag pin), saw me first. "Phoenix! We've all been so worried. How's Molly?"

Everyone stopped to listen.

I told the truth. "She's very ill. She needs complete rest today."

Bernadine said, "Good thing you had that key." She walked toward the stairs with Horse. "Hearing that girl's husband was coming here frightened me. It must have scared Molly silly."

Roland snorted and turned toward the back wing. "She was

already silly. She smiles all the time like Minnie Mouse." He'd topped off his black sweatpants with a purple knitted wool sweater. The dark color emphasized how pale he was and how dark the bags under his eyes were.

Jerrald opened the dining room door and held it for Clarissa and Connie.

Nancy came over to take my arm. "You look chilled, Phoenix. Come have some hot cocoa and Danish in the kitchen and warm up." Her lips twitched in amusement. "I guarantee you'll like the cocoa."

What was the deal with the cocoa? "Sounds wonderful." I had to get my hands on that folder. "I need a word with Annalynn first."

Nancy smiled. "She's in the kitchen. She made the cocoa with Stuart's recipe."

"How thoughtful of her." And she'd made sure no one could slip anything into the cocoa. I went on into the crowded kitchen with Nancy and surveyed the place for the folder before picking up a small slice of cherry Danish and a paper cup. As Annalynn poured my cocoa, I whispered, "Where's the folder?"

"Library," she whispered back. "Another marshmallow?"

I declined the marshmallow, told everyone not to wade through the drifts to visit Molly, and didn't watch Annalynn edge out of the kitchen while Connie took over pouring the cocoa. A moment later, I sauntered out and hurried to the library. Annalynn stood by a small table holding an empty folder. I closed the door.

She tossed the folder on a chair and picked up a yellow sheet of paper from a bookshelf. "Somebody emptied the folder. What did you expect to find besides the workload projections I passed out?"

"A printout of Molly's notes on what she planned to ask each of our three suspects this morning." I lifted the cushion on a chair and then surveyed the room for other hiding places. "Did you see anything but the projections in the folder?"

"No, and we won't find anything either." Annalynn pointed to the fire. "Why hide what you can burn? Who does Molly think shot her—umm—the mannequin?"

"She doesn't know, and neither do I. I doubt we'll find a smoking gun in her notes, but they're our best lead." I ran a poker through the ashes looking for bits of yellow paper and found none. "The notes are on her missing laptop, too. She left it on the middle shelf of the wardrobe."

"That shelf was empty." Annalynn bit her lower lip. "She couldn't have been thinking too clearly last night. Maybe she hid it somewhere else. Like under the bed."

"I'll do a thorough search of her room." It couldn't take more than five minutes. "What's on the schedule for the rest of the morning?"

"We'll gather here again in twenty minutes—at eleven. We're reviewing the procedures for choosing a candidate for the special election in June and for nominating one for a full term in August."

"If the hall's clear, I'll search the hall closet and her room now. I'll be done before eleven." I opened the library door, stepped out into an empty hall, and walked past the stairs to a short but wide door in the wall under the banister. I opened the door, ducked down to step inside, closed the door, and turned on my flashlight. Crowded into the space under the angled ceiling were cleaning and household supplies, an industrial vacuum cleaner, electrical cords, small tools and wrenches, and duct tape. I peered and touched but found no sign of a door to the bedroom or the tiny toilet. Dousing my light, I edged out into the empty hall and over to the bedroom door. Again I had to find the keyhole by feel in the unlit hall.

The window let in enough light to define the furniture and the figure on the bed, but I had to use my flashlight to see details. It took little more than a minute to recheck everything. No papers, no laptop, no hidden door.

Okay. I could understand not finding the printouts and the laptop, but the room had to have another door. Or at least an entry large enough for an adult to pass through. Where could it be? Wallpaper, probably a reproduction, covered the walls. I could see no break. Where and how would I conceal a door in this small room? Not in the same wall where the door opened into the hall. Not on the original outside wall. Not in the wall that ran along the hall closet and the toilet.

The built-in wardrobe filled more than half of the back wall. Behind that was the dumbwaiter and the butler's pantry. That left the wall between the toilet and the hall closet. I pulled back the accordion door and stepped into the tiny room, my body blocking most of the light from the bedroom window. The other door had to be in here. I shone my light on the walls next to the hall closet and the dining room inch by inch. Zip. Then I turned to the wall against the butler's pantry. I envisioned that room. It had to be parallel to the bathroom and bedroom. Cabinets would be directly behind this wall. Nothing.

A door in the ceiling? I turned my light upward. Solid. As I turned to leave, my beam flashed by the towel rack. Hmm. Tara had left a bath towel, a hand towel, and a washcloth on each bed in the bunkhouse, but the rack held only a salmon-colored bath towel and washcloth. Molly hadn't brought the towel with her. Maybe the hand towel was underneath. When I lifted off the bath towel, I saw a distinct line just above the rack. I trained my light on the wall beneath the rack and saw hinges two feet lower. I pulled hard on the rack and it moved. A door! I bent down to look behind it. The middle shelf of the wardrobe.

For a moment, I was stumped. Why would anyone want a concealed door between the wardrobe and the toilet? Then it hit me. The abolitionist Archers had used the tiny room to hide fugitive slaves when patrols came searching for them. What was now the toilet with a narrow accordion door had been an empty space with only the small entry from the wardrobe.

Brilliant deduction. Now all I had to do was figure out how the shooter got into the wardrobe. I inspected the back, top, and bottom of the wardrobe for another set of hinges. What about a trap door in the bedroom ceiling? Nothing. What could I be missing?

Frustrated, I decided to follow another clue: the missing hand towel. It was a good size to wrap around the revolver to muffle the sound or around the hand and wrist to capture most of the powder residue. Where was the towel now? If I were the shooter, I'd have put it into the laundry with the towels used by the Candon family in the last few days.

Or burnt it in a fireplace while on guard or in a stove in the music room or Bernadine's bedroom. But cloth burned more slowly and conspicuously than paper. What if someone stoking the fire noticed it? Perhaps the shooter hadn't yet destroyed the towel. Should I get Achilles to sniff through the laundry? No, I'd be less conspicuous alone, and I didn't need him to locate a salmon-colored hand towel.

I listened at the hall door for thirty seconds, heard nothing, and left as quietly as I could. The click of the lock sounded loud. Now to check the basement for the towel and the butler's pantry for an entry into Molly's bedroom. I abandoned both ideas when I opened the swinging door into the butler's pantry.

"Let's keep it simple, Clarissa," Nancy said from the kitchen. "I saw several packages of wienies and buns in the freezer when I went down for more Danish."

"I won't serve my guests hotdogs. We'll have three-bean salad, sourdough bread, and that canned beef stew Archer liked."

A chance to go unquestioned to the basement. "I'll be glad to carry up the stew."

"Thank you, Phoenix." Clarissa smiled her official smile. "I don't look forward to those steep stairs, but you won't need to carry anything up. The dumbwaiter is on the circuit powered by the generator."

I walked to the door leading to the enclosed porch. "I'll need the keys."

Clarissa pulled a loaded keychain from a pocket, unlocked the door to the porch, and went to the basement door. The lock on the old door refused to budge at first.

I checked the lock on the outside door. Good but not great. I'd barely heard the generator in the kitchen. From the porch, it sounded like someone mowing the snow. I gazed out a window and spotted wisps of steam rising from a huge drift some twenty-five feet away. "Your generator is remarkably quiet."

She laughed. "Close up it sounds like a tractor. It was so loud that we put it in an old storm cave and ran the connections underground." She opened the door. "Be careful, Phoenix. The steps are steep and worn."

I couldn't see beyond the top two steps so I turned on my flashlight. The walls and the steps were brick. Four steps from the bottom, I heard a faint sound. Someone moving? I switched off the light, put my right hand on my Glock, and flattened myself against the wall. I counted to sixty and heard nothing. The kitchen floor creaked above me. I waited another minute. Then I edged down two steps, held the flashlight as far to my left as I could reach, and turned it on.

A snowdrift blew at my head. What the hell? I fell backward onto the steps, doubtless diminishing the blow that landed on my bullet wound. Pain immobilized me for crucial seconds. A white bath towel, not snow, covered my face but didn't block out a light dancing down and to my left. The light went out. I pushed the towel off me as a mechanical buzz sounded. My attacker was escaping in the dumbwaiter.

I switched on my flashlight too late to see who it was. I'd have to catch the bastard on the first or, more likely, the second floor. I grasped the banister to pull myself up, but the bolt of lightning that shot under my ribs stopped me. I hadn't experienced such agony for two months. I lay back on the steps and tried not to move, not even to breathe. The pain eased. I gasped for air.

"Phoenix, are you all right?" Nancy spoke from the door above me.

The attacker mustn't learn how effective the blow had been, how vulnerable I was.

"I will be in a minute. I slipped on the steps."

"Don't move. I'll bring Annalynn."

I took a deep breath and then another. Nothing now but a dull ache. I knew from experience I could function with that. Moving cautiously, I sat up. I picked up the giant towel, got to my feet, and edged down the final steps. On the floor lay the attacker's weapon, a long-handled antique popcorn popper, the kind you use in a fireplace. A large freezer and shelves of food, both home canned and commercial, stood on the other side of the room near the dumbwaiter. A hotel-size washing machine and drier were on my left. Towels were scattered on the floor in front of the washer. None was salmon colored. The shooter had come back for Molly's towel. It was now headed toward a fireplace or stove.

Annalynn hurried down the stairs. "What happened?"

First things first. "Did anyone leave the library in the last five minutes?"

"Leave? No. The group hasn't reassembled for the meeting yet. Why?"

"The shooter tossed a towel over my head, whacked me with a popcorn popper, and escaped in the dumbwaiter." I shone my flashlight on the towels. "We both came down to find Molly's missing hand towel. I suspect the shooter used it to muffle the revolver."

Nancy gasped at the top of the steps. "Someone shot Molly last night?"

Scheisse! We'd have to let Nancy in on it. "Shut the door, please." I waited until she'd done that. "Someone tried but failed. To protect her, we're keeping that to ourselves. Did you see or hear anyone go into or come out of the butler's pantry in the last few minutes?"

"No, I was unloading the dishwasher when I realized you'd been down here too long."

Annalynn shone her light in my face. "Did you bring your emergency pain pills?"

"No. They knock me out." I could breathe normally now. "I'm okay."

"Damn it, Phoenix!" Annalynn's use of a swear word signaled that I looked awful. "You promised me you wouldn't go off without backup when you're investigating."

"I overestimated myself," I admitted. Achilles would have warned me someone was there. At least the weapon had been a popper rather than a machete. Next time I could expect something deadlier. I had to prevent that next time. I walked over to the dumbwaiter and pushed the button to call it down. Maybe I could figure out where the shooter got off. From the faintness of the sound, I judged that the dumbwaiter was coming from the second floor. "Let's load up the cans of beef stew and bean salad."

"I'll do it," Annalynn said. "Then I'm walking you back to the bunkhouse to lie down until lunch. Nancy, it's important that no one else knows Phoenix came down here after anything but the stew."

I added, "Don't mention I came down here unless someone asks."

"Of course. Is Molly really okay?"

Best to tell the truth. "No. If the roads weren't blocked, I'd drive her to a hospital right now." I had to let Nancy in on our plan. "We don't know who's trying to kill her, so we want that person to think that we're covering up her death. Just accept everything we say without question." One more pair of eyes wouldn't hurt. "And watch for reactions."

"Whom should I watch?"

Would she give us away? Then I remembered how well she'd played her role as Aunt Eller in Connie's production of *Oklahoma!* The minister could act. "Bernadine, Roland, and Horse."

"Oh, Lord," Nancy said, and it was more a prayer than an exclamation.

Annalynn put three large cans on the dumbwaiter. "Do you need help going up the steps, Phoenix?"

"No. I'm fine." I picked up the popcorn popper to lean on, but I regretted my refusal of help immediately. My legs supported me reluctantly, and my left shoulder ached from my fall.

Annalynn put her arm around my waist to support me. "Stop being an idiot. You endanger yourself and others."

I deserved that. I had to husband the strength I would need later today. Once up the stairs, my legs worked better. Still, I thought it a good idea to refuel before I went back to that icy bunkhouse. The kitchen worktable had two open shelves of pots and pans under it, so

I stuck the popper on the top shelf and sank into a chair at the small table by the window. "I could use some sugar and chocolate."

"Fine." Annalynn put the back of her hand on my forehead. "I'll go on to the meeting. I'll ask Connie to call Achilles in and make sure you rest."

Nancy put a big mug of cocoa with three marshmallows crowded on the top in front of me. "I'll stay with Phoenix."

Annalynn went into the butler's pantry and came back with cans of stew. "No sign of a passenger. I'll see you both later."

Nancy brought a paper plate with bite-size pieces of Danish to the table and sat down across from me. "Clarissa and I thought maybe the person intended to disable Molly with that extra caffeine, not kill her."

I'd speculated on that when I still thought Archer might have staged his accident. "The shooting was definitely meant to be fatal, Nancy." May as well pick her brain. "Has Clarissa said anything about any of our three suspects"—careful not to impugn Archer—"doing anything they wouldn't want made public?"

"Oh, Phoenix." Nancy twisted a paper napkin. "She's told me things in confidence."

"I appreciate that, but you know how well I can keep a secret. Something she's told you could help me prevent a murder."

Nancy closed her eyes and clasped her hands as though in prayer. I waited and waited.

She opened her eyes. "I can give you bits and pieces. They seem insignificant, but Connie says you take tiny bits of information and draw the big picture."

Praise from Connie? Incredible.

As though on cue, she came through the swinging door with Achilles. He rushed to me and tried to lick my face. He sniffed and whined.

Nancy reached out to stroke his back. "He really does know when you have a physical problem."

"I'm okay," I assured him, scratching behind his ears. "Connie, would you please give him some water?" She may as well receive the minister's confidences firsthand. "Go on, Nancy. Connie's part of the investigation."

In thirty seconds Connie had filled a plastic bowl with water for Achilles and a mug with cocoa for herself. She pulled up a chair.

Nancy untwisted the napkin. "Clarissa has worried for years that Horse disregarded the rules on campaigning and lobbying. He'd slip Archer a couple thousand in cash when they went out to dinner or invite him and Clarissa and a couple of other representatives for a week at a resort. Since that Citizens United court decision made election contributions so easy, she's worried mostly about the unofficial lobbying. Horse always couched whatever he wanted for his business in terms of helping Missouri's economy."

This sounded like standard operating procedure to me, penny-ante stuff. "How much under-the-table money are we talking about?"

"I don't know. My sister got upset when Archer came home from a Florida fishing trip with $10,000 in cash to finance something or other. She blew a gasket. She said if it were legal, Horse wouldn't have used cash. Archer brushed it off. During the last campaign, Horse was still stuffing hundred dollar bills into Archer's pockets. The point is, Molly didn't like it either. She told Archer that she gave Horse a copy of the laws he was breaking, and he laughed at her. As Archer—uhh—lost his grasp of things, Horse gave money and instructions for spending it to staff members."

This information had to be in Molly's notes. "Which staff members, Nancy?"

"Roland, for one. And at least one person, not Thor, in the Hill office."

I moved Horse and Roland to a tie at the top of my suspect list. "What about Roland?"

Nancy hesitated. "Archer kept shifting Roland around to find something he could do well, or at least do no harm. Thor certainly considers Roland expendable."

Connie stole one of my marshmallows. "My money for the

poisoning had been on Bernadine, but Horse and Roland both seem more likely to have used the antique gun. Can we eliminate her as a suspect?"

"No," Nancy answered, "Clarissa says Bernadine's ultra ambitious and vindictive. Molly refused to support Bernadine for a state Senate run because of something shady she did in a local campaign. She's been trying to undermine Molly with Archer and party committee members for months."

So Molly had opted not to speak ill of Bernadine and played down her possible motive. Damn. It would have been easier to focus on two rather than three suspects. "On another subject, Nancy, do you know where the antebellum Archers hid runaway slaves?"

She blinked in surprise. "In what's now the toilet off the sick room, Molly's bedroom. They crawled in there through the side of the wardrobe."

Connie lit up. "Clever." She frowned. "How did they get in the bedroom?"

Nancy stared at Connie, perplexed. "Through the door, I suppose."

Time to renew my search for the secret door. I took my cup to the sink and rinsed it out. "Thanks, Nancy. I'll rest for a few minutes before lunch."

Connie darted a suspicious look at me. "I'll go with you." She followed me into the dining room and whispered, "We're going to Molly's bedroom to find the secret door?"

"I already looked. We're going upstairs to see if it's in the floor of the game room." I headed up the stairs with no complaints from my body.

We walked the game room floor from the hall wall to the built-in storage cabinet that housed the dumbwaiter, moved the children's table to check under it, and checked the bottom shelves to see if they lifted up. All in vain.

I opened the cabinet doors. "It has to involve the dumbwaiter." I pumped my fist in triumph as I suddenly realized the secret entry's location. "I looked for hinges in the back of the wardrobe, but the entry must be a sliding door between the wardrobe and the dumbwaiter. The fugitive could access the wardrobe and the secret room from either floor or the basement."

"Just like entering Narnia."

"Where?"

"A place in a children's book. The kids entered it through the back of the wardrobe."

Light blasted in the windows as if nature had turned on a spotlight.

Connie darted to a window. "Thank goodness. The storm's over. Maybe we can get out of here this afternoon."

I joined her. Where she saw light, I saw darkness. We wouldn't be able to drive out, but Adam Augeri would do his damndest to drive in. I had double trouble.

CHAPTER TWENTY-EIGHT

With everyone else still in the morning meeting, I left Connie on guard at the top of the stairs and took Achilles down the hall to see whether he could smell black powder in the suspects' bedrooms. I didn't know how to tell Achilles what we were looking for, and he showed no interest in anything in Horse's room. I took note of a stack of Benjamin Franklins in Horse's overnight bag and a top-of-the-line computer on his dresser.

We went on to Bernadine's room. Achilles sneezed when he smelled her perfumed soap but reacted to nothing else. She had tucked a copy of the workload projections into a spiral notebook with some scrawled notes. No computer or tablet. No sign of yellow paper or a salmon towel among the coals in her stove. I rejoined Connie.

She shivered. "At least in the kitchen and the library you can't see your breath."

We trod lightly on the stairs and through the dining room into the butler's pantry.

Nancy came from the kitchen and watched with open mouth as I opened the inconspicuous door to the dumbwaiter and reached across to the back wall. I flinched and drew back as the outer edge of the shelf cut into my stomach and reawakened the pain.

Achilles whined, and Connie whispered, "Sit in the kitchen. I'll find the secret door."

I obeyed this once.

Nancy, mouth closed but eyes wide, stood guard by the swinging door. A minute later, she gave me a thumbs up and came into the kitchen. "Clarissa and Pete may know about that opening behind the dumbwaiter. I certainly didn't. No one would just happen on it." Her eyes widened. "Pete showed us the diary that told about hiding slaves. I saw Bernadine looking at it later. It may tell about that secret door."

I moved Bernadine to number one on the suspect list.

Nancy said, "She pointed out some diagrams to Horse."

Scheisse. "And I saw Roland reading an old ledger or diary by the light of the fire last night. Any of them could have read how escaped slaves got into that cubbyhole."

Connie joined us. "Somebody took a huge risk. It would be darned hard to crawl through that wall and out of the wardrobe without waking Molly up."

Nancy sighed. "Everyone knows about Molly's coffee, and everyone knows she sleeps through storms."

Connie paced the kitchen. "I don't think Roland or Horse is nimble enough to crawl through that little door and get out of the wardrobe without falling on his head. My money is still on Bernadine."

I considered Connie's point. They all seemed unlikely intruders, but people will out-do themselves when they're desperate. I put myself in the shooter's position. I would have figured going from the wardrobe into the bathroom upped my odds of not being discovered. Even if heard, I wouldn't be seen. The towels would have been right at hand, and creeping to the bed without turning on a light fairly easy. I would've shot as soon as I'd located the head (with a flashlight?), dropped the gun, and plunged through that wardrobe and across the dumbwaiter fast.

Connie touched my shoulder. "Phoenix, we better shuffle off to Buffalo before the meeting breaks up."

We walked to the back wing. Connie stayed at the door between the main house and the wing to keep watch, and I hurried with Achilles into Roland's bedroom.

One of the twin beds was rumpled, and photos of a woman and two teenagers were on the night table. Clothes hung neatly on hangers in an old wardrobe. I saw no towels or toiletries, so they must be in the

221

bathroom down the hall.

Achilles made a quick circuit and went out the door.

No paper anywhere, not even the yellow workload projection sheet. No laptop, but Roland probably carried either a large smart phone or a tablet.

Two taps on the door.

I stepped out and ran after Connie to the bunkhouse.

Achilles thought the sprint meant I was ready to play. He ducked under the bunk and came out with a white Frisbee in his mouth.

"I didn't pack a white Frisbee. Where did he get it?"

"He must have borrowed it from the collies." Connie turned on the heater. "Annalynn put in a fresh fuel cartridge. I'm dialing this up to high."

"I'm for that, but check it for tampering first." Shivering from the chill, I took my parka from the hook and curled up on the bunk with it over me. "If the water hasn't already frozen, better turn on the faucet enough to keep it dripping." I closed my eyes for a moment.

I opened them to hear Annalynn say softly to Connie, "Roland thinks the roads will be cleared before dark, but Clarissa says the plows may not come through until tomorrow morning." Annalynn pushed a loose strand of hair back into her French roll. "I'd love to get out of here with Tara and Molly this afternoon and leave solving both these cases to Sam Gist."

Sounded good to me. "Have the guests agreed on a departure time?"

"Not yet. Jerrald and Roland went out to the driveway to reconnoiter. We'll talk about what they find at lunch. We eat at twelve thirty." Annalynn sat on the edge of my bunk and studied my face. "Your color is good. Any pain?"

My shoulder ached enough to take an aspirin. My reawakened wound slept. "I'm fine."

Achilles barked three times.

Was he calling me a liar? Sometimes he seemed to understand our conversations.

"Thank you, Achilles." Annalynn stroked his head and then walked to the door. "Stay with Phoenix. Guard Phoenix."

Connie hurried after Annalynn.

I gave Achilles a light lunch and reviewed my findings while he ate. Depressing. I'd accomplished little but to confirm with Molly that I should continue investigating my—our—three suspects. If I could find her notes, maybe I'd see something she'd overlooked. Even eliminating one of the three would help. At least I'd smuggled Molly to a safe place, and certainly finding out who wanted to kill her was less important than keeping her alive. But if I didn't identify the would-be killer, I couldn't keep her alive after we left here.

Achilles nudged my hand with the white Frisbee.

"Later." I rubbed and stroked and scratched him to show I was sorry we couldn't play. I turned off the heater that kept the room above freezing. "Let's go."

He stuck by my side as we walked down the cold, dark hall to the main house.

Raised voices sounded behind the closed library door. I opened it, and the bright light coming through the windows made me blink.

"Calm down, everyone," Thor said from his perch on the low wall in front of the fireplace. He held a food tray on his lap. "No one wants to go home more than I do, but it would be foolhardy to leave here this afternoon if the roads aren't plowed. We could spend the night freezing in a drift."

Roland held up a portable radio. "The forecast says the temperature this afternoon will hit thirty-two. The snow will start to melt."

"Right," Jerrald said, his mouth half full. "About a quarter of an inch. After sundown the temperature will drop into the low twenties, and what's melted will freeze into a hard crust. I've got a souped-up motor and a four-wheel drive and I know how to drive, but right now I doubt I could make it to the front gate."

Bernadine waved her spoon. "I can't even see my car from my bedroom window. Just a mound of snow."

Annalynn turned to Jerrald. "Is the wind still blowing?"

"A little. Nothing like it was earlier."

"Good," she said. "I suggest we clear off our cars and the space around them. When the plow comes through, we'll be ready to leave."

Horse raised a paper cup to her. "A woman who knows how to solve problems."

Jerrald and Bernadine both frowned and ducked their heads at this sign of Horse's approval of Annalynn.

I'd have felt better about it if Horse weren't a suspect. I went to the kitchen to get a bowl of stew. Nancy and Connie were eating at the little kitchen table.

Connie said, "I'm going to meet with Clarissa and Nancy at one thirty to discuss the summer music program."

"Good." Hmm. The widow was proceeding with her plans. She must be tough. Or not as upset by her husband's sudden death as Annalynn had been at hers. In my head, I heard Annalynn say, "Don't always blame the spouse." I filled my bowl half full and buttered a thick slice of bread. I carried them to the table.

Horse came through the swinging door. "Phoenix, would you join me in the music room, please?"

Opportunity tapped. Not wanting to seem overeager, I glanced around the kitchen. "Is there a tray I can carry my lunch on, Nancy?"

"On the table's bottom shelf."

I found the tray, put my food on it, and went to the music room. It was cooler than the library or the kitchen but much more comfortable than the bunkhouse. I sat down near the stove.

Achilles lay down beside me, his eyes on Horse.

The man paced back and forth in front of the grand piano. "Annalynn tells me you've worked for firms specializing in venture capitalism in Eastern Europe since the Iron Curtain fell. You still doing that in Laycock?"

"I do a little consulting." I took a bite of the stew. Bland and salty. Heather's sourdough bread was much better.

"Do you know my company's products?"

Flatter with a yes? Not this guy. "No."

"We market proprietary business-management systems to major

companies. A big part of the business these days is updating systems for clients. A few years ago I wanted to increase the client base by going into Eastern Europe, but my advisers in New York told me the market there wasn't ready to pay for such sophisticated systems." He stopped in front of me. "Are they now?"

A huge question, one I couldn't answer properly without some research. If the bastard expected to barter a few thousands in campaign contributions for advice worth much more, he'd have to say so. "I never make recommendations without careful research and analysis. For which I get paid very well."

"I see." He drummed his fingers on the piano. "Paid enough to finance a big part of Annalynn's campaign? The June election alone will cost her half a million."

A threat to withhold support if I didn't give him valuable advice for nothing? A probe to judge how badly Annalynn needed his money? An attempt to scare us out of the race? Whatever he intended, letting him intimidate us would be a big mistake. "Annalynn doesn't expect me to become a super PAC and finance her campaign." Make it clear this winner set the bar high. "She also won't accept illegal contributions from me or anyone else. She follows the letter and spirit of the law."

He laughed. "That won't last long."

Annoyed at his assumption and confident I could fund a super PAC, I went a step farther: "Are illegal contributions the reason you and Molly don't get along?"

He glared at me. "Don't let your courtesy badge go to your head. I've done nothing you can arrest me for."

Achilles sprang to his feet and growled.

Horse stumbled back against the piano.

I picked up my lunch tray. "You're quite right, Horse. I can't arrest you for violating federal laws." I walked to the door and paused. I'd learned nothing to tell me whether he'd tried to kill Molly. I calculated risk on investment and decided to bait him. "Here's some free advice: Don't think the feds can't trace cash."

Exit right.

CHAPTER TWENTY-NINE

I joined the others in the library and took a chair where I could watch everyone and overhear most. Bernadine was arguing with Jerrald about whether to finance improvements to I-70 by making it a toll road or by raising gasoline taxes. Roland, his eyes bloodshot, faced them but obviously wasn't listening. No wonder he hadn't won over special constituents. Thor, a rueful smile on his lips, was telling Annalynn how newly elected members of Congress rewarded supporters, screened hundreds of eager poli sci graduates, and poached veteran Hill staffers from other offices. Was he assuming she'd need to know about staffing?

Outside the library, snow slid off the roof and plummeted to the ground.

Roland jumped up. "See? It's melting. I'm going to shovel out my car." He strode to the door.

The men responded like a pack of coon dogs drawn to the chase.

Bernadine heaved a sigh and pushed a strand of her blond hair behind her ear. "I didn't bring a shovel. My husband always handles that."

The men ignored her hint, and Bernadine got up to follow them out.

Annalynn winked at me. "Don't worry, Bernadine I'll lend you my shovel when I'm through." On her way out, she bent down to say in my ear, "Don't you dare come help me. Get some rest."

I closed the library door behind them and hustled to the family history shelf to search for the diary telling about hiding fugitive slaves. Not there. I scanned the shelves nearby. The books were all neatly aligned. They'd be a great place to hide Molly's notes. I pulled out random books to see if the diary or the yellow sheets had been stashed in the space behind the smaller books. After a good search of all the shelves except the top ones on the wall next to the music room, I moved to the shelves under the window. Rather than pulling books out, I turned on my flashlight and searched for any place dust had been wiped away from the edge of the shelves.

The door opened. To hide what I was doing, I reached for a copy of *In Mathematical Circles: A Selection of Mathematical Stories and Anecdotes.* Mrs. Roper owned a copy. Perhaps Kaysi would like to have one.

"Here you are." Connie came in and closed the door. "You said to watch for any problem with the heater. When I went to the room after lunch, I noticed it had been moved closer to the wall. I'm afraid somebody tampered with the sensor or the canister."

I'd anticipated that. "The killer must be afraid Annalynn and I recognized a fake suicide and is coming after us now." An "accident" fit this person's style. I had to minimize our risk. "Stay with other people, and don't be alone with any of our three suspects. Did you tell Annalynn?"

"No. She'd already gone out with Thor and Roland to shovel out their cars. She said you're not to go on patrol without her."

"Are the other guests shoveling, too?"

"Horse and Jerrald are. Bernadine is moping around waiting for someone to volunteer to clear her car." Connie opened the door. "I'll be with Clarissa and Nancy in the music room for the next hour or so. What are you going to do?"

"Devise a strategy for guarding us here and Tara and Molly at the other house."

Connie left.

Too bad she and Clarissa were meeting in the music room. Playing the piano, especially Mozart, helped me analyze my findings. I sat in front of the fireplace with my aching left shoulder to the heat. If we were stuck here another night, sleeping by the fire might be safer than staying in the bunkhouse with that heater. Anyone could have seen that

Connie, Annalynn, and I were in the main house, but getting in and out of the back wing unseen took daring. Desperation or arrogance? The shooter had to be wondering when I would announce Molly's death.

Roland was the only suspect with a reason to go into the wing. Wrong. All four men helped bring in firewood. It would take only seconds to go from the woodpile to our room and sabotage the heater.

Bernadine opened the door and nodded a greeting. She had her coat on, but she perched near me on the fireplace wall. "I understand you're Annalynn's financial adviser for the campaign."

"No, I'm the chief financial officer for the Coping After Crime Foundation." Lead her on. "You probably heard the adviser thing from Molly. I gather she's not always—umm—precise."

"You can say that again. You wouldn't believe all the bad information she's given me since—since people first asked me to run for public office."

"Really?" I gave her the wide-eyed innocent look I usually reserved for chauvinists. "I haven't lived in Missouri for years, so I don't know anything about politics here. You may have noticed I haven't come to the meetings."

She didn't quite buy it. "I thought you were watching for that man with the machete."

"As a matter of fact, I've been sitting here wondering how to watch for him at both the front and back. I'm going to need volunteers."

She leaned back a fraction of an inch. "I'll be glad to help, of course, but I don't know how to fire a gun or do any of those martial arts. Horse and Jerrald probably are good at that self-defense stuff."

She'd mentioned the two oldest and least likely men. "What about Roland? He looks like a hunter, a man who's comfortable with a gun."

"I've got no idea. I barely know the man."

A lie, one she expected to go unquestioned. She'd hired him to jumpstart her political career. Now she wanted something from me. Make her tell me. I switched topics. "You must be terribly anxious to get home to your children."

"Not really." She caught herself. "I mean, they're teenagers now. Very independent." She paused and added, "That's why I can finally devote myself to public service."

Why was she wasting these buffalo droppings on me? "Very commendable."

"Running for office is terribly expensive."

"So I've heard." These people's conversations always came back to money.

"My backers are urging me to run for Candon's seat, but I wonder if I should gain some experience in state government first."

The advice she'd rejected from Molly. I kept my face neutral.

She sat in profile but watched me out of the corner of her eye. "If an interested person would finance a campaign for the state House, I'd forget about going after the nomination for Congress."

I pretended to consider Bernadine's idiotic request that I bribe her to clear the way for Annalynn's nomination. "That sounds like a good idea." I paused to watch hope rise. Then I flattened it. "You should ask Roland for advice."

She stared at me, apparently not sure whether I was dense or deceptive. "I'll do that." She stood up and fished gloves from her pocket. "I better clean off my car. I don't want to spend another night in this miserable place." She hurried out.

I had to agree with Connie that powdered caffeine seemed like a weapon Bernadine Platt would choose. But what would she have gained by eliminating Molly last week? More to the point, perhaps, what did Bernadine have to lose if Molly met with her this morning?

Achilles roused himself from a doze at my feet and trotted to the door.

"You're right. I can't just sit here." First step, map out the surroundings to anticipate Augeri's most likely approach and the best places to intercept him. I walked to a library window to study the wide lawn and the formerly electrified fence separating it from a pasture. The sunlight bounced off the snow with such intensity that I could barely see. My sunglasses with the telescopic lenses were in my parka pocket. I walked back to the bunkhouse to get them, and even without the heater on, the room felt warmer than it had earlier.

With the magic glasses on, I looked out the bunkhouse windows on pristine snow.

Achilles nudged me with the Frisbee.

"It's not a good time to play." To convince him of that, I put his bullet-proof vest on him. He knew that meant danger.

Now what? The second-floor windows offered the best view of the surroundings. I walked back to the great hall and started up the stairs.

Bernadine burst through the front door. "He's coming!"

"Who?"

"The man with the machete!" She pointed behind her. "He's walking down the road. He'll be at the front gate in five minutes or so."

I ran up the stairs and down the hall to the French doors leading to the tiny balcony over the entrance. The trees blocked much of my view of the road, but I turned up my glasses to maximum distance and saw a man with a big bag slung over his shoulder. He was stumbling through snow above his knees. He waved both arms and shouted. Then he fell down.

Bernadine trotted up behind me. "Do you see him?"

"Yes." I watched him struggle to his feet. "It's not machete man. It's that damned documentarian." One more complication.

"Oh. I better freshen my makeup." Bernadine went into her bedroom.

Well, Bernadine thought like a politician. Or an actor. Connie would be putting on a fresh coat of paint for the camera, too.

A minute later, a treetop blocked my view of the man. At the end of the driveway, Annalynn and the men were shoveling snow away from the gate so they could open it. Thor and then Roland squeezed through the opening and pumped their arms to help propel themselves through the snow toward the newcomer. Annalynn continued to shovel at the gate.

If this man got through, Augeri could, too. I put the glasses on max but could see no one behind him. Augeri would be a fool to walk up that road. I ran to the window at the other end of the hall. No tracks between here and the barn but my own. Evergreen trees blocked my view of most of the farmhouse and of the lane leading to the other road. I'd have to go out there, but I couldn't cover much territory walking in the deep snow. Maybe Pete could use the generator to recharge the snowmobile.

I changed my focus to the hilly pasture visible behind the machine shed. A dozen buffalo played in the snow, running in circles, rolling over in drifts, dipping their heads into the snow and throwing up loose clumps. Amazing. Augeri wouldn't be coming through *that* pasture. I watched the giant animals frolic until the front door opened and half a dozen people spoke.

Annalynn's voice came through: "No, don't put him by the fire. Take him to the kitchen. He may have frostbite, and you treat that with warm water, not heat."

"She's right," Horse said. "And he needs to get out of these wet clothes. Somebody get him a pair of sweatpants."

"Phoenix," Annalynn called, "Phoenix, where are you?"

"Coming." I hurried downstairs.

"Wait here," Annalynn said to the people clustered in the great hall. She motioned for me to follow her through the dining room door.

In the kitchen, Horse eased the hiker's left arm from his coat sleeve. "You ladies get out of here. Thor and I will handle it."

"It's my toes and my fingers," the documentarian said.

Annalynn knelt and began unlacing his hiking boots. "How far did you walk?"

"Must have been about three miles. The driver ahead of me got stuck, and I couldn't drive backward or forward."

Augeri? I had to be sure. "What did he look like?"

"I don't know. He left before I got there. I stepped in his tracks until I got to the final turnoff coming here. He walked on straight."

Toward the younger Candons' gate. "What was he driving?"

"An old green pickup."

Machete man lurked somewhere close.

CHAPTER THIRTY

Half expecting to see Adam Augeri, I stared out the kitchen window. Whether by design or ignorance, he had walked past the road leading to Four Chimneys and to the lane leading to the house where Tara was hiding. Outside the gate, no longer secured by electricity, a mailbox identified the Candons' farm. I had no doubt Augeri already had gone through that gate.

The collies hadn't barked, so he hadn't approached the farmhouse yet. I recalled my view as Pete drove the snowmobile from the gate toward the farmhouse. On my left, a seven-foot-high wire fence separated the gently rising lane from the buffalos' pasture. On my right, scattered scrubby trees too small to hide anyone marked the side of the lane. When we topped the small rise, the roof of Four Chimneys—pictured on Archer Candon's official website—came into view. Full-grown trees often cut off that view for the next quarter of a mile. Four Chimneys' first floor didn't become visible from the lane until we neared the farmhouse.

But the big house would become visible much sooner if you cut across the snow toward it when you saw the chimneys.

Annalynn broke into my thoughts: "Phoenix, do you think Augeri's already on the property?" She eased off the documentarian's boot.

"Yes." I pointed toward the orchard south of us and behind the farmhouse. "Somewhere back there probably." I'd been right to look out the upstairs window, but I may well have watched from the wrong vantage point. I noticed Connie standing in the archway. "Tell everyone to come indoors and take a coffee break."

Horse held a pan of tepid water for the man's fingers. "What possessed you to drive up here before the plows came through?"

The documentarian grimaced. "I thought a four-wheel would bring me through. I had no idea how high the snow had drifted north of Highway 36."

He had no more information to offer me. I motioned to Annalynn to come with me into the dining room. Keeping my voice low, I said, "You set up watches in the upstairs windows. I'll alert the younger Candons. Then I'll take the dogs out to look for Augeri." I feared she'd insist on coming along, so I added, "He should be cold enough to be glad to be found."

Annalynn shook her head. "He didn't drive over here to be found. If he had, we'd have seen him by now. I'm going with you." She turned as Jerrald and Clarissa came into the dining room from the hall. "Jerrald, we're fairly sure machete man is hiding on the property. Could you please watch from your bedroom window and ask someone to watch from the game room while Phoenix and I go after him?"

"Of course." He hesitated. "What do we do if we see him?"

"I have an old hand bell from a one-room school," Clarissa said. "You can open the window and ring it. The sound carries a long way."

"Good." No time to talk. I jogged back to the bunkhouse with Achilles running ahead and Annalynn following.

I put on my parka and stowed my Glock, sunglasses, and other tools in my pockets. "We'll walk and talk casually," I said to Annalynn as we went out the back door. "I doubt that he's close enough to see us."

"Phoenix, are you sure you want to see him?"

"What do you mean?"

"All he's done at this point is come onto farm property after his pickup got stuck in the snow. We can't even charge him with trespassing."

A sobering point. "And Tara would be on the run again indefinitely." What was our alternative? "I don't want to shoot him unless I have to."

"Good Lord, no." She grabbed my arm. "I'm not suggesting that. We've shot more than enough people this last six months. I don't want to shoot anyone else."

Achilles nudged me with the white Frisbee. He obviously didn't smell trouble.

I took it and sailed it toward the barn. "What do you suggest?"

"That you outsmart him instead." She smiled. "You're good at trapping people. Encourage him to break in and disarm him immediately. Armed B&E is an easier case to prosecute than domestic abuse."

"A great idea, but it's a little sketchy." I made a snowball and threw it at the barn door. "Would it count if he went into the barn?"

"It's much better to entice him to break into the late Congressman Archer Candon's historic home. Ohhh! Our chilled friend could film it. We'd have irrefutable proof."

"Right." Could I tolerate working with that guy? I walked on toward the farmhouse. "You've spent too much time with Connie. This scheme is all fantasy and no substance."

"You'll figure it out." She smiled. "You may need Connie's help, of course."

Very funny.

Iron and Steel came running out to greet us, barking and romping around us with Achilles until Annalynn talked them into coming up to her for some stroking, something she would never have dared to do before Achilles became part of our household.

I was pleased with their noise. Augeri would avoid a house with guard dogs.

Heather opened the door and waved to us. "I hope you're coming to give us an all clear."

"Just the opposite," I said. "Is Molly okay?"

"No, but she's feeling better than she did when you left." Heather fiddled with the end of her long braid. "You stressed her out, Phoenix. I know you thought it was necessary, but her blood pressure really worried me. Please don't talk to her again."

Annalynn took off her coat. "I'll give Molly a report on this morning's meeting while Phoenix briefs your family and Tara."

Heather pursed her lips and brushed her cheek with the tip of the braid. Finally she took a step toward the hall and said, "I'll see if she's up to it."

A moment later, I whispered. "We have to know what's in her notes."

Annalynn gave me a look reminding me she knew that as well as I did.

I shut up, but another thing had been niggling at me. "The whole staff went to the morning coffees and lunch. Only Molly and Archer attended the afternoon coffees. Find out why. The motive and opportunity for the poisoning both may be linked to that."

Heather motioned to Annalynn from an open door down the hall.

I gave Annalynn an encouraging pat on the back as she walked away.

Heather led me into the living room where Pete sat at a computer, Junior read a business magazine, and Tara knitted a dark green sweater. They all focused on me.

Distract and relax them with a normal comment. Vertical bamboo blinds made the room quite dim except near the battery lamps, but I noted a stunning four-by-seven textile collage in desert colors over the comfortable sofa and walked over to it. "What a lovely piece."

"Thank you," Heather said. "That was Junior's winter project two years ago."

Tara, her face pale, took a deep breath. "Adam's here, isn't he?"

"Most likely." I told them about the documentarian's arrival and the abandoned pickup.

The Candons quickly reached the same conclusion I had: Augeri had walked to their gate, seen the mailbox, and headed toward Four Chimneys.

Tara shivered. "He'll find a place in the snow to hide and watch for me. He's a regular snowman. He made me go camping with him during a snowstorm last winter. I about froze, but he had sock warmers and all that stuff. It didn't bother him."

Worse than I thought. "What color coat and pants did he wear?"

"A real light gray, hard to see in the snow," she said.

"The dogs will find him easily enough," Junior said. "We've got two hours of good light left. We'll track him down."

"No! You can't do that!" Tara buried her face in her hands. "He'll hurt you! He'll jump up out of the snow and shoot you, and it will be all my fault." Sobs cut off her words.

Heather leaned over Tara to stroke her hair and rub her shoulder. "Deputy Smith knows what she's doing. She won't let Adam hurt anyone."

Pete bounded out of his chair and toward the door. "I'll shoot the crazy bastard! He's on our land. Nobody will blame me for shooting him."

Time to lay down the (not quite) law. "Everyone sit down. We're not going to risk injury to ourselves or our dogs by going after him." What were we going to do? "Annalynn and I are going to draw him into a trap and arrest him." How? A plan began to form, but only the first step was clear. "You stay in the house and out of sight, all of you." Especially Pete. Adam would be even more dangerous if he knew Tara and a young man lived in the same house. "Adam expects Tara to be in Four Chimneys because that's where he saw her on television. Confirm that by playing some music she never listened to. A symphony? Chamber music? Opera?"

Heather pointed to an entertainment center. "Rampal playing classical flute?"

"Excellent." Next problem: How could we use the dogs to give the alarm without endangering them? Augeri would probably swing the familiar machete rather than fire the unfamiliar and noisy gun. "Bring your collies into the house. Their barking will drive him away, but they won't be exposed to his weapons."

Pete pounded his right fist into his left palm. "What if he climbs through a window or shoots his way through a door anyway?"

Give it to them straight. "If he breaks into the house, shoot him in the chest. Not the legs. Not the head. The chest." Tell them the rest. "Shoot him before he gets close, no closer than from the free-throw line to the basket. You know how fast you can cover that, Pete."

He nodded vigorously.

Sobbing uncontrollably, Tara curled up in a fetal position in her chair.

Heather and Junior exchanged glances that I couldn't interpret. I'd credited them with courage for guarding the girl against physical violence. Now I admired them for their compassion and skill in dealing with her emotional trauma.

He said, "You figure to draw him to Four Chimneys. Do you plan to shoot him?"

"No," Annalynn said, standing in the door with Molly. "We'll use no more force than is absolutely necessary."

Be positive. "Good to see you up, Molly. You rest here tonight. I'll come by for you tomorrow morning after we've wrapped things up."

Her big smile in place but shaky, she said, "Thank you, Phoenix."

My immediate concern was making sure Augeri had entered the property. "Pete, does the snowmobile have enough juice to take Annalynn and me to the gate and back?"

The boy raised his eyebrows. "Yeah, but I thought you weren't going after him."

"I'm not, but I intend to find out whether he's actually on the property."

Junior got to his feet. "If the dogs get his scent, they'll go after him. I'll lock them in the breezeway. Do you want to leave your dog here, too?"

"No." Annalynn walked toward the kitchen. "He'll stay with us."

I realized her insistence on taking Achilles meant our little jaunt frightened her. For me, it fell well within the acceptable-risk zone.

We got into our coats quickly. The sunlight still bounced off the snow, but dirty little clouds moved through the sky. The light wouldn't linger much past five.

Junior went through the breezeway to unlock the garage and bring the snowmobile out for us. "By the way, the radio says most of the secondary roads will be cleared by tonight. They'll work on the little roads like ours tomorrow."

We'd be lucky to get out of here by noon. I set my sunglasses for distant viewing and racked my Glock before mounting the snowmobile and moving off at about ten miles an hour. To Annalynn, riding behind me, I said, "If Augeri fires, dive into the snow." To Achilles, who had loped over to the fence to stare at the buffalo, I said, "Stay close. Alert."

"The wind has changed directions," Annalynn said. "It's blowing southeast toward the road that runs past the front entrance now. Achilles may not smell Augeri."

No human tracks marred the snow in the pasture or on the lane. I projected my voice. "Yes, they're fascinating animals. Easier to care for than Herefords, especially in winter."

A moment later, Annalynn said, "They weigh twice as much, and the meat contains less fat. The Candons sell most of the young bulls for meat."

We'd pretty much exhausted our knowledge of buffalo.

Achilles raised his head and plunged through the snow to our left.

"Achilles! Stay!" I could see nothing hidden in the snow, but the snowman could burrow into a drift and be completely hidden.

Achilles barked, a rapid baritone cadence that set a calf running.

No human head popped up. "Quiet, boy. You're scaring the animals," I called. I added softly, "Stay close. Guard." We approached the rise. For once, I wished Connie had come with me. She picked up on my ruses immediately and fed me lines. "Play along with whatever I say," I murmured to Annalynn.

I stopped the snowmobile on the rise, adjusted my lenses, and projected my voice: "They haven't plowed this road yet either." He'd walked up the road, stopped a little before the mailbox, and retraced his steps. "He's here," I whispered.

"Where? I don't see anything."

Thanks to my telescopic lenses, I spotted where he'd gone off the road behind a drift, burrowed under the wire, and walked parallel to the lane. At the top of the rise, the tracks angled. "Near Four Chimneys."

She said loudly, "I'm cold. Let's go back."

"I just felt a chill myself." I drove to Junior's garage as fast as Achilles could run in the snowmobile's track.

Junior opened the garage door. He held a .22 rifle. "See him?"

"Only his tracks," I said. "He headed through the field toward Four Chimneys. I expect him to hunker down out of sight until dark. Where would you guess he'd hole up?"

Junior rubbed his hand along the rifle's stock absentmindedly. "We got a little shed—more like a big box—in the orchard between the peach and apple trees."

"Would he be able to see the dining room and kitchen windows from there?"

"Sure," Junior said, "but he'd be too far away to recognize faces."

Then the windows would draw him like a moth.

Annalynn said, "The barn would be warmer."

Junior pointed at one of his dogs. "Nobody gets near that barn unannounced."

I dismissed the barn from my mind to focus on the real problem. "He didn't come here to hide and watch. He came to snatch"—or kill—"and run. Junior, get back in the house, check all your locks, and keep everybody out of sight and away from your windows until you hear from me."

I strode back toward the main house forming part two of my plan.

CHAPTER THIRTY-ONE

Connie met us at the back door. "Everyone is in the library waiting to hear whether it's safe to go outside again."

Was it? "Tell them we'll be there in a minute." We cleaned the clumps of snow from our boots and pants legs.

Annalynn unbuttoned her coat but didn't take it off. "Well, Phoenix? What are you going to tell them?"

I didn't trust these people, but almost any group will pull together for self-preservation. "The truth, but not the whole truth, at least not until I can pin down some essential details."

She sighed. "You mean your version of the truth. Fine, but you do all the talking, Deputy Smith."

"Just this once." I didn't like stepping out front and drawing attention to my inexplicable skills. I thought about what to leave unsaid as we hurried through the freezing back hall into the cold great hall. Fortunately the library was warm enough to be comfortable.

The room went dead still when we came in the door, Annalynn a step behind me.

I moved toward the fireplace. "Thanks for your cooperation. To keep us all safe, we need to continue to work together." I glanced at Annalynn, who stayed by the door. She handled public occasions better than I did. She gave me a tiny nod of encouragement. Okay. Run this like a business meeting. "Tara's husband is hiding somewhere behind the orchard. If he hadn't come to harm her, he would have walked to this house or the farmhouse and asked for help,

240

so he's come after Tara, but he's a danger to anyone who gets in his way." I let this sink in. "Fortunately, he doesn't know we realize he's out there."

Achilles came to my side and frowned at my listeners, reinforcing my words.

"Confronting him directly would almost certainly end in bloodshed. We intend to capture him without anyone getting hurt. We'll need your help later. Right now, I'd like for you to finish shoveling as though we have no idea he's in the area. Annalynn will keep watch with the group at the front gate. Achilles and I will guard the group in the circle drive. Oh, be sure to lock your cars when you're done."

Connie frowned.

I added, "Connie and Nancy, I'd like for you to keep watch for Adam Augeri from upstairs windows."

Connie's frown vanished. "Do we ring the bell if we see him?"

That would give my game away. "Unless he's holding a gun, sing 'Winter Wonderland' from the balcony. We'll reserve the bell as a signal to take cover."

"Let's go," Annalynn said. "We have only an hour or so before it gets dark. Junior heard the plows will go through early tomorrow."

Thor led the way, and the others followed.

I pushed through to Connie in the hall. "Augeri's probably in the orchard behind a drift. He may move up to a small shed among the fruit trees." I hustled her into the dining room and said softly, "I need a fake Tara to use as bait tonight."

Connie's eyes sparkled. "We're going to trick him into coming to us."

Clarissa stuck her head in the dining room. "I gave Nancy the binoculars. Here's a pair of opera glasses for you, Connie."

"Come with me, Clarissa," Connie said. "We can brainstorm while I keep watch."

I hurried to the front door with Achilles.

Bernadine waited there. "Are you sure it's safe to go out in the open?"

Never assume safety. "You'll be two seconds from the door."

The air grew colder and colder over the next hour, but I kept warm by playing fetch in the snow with Achilles. As the light dimmed, he went on high alert and led me back to the front door. I couldn't see the snowman, but I whistled "Silver Bells" to clue everyone to go inside.

They hurried into the house flushed from their exercise and the cold, and from the excitement of working while an unseen man with a machete watched.

"Great job, everyone," Annalynn called as her crew came into the great hall. She earned an unexpected high-five from an exuberant Bernadine.

Nancy called from the top of the stairs, "Phoenix, Connie spotted him right before you started back in. She's watching him."

I ran up the stairs.

Connie waited in Jerrald's bedroom, which stood next to the balcony. She said calmly, "I spotted him crawling through the snow a few minutes ago. He moved a few feet and then flattened out. About a minute ago, he settled down behind a big mound of snow. He hasn't moved since."

"That mound must be the shed. Show me."

I looked through the opera glasses while she pointed. I found the mound and lowered the glasses. "He's about two football fields away. From there, he can't see anything in the house but lights and silhouettes."

"Yes, and he won't be able to resist coming closer when it's dark enough to hide him. That's when he'll see Tara in the kitchen. All alone."

Hmm. "That plan may be too obvious."

She pouted in the same annoying way she had in high school. "Why? Because I thought of it?"

"No, because we both thought of it."

She smiled. "Then it's sure to work. I, of course, will star in and direct the production. You will supply the muscle, and Annalynn will give the whole thing class."

The sun slipped down another notch, and I could no longer

distinguish the mound of snow that marked Augeri's hiding place. "Let's find Annalynn and work out the details."

"Clarissa and Nancy will meet us in the music room at five thirty—in five minutes."

I groaned. Every additional amateur we involved multiplied the danger.

"Calm down, Phoenix. It's Clarissa's house, and Nancy feels responsible for Tara. Besides, they both had some really good ideas."

I counted to three and said, "Connie, this isn't an improv. If anything goes wrong, someone could get killed."

Achilles licked my hand.

I scratched behind his ears. "Achilles is particularly vulnerable. He knows nothing about countering a machete."

Connie stroked his back. "Neither do you and Annalynn. You need all the help you can get. Accept that for once."

Arguing with Connie would do nothing but burn crucial energy. "I gladly accept help—as long as it doesn't endanger me or anyone else."

"For Pete's sake, Phoenix, you're the only one who takes risks. The rest of us have too much sense."

Bernadine had walked in while we argued. "I have good night vision. Want me to watch for machete man?"

I figured Augeri wouldn't move closer until later, and Bernadine was gung-ho, so we pointed out where he'd hidden, gave her the binoculars, and went downstairs.

Nancy met us at the bottom of the steps carrying a tray with six steaming glass cups. "I hope you like hot cider. Heather made it from heritage apples in the orchard."

The aroma raised my spirits. Until I thought what a pall two wannabe killers threw over our visit to the beautiful old home.

A semicircle of chairs stood in front of the ceramic stove in the music room. Clarissa, Annalynn, and Thor occupied three of them. I wondered who had invited Thor.

Clarissa held up a red wig in her right hand. "I darkened it a little with a colored hair spray. What do you think? Does it look like Tara's hair?"

I studied it. Through a window from thirty feet, close enough.

Not for Connie and Nancy. They peered at it up close and suggested improvements.

I shed my coat and sat down in the chair closest to the stove with my cider. "The wig is fine as is. What do we have to put it on?"

Connie took the wig from Clarissa. "Me. I'm a little taller than Tara, but I'll take off my shoes." She cocked her head to the right and looked up exactly the way Tara did.

Bloody hell! Connie could get herself killed. "Using a person as bait is too dangerous. He has a pistol. He might decide to shoot you through the window."

"Then I'll stay away from the window when he sneaks up close." Connie walked across the music room with Tara's short, quick steps. "We're not going to fool the abominable snowman with a wig on a mop, Phoenix. We've thought out a three-act sequence and how to stage the whole thing in the dining room and kitchen. It will work." She shook her finger at me. "And you know you can't play Tara nearly as well as I can."

True. Concede her points. If a CIA team were planning this operation with me, I'd at least listen to them. "Give me the gist of your three acts."

Clarissa smiled. "Act one, scene one: Tara is helping prepare dinner in the kitchen. She walks by the side window with her head turned. When our watcher upstairs signals that machete man is moving closer, she stands by the window a moment with the light glinting off her hair."

Nancy clinked her glass cup against her sister's. "Act one, scene two: The group eats in the dining room, and Tara serves us."

"By the end of dinner," Connie said, "we'll know whether it's working, whether he's come close. If he has, we go onto act two. Everybody but Tara—as far as he can see—comes to the music room and sings. Act three: He breaks in the back door. Happy ending for everyone but machete man."

Some huge holes, but not a bad start. "The third act needs a little work."

Annalynn spoke for the first time. "Phoenix and I will rewrite act three. Connie, it's time for you to get into costume and go on stage."

CHAPTER THIRTY-TWO

As soon as Connie, Clarissa, and Nancy left the music room, Thor cleared his throat and said, "I don't quite get your drama in three acts. Obviously I'm here for my brawn rather than my brain. What do you want me to do?"

The last thing I needed was a chivalrous but untrained male in my way when I confronted Augeri, but Thor had shown himself to be reliable and intelligent. "It's critical to know when Augeri comes close. I'm guessing he's eating power bars or a peanut butter sandwich and waiting for complete darkness. Bernadine is watching from Jerrald's room, but we need another set of eyes. I'll bring up some night-vision goggles for one of you to use in the game room. It's easier to communicate from there."

Thor and I went our separate ways. When I reached the game room minutes later, he and Bernadine stood in the dark staring out the windows. I saw no disturbance in the snow with the night goggles and turned them over to Thor. We agreed he or Bernadine would call any urgent alerts down the dumbwaiter shaft.

I went back downstairs.

Annalynn waited for me by the hall fireplace. "What if machete man comes in one of the doors in the back wing instead of the kitchen door?"

I didn't want to face that machete or a pistol in the dark, narrow hall with no room to dodge. "We have to discourage that." He would avoid lights. "We'll leave lanterns on in the wing bedrooms so he'll think those are occupied, that someone could hear him breaking in."

"He'll worry about the same thing at the kitchen door." She bit her lower lip. "Unless he thinks it's unlocked."

"Right. Which means we have to open the door to the porch to show him he can get in."

I could think of only one way to do that. "I'll take Achilles outside to do his business."

"No! He might charge Augeri before you could stop him. Much too risky!" She stood in silence a moment and then thrust a fist into the air, an uncharacteristic gesture. "I know how to do it. Connie must be rubbing off on me. I'll recruit two volunteers."

Bad idea. "No more volunteers!"

She leaned close to say softly, "If we want these people to stick with us, we have to involve them, to give everyone something to do they can brag about later."

That's leadership. I didn't have the patience for it. "Okay. You handle that."

Connie came from Clarissa's bedroom next to the library wearing the red wig. She'd combed it to hide as much of her face as possible. To conceal that she wasn't as lithe as Tara, she'd donned a loose-fitting sky-blue fleece jacket.

I nodded approval. The light-colored jacket contrasted with the dark sweatshirts and jackets everyone else wore. Augeri would be able to track fake Tara's movements by the color of her hair and her jacket. Once he saw the hair and assumed it was Tara, he wouldn't bother to look too closely at her face.

Annalynn walked over to the library and stuck her head in the door. "We want a man in the kitchen with Tara while she and Nancy are fixing sandwiches for dinner. Jerrald, would you mind? Roland, please close the blinds and turn on lanterns in the back bedrooms."

Not waiting to hear what she'd cooked up for Horse, I went through the dining room and opened the pocket doors into the parlor enough to slip through them. I wanted to see for myself whether Adam reacted to a redhead in the kitchen. I chose a window with an unobstructed view of the orchard. As soon as my eyes adjusted to the darkness, I put on my magic sunglasses. Fortunately the snow reflected enough of the sky's light that I could discern the contour of the landscape. I adjusted the glasses' lenses and picked out the garden shed's mound. Ten tense minutes later, a blob popped up above it. I adjusted the glasses again but couldn't distinguish the oval of his head. He must be wearing a hooded coat.

Then the blob disappeared. A much larger blob appeared near the bottom of the mound and began to move toward the house. "He's on his way," I told Achilles. If I hadn't known better, I might have mistaken the figure for a polar bear.

Achilles placed his paws on the windowsill so he could see better. "Quiet!"

The blob moved forward in an awkward crouch, sometimes disappearing behind a drift for a minute or so before pushing forward.

Clarissa spoke through the door. "Phoenix, he's moving toward the house."

"I see him. Tell 'Tara' to prepare to show the colors in about two minutes. I'll signal when."

Clarissa's steps moved across the dining room.

Augeri had reached the edge of the orchard a good thirty yards away. He hunkered down behind a drift and stuck up his head.

"Now! Have her bring something from the kitchen to the dining room."

Connie did her stuff and returned to the kitchen.

No movement. "He's watching. Keep moving around near the windows." I stared at his head as Connie and Nancy set the table.

He popped up, dove over the drift, and scrambled forward.

"He bit! Get away from the windows." As he came closer, I saw that his hands were empty and he wore a small pack on his back.

"Everyone to the table," Annalynn called from the hall. "Show him a lot of people are in the house. We want him to think about the best time and place to catch Tara alone."

I lost sight of Augeri as he lifted his knees high to run toward the only place to hide, the storm cave. Would he go into the cave and endure the generator's noise and fumes? Maybe long enough to warm up a bit. No matter how well he'd prepared for this expedition, he had to be chilled and, mostly likely, afraid of frostbite. Hmm. His hands might be too stiff with cold to hold the pistol he'd bought yesterday morning.

I strolled into the dining room and glanced out the row of windows. I could see nothing but reflections from the lanterns. I propped back the butler's pantry swinging door. With it open, I had a direct view through the kitchen archway to the door leading from the enclosed porch. The kitchen extended approximately sixteen feet from the original house. Augeri would be no more than fifteen feet away from me when he stepped into the kitchen. Too close for comfort.

If we didn't scare him into dropping whatever weapon he held, I'd have to shoot to kill. Why risk serious injury? Why not go upstairs, aim through a window, and take him out? All my training and experience told me to do just that. But I didn't live in that world anymore. And I didn't want to. I stepped into the butler's pantry to make sure the dumbwaiter door was open.

The scuffing of chairs at the dining room table stopped. I took a seat where I could see the back door. Three people were missing: Thor, Bernadine, and the documentarian. All three must be upstairs watching Augeri.

Nancy said a short blessing.

Connie/Tara brought in platters of hot sliced ham and turkey. In a moment she was back with a plate of cheeses and a basket of sourdough bread.

Annalynn said, "Thank you for your help, everyone. Please talk about something pleasant and give the appearance of normal dinner conversation."

Horse raised a wine glass. "Here's to Archer, the man who changed my life." He waited while glasses clinked. "Without Archer, I'd never taken my company national. Back in the eighties, I was a software pioneer way outside the tech centers. Archer was running Candon Enterprises, the biggest client for my new-fangled proprietary business-management software. I reached one of those turning points Phoenix here would know about. I had to expand overnight or lose out to well-financed competitors. The banks and venture capitalists turned down this nobody from Missouri. Archer bankrolled me out of his own pocket." He lifted his glass again. "That's the kind of debt you can't repay."

I glanced at Annalynn to see if she realized Horse was justifying the money he'd given Archer off the books over the years. She had on her inscrutable public face. No one exclaimed or commented.

Horse directed his gaze at me. "Molly, for one, thought I was a little careless about following the rules. Archer earned every penny I ever gave him, and I'm damned well not sorry I played by Missouri rules instead of the federal ones."

Clarissa patted her mouth with her napkin and remained silent.

Roland said, "Archer didn't take Molly's nagging seriously." He passed the bread to Jerrald. "She's terrible at numbers. She had trouble balancing the books every single month. All anyone has to do is input the right numbers to the spreadsheet."

His use of the word "nagging" irritated me. Men used that term to dismiss women's factual criticism.

Quick steps sounded on the stairs. "Phoenix!" Bernadine rushed in. "That man's trying to get in the wing's side door."

"Bloody hell!" If he came in there, he'd probably force me to shoot him to protect Achilles and myself. I ran into the great hall and, Glock in hand, eased open the door to the wing. I couldn't hear anything.

Achilles stood by me on alert.

"Quiet, boy." I turned on my flashlight. No one in the hall. "Bernadine, don't let anyone come after me."

I ran down the dark hall on tiptoe with Achilles at my side and listened at the door to the former porch. I could hear sounds of metal on metal at the outside door. Scare him off. I opened the door to the bathroom and flushed the toilet. The plumbing rewarded me with a loud cascade of water. I listened and heard faint sounds of footsteps crunching through the snow.

Achilles licked my hand.

A few seconds later, Bernadine called softly, "He's running to his hiding place."

I hurried back to the great hall. "Thanks, Bernadine. He'll probably stay hidden a little while." It occurred to me the volunteers upstairs were hungry. "I'll ask Connie to send up some food for you."

"Thanks. We're starving." She ran up the steps.

I went to the pantry door and asked Connie to fix sandwiches before taking my seat at the table again. Tension had curbed my hunger, but I placed some ham, cheese, and lettuce on a slice of bread. If I didn't eat now, I'd regret it during the stakeout.

Thor came in and took an empty chair. "We don't need three people upstairs. Phoenix, I saw the handle of the machete sticking out of a backpack. I suggest we scare him off and let the police run him down tomorrow."

Tempting. I had to knock down the idea fast. "I am the police, and I came here to protect that young woman. Leaving him free tonight might well result in his harming her or someone else trying to reach her."

"Phoenix is right," Annalynn said. "Our plan is working. We'll play it out. Jerrald, what's your position on raising the state's cigarette tax to increase funding for schools or roads or healthcare?"

Politicians never tired of that topic. I tuned it out to think. Augeri couldn't see in the kitchen from where he was. We'd established that Tara was the servant. He'd expect her to be in the kitchen alone after dinner. He'd probably try for another look, a closer one, when the dining room lanterns went out. We had to know when he made that move. "Excuse me. I need to get another glass of water." I strolled into the pantry, went to the dumbwaiter, and called, "Bernadine!"

A moment later: "Yes?"

"Let us know when he moves over to look in the kitchen window again."

"Right."

Connie had come up behind me. "I'll stay here and listen for her

251

signal. Then a quick show of red at the kitchen windows and out of sight in the pantry."

"You got it." I added, "To make sure he doesn't get a good look at you, flip off that generator-powered kitchen light and use only a lantern."

My tablemates had moved on to ways to lower student debt by the time Bernadine sent down the word that Augeri had moved to take a closer peek.

I stood up as soon as Connie finished her quick parade in front of the windows. "Tara, Annalynn, and I will clear the table. The rest of you go into the music room and sing loudly enough to be heard outside."

They all filed out, and Annalynn and I stacked dishes.

Thor came into the dining room carrying a stick of firewood at his side. "I don't sing. I'll stay by the dumbwaiter to pass on messages." He raised his stick slightly. "And provide backup."

He'd also provide a credible witness if I had to shoot. "Thanks, but stay back out of the way. Annalynn and I are wearing bullet-proof vests. You aren't."

We completed a normal cleanup, with Annalynn and I going back and forth past the windows and fake Tara cleaning off the worktable. At the front of the house in the music room, the others belted out "Jingle Bells."

I had a moment of panic. Augeri would stay away if he realized Achilles was right here. "No singing, Achilles. No singing."

He stayed with me as I turned off all the lanterns except the one on the china cabinet on the parlor wall. I intended for Augeri to see little more than my silhouette when I confronted him. I stood in the doorframe, and Connie approved my backlighting.

"I'll duck down behind the worktable," Annalynn said. "The pans and appliances on the shelves underneath it will hide me."

I hesitated a moment and then nodded. The table would be about six feet to Augeri's left as he came in. She'd be closer to him than I liked, but out of the line of fire.

From his place by the dumbwaiter, Thor said softly, "He's behind the cave. Bernadine thinks he's resting."

And getting cold. Time to pull the fly into our parlor. "Annalynn, you said you have a way to convince him to come in the back door."

"Yes, and please don't argue, Phoenix. Horse and Roland volunteered to go outside to smoke after-dinner cigars." She left.

Ironic. All of my suspects had stepped forward to help trap another wannabe killer. I evaluated the risk. The entrepreneur and the political hack would be vulnerable, but Augeri wouldn't attack two men and announce his presence. I unlocked the kitchen door.

Horse and Roland walked into the kitchen with their coats on as the three remaining singers began "Joy to the World."

I handed Horse the key to the porch door. "He needs to hear you coming."

"Clarissa already coached us," he said. "I think you crazy women are enjoying this."

This one wasn't.

Annalynn and I reviewed our plan for Augeri's entrance while we waited for the smokers to return. We turned off all the kitchen's generator-powered lights and left a lantern on a cabinet by the porch door. I'd have a much better view of Augeri than he'd have of me.

Roland came inside first. His teeth were chattering from cold or fear, or both.

Horse boomed out, "Thanks for cleaning up, Tara. Goodnight."

Connie grabbed the door before he could close it. "And Tara, could you please bring in the coffee cups and glasses from the library and turn on the dishwasher?" She gave Horse a little shove, closed the door, and whispered, "I'm staying, Phoenix. I have a weapon." She darted to the worktable, reached down to the top shelf under it, and pulled out a sword almost a yard long.

Scheisse! Another stage prop. "Get the hell out of here!"

"Let her stay," Annalynn said. She racked her Glock and crouched in her designated spot beside the worktable. Achilles joined her. They were barely visible in the table's shadow. I let him stay by her. He would be safer attacking from the side than from the front.

Thor said, "He's moving toward the porch door."

Connie emptied a bowl of potato chips on the floor two feet in front of the door and ducked down behind the far end of the worktable.

No time to argue. Glock in hand, I stepped back into the pantry away from the arch and whispered. "I'll give him time to get all the way into the room."

Complete silence. "Frosty the Snowman" sounded from the music room. I breathed deeply three times and visualized the sinister snowman holding a pistol in his right hand and a machete in his left. Wrong. He'd thrown the ball with his left hand. He'd use that hand to hold his new pistol.

A faint sound from the porch. Silence. A footstep in the dining room. Ignore that. The kitchen door latch clicked. Silence. A potato chip crunched.

I spun into the doorway with the Glock ready to fire. "Police. Hands on your head!"

A bright light from behind me lit up a bulky gray ninja menacing me with a machete held in both hands.

Achilles leapt out of the darkness and closed his teeth over Augeri's left wrist.

He screamed but held onto the machete.

Connie poked her sword into his back. "Drop it or I'll cut off your head."

Annalynn swung the popcorn popper down over the machete, knocking it out of his hands and out of his reach. "On the floor, Augeri."

He dropped to his knees. "I came to see my wife." He struck out at Achilles, clamped on his left arm, with his right fist.

Annalynn hit machete man on his hooded head with the popper, sending him flat on his face. "Back, Achilles. Watch."

Augeri recovered enough to yell, "Tara! Tara! I love you. Tara, help me!"

I planted my right foot on his left hand and, ignoring his anguished protest, reached over to his coat pocket. No pistol. "He's got the pistol on him." I ground my left heel into his other hand and said over his screams. "Where is it, Augeri?"

"Tucked into my belt," he yelped. "In the back."

Annalynn pulled up the tail of his coat and extracted the pistol. She put it on the far end of the worktable and frisked him for other weapons. She found none. "We're ready for the duct tape, Jerrald."

A round of applause came from the dining room.

Bernadine said breathily, "Did you get it all on film?"

"Every second," the documentarian said. "A good thing. Nobody would believe it otherwise."

CHAPTER THIRTY-THREE

Five minutes later Jerrald had wrapped Augeri in enough duct tape to hold a wrecked racecar together. With no advice sought from me, the men decided to leave Augeri, now sullen and silent, in the great hall by the fire until the police arrived.

That could take a while. Neither Clarissa's landlines nor our mobiles worked. Even so, the group remained exuberant. The singers returned to the music room to sing more carols. Thor, holding his stick of firewood, stood in the door to keep an eye on the prisoner.

I couldn't share their elation. We still had a killer loose in the house. And I hadn't fed Achilles anything except treats for hours. Grabbing a lantern and the garbage bag containing the machete and the pistol, I went into the wing with Achilles. The temperature in the hall had dropped to the upper thirties, I guessed, and the bunkhouse felt even colder. I didn't dare turn on the propane heater, so I put on my parka. Then I prepared a generous dinner for my hero.

"Sorry, boy. I should have fed you earlier. As soon as you finish, we'll go give Tara the good news." To keep moving while he ate, I folded the blanket that Molly had pulled up over her bunk. I decided to strip the bed and lifted the pillow to remove the white slip. Even by the lantern's dim light, I couldn't miss the pieces of yellow paper. Molly's notes. She'd removed them from the folder and forgotten doing it in the excitement.

I put the lantern down beside me on the bunk and peered at the top page. It was labeled Bernadine. I skimmed a mix of sentence fragments and dates. They summarized what Bernadine had hired Roland to do for her. Four other names at the bottom meant nothing to me. Were these other local politicians Molly suspected Roland was working for? She had underlined *moonlighting in violation of contract.* No big deal, at least from Bernadine's point of view.

Annalynn came in the door. "What are you studying? Oh, good! You found the notes!"

"Just now." I handed her the page. "Do you recognize the names?"

She shone her flashlight on them. "Two of them are reaching their term limit in the state House and planning to run for the state Senate. Or maybe they'll join the crowd running for Archer's vacant seat."

"So they're candidates for something. Molly was tracking Roland's moonlighting as a political consultant. Did she tell you anything new this afternoon?"

"Nothing useful, or at least I didn't think it was. She said she'd pulled together figures from several places and the totals didn't make sense to her. She intended to turn over the whole problem— whatever's in those notes—to Archer. That's why she agreed to take him to the afternoon coffees without Clarissa."

Hmm. Those figures endangered someone. "What did he tell her?"

"Nothing. He'd done fine greeting people at the events, but he couldn't absorb what she told him. He did say, several times, the vote on the agricultural bill would be his last one. That's one more verification he didn't intend to kill himself."

Or that he could still think well enough to lay the groundwork for concealing a suicide. Even though the caffeine in his system could have precipitated the crash, the fact that he'd chosen to drive kept me from eliminating suicide as a possibility.

Annalynn handed the sheet back to me and put on her coat. "You read numbers like poets read poetry. Maybe you can see what she missed."

I turned to the next page, labeled "Roland's Moonlighting." It had a list of campaign functions and dollar signs with question marks. Molly must have thought Bernadine could supply the amounts. His moonlighting constituted grounds for dismissal, but not a motivation for murder for him or Bernadine.

Next came a spreadsheet labeled "Roland's Solicitations." It showed roughly twenty-five cash and in-kind contributions from special interests over this calendar year. Molly had circled nine numbers, four of them contributions of $3,000 to $5,000 from Horse. The other five, in similar amounts, came from different sources, none of which I recognized. The largest number on the spreadsheet was $12,000 for financing a discussion group at a Lake of the Ozarks resort last April. I ran my finger down the page and came up with $49,400. No big bucks here.

I handed the page to Annalynn. "Molly will have to explain this. Or do the names give you any ideas?"

She sat down on the other side of the lantern. "Not at first glance. Give me a minute."

The next sheet, unlabeled, covered the previous calendar year. It contained more entries but showed contributions from many of the same donors. Molly had circled the amounts from the same contributors. All were several thousand dollars higher last year than this year. I leaned over to compare the two sheets. "Roland solicited roughly $27,000 less this year. That may prove he's incompetent, but it doesn't indicate he's a killer." I handed my page to Annalynn.

"Last year was an election year. People would have given more, but I would have expected most of this money to have gone to PACs." She studied the pages side by side. "These are regular contributors, but amounts go up and down according to what they're lobbying for. Some contributions, like that resort junket, probably bought long-term goodwill. After all, most companies write off lobbying costs as business expenses. Anything else?"

I peered at the last sheet. "A spreadsheet labeled 'Questions.' Let's hope it tells us more than the others do." This one duplicated the names on "Roland's Solicitations," but the amounts on Horse's and three others' circled entries were higher. I did some quick arithmetic. "This spreadsheet shows $18,000 more in contributions,

$7,000 of them from Horse, for this calendar year. Why don't these two sets of figures match?"

Annalynn sucked in her breath. "That's what Molly planned to ask Roland and then Horse. What's the answer?"

"No way to know without checking bank records." I'd seen many mismatched sets of numbers over the last thirty years.

Annalynn sprang up, pressing her fingers against her forehead. "Either Horse or Roland could have poisoned the coffee or shot the mannequin. Would either one of them kill for a few thousand dollars?"

Many people killed for less than that. I thought it through. "The logical assumption is that Roland reported less than the four 'special constituents' gave him. We know Horse often used cash. I doubt anyone else handed over bundles of hundreds, but Roland could have conned the other three into writing checks to him, deposited those to his account, and written checks or taken in cash for lesser amounts. Once you start looking for discrepancies, it's easy for banks to trace."

"Could he really get by with that?"

"For a while. He probably skimmed off a few hundred here, a thousand there—amounts he could claim were numerical typos. Then one or more contributors, Horse for sure, complained Molly had the wrong figures. Roland either knew or guessed she was going to tell Archer. And he knew she was going to talk to Horse and Bernadine this morning."

"Yes, Molly was determined to talk to all three before accusing anyone." Annalynn shook her finger at me. "Before you condemn her for not reporting the problem to the police, remember that no congressional office wants a financial scandal involving their own staff."

"Roland certainly knew that, and he probably counted on paying the money back—or getting his father to do it—if someone discovered the theft. Stealing from an employer sometimes starts with 'borrowing' to meet a personal emergency. If it goes undiscovered, the thief takes more—like a kid taking candy from an unguarded candy bowl."

Connie burst through the door. "Avast, me hearties!" She pointed her pirate sword at the yellow pages. "Oh, heck. You've already figured out who done it. My bet is on Bernadine. Poison is a woman's weapon."

"You lose," Annalynn said. "It looks like Roland skimmed money from contributors. The missing money meant much more to him than to Horse."

Yes, the wealthy steal much bigger amounts. I tossed the sheets down on the bed. "These numbers don't prove anything. To get court orders or whatever prosecutors use to gather evidence, we need more than a strong hunch."

Connie tapped her foot. "Why can't we just ask the contributors how much they gave?"

Annalynn answered: "Because they gave at least some of it under the table. That may be why Molly didn't tell us what was going on."

Proving the theft at a trial didn't worry me. To protect ourselves tonight and Molly in the coming days, we had to establish that Roland—or Horse—had attempted murder and arrest him. How to do that? Connie's sword inspired me. "The play's the thing in which we'll—whatever Shakespeare said. If we're right about Roland, he thinks Molly is dead. Let's spring her on him and scare a public confession out of him."

Connie looked at me openmouthed. "Oh, Phoenix, nobody believes in ghosts anymore."

Wrong, but I didn't argue the point. "Forget the ghost. We set the stage for Molly to walk in and surprise everyone—and shock Roland." Hedging my bets, I added, "Or Horse."

Connie beamed. "The second bill of a double feature."

Annalynn smiled. "And with the whole scene on tape. I'm game, but Connie, please put down that sword before you cut someone."

We huddled in our coats for ten minutes working out a simple staging of Molly's dramatic entrance. Then Connie left to initiate the first step: encouraging everyone to risk Clarissa's disapproval and imbibe freely.

Annalynn and I bundled up and walked briskly toward the

farmhouse. A hard crust had formed on the snow, making our progress noisy. Achilles loped around us atop the snow, not at all bothered by an occasional slide or drop into deep snow. We didn't need the flashlight. The sky had cleared, and a lone star blinked an invitation for others to come out to enjoy the winter wonderland. The night's beauty lifted my spirits much as Mozart's music did. And this snow, unlike in a city or even Laycock, wouldn't turn a dirty gray tomorrow morning.

Annalynn stopped. "Look! The lights just came on outside the farmhouse." She glanced over her shoulder. "And in Four Chimneys. Thank God the heat will be on tonight."

"Yes, but no way Molly can suddenly emerge ghostlike from the darkness."

The collies started to bark, and Achilles responded, almost drowning out our calls identifying ourselves.

Junior opened the door with the rifle in his hand. "You got that maniac?"

"Yes," Annalynn said. "The charges will be assault with a deadly weapon and breaking and entering."

The collies darted outside as Junior opened the door wide for us. He ushered us into the kitchen.

Tara, eyes enormous, put down a mug of hot cider. "Did you shoot him?"

"No," I said, not sure what answer she wanted. "Annalynn disarmed him with a popcorn popper." People would joke about our using a sword and an antique popper as weapons, but the alternative had been multiple bullets. At least no one would suspect a former CIA operative had participated in the capture.

"We'll give you details later," Annalynn said. "How's Molly feeling?"

"Much better." Molly, dressed in the winter sweats uniform, walked in from the hall. She wore her red lipstick and her smile. "Can you tell from my notes who tried to kill me?"

Although ninety-five percent certain Roland was guilty, I hesitated to commit myself. After all, Molly knew facts and personalities I didn't.

I hedged, hoping to draw her out. "Those figures offer no evidence of attempted murder. They do hint at a diversion of contributions." I waited a moment, but she clamped her lips shut, still unwilling to voice an accusation. I needed at least a confirmation. I resorted to corporate speak. "It seems probable that Roland was, in effect, embezzling funds. The situation requires an investigation to ascertain whether he was reporting all of the monies funneled through him."

Tara tilted her head and looked up at me. "You mean that man who wears the fancy flag pin is a thief?"

Instead of answering, I said, "Well, Molly? Is Roland a thief?"

She licked her lips. "I'm afraid he is, but I can't prove anything, so you can't arrest him."

Annalynn patted Molly on her shoulder. "We have a plan."

I explained it to her. She wanted to think about it overnight, to wait until Captain Sam Gist arrived. I knew he would never go along. Besides, delay endangered us. I signaled to Annalynn to take over. Heather chimed in, too, but the Missouri mule wouldn't budge.

Persuasion be damned. I grabbed a coat on a peg in the foyer and held it for Molly. "This can't wait. Put on the coat or I'll drag you across the snow without one."

Annalynn walked to the door and opened it. "Please."

Molly put her arm in a sleeve. "I have to put on my boots."

Heather threw her arms in the air. "Hallelujah! Don't go without us. I'm not missing this."

Only Tara wavered, but her fear of staying alone proved stronger than her dread of seeing her husband. She stayed at Heather's elbow as we walked toward Four Chimneys' back wing, the Candon men leading the parade and stomping down the snow to make sure Molly had an easy path to follow.

From the end of the line, I kept an eye on the windows, all bright with light. If someone saw Molly coming, we'd lose the element of surprise. No one moved at a window. All were partying, I hoped.

Junior went in first to shut off the alarm and make sure no one was in the wing hall. We shed our coats in the bunkhouse and waited there for Annalynn to go into the main house and gather everyone into the library.

I took off Achilles' black winter coat but left on his bulletproof vest. When he whined a protest, I knelt beside him and whispered, "Danger. Stay alert. Alert."

He growled deep in his throat. He understood danger and alert.

When the curtain came down tonight, I'd have to calm him by letting him sing.

Nancy opened the door. "Everyone's in the library, Phoenix."

I was on, and I'd better be good. The Candons hurried down the hall with me with Tara hidden among them while Nancy and Molly trailed behind. They would wait in Clarissa's bedroom for five minutes and then creep into the hall to listen for Molly's cue.

Heather and Tara went to sit in the back of the library. Pete stood in the back corner by the family history shelf, and Junior leaned against the wall by the door. Achilles and I joined Annalynn, who was standing in front of the fireplace.

Her face and voice calm, Annalynn said, "Phoenix will give you instructions on writing your witness statements so you won't be delayed tomorrow." Annalynn took a chair to my right with a clear view of all three suspects. Bernadine and Horse sat directly in front of me on a loveseat and Roland to my left in a wingchair.

The documentarian, grinning like the Cheshire cat, waved at me from a kitchen stool against the wall to my right. He would have a good angle for capturing reactions to Molly's entrance. He lifted his camera.

Achilles growled and bared his teeth.

That expressed my sentiments, but I'd committed myself to playing the scene on camera. "It's okay, boy." I stroked his head. "Before I talk about the statements, I have some bad news. You have the right to hear it before you see it in the press." Same tense reaction from everyone. "At dinner last night, I told you Archer ran off the road as a reaction to drinking coffee from Molly's thermos. What I didn't tell you was this: The coffee contained a large dose of caffeine powder that almost killed Molly."

Gasps all around.

Roland's hand shot up. "Are you telling us machete man poisoned Molly's coffee?"

Well played, advance man. Set up someone else.

Horse snorted. "How in hell could that kid put poison in Molly's thermos?"

"Somebody did," Jerrald said. "Everybody knew about her coffee. Even me." His mouth snapped shut as he realized what he'd said.

I raised my hand for silence. "I suspected Adam Augeri initially, especially when I found out he didn't have an alibi. Captain Gist has been investigating him." Intense attention. No fear evident. "The coffee remaining in the thermos has gone to a special Drug Enforcement Administration lab for testing." Now to bluff. "Powdered caffeine processed by each manufacturer leaves a marker. Today the DEA matched that marker to its source. Tomorrow the computers will identify possible vendors. We'll identify the buyer within days."

Exhalations of relief. Except from Roland. He rubbed the bridge of his nose with his left hand, obscuring my view of his face.

Thor raised his hand. "You said you suspected machete man *initially.* Do still suspect him?"

"No." I brushed back a strand of hair to signal Connie to call Molly. "Shall I tell them, Annalynn?"

With all eyes on Annalynn, Connie crept to the closed door and opened it an inch before edging away to stand by Junior.

Annalynn said, "I trust your judgment, Phoenix."

"This goes against police procedure," I said, "but you need to know." I heard movement in the hall. "Have you wondered why Molly didn't keep her appointments this morning? Why she hasn't been seen all day?"

Their reactions indicated they were wondering now.

Roland shifted in his chair and said earnestly, "She felt real bad last night about her coffee causing Archer's accident. I thought she— uhh, she just couldn't face us—uhh, couldn't face herself."

His skill as a liar removed any doubts of his guilt. I shifted my right hand to my Glock.

Molly opened the door. She smiled. "On the contrary, Roland. I've come to face the man who shot me."

His mouth flew open, his body went slack, and he slid from his chair onto the floor.

"Sit! Quiet!" I ordered as several people moved to help him.

Annalynn backed me up by standing beside me, holding up both hands, and motioning them to stay back.

I'd anticipated Roland's blurting something that revealed his guilt or trying to run or to bluster his way out of Molly's accusations. It hadn't occurred to me he'd pass out. Or have a heart attack? I knelt and felt his pulse. Fast but strong. He'd fainted. I needed for him to say something revelatory, but I didn't dare interrogate him in a way that would violate his Miranda rights, whatever they were. Time to improvise.

When he groaned, I motioned Molly and Nancy to sit down in the back of the room. Kneeling beside him, I cradled his left hand. In my sweetest tone, I said, "Are you okay, Roland?"

Face drained of blood, he looked up at me and blinked. Panic moved across his face, and he covered his trembling lips with his free hand.

"Don't try to get up. Relax. Take deep breaths."

He jerked away from me and pushed himself up to stare at the door, now closed. He collapsed onto the floor again. "I—I—what happened?"

"You passed out. Right after you said you shot Molly with the antique revolver."

He closed his eyes and his Adam's apple bobbed. "I couldn't have shot her. She was in a locked room."

Don't argue. Keep the voice soothing. "Crawling through the wardrobe with that hair-trigger pistol in your hand was daring. You could have shot yourself."

"I knew how to handle it." His voice held pride. His eyes remained closed. "I fired a revolver just like it at the re-enactment of the Battle of Lexington."

Go for the kill. I smiled to soften my tone. "I'm surprised you missed her at such short range."

"I didn't miss!" He opened his eyes, came back to reality, and rolled away from me. "I meant to say I didn't shoot her. You're tricking a sick man." He staggered to his feet.

Achilles growled and advanced on Roland with bared teeth, backing him against the wall.

"Jerrald," Annalynn said, "we're ready for the duct tape."

"Fantastic," the documentarian said. "That True/False Festival in Columbia won't turn this one down."

Bloody hell! I'd never be able to go undercover again without a full disguise.

CHAPTER THIRTY-FOUR

As soon as Roland was trussed up, I sneaked into the parlor to try my cell phone again. After a long time searching, it connected. I had sixteen messages, the first two and the last ten from Stuart. His final three were one-word text messages: "URGENT." Vernon had left three voice messages and Captain Gist one. I dialed the one person I was sure would answer and act: Stuart.

"Phoenix! I've been worried sick. Are you okay?"

"We're fine, but we're still snowed in. What's urgent?"

"A message from Captain Gist. Augeri disappeared early this morning."

Scheisse! Gist knew machete man might head this way but failed to stop him. "We caught Augeri and the man who tried to kill Molly." My phone went dead. I'd used it on mountains and in valleys on three continents. Why didn't it work in rolling hills in Missouri? I'd almost given up when the phone found service again. Fearing the connection wouldn't last, I rang Stuart's cell. Speaking fast, I said, "Tell Gist to come pick up two would-be killers. Then call Vernon and tell him Roland Renmar embezzled and tried to kill Molly to cover it up."

"That makes sense. Vernon's AP friend tracked the suicide leak to the same man."

Of course. "Has AP released the source of the leak yet?"

No answer. The phone had gone dead again. Oh, well. Stuart would call Gist and Vernon.

"Phoenix," Connie called from the hall, "we're all meeting in the library."

I thought of ignoring her, but no one could deny hearing Connie when she used her stage voice. "I'm coming." I put my phone away and went into the hall to cast an evil eye on the prisoners before going to the library. I stayed at the door to make sure the two didn't help each other loosen the tapes.

Clarissa stood in front of the fireplace. She smiled at me. "First, I want to thank Phoenix for her courage and her commitment in finding out who caused my husband's death. She came here to protect Molly and Tara and all of us, people she didn't even know six days ago. I thank God for her presence and pray He will continue to bless her marvelous work with the foundation."

First time anyone wished a blessing on my work. I bowed to the round of applause.

Clarissa closed her eyes and lowered her head for a moment. She took a deep breath and said in a firm voice, "I went ahead with this meeting out of a sense of obligation to Archer and his supporters. I didn't intend to name my candidate to succeed him, but I can't imagine anyone more qualified and more electable than Annalynn Carr Keyser. When she has established her campaign committee, I will authorize the transfer of the surplus funds from Archer's last campaign to that committee."

Annalynn rose to thank Clarissa, and Horse stepped up to congratulate both of them. Then so did everyone else, even Bernadine. I guessed she expected to get a lot of mileage out of taking part in Augeri's capture. I feared she would insist on campaigning for Annalynn as a way of introducing herself to voters.

I glanced at my watch. Not quite nine. With luck, Gist would commandeer a snowplow and arrive before I had to set up a guard system for the night.

Thor came over to me. "What about our statements?"

I'd used instructing them on writing statements as an excuse to set up Molly's entrance, but having those ready would save time for everyone. "Thank you for reminding me."

He clapped for attention. "Listen to Phoenix, please."

I had only my own experience in writing statements to guide me. "Write two statements, please, one about Adam Augeri breaking in and one about Roland's reactions when he saw Molly. Facts only, no feelings. Save your emotions and impressions for social media and speeches."

Bernadine and Jerrald both brightened at my last suggestion.

"Please give them to me or Annalynn before you go to bed."

Clarissa went to Archer's office and returned with paper and pens for everyone. Soon they were all scribbling like a bunch of students taking an essay exam. I pulled a chair from the library into the hall so I could watch the prisoners and wrote my own accounts on a laptop that Clarissa provided.

One by one the witnesses turned in their papers.

As Connie handed in her *magnum opus,* I remembered my promise to Achilles that he could sing. "Would you mind doing a number with Achilles? Singing will relax him."

"Sure. Any requests?"

"Something short." I figured even "Mary Had a Little Lamb" would be long enough to encourage the houseguests to stop chatting about what they'd done to capture both men and hurry to their rooms. Their accounts were soon going to be less accurate than fish stories.

Connie chose one of Achilles' favorites: "If I Loved You."

The houseguests opted for bed almost immediately. Roland complained of being tortured by sound and cold. Thor spread blankets over him and Augeri before escaping the duet.

When Connie and Achilles finished on long-held high notes that made me shudder, she came back into the hall and said solemnly, "We dedicated that to Stuart."

With the house quiet, I finished writing my report, including a reminder to look for a towel and clothing with black powder on them. Exhausted, I didn't object when Thor and Annalynn came to relieve me. On my way to the wing, I stopped off at Archer's office to print out my report. The phone jingled. When I picked it up, I heard a dial tone.

Opening the Internet connection on Clarissa's laptop, I emailed a copy of my report to Gist, Stuart, and myself. After debating a moment, I sent a copy to Vernon with my usual off-the-record warning. I didn't want the annoying documentarian to scoop the dedicated newspaperman.

I heard a vehicle approaching and rushed into the great hall.

Annalynn came in from the vestibule. "It's not Captain Gist. It's a sheriff's department pickup with a snowplow. The county should take both prisoners, but it may have jurisdiction only over Augeri. Roland's offenses took place in multiple jurisdictions. It will go more smoothly if I talk to the deputies as a former sheriff. Go on to bed, Phoenix. It's too late for us to leave tonight."

I gladly left the turnover to her. Within minutes, I slept the sleep of the self-satisfied.

Annalynn woke me the next morning. "Phoenix, get up. I've already taken Achilles out."

Connie yawned. "It's barely light. What's the hurry?"

Annalynn began to strip her bunk. "It's almost seven thirty. I need to get back to Laycock before noon, and Phoenix always has work to do."

Connie and I exchanged raised eyebrows. Why was Annalynn in such a rush?

She tugged the sheet off her thin mattress. "I'll feed Achilles while you use the bathroom, Phoenix. Oh, Clarissa wants to talk to you privately before we leave."

Connie sat up. "To Phoenix or to me?"

Annalynn, her back to Connie, rolled her eyes. "To both of you, I'm sure, but separately."

I dawdled with my morning ablutions in hopes of provoking Annalynn into revealing what had her so hyper. Neither Connie nor I got anything out of her as she packed her bag and left to take it to the front door.

A little after eight, I ambled into the dining room. Everyone but the documentarian was there eating pancakes.

Clarissa motioned me to a chair. "Sam—Captain Gist—got here an hour ago. He's at the farmhouse talking to Molly. He said you're not to leave until he can talk to you."

Bernadine, beaming at me as though we were best buds, said, "A CSI officer is in Roland's room now. Do you have the key to the bedroom with the dead mannequin?"

I handed the key to Clarissa and helped myself to pancakes, bacon, and coffee.

Two and a half hours later, I was glad I'd fortified myself. Gist, looking even leaner and meaner than usual, had taken me into the library to demand a detailed oral account of events, ask unnecessary questions about my written report on the attempts on Molly's life, and lecture me on my violations of standard police procedures.

Finally a new tension in his voice and his posture told me that he'd come to the real point of the prolonged interrogation. "You know, Phoenix, the prosecutor will ask whether Roland Renmar should be charged with contributing to Archer Candon's death. What's your recommendation?"

Nothing to do with me. I didn't know the fine points of the law. I shrugged.

Gist raised his voice. "You spotted the possibility of foul play immediately. Is that because you were there to prove or disprove a suicide?"

We hadn't discussed the possibility of suicide. "I wasn't there to prove anything. I analyzed what I found. What makes you think it was suicide?" I waited as he frowned and looked away. Goad him. "One thing my observation told me: Archer Candon was driving much too fast for a man with poor night vision, slowed reflexes, and encroaching dementia."

Gist slumped in his chair and stared at the floor. "I know. I expected to drive him to Laycock, not escort him. He insisted on taking Molly's car, and he told me to 'put the pedal to the metal.'" The captain straightened and faced me. "When I heard the suicide rumor on the news, I thought, 'My God, did the old man outfox me? Did he plan to die on that road?' What's your analysis?"

I analyzed the family members. They didn't want the death to be a suicide, and no one could prove it had been. "Neither of us found physical evidence he crashed the car on purpose. The medical examiner can't say whether the coffee caused him to veer off the road. It would be easy to argue reasonable doubt on negligent homicide or whatever. I'm willing to forget what you just told me if you are."

He took a deep breath and extended his hand. "It's forgotten. Thanks for your help, Deputy Smith." He stood up and adjusted his holster. "Tell Annalynn she's got my vote."

The moment he opened the library door, Clarissa hurried from the dining room. "Sam, a news channel is running 'the exclusive true story' of Archer's death at eleven. With taped coverage from here."

Gist went heart-attack red. "Those deputies should never have let that guy leave here without confiscating the footage as evidence. I'll put a stop to this." He strode from the room.

Clarissa came in, closed the door behind her, and motioned me to a seat. "He's too late for that. I'm glad the truth will come out. Besides, the publicity will be wonderful for Annalynn's campaign." Clarissa sat down opposite me. "I'd like just a moment of your time. Nancy told me a bit about your—umm—romantic situation. I don't want to interfere, but my personal experience may give you a new perspective."

Good grief! Was this virtual stranger following my soap opera, too? With Annalynn's interests in mind, I mumbled, "Experience is the best teacher."

Clarissa twisted her wedding ring around her finger with her thumb. "I was in my forties, single, and satisfied with my life when Archer and I met at a concert. His wife had died, and he was terribly lonely. I realized he was serious when he invited me to a family picnic here." She grimaced. "It was a terrible day. No one welcomed me, and his mother and two of his sons—not Junior—were openly hostile. The next time Archer called, I told him I was busy." She cleared her throat and stared into the fire. "He called and called until he wore me down. The first time he proposed, I said no. I loved him, but I didn't relish dealing with his family. His mother died shortly after that. The sons still resented me, but I decided Archer was worth the aggravation."

Gott im Himmel! Was she comparing Archer's grown sons to Stuart's teenagers?

She met my eyes and smiled. "It took a while for them to realize I was good for him." She leaned forward. "Here's the important part. The little ones accepted me from the beginning. One of my great joys has been Archer's grandchildren—*my* grandchildren."

"Pete certainly adores you." Kaysi and Zeke wouldn't be producing cuddly little playmates for Achilles for years. "Thank you for sharing that."

Clarissa patted my hand. "You have a great advantage. His mother wants you in the family." She stood up. "Annalynn is anxious to leave. She drove the SUV to the front door and loaded your things. She's packing a lunch so you won't have to stop on the way home."

I'd barely recovered from Clarissa's lecture when Annalynn stuck her head in the door. "What were you and Clarissa talking about?"

"Delayed gratification."

"The others left in a convoy ages ago. Are you ready?"

She'd ignored my clever reply to her question. Very unlike Annalynn. "Don't you want to see that newscast first?"

"No, it will play over and over. We can watch it in Laycock." She studied her fingernails. "I have an important appointment early this afternoon."

She reminded me of an insecure teenager. This must have something to do with that coy phone call on the way up. I joined her in the great hall. "Where are our passengers?"

"A trooper took Molly home, and Tara is staying here. Clarissa went to call Connie and Nancy from the barn. They're measuring it to see if they can turn it into a summer theater."

Connie, the sisters, and Achilles came in from the back wing, all wearing their coats and boots.

273

Annalynn, not one for hugging, held out her hand to Clarissa. "Thank you so much for your support. And do call me if you want to talk. The first weeks of being alone are so difficult."

Clarissa drew Annalynn into an embrace. "I look forward to getting to know your extraordinary trio much better."

As Annalynn went on out, Clarissa held me back a moment and said softly, "She's going to have a tough race, Phoenix. If she wins, she'll be a force on the Hill within a year."

I'd promised Annalynn my help if she ran. My education in politics was about to begin.

Although a plow had cleared a wide lane, driving required my full attention most of the way to Highway 36. Everyone else except Achilles rode immersed in her own thoughts. He took a nap at Annalynn's feet.

To my surprise, she didn't make a call when we hit the service zone.

A little before one o'clock we reached Laycock. The streets were clear, and only two or three inches of snow covered the grass. I decided to make one more try at finding out why Annalynn was so anxious to get home. "Does anyone want to stop at Hy-Vee for groceries before I drop you off?"

In the rearview mirror, I saw Connie wink at me. "I need some milk."

Annalynn looked out the window. "Take me home first, please. I'll shop for groceries when I pick up our Thanksgiving turkey tomorrow morning. What are your plans for Thanksgiving, Nancy?"

"Clarissa is bringing Tara over to celebrate with her mother and members of our congregation who don't have family nearby."

Tara's mother?

Connie said, "Nicole will be so relieved that Adam Augeri is behind bars."

Nicole. The dog walker who had hidden her face when he came to the park. Of course. She said naïve things and cocked her head the same way Tara did.

As we turned the corner a half block from the castle, I noticed a red sports car parked in front of our neighbor's house. The license plate identified it as the one I'd rented at the Kansas City airport in

August. The person behind the wheel held an open newspaper in front of his face.

Annalynn's face lit up. She ducked her head and pretended to be searching for her keys.

Burning with curiosity but reminding myself she was old enough to have a secret rendezvous, I pulled into the driveway.

She jumped out and closed the door. "Bye." She hurried toward the house without taking her bag from the back.

I couldn't take chances. I opened my door. "Achilles, go with Annalynn."

He leapt over my lap and raced after her, delighted to be home.

I backed out, and the man moved the newspaper to block my view of his face as we went by. I drove on down the block, turned right, and pulled into a driveway to turn around. "I forgot something. I need to go by the house a moment."

Nancy leaned forward. "Are you worried about the man in that car?"

Connie giggled. "Phoenix, I'll bet you a hundred dollars he was Annalynn's secret crush in high school."

It would be worth a hundred to find out who the guy was. "You're on." I pulled up alongside the red car just as a tall, slim man in a leather jacket rang the doorbell. I watched as Annalynn opened the door and, to my amazement, held out her arms to him. He lifted her off her feet and swung her around.

If I'd had false teeth, they would have fallen out. "It's Ulysses! Annalynn had a crush on my big brother? He teased both of us unmercifully." Until he came home the summer after his freshman year in college.

"Pay up," Connie crowed.

Nancy said, "Annalynn told me you'd be surprised that your brother came for Thanksgiving."

"She was right." How could I not have seen the attraction in high school? How could I not have noticed how often she'd mentioned Uly in the last few weeks? No wonder he'd stopped emailing me questions about what I was doing in Laycock. He was getting all the answers, plus more, from Annalynn.

I released the brake and drove on unnoticed as Achilles offered Uly a paw, something my suspicious dog rarely did when he met a man.

I would've fought a romantic relationship between my best friend and my annoying brother claw and fang as a teenager. Could I stay in a neutral corner this time? Not without great effort. Careful, Phoenix. Don't jump to conclusions. I remembered the fights I'd had with Annalynn when she and Mrs. Roper pushed me to take Stuart seriously. "No teasing Annalynn, Connie. Give her and Uly a chance to get to know each other again and find out if there's anything beyond friendship there."

Connie chuckled. "That's what Annalynn says about you and Stuart. I hope you follow your own advice better than she does."

I drove Nancy and then Connie home and went to Hy-Vee to dawdle and buy some of Uly's favorite childhood foods. I debated over steaks. Hadn't he gone through a vegetarian period? He'd become very Californian during his student days. I told myself I was giving Annalynn and Uly time alone. Then I admitted I was allowing myself time to adjust to the possibility of them becoming a couple. An hour wouldn't do it. Would a week? A month?

But I was anticipating trouble. My friendship with Annalynn had survived her marriage to a charming jock. Besides, any teenage attraction might fizzle fast. Ulysses had a hectic professional life in California. She was pursuing her long-delayed dream of running for Congress. *Que sera sera.*

Scheisse! Whatever happened, I'd be stuck dealing with "despirit for car" and the like. No way. I'd recruit a part-time work-from-home assistant right after Thanksgiving. Inspiration hit: Willetta Volcker, outstanding deputy and brand new mother on maternity leave for three months. A load lifted.

I was putting my groceries in the SUV when my phone rang. Stuart. I wanted a hug. I wanted more than a hug. Not a mythical happily-ever-after, but more than a hug.

Why not tell him so? I answered, "Hi, hon. I've decided to accept your invitation to stay with you while Achilles and I are in training."

A moment of silence. "Great," Kaysi said, "I'll tell him."

My brain went blank.

Kaysi broke the silence. "The Cyber Defenders are dying to meet you. We saw the video of you facing down that machete."

Another surprise that I didn't know how to handle. I recovered enough to say, "The Defenders were a great help. Thank you."

Stuart said something in the background. "Dad's afraid you were hurt when you got ambushed in the basement. He's coming to see for himself whether you're really okay. We'll be at the castle in about an hour and a half. Zeke, too."

All three of them. They outnumbered me. "I'll be waiting." We disconnected.

I closed the SUV's back door, crawled into the driver's seat, and took deep, calming breaths. I'd faced a machete without flinching. How scary could two temporarily friendly teenagers be? Damned scary.

But fear had never stopped me before. Annalynn had accused me of being addicted to excitement. During my six months back in dull old Laycock, I'd dealt with one crisis after another. Annalynn, Connie, and I had all struggled not only with crime but also with life-altering challenges. Annalynn had gone from a devastated widow to a respected sheriff and now dared to run for the House. Connie had metamorphosed from an undervalued singer to an admired musical director. More surprising to me, Connie and I had overcome our mutual antipathy to function with Annalynn as a trio, not a duet.

My former colleagues in Vienna thought I'd wasted my skills. I knew better. The bullet that ended my dual careers in Eastern Europe had forced me to envision a new future. For another six months or so, that meant staying in Missouri, running a nonprofit charity, and testing the possibility of living a normal life. Ironic. I'd never expected to do any of those things. On the plus side, they provided a great cover story for anyone who suspected I'd been a spy.

ABOUT THE AUTHOR

Carolyn Mulford decided to become a writer while attending a one-room school near Kirksville, Missouri. After earning an M.A. in journalism at the University of Missouri, she received a different kind of education as a Peace Corps Volunteer in Ethiopia. That experience prompted an enduring interest in other cultures, travel, and international affairs. She became a magazine editor in Vienna, Austria, and Washington, D.C., and then a freelancer. She wrote thousands of articles, five nonfiction books, and other materials ranging from calendars to manuals.

After working on five continents, she moved to Columbia, Missouri, to focus on fiction. Her first novel, *The Feedsack Dress,* was named Missouri's Great Read at the 2009 National Book Festival. The Missouri Writers' Guild awarded her first mystery, *Show Me the Murder,* the 2014 Walter Williams Major Work Award. Her third mystery, *Show Me the Gold,* won the Guild's 2015 Best Book Award. In 2016, publishers released her fourth mystery, *Show Me the Ashes,* and her second historical novel, *Thunder Beneath My Feet.*

To read the first chapters of all the novels and blogs about them or to contact the author, go to http://CarolynMulford.com.

8c 1/19 1/20

CPSIA information can be obtained
at www.ICGtesting.com
Printed in the USA
LVOW12s2327120517
534377LV00001B/156/P

9 780971 349797